P9-CQG-125

Wanda Seasongood

and the
Mostly True Secret

Wanda Seasongood
and the
Mostly True Secret

BY Susan Lurie

ILLUSTRATED BY Jenn Harney

DISNEP • HYPERION

Los Angeles   New York

Text copyright © 2020 by Susan Lurie
Illustrations copyright © 2020 by Jennifer Harney

First Edition, February 2020

1 3 5 7 9 10 8 6 4 2

FAC-020093-19361

Printed in the United States of America

This book is set in Albertina MT Pro/Monotype; Eames Century Modern/House Industries; Billy Serif; Eyeful; Cherily Blussom; and P22 Garamouche/Fontspring.

Designed by Tyler Nevins

Library of Congress Cataloging-in-Publication Data

Names: Lurie, Susan (Susan L.), author. • Harney, Jennifer, illustrator.
Title: Wanda Seasongood and the mostly true secret / by Susan Lurie ; illustrated by Jenn Harney.
Description: First edition. • Los Angeles ; New York : Disney - Hyperion, 2020. • Summary: "Wanda doesn't fit in with her family and is always searching for clues about her past. On her eleventh birthday, a talking bluebird named Voltaire shows up and takes her on a quest through the Scary Wood to find her true parents"— Provided by publisher.
Identifiers: LCCN 2018026164 • ISBN 9781368043151
Subjects: • CYAC: Identity—Fiction. • Witches—Fiction. • Magic—Fiction. • Brothers and sisters—Fiction. • Bluebirds—Fiction. • Memory—Fiction.
Classification: LCC PZ7.1.L87 Wan 2020 • DDC [Fic]—dc23
LC record available at https://lccn.loc.gov/2018026164

Reinforced binding

www.DisneyBooks.com

SUSTAINABLE FORESTRY INITIATIVE
Certified Sourcing
www.sfiprogram.org
SFI-00993
Logo Applies to Text Stock Only

*For my mother, who lives on
every page of this book.*

For my father, an extraordinary adventurer.

And always, in all ways, for Lou.

ONE

It Started with a Thud

On Wanda Seasongood's eleventh birthday, a bright and bouncy bluebird flew toward her bedroom window. *Just like in a fairy tale,* she thought as she watched it flutter her way. But the window wasn't open, and the little bird's head smacked into the glass, making quite a thud. Then it dropped, lifeless, into the tangled garden below.

That was Wanda's first birthday surprise.

Wanda hoped against reason that the bird was all right. She ran from her room and leaped down the stairs, two at a time, her frizzy reddish-brown hair flying behind her.

"Wanda, where are you going?" her mother shouted

from the kitchen. "Such a racket you're making! You'll drive Zane crazy."

Zane was Wanda's horrible eight-year-old brother, and quite frankly, he was already crazy. He kicked things and howled all day long, and her parents could not restrain him. And yet they only had praise for him. They yelled at Wanda for all the awful things he did. And they demanded that she take him wherever she went. Which is why Wanda had no friends, not even one.

When Wanda reached the bottom of the stairs, her parents were waiting for her, with Zane standing squarely in front of them. His wavy dark hair was matted with dirt. He glared at Wanda with his cold blue eyes.

"I'm just going into the yard," Wanda said.

"Take him with you." Her mother's hands rested on Zane's shoulders. "He needs some fresh air."

"Yes," her father added. "Besides, it's your turn to watch him."

Wanda's shoulders sagged. It *always* seemed to be her turn. "Come on, Zane." She gently took his hand—

And he bit her arm.

"Ow!" she cried, pulling away and spotting his teeth marks clearly pressed into her skin.

"Wanda, why did you grab him so tightly?" her mother scolded.

"When will you learn?" Her father shook his head in disgust.

"*When will you learn, Wanda?*" Zane shrieked with glee. "*When will you learn?*" He stomped on her foot and bolted out the front door.

Zane ran into the street. Into the path of an oncoming car. It braked with a loud screech, but Zane just giggled. He continued to the other side and promptly started yanking leaves off the neighbors' shrubs.

"Now look what you've done, Wanda!" Her mother's cheeks flushed with anger.

Wanda swallowed the hurt, as she was accustomed to doing, and watched her parents take off after Zane. Then she rushed through the kitchen and into the yard to search for the bluebird.

I hope I'm not too late. She tore through the creeping thistle that choked the garden. Its spiky leaves cut her hands as she parted the stalks, searching for the little bird.

Please don't be dead. Please don't be dead. Not on my birthday. That would be such bad luck, Wanda thought. As she combed through the plants, her eyeglasses, large brown frames perched on her freckled nose, slipped down until she was peering over them.

"There you are!" She finally caught a glimpse of the

bird's feathers. She could tell it was a male from his bright blue color. A note was tied around his neck, but Wanda didn't see it at first.

She pushed her glasses up, stared at the bird for a moment, and let out a long, heavy sigh.

"Happy birthday, Wanda," she said. "Here's a dead bird to help you celebrate." She poked the bird with her pinkie. "Well, I guess it won't be having any cake."

The truth was, Wanda wouldn't be having any cake, either. Her parents always forgot her birthday. But she still planned on lighting a candle so she could make the wish she'd been wishing on every birthday for as long as she could remember.

Wanda lived at the foot of the Catskill Mountains. When she was six, she had heard the tale of a man named Rip Van Winkle, and that's when this wish had taken shape and burrowed into the chambers of her heart.

Rip lived in the Catskill Mountains, too, and one day he took a nap in the woods. When he awakened, everything had changed. It seemed he had slept for twenty years.

The moment Wanda heard this story, she wished that she, too, would fall into an enchanted sleep, and when she awakened, she would also find that everything had changed. She would discover, much to her delight, that she was an orphan, free of Zane and her parents.

Now, if you've ever made wishes, birthday or otherwise, you know they're usually as light as a petal and as smooth as silk. They sparkle and shimmer, and the mere thought of them can send you whirling like a dervish.

Most of Wanda's wishes were like that. But not this one. This one was heavy and dark, and her shoulders slumped under the weight of it. But on each birthday, she made the wish with greater conviction and increased fervor. And to be absolutely clear about it, she would add, "Disappearance is preferred, but dead would be okay, too."

On first hearing, and probably second and third, that might seem like a cold, harsh wish, and it might turn you against Wanda—but it shouldn't. Wanda's brother truly was a beast of a boy. He ate with his hands, chomped loudly on his food, and let it dribble down his chin.

When asked politely to pass the peas, he'd help himself first, fill his mouth to brimming, then spit them onto her plate. He blew his nose in Wanda's best dresses. He never combed his bushy brown hair. Never brushed his teeth. Never took a bath. When he was especially muddy, he slept in Wanda's bed instead of his own. Shoes and all. And he bit her whenever he had the chance.

And where were Wanda's parents through all this?

Did they ever reprimand Zane, as any reasonable parent would? Did they even once offer their good daughter kind and soothing words?

No. They blamed her instead. They blamed her for all of Zane's bad behavior. Tossing the breakfast bowls out with the trash. Watering the plants with vinegar. Once even setting the kitchen curtains on fire. How could they believe for an instant that Wanda was behind these things? It was bewildering.

Zane was allowed to do whatever he pleased, and their parents were pleased with whatever he did.

Wanda could not make any sense of it. She seemed to

remember a time when her life was brighter. But when she tried to recall those moments, her memory clouded and she could not pierce the fog. No, this dark life was hers and always had been. So she wished and wished and wished.

And while she waited for her wish to come true, did she mope and moan about how unfair her life was? No, not Wanda. Which was very admirable, you'd have to agree. Wanda had the good sense to go her own way. Each afternoon, when she returned from school, she'd lock herself in her bedroom, tend to her homework, then paint or write in her diary. And she found another excellent way to escape. She'd read and read and read, sometimes two or three books at a time. Schoolbooks, novels from the library, the classics on her parents' bookshelves, she'd read them all.

Or, sometimes, if no one was home, she'd snoop.

She'd look in every drawer. In every closet and cupboard. Under every loose floorboard and behind every sooty fireplace brick. Wanda was so different from the three people she lived with, she was certain that a secret kept her imprisoned with them, and if she could find a single clue, even a tiny one, she could venture forth and search for her real family.

But today was Saturday and everyone was home, so there would be no snooping.

And it was Wanda's birthday.

And a dead bluebird sat at her feet.

She looked at him and sighed another long sigh—and the bluebird's head suddenly popped up.

He hopped to his feet, wobbling a bit on his spindly bird legs. He stared at her for a moment, then shook his head, as if to clear it.

"I thought you were dead!" Wanda cried out.

"I thought I was, too," the bird replied.

That was Wanda's second birthday surprise.

TWO

Have You Been Waiting for a Secret?

"Eiii!" Wanda shrieked. "You can speak!"

"Evidently," the bird said calmly. He slowly turned, taking one small step after another, making a complete circle, observing his surroundings.

"Nice garden. Somewhat overgrown," he said, opening and closing his small black eyes, trying to focus. "I'm sorry, but I'm feeling a bit dizzy." He gazed down to find a soft place to sit—and caught sight of his matted feathers, crusty and coated with blood.

"What happened to me?" His voice rose in alarm. He searched Wanda's face for an answer and his glance fell to her cut, bloodied hands. He leaped back in a flurry of feathers. "Did you try to kill me?"

"No! No!" Wanda said. "I cut my hands on the thistle. You flew into my window." Wanda pointed to her bedroom above. "Don't you remember?"

"No, I don't." He glanced up at the window, then eyed her suspiciously. "What proof do you have?"

"I would never want to hurt anything," Wanda said, peeved that the bird could think ill of her. "Except for my brother and parents, who I wish were dead," she admitted, feeling absolutely dreadful just saying those words. But if nothing else, Wanda was honest.

"All right, then," the little bird said. "I choose to believe you." But he took a small hop away. "Let's get on with it."

"Let's get on with what?" Wanda's eyes narrowed in confusion.

"The mission, of course," he said. "I'm on an important mission. And there's no time to waste." In a flash, his body stiffened and the bird suddenly appeared alert. Then, just as quickly, he let out a *whoosh* of air so great, he seemed to shrink. "If only I could remember what the mission was . . ."

Wanda watched the bird as he paced back and forth, trying to recall what it was he was supposed to be doing. And that's when Wanda saw it—the note, tucked under a thin vine that was tied around his neck.

"Would it have something to do with that paper you're carrying?" She pointed to the note.

"Yes! That's it!" The bird leaped up with joy. "You are a clever one. I'm supposed to deliver this secret tied around my neck!" His blue-feathered chest puffed out with confidence and pride. "I'm supposed to deliver this secret to—" Then his body slumped. "I'm not really sure. . . ."

"Don't feel bad." Wanda tried to cheer up the bird. "I bet it's hard to remember things with a brain as small as yours." As soon as these words were said, she knew she'd made a big mistake.

But the bird didn't seem to hear her. He concentrated hard, trying to remember. "Who am I supposed to deliver this to? Who? Who?" He pecked the ground with his beak in an effort to jog his memory. "I'm sure I was sure I knew who it was when I started out, but now I'm not sure at all.

"Wait! I know!" His face lit up. "It must be you, because, well, here I am. Have you been waiting for a secret?"

THREE

Read It! Read It!

"**Y**es! Yes! I *have* been waiting for a secret!" Wanda was astounded by the bird's words.

"Well then," the bird said, lifting a foot to scratch his head. "That means that you must be the One, and if you are the One, then you should read this message tied around my neck."

The secret that had escaped her for so long was now just a fingertip away. Wanda jumped up and flung her arms wide, as if she were about to take flight. Today was her birthday, and even though there would be no cake or song, she knew she would remember this as her best birthday by far. She reached out to the bird to take the note.

"Whoa! Steady there." The bird quickly hopped a few steps back. "What if I'm wrong? What if you aren't the One?"

"But I'm sure I am," Wanda said. The muscles in her forehead twitched, and her brow creased with concern. "I'm absolutely certain of it."

"Hmm . . . Doubt is not a pleasant condition. But certainty is an absurd one," the little bird said.

"Who said *that*?" Wanda asked, because she didn't think the small bird was capable of such a grand thought.

"I did," the bird replied. "My name is Voltaire, and that is my saying."

"Voltaire?" Wanda laughed. "You aren't Voltaire. Voltaire was a French writer from the 1700s. I've read all about him. He was a wise, witty person who wrote plays and poems and novels. A writer of great fame."

"Well, I am a bird of great distinction." The bird ruffled his feathers. "My name is Voltaire."

Wanda didn't know what to make of this creature—a bird who could talk and quote the famous writer Voltaire. If she had tried to get to the bottom of this, it might have saved her from certain danger to come. But rather than prolong the discussion or argue with the bird, Wanda thought it best to turn their attention to what mattered most—the note.

"I know how we can settle this," she told the bird. "The secret I am waiting for will tell me where I truly belong. Is that what the note says?" Wanda's heart skipped with anticipation.

The bird peered up, then side to side. Wanda held her breath and tried not to fidget while she waited for his reply.

Finally, he spoke. "I don't know," he said. "I can't seem to remember. I know I knew it when I left, but now I know I don't know it all." He exhaled a wobbly whistle of a wheeze. "How about we just read the note?"

Wanda reached for it quickly and pulled it away before the bird could change his mind.

Her fingers trembled as she unfolded the tiny piece of paper. She stared at the words, and her mouth turned down in dismay.

"Well, what does it say?" The bird flapped his wings. "Read it! Read it!"

Wanda gazed up from the note. She shook her head. "It says, 'The bird will tell you a secret.'"

FOUR

But How?

Voltaire leaped up from the ground. His small wings beat furiously as he rose in the air. "All right, then!" he cheered. "We're making progress at last!" His head jerked this way and that. He appeared to be searching for something that kept bolting from view.

Could there be more to this message than I realize? Wanda brightened at the thought. She followed the bird's frantic glances. "What are you looking for?" she asked.

"For the bird! For the bird!" Voltaire squawked. "I'm looking for the bird who knows the secret!"

"Oh."

Anyone, even a bird as befuddled as Voltaire, would

have been able to hear Wanda's deep disappointment. His wings stopped beating, and he crashed to the ground. "I see. I see now. I am that bird."

Wanda flopped down on a rock beside the bird and rested her head in her hands. "Well, I suppose this is simply not meant to be. If there *is* a secret, it's not mine to discover."

"Utter nonsense." Voltaire hopped up on her knee. "I don't know you very well. Come to think of it, I don't know you at all. But you don't seem the surrendering sort. And of course there's a secret. And of course it's for you. We just need to find it."

Wanda liked the sound of that. She lifted her head and smiled. "Yes! Let's find it." Then matters of practicality set in, and her head drooped once more. "But how?"

"But how? But how?" The bird's little feet paced up and down Wanda's leg. "I've got it!" He halted his mini march. "We will head into the woods. We will follow the path I traveled, and the secret will return to me. It makes perfect sense. When I left, I knew the secret. When I arrived here, I didn't. That means I lost it somewhere in between. And that spot in between is the woods. So that is where we will go."

Wanda shook her head. "No. I don't think so. I don't think that will work." She let out a sigh, and if a sigh could hold all the sadness in the world, this one did. "I know you are trying to help, but it's useless. I think I am doomed to live this terrible life forever."

"Well," the bird said with a huff, "I think you are feeling sorry for yourself. And what's worse—I think you *like* feeling sorry for yourself!"

"That isn't true!" Wanda leaped from the rock, catapulting the bird into the air.

And it wasn't. Wanda wasn't given to long periods of moping. She had simply briefly lost hope. These things happen.

"That isn't true at all." She said it again to be perfectly clear.

"If you say so." Voltaire shrugged. "But the longer we dwell on our misfortunes, the greater is their power to harm us. So let us *do* something about them and set off on our little journey."

Wanda thought about Voltaire's words, and she knew he was right. Because, lately, the more she thought about her terrible life, the more helpless she felt. And *that* feeling felt worst of all.

But still Wanda hesitated. Was the bird's secret really meant for her? Had he ever known it? Could he really remember it with a simple walk in the woods?

Wanda answered those questions with a *no, no,* and

no. The three little *noes* echoed and bounced and banged about in her head.

But the bird wouldn't give up. He might have forgotten the secret, but it seemed to Wanda that he was somehow certain that the woods held the clues he was seeking. And it was almost as if something was compelling him to take her there—to take her there *now.* He chirped on and on until Wanda had to agree.

"Before we leave, I must tell my parents that I'm going," Wanda said. "We might be gone for days, and they will worry about me. I wouldn't want to cause them grief."

It is true that most of the time Wanda thought her parents weren't her real parents. And she often wished they would disappear. But sometimes, during lonely nights in the stillness of her bedroom, she thought they *could* actually be her parents. And even if they didn't show it with hugs and kisses or praise the way other parents did, they loved her deep down. This made the idea of her quest that much harder. But she summoned her determination, swept aside her uncertainty, and headed off to find them.

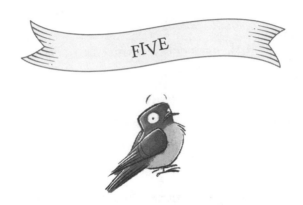

FIVE

Stay Away

W anda heard her parents whispering in the kitchen. Were they planning a surprise for her birthday? Maybe this year they had remembered it. At the sound of their voices, Wanda's will to leave grew weak.

"I don't think I can do this," she said quietly to Voltaire, who was perched on her shoulder.

"You can and you must," he said. He pecked her head to urge her along, then took flight to meet up with her outside.

So Wanda entered the kitchen and told her parents that she was going off for a few days. Staying with a friend, she said, then waited to hear their protests, how this would ruin their birthday surprise.

"What a wonderful idea!" Her mother's face lit up.

"Yes, yes it is!" Her father wholly agreed. "In fact, that's just what we were discussing. This makes everything so much easier." Her parents shared a knowing look.

"Zane is so difficult," her father continued. "You see the way he is around you. You might be the cause of the problem here. So we were thinking that you should move out. Just for a while. Until he gets a little older." He smiled broadly.

"But I'll be gone for just a few days," Wanda said, growing dizzy. "I planned on coming back."

"Well, don't hurry, dear." Her mother patted her on the head. "Stay away as long as you can."

And with that, they ushered her through the back door and closed it firmly behind her.

Wanda stood in the yard next to a tall flowerpot filled with weeds. She gripped its rim, trying to steady herself. She took great gulps of air. It seemed that her birthday wish to be an orphan had finally come true.

"Well, it looks like you're ready!" Voltaire met Wanda in the yard. "Shall we go?"

"Yes," Wanda said. "Unfortunately, things turned out

better than I had expected." She told the bird what her parents had said.

"All the more reason to start this adventure," he chirped. "What luck, Wanda! No one will miss you!"

No one loves me, Wanda thought.

No one really cares about me.

No one cares what happens to me.

No one.

It was hard for Wanda to share Voltaire's good cheer with these thoughts circling around and around in her mind. But she tried. She took some fortifying breaths. She attempted to shake off the gloom that hugged her, and after a while, she did feel calmer. Soon her heart began to stir with optimism and hope. She went up to her room and quickly packed as much as her rucksack would hold; then the two headed off.

As Voltaire led her away from her home, she glanced back at the withered trees that framed the house. The once bright and welcoming front door was cracked and peeling, and the yellow shutters had turned grimy and gray. When had it all fallen apart? She couldn't say exactly. *Sometimes being close to a thing doesn't mean you can see it clearly,* she thought as she turned to the road again.

It was time to leave this dreary place behind.

It was time to find out the truth about her life.

SIX

The Scary Wood

Wanda and Voltaire stood at the edge of the forest.

They had traveled hours and hours to reach these woods, crossing meadows and valleys Wanda had never seen. Sometimes Voltaire flew just ahead of her, leading the way. Other times he perched on her shoulder, issuing orders.

"Turn left. Turn right. No, pardon me. That would be left, no, turn here, no, there, no, straight." His sense of direction was somewhat askew, and the way back to the woods took longer than either could have imagined. But as the sun began to set, they had reached their destination.

"Here we are. At last," Voltaire chirped. "Not to complain, your company is marvelous, really—except when you go all gloomy, that is—but flying alone is so much faster." He stretched his tired neck.

"Really," Wanda said with an arch of one eyebrow. Then she peered into the forest. She gazed up and up— over a hundred feet high—at the silvery gray trees that towered before her. Their leafy tops blocked out the remaining light of day.

She stepped between two of these giants, into their cool, dark shade, and shivered. "I'm not familiar with these woods. I've never traveled this way before."

"No need to worry. I am your guide." The bird flew a few feet ahead. "Just follow me. Into the Scary Wood."

"What? Wait! The Scary Wood? Why is it called the Scary Wood?"

"Because that's what it is. Smaller than a forest but more than a few trees. That's a wood."

"But why is it called the *Scary* Wood?" Wanda pressed.

"Because that's its name, dear girl. Come now, follow me. Into the Scary Wood we go. No need to be frightened. At least I don't think so."

Within two or three steps, they came to a fork in the path and stopped. Voltaire landed on Wanda's shoulder, trying to decide which way to turn.

Finally, he took off. "This way!" he called.

"Are you sure?" Wanda asked, hesitating.

"Not in the least," he answered. "But if we do not find anything pleasant, at least we shall find something new. So don't dawdle!"

Wanda shook her head. Should she follow or not?

She thought about her life back home. She couldn't go back there, at least not yet. And not just because her parents had told her to stay away. And not because she obviously didn't matter to them anymore—although this last reason would be reason enough.

No, it was something else.

For a long time now, she'd felt that something wasn't right. As if she'd been walking in a dream and couldn't see clearly. As if she'd been trying to look through blueberry jam.

She was determined to find out why. And something told her that this bird would lead her to the answers. She would have to summon all her courage and follow him into the unknown. Because one thing was certain—if there was a mystery to solve, she wouldn't find the answers at home.

"Wait up! I'm coming!" she called to the bird, who had flown out of sight.

In the few minutes that had passed, the air had grown chillier. The path had turned darker.

If we do not find anything pleasant, at least we shall find something new. Wanda shivered as she stepped onto the trail. She thought it strange that she knew nothing about these woods. But she would soon learn something very important about them. She would soon find out why no one *ever, ever* entered them.

SEVEN

Groods

"Does *any* of this look familiar?" Wanda stopped and slipped her rucksack off her shoulders. They ached from the weight of everything she had brought from home.

Voltaire settled close to her ear. It was night, although what time precisely, Wanda couldn't say. The air held a chill, but nothing more threatening. This part of the forest wasn't as dense, and the glow of the moon lit up the trees. Above, the sky was clear, with clusters of stars winking their arrival.

"Hmm." Voltaire nodded, looking at the branches above. "Ahhh," he said, gazing with intensity at the shrubs that surrounded them.

"Well?" said Wanda. Her eyes crossed in an effort to see the bird so close up. "Do you remember anything about the secret now?"

"Not a thing," he said.

Wanda frowned.

"I admit I am vexed by the lack of clues here," Voltaire said, flying up to the top of her head. "I was thoroughly convinced that a walk through the woods would jar my memory."

"So . . . what do you think we should do next?" Wanda asked.

"I suggest we stay right here and think for a spell," the bird said, fluffing his feathers, making himself comfortable. "Your hair has a lovely nest-like quality."

"We can rest for a while," Wanda agreed, "but could you please come down where I can see you?"

Wanda placed her rucksack against a tree, then sat on the ground and leaned against it. The bird hopped from her head to perch on her knee.

"Time to review," the bird said. "What do we know?"

Wanda was about to answer when she heard the crunch of a leaf. She gazed between the trees, but nothing unusual caught her eye.

Just the scurry of a forest animal, she thought.

Wanda scratched her head. "I don't think we know any more now than we knew an hour ago, or an hour before that, or an hour before that."

"Well said," Voltaire chirped, and Wanda sighed. At the end of her long breath, her ears picked up another sound. This time, the sharp snap of a twig.

"Did you hear that?" Wanda sat up straight, her whole body rigid.

"Yes." The bird nodded. "It's the sound of the woods. Night creatures, that's all."

Wanda slumped against the tree, relieved, and turned her attention back to their problem. *There must be something I can do or say to help him remember the secret.*

And then it came to her.

Why didn't I think of this before?

"Voltaire, I know you can't remember the secret, but can you remember who told it to you?"

"Well, of course I can," he said.

Wanda's eyebrows leaped up in surprise.

"I know, I know. You think I'm quite limited, with my small brain and all. Yes, Wanda, I heard you say it earlier, clear as a bell, but even though you believe—"

"Voltaire!" Wanda interrupted the bird. "Who told you the secret?"

"It was a lady."

"What lady—AAAIII!"

Wanda's rucksack was suddenly whipped out from behind her. She fell back and hit her head hard against the tree. And by the time she sat up, which was less than an instant later, she and Voltaire were surrounded.

Wanda tried to speak. But she could never have imagined the creatures that stood before her—no one could have—and she fell silent in fear.

There were at least ten of them of varying heights and heft, all dressed in rags. They were part human, part tree, part beast, and part bird.

The creature standing closest to Wanda stood at least six feet tall. Its arms and hands were covered in dark, craggy bark. On its head, leaves and green vines sprouted along with thick brown hair.

The beast to the left of it had a face covered in fur, with a nose shaped like a mushroom. On its right stood a very short creature with skin the texture of pinecones. Others had feathers. A few had skin that resembled the scales on bird legs.

If some were female and some were male, it would be impossible to say. Their clothes—torn pants, muddy shirts, shredded vests, ripped shoes—gave nothing away.

Any of this could have made Wanda's heart stop, but it was their eyes that kidnapped her breath. Cold eyes of stone, both vacant and menacing, stared at her.

"What do we have here?" said the tallest one, who had swiped her rucksack. Its voice was very deep. *This one's a male,* Wanda thought. He rifled through her bag, flinging things out as he noted each item.

"Shirt," he said, and Wanda watched as her favorite purple sweater landed in the shrubbery.

"Pants." These were caught by the short creature, who held them up like a coveted trophy. His face broke out in a lopsided grin, and Wanda saw that his rotted teeth were covered in moss.

"Book." With a flick of the wrist, Wanda's diary was hurled into the mud.

"STOP THAT!" Wanda couldn't help herself.

"Don't anger the Groods!" Voltaire whispered. "They're . . . unpredictable." Then he fluttered above her and tucked himself into the shadows of a branch overhead.

Groods? Wanda had never heard of such a thing. What were these creatures, exactly? Were they civilized or wild? They knew human words, but they had no manners at all.

She leaned forward to rescue her diary. Then she turned and snatched her sweater from the shrubbery beside her. "These things belong to me!"

The thieves broke out into laughter that was gruff and growly, surly and sour.

"Nothing belongs to you in the Scary Wood," the tall beast said. "In the Scary Wood, everything belongs to us." He stepped closer and leaned over her. "Including you." And with that, they trapped Wanda in a net made of rope and carried her away.

EIGHT

Let's Cook Her and Eat Her

"What if they cook me and eat me?" Wanda whispered to Voltaire, who had stowed away in her rope prison.

"Pure drivel," Voltaire whispered back as the Groods carried Wanda through the woods to their home. "They're gruesome, yes. To be feared, absolutely. But they're not cannibals. They don't eat humans."

"Let's cook her and eat her." The smallest creature kicked the net, jabbing Wanda in the ribs.

Voltaire's body stiffened. His head jerked up in surprise.

"We don't eat humans," the one with the mushroom nose said.

Voltaire relaxed. "Ah. That's better."

"But we could feed her to the bears. That might be fun."

"Oh, dear," the bird said, and he remained silent the rest of the journey.

When the Groods reached their home—a garbage-strewn campsite—they dumped the net on the ground, with Wanda still inside it. Voltaire flew to safety, hiding in a tangle of branches close by.

Wanda took in the details of the clearing. It was surrounded by trees and dotted with large boulders. A huge fallen trunk marked one of its boundaries.

She inhaled deeply to calm herself—and choked on the stench of rancid meat, the remains of past meals scattered about, circled by flies and swarming with maggots.

And then there was the Groods' bounty. Old, muddy backpacks in every color, large and small, piled higher than the tallest boulder. A variety of shoes and mismatched socks. Shredded jackets missing sleeves. Ragged pants missing legs. Torn books; old water bottles; pots and pans; a sleeping bag, slashed; a teddy bear, hacked to bits. And more. It all littered the forest floor.

What had happened to the children who owned these things? A shiver ran down Wanda's spine.

One of the Groods turned Wanda's rucksack upside down and shook it hard. Then the others pounced in a frenzy, grabbing, shoving, pulling, fighting for every piece.

Riiip. Off came a sleeve.

Yaaank. Pants split in two.

"Put those down!" Wanda yelled. "I need those clothes!"

Her shouts were ignored.

Buttons popped.

Collars and cuffs soared high in the air.

The woods echoed with the Groods' savage tug-of-war grunts.

It was clear to Wanda that this battle was for the sake only of claiming and destroying, and it made her heart race and her pulse pound.

Then, just as suddenly as the frenzy began, it ended, as if all at once they had become bored with the whole thing. The Groods drifted their separate ways except for one, who wandered over to Wanda.

"Beastly, wasn't it?" The Grood shook his head sadly.

"Yes." Wanda's voice came out in a whisper.

"A real pity," he said, turning to leave. "You're next."

"Voltaire!" Wanda called out to the bird after the Grood was a safe distance away.

Voltaire fluttered to the ground.

"Did you hear that? We have to escape—now." Wanda pulled hard at the net, trying to tear a hole in it. She tugged and tugged, but the rope was too strong. Her hands turned red in the struggle as the rope burned her palms.

"Yes. Escape. Not to worry. I've been devising a plan for that very thing," Voltaire said. "As I see it, we can accomplish this in two simple steps."

"Great!" Wanda said, rubbing her raw fingers. "What are they?"

"To escape," Voltaire said, "the first thing we must do is free you from the net. The second is to run."

I'm doomed, Wanda thought.

And she was right for more reasons than she knew, because just then the tallest of the beasts, the one with bark for skin, stomped toward her.

"Who were you talking to?" the Grood demanded, gazing about for the source of the other voice.

Given her circumstances, Wanda thought it would be best not to anger the creature, so she answered quickly and in a most straightforward manner.

"I was talking to this bird," she said, pointing to Voltaire.

"It is not wise to taunt me. Birds can't speak." The

beast's voice boomed. "WHO . . . WERE . . . YOU . . . TALKING . . . TO?"

"I don't mean to anger you," Wanda said in her sweetest voice. "Truly, I was talking to this bird."

The Grood's fury brought one of the other creatures scampering close, curious to see what the commotion was about. He was nearly Wanda's height, smaller than all the others—shorter than the shortest one she had seen earlier. The skin on his body looked like human skin, but hairier. His face had fuzzy cheeks, a small mouth, and a nose that resembled the nose of a deer.

Wanda might have gone so far as to say he was cute—for a Grood, of course. But his stony-eyed gaze crushed any kind thoughts.

The tall beast bowed at the waist, practically bending in half. He leaned so close to Wanda she could inhale his breath. It smelled like damp earth and wet leaves, more woodsy than human, and it made Wanda jerk back and shudder.

"Do you know what we do with troublemakers?" The tall Grood lowered his voice to a most-menacing timbre.

Wanda shook her head no.

"We slice 'em up." His cold rock eyes remained fixed

and unblinking. Wanda's temples began to throb under their stare.

"She looks like a nice person," the littlest one said in a high-pitched voice similar to Wanda's.

This creature is a girl, Wanda realized.

The female Grood gave Wanda an encouraging smile.

"I am. Really. I *am* a very nice person," Wanda tried to assure them.

The tall Grood snickered. "A nice person. We like nice people, don't we, Kitten?" he said to the little Grood, who nodded with enthusiasm.

Kitten? Really? Wanda stared at the little Grood's cold eyes and fang-like teeth.

"The nice ones—we slice 'em up extra thin. More to go around that way."

"That's what we do! That's what we do!" Kitten agreed.

"Now—who were you talking to?" the big Grood asked Wanda once again.

"I was talking to this bird. I mean no disrespect." Wanda turned to Voltaire. "Tell them, Voltaire. Tell them that I was talking to you."

Voltaire's head cocked to one side, then to the other. He gazed up into the giant's face, opened his beak, and— tweeted. *Tweet. Tweet. Tweet.* Then he spread his little blue wings and flew to a distant tree.

Wanda was stunned, but there was no time to dwell on what had just happened. The tall Grood lifted her, net and all, and raised her high in the air. Then he shook her with great cruelty and force.

Her arms and legs flew every which way. Her head bobbed and jerked. There was no doubt he would soon shake Wanda's skin from her bones.

But suddenly, he stopped. And grunted. And dropped her back to the ground.

"It's late," he said. "I'm tired. It's time for bed. I think I'll kill you at sunrise, when I feel more refreshed. It's such a treat to tear people limb from limb first thing in the morning."

"Yes! Yes!" cried Kitten, clapping her hands with delight. "We'll pull her completely apart in the morning!"

While Wanda tried to calm her thumping heart, each of the Groods lay down on the grass and fell asleep. Soon the clearing echoed with their groans, grumbles, and snores.

Wanda curled up in her rope prison, wishing her head would stop spinning. She could not fathom why Voltaire had behaved this way. He was her one and only friend, and he had betrayed her. She waited for him to return and explain. She waited and waited. But he never came back.

When the dizziness passed, she sat up to think. *What should I do now?* She shivered in the chilly night air.

She saw her favorite purple sweater snagged on a nearby shrub. She reached out, pulled it into her net, and raised it to her cheek. Its softness soothed her jagged spirit.

Then she put her mind to work. How would she escape? Just before she drifted off into a restless sleep, the answer became clear.

NINE

A Very Sharp Knife

"P*sst!* Kitten!"

It was just before dawn when Wanda called out to the smallest Grood.

The darkness of night was beginning to lift, but the clearing was still sheltered by shadow. Wanda could tell that the Groods would soon be awake—their snores had gone from deep rumbles to light snorts. It was important that Wanda talk to Kitten before they woke up.

"Kitten!" Wanda called out again. . . .

And the small Grood stirred. She placed a hairy hand over her ear as if to block Wanda's voice.

"Kitten!" Wanda tried once more.

"What?!" The little Grood sprang up. Her gaze traveled the campsite to see who had annoyed her.

"Over here," Wanda whispered.

The Grood stood and approached Wanda with great curiosity.

"My arms and legs have gone numb in this net." Wanda grimaced. "A small favor. Could you please cut me free—just so I can stretch?" Wanda asked. "If you could, I have something very special for you."

The Grood cocked her head, considering Wanda's offer. "What do you have?"

Wanda held up her favorite purple sweater. "I would give this to you—it's very silky and soft. I'm sure the others would like it, too. But you wouldn't have to fight for it. It would be all yours."

The Grood pursed her small lips, then nodded in agreement. "I'll be right back."

Wanda grew anxious as she waited for Kitten to return. What was taking her so long? Had the little Grood gone to wake her leader? The sky was growing lighter. The sun would soon rise. The other Groods began to twist and turn. They were nearing the end of their sleep.

Finally, Kitten came into view. She was alone and Wanda was relieved—until she saw what Kitten was

holding. She was grinning and gripping a knife. A very large, very sharp knife.

And what was that crusted on the tip of the blade?

It looked like dried blood.

Wanda's relief quickly turned to fear.

What had made her think she could trust this little Grood? She chided herself for a plan that now seemed not only foolish but fatal.

Kitten held out the knife.

Wanda held her breath.

Kitten jabbed the knife forward—and Wanda gasped. But the Grood began to saw away at the thick rope. She was astonishingly strong, and Wanda was quickly freed.

"Thank you." Wanda offered her the purple sweater, and the young Grood snatched it. Wanda wasn't surprised. The grimy shirt the girl wore had holes and tears, and the color had become impossible to tell. It was probably the same shirt she'd worn every day last week, last month, last year.

Wanda watched for her to put the sweater on, but instead, with a loud shriek, the little Grood joyfully set to ripping it to shreds.

Wanda was so startled by this that she forgot to flee. And by the time she did remember, the other Groods were awake.

One of them jumped up and shouted, "Get her!"

Wanda turned to run.

"Wait!" Kitten cried, grabbing her arm. "I want your hair, too." She lashed out with her knife, slicing an inch off Wanda's mane.

Wanda charged out of the clearing.

The ground vibrated with pounding Grood footsteps. She could hear their grunts as they chased her.

She ran and ran without direction or plan. But in this instance, she had something more important than strategy. She had luck.

Because, as Groods often do, they grew bored with the hunt. They slogged back to their clearing with the fresh hope that they'd find something already dead to rip to shreds.

When Wanda was confident that she was safe, she collapsed against the nearest tree. A cool, heavy fog hung over the forest, and Wanda shivered as she tried to catch her breath.

"Ah. Very good. Escape accomplished in two easy steps," a voice chirped overhead. "Just as I said. Simple, really. Just required some good common sense, I'd wager."

Voltaire had returned.

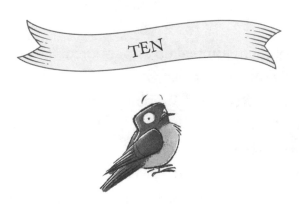

TEN

A Breeze Most Foul

"Voltaire! What happened to you? Why did you fly off?" Wanda leaped up to face the bird. "How could you leave me that way?"

How strange it is to feel both happy and angry at the sight of him, she thought. And it was even stranger, she realized, that her lips could smile while her fists were clenched at her sides.

"I went to seek help," Voltaire began to explain.

"But why wouldn't you speak to the Grood?" Wanda pressed. "Your silence put me in great danger."

"I am many things, Wanda, but I'm no match for Groods. You saw how wild and unpredictable they are.

A talking bird? Mangled in minutes, I'd say. Then just feathers and bone. No good to anyone, especially you."

Wanda's anger softened a bit. It was true that the Groods were unstable and nasty. She shuddered at the thought of them.

Voltaire fluttered down and landed on her shoulder. "I took to the trees, searching for someone to assist us," he went on. "No easy task in the Scary Wood, I might add."

Wanda's anger lightened a bit more.

"Then I heard Grood footsteps. Thundering footsteps. What a fright!" His blue head bobbed as he spoke. "But here you are. And now I must say, I am relieved and delighted to see that you're safe."

Wanda had to admit it all made sense, and her feelings of betrayal began to dissolve in the morning mist. And yet some doubt lingered.

"Voltaire, I'm sorry to say that I still don't know if I can rely on you."

"Well," he answered, "'the best way to find out if you can trust somebody is to trust them.'"

Hmm. Wanda thought about that. It seemed logical and wise. "Is that a quote from Voltaire? The writer, I mean."

"Dear girl, how many times must I tell you? I *am*

Voltaire. But if I quoted only myself, I'd be quite a bore. No, that was from Hemingway, another writer of some talent, I've heard."

Well, anyone who could quote the great writer Hemingway definitely deserved another chance, Wanda concluded. She decided to trust the bird. In less than two days, she had grown very attached to him, and she couldn't imagine their friendship ending.

Her faith in Voltaire mended, the two took off . . . and that's when Wanda remembered why they were there at all.

"Wait!" she said. "The secret. We were getting closer to unraveling this mystery. And then those horrible Groods showed up."

"Yes! That's right!" Voltaire said, hopping into the palm of Wanda's outstretched hand.

"Who did you say told you the secret?"

"It was the lady," he said.

"Which lady?" Wanda stopped and gazed into Voltaire's eyes, hoping to get him to focus.

"How odd," he said. "I can't seem to recall a thing about her."

"Concentrate. Close your eyes and try to imagine her," Wanda suggested.

Voltaire did as she asked. "I've got it!" he said.

"Who is she?" Wanda was very excited now. "Who is the lady?"

"I don't know! But I think we're meant to go to the top of a mountain. To a cave. Yes. No. Hold on. Not a cave. It's a castle. No, it's a cave. It's coming back to me. Slowly."

This wasn't what Wanda expected to hear, but it was a clue, and for that she was grateful and thrilled.

Voltaire tried to remember more. He tried very hard, but nothing else came to mind. So the two decided to take an uphill path to the mountaintop, where they would search for a cave.

Along the way, Voltaire settled in the crook of her arm, and they talked about all sorts of things. . . .

"Were you always able to speak?" Wanda asked.

"Yes," he said. "I can't remember a time when I couldn't."

"Of course you can't. You don't remember much." Wanda laughed.

"Where are your friends? Doesn't anybody like you?" he volleyed.

"Why do you think you're the writer Voltaire?" she shot back, which riled the bird, as she knew it would.

"I don't know why you insist I am not who I say I am. You are most difficult when it comes to this point."

Voltaire ruffled his feathers. "I am me. Voltaire. And quite pleased about it."

Wanda admired the bird's self-confidence. Sometimes she wished she were a different person. A person who shined. A person she could feel quite pleased about, too. Usually, she was able to dull the sharp edges of these thoughts. *Everyone has self-doubts,* she would tell herself, which was true enough and somewhat soothing. Now, though, after her parents had cast her out, she felt slight and small and hobbled.

Wanda had never shared these self-doubts with anyone, and she didn't want to share them with the bird. But she wasn't one to wallow in self-pity. She was quite the opposite, in fact. So right then, she came to a sudden decision. *I will show my parents that I count. Somehow, someday, I will prove to them that they were wrong to treat me so poorly. I am SOMEBODY, and I will make them see it.*

With this settled, Wanda turned her attention back to the bird. "If you are Voltaire, tell me, what have you written?"

"Wanda, dear, have you lost your senses? Birds do not write. My talent is to dispense wise thoughts to those in need." He gave Wanda a pointed look.

Wanda decided to abandon this argument. Voltaire did seem wise, and she wanted to seek his opinion on a nagging matter. It would mean sharing a secret with him. A secret she had never revealed to anyone before.

"All right, then," she said. "There's something that's been puzzling me. I'm wondering if you could help me figure it out."

Voltaire puffed out his chest. "Certainly, Wanda!"

"Sometimes, I have visions," she told him.

"What kind of visions?" the bird asked.

"I see my house, my garden. There's a little girl, dressed in yellow from cap to shoes, happily running through the flower beds."

"Is the little girl you?" Voltaire asked.

"That's the puzzle," Wanda said. "I think she must be, but it isn't a time I actually remember. What do you make of it?"

"Hmm. Let me think." Voltaire's head bobbed from side to side. Then he gazed up at the sky. He looked like he was about to pluck the answer right out of the air. Finally he spoke.

"Unfortunately, I don't have a clue."

"Well, *that* isn't very helpful," Wanda said.

"Wanda, dear, how could I possibly know what happened in *your* past? Haven't you noticed that I have enough trouble remembering *mine*?" He flew up to Wanda's shoulder to avoid her glare.

They walked in silence for a while. After several minutes, their argument faded from Wanda's mind. Something new had taken its place. She kept peering behind her. Casting sideways glances.

"What's wrong?" Voltaire asked.

"I can't shake the feeling we're being watched."

Voltaire craned his neck in every direction. "There's no one else here."

Wanda stopped short.

"Over there," she whispered, "in the shrubs. I see eyes."

Voltaire peered where instructed. "I don't see anything," he replied. "No insult intended, really, but I think you must be imagining them."

But Wanda was certain she had seen them—two dark, blinking eyes.

Was it a Grood? Had one followed her trail?

Wanda and Voltaire walked a bit farther, and she felt someone staring each step of the way.

This would have been enough to set her nerves tingling, but then a breeze began to blow.

It picked up quite suddenly. As if on command.

As she peered through the trees, the breeze seemed almost visible. Touchable. It swirled between the leaves, winding its way directly to her. Warm and charged and foul.

And as it grew closer, it began calling to her.

Wanda. Wanda. Her name rode on its wave.

"Voltaire, do you hear that?" She shuddered. "A voice. It's calling me."

"Yes, I hear it," the bird said with a flap of his wings. "A man's voice."

Wanda. Wanda.

A whisper on the wind.

Wanda. Wanda.

Her name floated toward her.

Beckoning her.

Wanda. Wanda. Come this way.

ELEVEN

The Swamp Gnome

anda. Wanda. Come this way.

"That voice. It's so frightening." Wanda shivered in spite of the morning sun that had warmed up the woods. "Who's calling my name? Who knows me here?"

Voltaire flew up to a tree limb to peer into the distance. "Those are very good questions," he said. "We must follow the voice to find out."

"But it sounds so evil." Wanda shook her head. "No, I think you're wrong. We should stay far away from it."

"I'm sure we should follow it," Voltaire insisted. "That way," he said, pointing to a path going off to the left.

"I'm sure we should not," Wanda said, noticing that the bird suddenly looked a bit woozy.

"But it will lead us to the mountaintop," Voltaire said, now sounding as if he were in a trance.

"What makes you think that?" Wanda asked as a glazed look settled in the bird's eyes. "Voltaire, are you all right?"

"I do feel a bit odd," he admitted. "Somewhat light-headed."

Wanda hoped that all their bickering hadn't made the bird sick. After all, he was just a little thing, not really built to bear much stress.

"I do think this path will lead to the mountaintop," Voltaire spoke slowly. "Something deep inside me is telling me so. And listen . . . whoever was calling your name has stopped. He's gone now."

Wanda still had a bad feeling about this path, but Voltaire had already taken flight, so she dashed after him. They moved through the trees, the bird fluttering just slightly ahead of her. From time to time, she thought she saw the blinking black eyes in the bushes they passed. But she couldn't be certain.

The forest was strangely quiet. No chirps. No rustling. No buzzing. Except for the soft patter of Voltaire's wings, no sounds at all.

It made Wanda wary, but the path began to lead uphill, and this gave her some hope that they were headed in the right direction.

As they continued on, the air became misty. Soon it turned into a gray fog that was difficult to see through. Even though Voltaire flew just ahead of her, she couldn't spot him anymore. And she wasn't sure, but she thought the path had started to go *down* again.

"Do you think we're still headed in the right direction?" she called out, but the bird didn't reply.

Finally, she came to the end of the path, where the fog had lifted slightly. Instead of finding a cave at the top of a mountain, she found herself standing at the edge of a swamp. "Oh, nooo!" she moaned.

Voltaire flew onto her shoulder.

The swamp water was thick and milky green. It surrounded the trees, and a white swirling smoke drifted up from its surface.

"We've made a mistake," Wanda said. "This swamp is too big and there's no way to cross it. We took the wrong path."

"You took the right path," a deep voice said from inside the smoke.

It was the same voice she had heard calling to her

before. "Where is he?" Wanda whispered to Voltaire. "Can you see who it is?"

But before the bird could answer, a figure stepped out of the swirling mist.

He was taller than a boy and shorter than a man, but he was neither.

His strange green skin matched the color of the swamp. His long pointy ears stood out from his bald, lumpy head. Around his middle he wore a brown tattered rag that hung like a skirt to his knobby knees. His round belly bulged over it.

"Who are you?" Wanda asked.

"I am the swamp goblin. I rule this bog," he replied. "Follow me." Then he smiled at Wanda, and his eyes glowed red. She leaped back at the sight of them.

Wanda started backing down the path. "Er, we'll just be going now. We've come the wrong way."

"No, you haven't. You're exactly where you should be," he said.

Then he reached out and touched Wanda's arm with a wet green hand—and she suddenly and completely disappeared.

TWELVE

Vanishing Wanda

Voltaire let out a shriek as Wanda disappeared right out from under him. He fluttered wildly to avoid hitting the ground.

"Voltaire!" Wanda called out. She saw his eyes dart about, searching for her. "This way!"

Wanda had reappeared in the middle of the swamp. She stood on a patch of land the size of a doormat. The goblin stood on it, too, still clutching her arm.

"Oh, there you are! That was quite a trick!" Voltaire said, mesmerized at her sudden vanishing. He hopped up and down at the swamp's edge. "This is excellent, Wanda! You may have discovered a new talent."

"Voltaire, I think I'm in trouble here," she said as the goblin grabbed her arm tighter.

"Yes, indeedy," the goblin said with glee. "You're in very big trouble! The finest kind." Then his free arm swept forward, and Wanda could see he was holding a cane. It was a stick of old wood, crooked and gnarled, with an image of his face crudely carved into its top.

He waved the cane over the swamp, and the swirling smoke began to take shape. It churned and twisted, forming figures of men and women, young and old.

As the hazy forms floated through the trees, more smoke rose from the water, turning into children, boys and girls of fog and mist.

With eyes and mouths opened wide in terror, they all cried out, "Help me! Who am I? Tell me my name!"

Wanda gasped at the horrifying sight.

"Welcome to Gravesend Landing." The goblin gave a short bow. "Your new home."

He tapped his cane on the ground, and Wanda felt a tingling in her arms and her hands. Then from the top of her head all the way down to her toes.

She gazed at her feet and cried out, "I can see right through them!" And it was true. Her shoes and feet had

turned to vapor, and she could see straight through to the ground they stood on.

She held up her hands and shuddered as the gauzy swamp sunlight set them aglow, inside and out.

In a wave of shock, she hugged herself tightly, and her breath caught in her throat. Her arms were as soft as cotton candy.

Every part of her had begun to fade. She started to feel lighter and lighter—until she felt as light as the air.

"Help me!" Her cry joined the others. "I—I'm disappearing!"

She faded and faded, and the more she did, the less she could remember. "Help me! Help me! I can't remember my name."

"Wanda!" Voltaire shouted to her. "You are Wanda!"

"Wanda! Wanda!" she repeated, and the tingling weakened, but it didn't stop.

"Keep at it, Wanda! Don't forget who you are!" Voltaire said.

"Wanda! Wanda!" she cried out. She yelled loud and strong and without pause. "Wanda! Wanda! Wanda! Wanda!" And the fading began to slow.

"That's it!" Voltaire cheered.

"I am Wanda Seasongood!" she shouted with great force. And with her last name declared, the fading halted.

"Wanda! Wanda! Wanda Seasongood!" she shouted again and again, but her name didn't hold the power she needed to reverse the goblin's magic. Her heart began to race in fright. She was still see-through, still a body of mist.

"Enough of this. It is time to join the others." The little man sneered and raised his cane. He aimed its carved head at Wanda. . . .

And a breeze began to blow.

It was warm and charged and foul—just like the breeze that had carried her name.

And it started to blow Wanda apart.

THIRTEEN

Have Courage!

"Help me! I'm breaking up!" Wanda cried as the breeze swirled around her.

"Don't forget who you are!" Voltaire called out. "Have courage!"

"I'm Wanda! I'm brave!"

"That's working! I think you're becoming more solid! Say more! Say more!"

"I'm smart and I'm careful!" Wanda shouted, and indeed she could feel herself growing a bit more substantial.

"Good! Good!" the bird cheered.

"I'm always polite!"

"No. Don't think so. You're fading again."

The breeze picked up and started blowing Wanda to pieces.

"I'm very kind!" she yelled in a panic.

"Uh, that doesn't appear to be true, either. You're going all ghosty. And your legs are drifting away."

Voltaire beat his wings frantically, trying to send Wanda's legs back to her.

"So touching." The goblin laughed at the sight. He sucked in a bucket of air and filled his cheeks to bursting. Then, with one mighty blow, he blasted Wanda again. Her arms blew away at the elbows. Her head bobbed in the wind.

"Oh, noooo!" Wanda wailed. But she took a moment to calm herself, then focused on remembering who she was.

"I'm thoughtful! I'm honest! I'm trustworthy!" she cried out.

"That's better! More! More!" Voltaire chirped.

"I can't sing! I have no friends!" Wanda yelled, and her limbs began to float back to her.

"Sad, but true," Voltaire agreed. "Go on! Go on!"

"I'm a good listener!"

"Hmm. Maybe not." Voltaire watched Wanda's ears drift away from her head.

"I'm loyal! Responsible! Hopeful!" Wanda shouted, and she could feel herself going from wispy to weighty.

"Yes! Yes! Yes!" Voltaire whooped with joy.

"No! No! No!" The swamp goblin stomped his feet. "I cannot allow this." He raised his arms and the air around Wanda churned and set her whirling—but she fought back hard.

She continued to shout every true thing she could say of herself . . .

And it worked.

She went from smoky to see-through and back to solid—and became Wanda again. And she was never happier to be who she was.

FOURTEEN

An Awful Screech

"Well done, Wanda!" Voltaire flew circles around her as she tested her arms and legs. She was a bit dizzy from the whirling and twirling, and it took a few moments for her head to stop spinning. But when it did, she became aware of an awful screech.

"What's that terrible sound?" Wanda's gaze traveled the swamp and came to rest on the goblin, who sat hunched on a rock a few feet away.

His piercing sobs echoed through the bog. Fat tears rolled down his cheeks and plopped into the folds of his skirt. "They all forget who they are without fail." He lifted his head to peer at Wanda. "And as soon as they do, they turn to smoke. Then they're trapped here at Gravesend Landing, and they belong to me. I've never lost one. Never ever. Until you."

Then his head dropped down, nearly touching his lap, and he wailed and wailed.

Wanda quickly looked around for the other ghost figures. Perhaps there was some way she could help them. But she saw in an instant that nothing could be done. They had scattered in the breeze, and the swamp air swirled once more with their smoky remains.

"Follow me," Wanda whispered to Voltaire as the goblin continued to howl. She leaped from stone to stone to the edge of the bog. Then she and Voltaire stepped through the trees and crept silently away.

Wanda was proud of her excellent escape. But her joy was mixed with confusion. She had always considered herself kind. So why, then, had she continued to disappear when she shouted it out?

I'm a nice person. I'm definitely a nice person, she thought, trying to console herself.

After all, no matter how unfairly her parents had treated her, hadn't she always been respectful and helpful? And no matter how horribly Zane had behaved, hadn't she always been nice to him? Had she ever struck back at him? Had she ever tried to get even? Never. Not once.

And just now—after she had escaped—wasn't her first thought to save the ghost people in the swamp? Weren't all of those signs of a kind person?

What was the unkind thing she had done?

Wanda was stumped.

FIFTEEN

The Key to the Secret

"Voltaire, I don't think I've ever been that frightened before." Wanda pinched her arm to make sure she was still solid. "I nearly disappeared."

"Yes! It was quite exciting. Dreadful, yet thrilling," he chirped.

"Evaporating is not thrilling." Wanda had recovered, but there was still a toll to pay for fading to smoke. Her arms felt rubbery and her legs were unsteady, and she moved through the forest with a definite wobble.

She walked through the woods slowly. And twice she glimpsed the blinking black eyes. Hidden in the shrubbery. Following her path. Each time she saw them, her chest tightened and a sharp pain of fear shot through her forehead.

But when the eyes didn't reappear a third time, she wondered if she had seen them at all. There and gone. There and gone. Was her mind playing tricks on her?

I'm still very shaken and on edge, Wanda thought. *I need to calm down. That must be the problem.*

"Let's sit," she suggested. "My legs feel like jelly."

They found a spot near a blueberry bush. Wanda and Voltaire were so famished, they immediately began to pick the berries. This was the perfect place to rest.

As they ate, they talked about the swamp goblin and Wanda's amazing escape. It was exhilarating to relive now that she was safe.

"You know," Wanda said, "it's very disturbing to think I'm unkind."

"Yes, that was baffling." Voltaire pecked at a berry. "After all, you seem nice. Well, nice enough."

"I *am* nice," Wanda insisted. "And I can't imagine why anyone would think . . ."

And then it came to her.

"Oh, noooo," she moaned. "Voltaire, I *have* been unkind! Actually, I've been very, very mean."

Then she told Voltaire about her birthday wishes.

"It's a very bad thing, hoping your brother and parents disappear. But I've wished it year after year. And now that I've actually disappeared myself, I know how terrible it is. It's terrifying. No, I'll never make that wish again."

"Hold on! Did you say something about a brother?"

"Yes, I have a brother. He's repulsive and nasty. Like a pig and a mole and a snake all in one. But I will no longer wish him harm."

"That's it! That's it!" Voltaire's wings beat in a flapping fit. "I remember the secret! I remember it!"

"Really?" Wanda said, forcing herself to remain composed. She'd been down this path of false hope before.

"It's about a brother! Your brother is being held captive in the Scary Wood."

Wanda jumped up. "I knew it! I knew it! I knew there was a secret in my family. All that hunting and prying and snooping—and at last I have discovered it. I can hardly believe it—I have another brother!"

Voltaire was quite pleased with himself. "Once you free your brother, you will know the truth about your life! Your brother is the key."

The secret she finally found was all too much. Wanda grabbed on to a tree, trying to catch her breath. Finally,

finally, she possessed the clue she'd been searching for—
the clue that might change her life forever.

Wanda's spirit soared to the sky and circled the sun.
"Thank you, Voltaire! Thank you so much!" She kissed
the bird on the crest of his head.

I will find my brother and bring him home, Wanda thought.
*And my parents will finally respect me. I will rescue him, and
they will see how wrong they were to toss me out so easily.*

"I have another brother!" Wanda was beside herself with the news and filled to the top with questions.
*What's he like? Does he know about me? Do we resemble each
other? Why is he in the woods?* she wondered.

"Voltaire, can you tell me who is holding my brother?
And why?"

"Hmm. That's a tough one." Voltaire thought very
hard. "Well, I don't know," he concluded. "But I might
have known it once. So there's hope that I'll know it
again."

"Where do you think we should look for him?" Wanda
asked. "We must find him. Let's start right now!"

"Where should we look? Where should we look?"
Voltaire paced the ground, head down, pecking at
blueberries while he thought.

"I know!" His head jerked up, a blueberry stuck to the

top half of his beak. "In the cave. That must be it. He must be in the cave."

"The cave. Of course!" Wanda said. "But there are so many paths in the Scary Wood. And there's so much danger here. How will we stay alive to find it?"

Wanda stared off, mulling over the problem—when a pair of eyes appeared in the nearby shrub.

Blinking black eyes.

They disappeared. Then they came back again. This time nearer, because whoever it was had moved closer.

They blinked again. And came closer still.

"Voltaire, look," Wanda whispered. "The eyes."

Blink.

Closer.

Blink.

Still closer.

Then a voice.

Eyes and a voice.

"I know where the cave is," the voice said. "I'll tell you where it is."

SIXTEEN

Prince Frog

With another blink, the mystery figure leaped from the shrubbery and landed precisely before them.

"You're a frog!" Wanda said. "And you talk, too!"

"You're a genius," the frog replied. "Very sharp of you to notice."

That's all it took for Wanda to form an instant dislike for the frog.

"You've been following us for hours," Wanda said. "You nearly scared me to death, stalking us that way. That wasn't very nice. What do you want?"

"You're my princess," the frog said. "I want a kiss. Kiss me."

"Ha! That's not likely to happen," she said. Wanda had never met a creature so bold and so irritating. And that would have been enough by itself to make her refuse his kiss. But there was something else. Wanda liked fairy tales, but she did not believe for one moment that a kiss could turn any frog, even one that could talk, into a prince. She was not about to be tricked.

"Just one kiss," the frog said. "One kiss will be all that it takes. Kiss me."

She looked at the frog's green slimy skin. His bulgy black eyes. His big froggy mouth. And the issue was settled. "No. I would never kiss a frog."

"But I know the cave you're searching for." The frog gave a sly grin. "Kiss me and I'll tell you where it is. Kiss me. Kiss me."

More than anything, Wanda wanted to find her brother. But her glance settled on the frog's mucousy skin, and she couldn't bear the thought of a kiss, not even one. "No, I cannot kiss you."

"Just one kiss!" he cried with a wide-open jaw, and a glob of frog spit flew from his mouth.

"Yuck! No!"

"Kiss me. Kiss me. Kiss me."

"Never. Never. Never."

"If I may interrupt . . ." Voltaire entered the fray.

"Wanda, a word, please." Voltaire turned to the frog.
"Would you excuse us, sir?"

"Sure." The frog shrugged. "She's my one true love. I
can wait."

"Perhaps just one kiss," Voltaire suggested to Wanda.
"It might prove to be helpful."

"I won't kiss a frog. Especially that one."

"But he really might know where the cave is," Voltaire said, trying to persuade her.

"Then *you* kiss him." Wanda shook her head.

"Please, just think about it...."

Then, at that moment, they both looked at the frog, and it was exactly the wrong moment because—WHAP!—the frog flicked out his tongue, caught a fly, and gulped it down. "Ahh. Delish." He burped, then grinned at Wanda. "Kiss me."

"Would you kiss that?" Wanda shook her head. "No," she answered for Voltaire. "But I have an idea."

They returned to the frog, and Wanda smiled sweetly, hoping to charm him into helping them.

"My name is Wanda," she said in her friendliest voice.

"I am the royal Prince Frog," the frog replied.

"The royal Prince Frog?" Wanda said. "That doesn't sound right. Don't you mean the royal Frog Prince?"

"I know who I am," the frog said. "You're very difficult. But you're still my princess. Kiss me. KISS ME. KISS ME. KISS ME. KISS ME. KISS

ME. KISS ME. KISS ME. KISS ME. KISS ME. KISS ME.
KISS ME. KISS ME. KISS ME."

"ABSOLUTELY NOT."

"Well then, I won't tell you which path to take. You
will never find the cave."

"We will find it on our own," Wanda said in a huff.
She turned to the bird. "Which way, Voltaire?"

Voltaire studied the paths. There were three, and it
looked like he had no idea which one to choose. But
then his eyes glazed over. And when they cleared again,
he pointed. "This way."

He hopped onto Wanda's shoulder and they
started off.

"Wrong. Wrong. Wrong," the frog said. "Kiss me, and
I'll set you straight."

Wanda and Voltaire ignored the frog and continued
on their way.

"Kiss me. Kiss me. Kiss me." They could hear the frog
croaking even at a distance. But Wanda had made up her
mind. She would find her brother on her own and there
would be no kiss.

The frog headed back into the shrubs. "If that's what
you want," he grumbled. "But you're making a mistake.
A big mistake." He slurped up another fly. "And, really, I
wouldn't go that way if I were you. . . ."

SEVENTEEN

The Nixie

After walking for miles and getting nowhere, Wanda had second thoughts about the frog. "Maybe I *should* have kissed that slimy creature."

"'The course of true love never did run smooth,'" Voltaire chirped. "A quote from Shakespeare," he told Wanda before she could ask.

"True love? Really, Voltaire?" Wanda pictured the frog and laughed.

It was mid-afternoon, the sun was shining, and the woods buzzed with activity. Yellow and purple wildflowers grew alongside the path, with bees and butterflies darting among them. Wanda spotted a doe eating berries under the shade of a tree. Sweet birdsong filled the air, and somewhere nearby there was a stream— Wanda could hear the sounds of water splashing over rocks. The loveliness of it all made Wanda forget how frightful a place this was.

Wanda strayed off the path to find the stream. Then she and Voltaire walked along its shore. The flowing water glinted under the sunlight, and every now and then, they caught sight of a trout leaping into the air. So peaceful.

They followed the river to the end, where it flowed into a clear blue lake.

"This part of the Scary Wood looks so different," Wanda said. "Bright and open and fresh. And the water—I feel like it's calling to me."

She lowered her hand into the lake. It was warm and comforting. A sudden calm came over her and every muscle in her body relaxed. She hadn't realized how tense she was until now.

"This is magical," she said to Voltaire. "This water is so soothing."

She cupped her hand and filled it with water. She wanted to splash some on her face. But when she tried to lift her hand out of the water, she couldn't. She twisted

and turned. She grabbed her arm with her free hand and tugged. Nothing worked.

"Is there a problem?" Voltaire asked, observing Wanda's strange contortions.

"The lake has my hand and it won't give it back!" Wanda said, her calm replaced with alarm.

Then the center of the lake began to churn, and rising from the bubbling water, a woman appeared. She was the most beautiful creature Wanda had ever seen.

Her eyes matched the green of the lily pads. Her skin shimmered a silvery blue. When Wanda took a closer look she could see why. Her skin was made of the smallest scales, delicate and pearly.

Her silky blue hair hung down to her waist. Her arms and legs were long and elegant, with hands and feet that were slender and graceful. Webbing grew between her fingers and between her toes.

"Who are you?" Wanda asked, mesmerized.

"I am a nixie, a water spirit," she replied, her voice as light as a raindrop.

"Are you holding me here?" Wanda asked, still unable to pull her arm out of the water.

"I am *helping* you," she said. "There's no need to

struggle. Come with me beneath the water, where there is no misery and despair."

"I am not miserable. Really," Wanda said, her heart beginning to thump with fear. "And I'm not in despair. I'm fine. I'm totally fine. Please let me go."

"But you're not fine," the nixie said. "You're not fine at all."

The nixie rose above the water. Surrounded by a pearly blue mist, she drifted through the air to stand next to Wanda. Her eyes met Wanda's—and with only her glance, she robbed Wanda of her will. Then she filled her with anguish.

Wanda's thoughts turned dark with woe: *Life is too hard. There is no point in trying. Nothing gets better. Things only get worse.*

All at once, Wanda was overcome with sorrow and grief and bleakness and gloom.

She thought about finding her brother—and now expected that she would fail in her quest. They would never find the cave. Or leave here alive. She wouldn't be able to prove to her parents that they'd been wrong to treat her so badly. They would never offer the apology that she deserved to hear.

The nixie touched her shoulder, and Wanda felt every bit of joy drain from her. Her spirit sunk to the darkest depths, and her body felt foreign to her, like an empty vessel.

With all hope gone, she mourned everything that would never come to pass. No brother. No wishes. No dreams. No possibilities at all. The pain of it was too much to endure—and she began to cry.

Her eyes filled with tears that streamed down her face. Tears poured from her skin. Her shoes filled with puddles. Her clothes became drenched in her sadness.

"Leave her alone!" Voltaire squawked at the nixie.

"She's mine now." The nixie laughed, revealing sharp, pointy teeth. She was a hideous creature under false beauty.

"Voltaire, I'm feeling so lost and so weak." Wanda tried to break free of the nixie's grip. She tried to fill her mind with happy, hopeful thoughts.

And it was beginning to work. For an instant, Wanda felt the nixie's power weaken. Then it took hold again, and Wanda felt something else. A squishy feeling in her feet. She tried to look down, but she was frozen in the nixie's spell.

"Voltaire! My feet—they feel strange. I think they're dissolving. Or wait—no. I think she's trying to turn me into a mermaid. I don't want to be a mermaid!"

Voltaire gazed down. "No worries there. She's not turning you into a mermaid."

Wanda felt some relief. "Thank goodness. I wouldn't want to lose my legs!"

"Your legs are still there—and you'll have so many more," he told her. "She's turning you into a squid."

EIGHTEEN

Pucker Up

"A squid?! I don't want to be a squid!" Wanda wailed. "Somebody help me!"

A tentacle wriggled out of Wanda's left knee. Another burst from her right one.

"Help! Help!" she cried out.

"Hello, Princess. Did I hear you calling for help?"

"Oh, noooo! Not you!" At the sight of the frog, Wanda's distress doubled in size.

"Princess, I tried to warn you. 'Wrong path,' I said. Did you listen? No." The frog shook his head. "And now look—you have tentacles, and they're sprouting little suction cups. Very attractive."

"Suction cups!" Wanda moaned. "No! No! No!"

"Frog, be gone." The nixie sneered. "You're disturbing my concentration. I must focus now to capture this girl for the lake."

"But you'll surely kill her," Voltaire said. "A squid needs the ocean."

"And why would I care about that?" the nixie replied. "I simply want to turn this girl into a squid."

Wanda felt her foot disappear—and three arms grow in its place. "Voltaire, my foot is gone—and my head is growing larger!" Wanda's voice quivered with fear.

"It's not very practical," Voltaire said to the nixie. "A squid cannot survive in a lake."

"Voltaire, I think my head is going flat. Somebody, help me!"

"Kiss me and your troubles will be over, Princess. Kiss me. Kiss me."

"Voltaire! At least tell this frog to GO AWAY!"

"You two are distracting me." The nixie turned to the frog and the bird. "I think I'll change you both into guppies."

"Wanda," Voltaire whispered in her ear, "you must kiss the frog. It's our last hope. He might turn into a human, and then he could help us."

Wanda felt her tentacles writhing, and though she

hated to admit it, kissing the frog was the only sensible thing to do.

"All right, frog. Come here." She took a deep breath. "I'll kiss you."

The frog leaped up.

The nixie swung at him to swat him away. The frog was too quick, and she missed.

He puckered his lips.

Wanda closed her eyes as he reached her mouth.

His lips were cold and wet and slimy.

With a loud *smack*, they kissed. Then the frog landed on the ground next to Wanda's remaining foot.

They stared deeply into each other's eyes.

And waited in silence.

Even the nixie watched to see what would happen next.

They waited.

And waited.

And waited.

And nothing happened.

"*Ack!*" said the frog. "It didn't work. How disappointing. You're still a girl."

NINETEEN

Phfft!

The nixie laughed. "You are all so foolish."

Although the kiss had been an out-and-out failure, it still proved to be helpful. While the nixie had been watching, her magic had slipped. Wanda noticed that her tentacles had started to shrink, and her foot had quickly grown back. And suddenly she knew how to escape the nixie—they had to distract her!

"Frog!" she whispered. "I need your help. Kiss the nixie!"

The frog turned to the nixie at once. "Kiss me. Kiss me." He puckered his lips. "Kiss me! Kiss me! Kiss me!"

"Go away, you pest!" She swiped at the frog, forgetting

about Wanda for just a moment—but that was all that it took.

Wanda's hand came free of the lake. She yanked it hard—and it flew out. But it flew with such force that she lost her balance and fell into the water.

SPLASH!

The nixie spun and let out a shriek. "My hex on the lake has been broken! Look at me, girl!" She tried to recapture Wanda in a spell.

"Don't look! Don't look!" croaked the frog. "Run!"

Wanda took off. Voltaire soared by her side. The two moved as fast as they could. They ran into the woods, but soon their chests burned with fatigue. Panting, they stopped to rest behind a large tree.

"That frog turned out to be much better than a prince," Wanda said between gasps. "He saved my life."

"Indeed," Voltaire wheezed from a branch above.

"I think I should follow *him* from now on!" Wanda bent down to tie her shoe. "Because you seem to deliver me into all kinds of trouble. Groods. A goblin. A nixie. I've nearly lost my life three times."

Hmm. That set Wanda to thinking. *Was it strange that Voltaire's choices were all bad ones?*

"I wonder, Voltaire, if I should continue on my own? Can I really trust you?"

The words flew out of her mouth before she could consider them. And by the time her lace was tied and she had straightened up, Voltaire had spread his wings and flown away.

"Voltaire! Wait!" Wanda cried out, but the bird didn't reply. "Well, fine. Just leave. I can do this on my own." Wanda was shocked by Voltaire's hasty departure. And if truth be told, she was hurt, too. As she considered what to do next, a silvery blue mist formed in the air. The pearly haze could mean only one thing: The nixie had followed her.

Wanda ran.

"I will find you!" The nixie's shrill cry chased her through the forest.

Wanda raced through the trees in terror. She took twists and turns, then doubled back, then changed direction again, trying to lose the dreadful creature. In a frenzy, she left the trail altogether, leaped over logs, crawled beneath shrubs, and finally found herself in a darker part of the forest.

The trees looked very different here. They were all short and blackened, as if their crowns had been scorched.

And the ground was bare. No grass grew. No flowers. Not even weeds.

Heart pounding, Wanda stopped. She had come to a bridge that hung over a river. She couldn't tell how deep the water was. The bridge was rickety, the kind made of vines and planks, and it swung wildly in the breeze.

This bridge is dangerous, but the nixie is worse, Wanda thought. *I must try to cross it.* She grabbed its rope railing to steady herself—and a mouse scampered through her legs.

"Ohhh!" Wanda jumped in surprise.

The mouse dashed across the creaky planks, and when it reached the center of the bridge—*Phfft!*—it exploded in a small puff of smoke.

Wanda didn't trust her eyes. Had that really happened? She had nearly convinced herself that it hadn't, when she spotted a squirrel. It stood on the other side of the bridge. It waved its tail at Wanda. It twitched its cute nose. Then it scampered toward her. When it reached halfway—*Phfft!*—a flame shot up out of nowhere and roasted the creature. It disappeared in a cloud of gray.

"How awful!" Wanda leaped off the bridge and back onto the riverbank.

The mist had turned to a light blue rain, and Wanda was thoroughly drenched in it. She listened for the nixie's cries—they were growing louder and closer.

Wanda looked under the bridge, planning to swim beneath it. *I'll follow that duck paddling there,* she thought.

She took a step toward the water, and—*Phfft!* As the duck passed under the bridge, it was blasted to bits. Its soft downy feathers hung in the air, then blew away in the breeze.

Wanda trembled in shock. Clearly, there was no way to cross this river. And there was no going back the way she came, either, with the nixie chasing her. She was trapped.

"This way!" A girl's voice cut through her fear. It was Kitten, the Grood. She stood on the other side of the creek, waving Wanda over.

"I can't cross the bridge. I'll explode."

"No, you won't! You can cross!" Kitten said. "You are covered in pearly blue mist. It will keep you safe."

Was the Grood telling the truth? Why would she want to help?

"Wanda!" The nixie broke through the trees.

"Hurry!" the Grood called. "She can't cross the bridge. She can't stray that far from the lake."

"I've got you!" The nixie reached out with her long webbed hand, grabbing for Wanda.

Wanda looked at the nixie.

She looked at the Grood.

She looked at the bridge.

All bad choices.

All right, she thought. *Which way should I die?*

TWENTY

Sizzle and Steam

"Wanda, you're mine!" The nixie's long fingers caught Wanda's sleeve in a pinch. Wanda's heart skipped as she twisted away.

"Do not cross that river." The nixie gurgled and spat. "You belong to me. You belong to the lake."

"Hurry! Hurry!" The Grood waved to Wanda. "Cross the bridge now!" She jumped up and down, trying to convince Wanda that there was no time to spare.

Wanda stepped onto the bridge again. She checked her arms and her legs, her head and her feet. She was still covered in the pearly blue mist. Would it really keep her from exploding?

Wanda's hands trembled as she grabbed hold of the

bridge's rope railing. Then she slowly placed a foot on a plank.

The bridge swung and dipped, and Wanda careened wildly, first left, then right. She gasped and waited for it to stop lurching, but the Grood was shouting, "Keep going! Keep going!" so she took another step.

"No! Stop! You'll explode!" the nixie cried out.

Wanda turned to the nixie. Her green eyes glowed a fiery orange, and Wanda's heart fluttered with fear. She stepped onto the next plank.

"That's it!" the Grood shouted. Her lips curled in a menacing smile. The fuzz on her cheeks stood on end. Her nostrils twitched with an air of excitement, as if she was already imagining the horrible things she would do to Wanda, her splendid prize.

I will make it to the other side, and then I'll reason with the Grood, Wanda thought. *I'll convince her not to tear me to shreds. Yes, that's exactly what I'll do, and all will be well.*

Wanda took another step on the bridge and another. And then a bunny streaked across her path. She froze as it started over the bridge. In the middle of the bridge, it stopped.

Wanda's breath caught in her throat as she watched the bunny glance about. It sniffed at the air with its little pink nose. It lifted a foot and scratched an ear. Wanda

sighed with relief. The rabbit was fine. Did that mean she would be, too?

The bunny hopped to the next plank—and its fluffy white cotton tail burst into flames.

"Oh, noooo!" Wanda cried as the animal was blasted from sight.

"Don't be afraid!" the Grood called. "The pearly blue mist will protect you, I promise. Keep going!"

Small beads of sweat dotted Wanda's forehead. There was nothing to do but continue. She took one more step, then another. She swallowed a great gulp of air—and stepped on the plank where the bunny had blown up.

She struggled to breathe as the wood sizzled and steamed under her foot.

But she did not explode.

Another step. Sizzle. Another step. Steam. Step after step, sizzle and steam. She walked faster and faster, sparks flying as she lifted her heels.

The bridge lurched and swayed under her weight— but she was close to the end now. She broke into a run— and red embers burned under the soles of her shoes.

As she reached the far side, the nixie howled a long wail of defeat.

Breathless, Wanda took one final leap off the bridge— and nearly landed right in the arms of the waiting Grood.

"See! I told you!" The Grood nodded happily at Wanda's success. "You did it! You crossed the bridge. You're alive!"

The Groods were not Wanda's friends, but Wanda knew what had to be said. "Thank you, Kitten. Thank you so much. You saved my life."

The Grood shrugged, as if saving people was what she naturally did.

The sun was setting over the woods. The two girls stood in its gentle glow and peered down the bridge. On the other side, the nixie was melting into a pearly blue puddle.

"That's what she does whenever she loses." Kitten smiled and laughed. Then she gazed up at Wanda—and stared at her with her cold stone eyes.

"You crossed the bridge," she said, her smile slowly collapsing into a sneer. "Now it's time to pay the toll."

TWENTY-ONE

Follow the Bunchberries

"The toll? What toll?" Wanda asked, taking a giant step back.

"Your purple sweater was very nice," the Grood said, eyeing Wanda's shirt. "I want more clothes."

"But you already have all my clothes," Wanda said. "That tall Grood took my rucksack with everything in it. You have all my possessions. These are the only clothes I have left." Wanda pointed to what she was wearing.

"That's what I want! That's what I want!" The Grood nodded. "I want what you're wearing."

"That's impossible. I will not walk through the forest naked," Wanda said, shocked at the notion.

"Then give me your eyeglasses. I want to break them apart and shatter them to pieces."

"I will not give you my glasses." Wanda reached up to make sure they sat securely on her nose. "I can't see without them."

"Well, it's not fair." The Grood jammed a hand into her pocket and pulled out a pair of very sharp scissors. "I helped you cross the bridge. Now you have to pay the toll. I want a prize."

"The biggest reward for a thing well done is to have done it," a voice called out.

"Who said that?" the Grood asked, puzzled because clearly no one was there but Wanda.

"I said it, young creature. My name is Voltaire, and those are my words! It is I who have spoken!"

"Voltaire, you're back!" Wanda's voice lifted with joy.

"Of course I'm back. Where else would I be?"

"Where is that voice coming from?" The Grood spun in a circle, searching for the other person who was speaking.

"Up there. In the tree." Wanda pointed to a branch overhead.

"A bird? A talking bird?" The Grood was amazed but quickly overcame her surprise. "I don't care if you're a bird who can talk. I don't care what you're saying. I want a reward." The Grood walked toward Wanda, opening and closing the very sharp scissors.

"Oh, I wouldn't do that. Don't you know, opening scissors without cutting is very bad luck," Wanda said, which was exactly the wrong thing to say.

"Bad luck for you!" said the Grood, and she lunged for Wanda. "And bad luck for your hair!"

Wanda ducked and dodged. She twisted and turned. The scissors missed Wanda's head by a mile. But they caught her nonetheless, and slit her back pocket. And out fell the one thing Wanda had managed to keep safe from the Groods—her diary.

"A book!" The Grood snatched it up and flipped through the pages. "I'll rip it to shreds. Then I'll chew on the paper. That will be fun. My very own book to devour."

"No!" Wanda couldn't bear losing her diary that way.

"Little Grood, why don't you *read* the diary instead?" Voltaire came to Wanda's rescue. "Diaries are filled with all sorts of secrets. Things I'm sure Wanda wouldn't want anyone to know. Juicy tidbits, I daresay, and more. Snooping in someone's diary is always such fun."

"Yes! Wanda's secrets!" The Grood opened the book,

and then she remembered—"I can't read," she said with immense disappointment. "I have no choice. I will have to eat it." She lifted the book to her mouth.

"No! No!" Wanda grabbed the book away from the Grood. "I'll read it to you! Let's sit."

The Grood plopped right down in front of a tree, eager to hear Wanda's most private thoughts. Even

Voltaire was curious about what Wanda had written. So the three leaned against the tree's extremely wide trunk and Wanda began to read.

"'I was born in the late afternoon, on a partly sunny day, not too hot, not too cold, on the fifth day of the fifth month, twenty-three minutes past four. I wasn't a small baby nor a big one. An average-size baby, I would say, if that's a thing that can be said about a baby. . . .'"

Wanda read and read and read. The Grood listened. Voltaire listened.

And the woods grew silent. So silent that after a while Wanda gazed up from the page—and saw that Kitten's mouth hung open and a strand of drool dribbled down her chin. Her eyes were shut tight. It appeared that Wanda's life was so dull, it had knocked the Grood out cold. Every creature nearby had also fallen fast asleep.

***

"Fascinating diary," Voltaire said politely. They were both a safe distance away now from the sleeping Grood.

"Then why are you still yawning?" Wanda frowned.

"Cheer up, dear girl. A book is a magical thing—and this one has proven it. It saved your life."

Wanda couldn't argue with that.

"And yet," he went on, "one should always aim at being interesting rather than exact."

Normally, that would have riled Wanda, but this time she replied with a simple "Uh-huh."

Voltaire flew in circles around her. "Wanda, your mind has drifted to a disagreeable place. You should order it to return at once!"

"Voltaire," she said sadly, "we've taken many different paths, and we are no closer to the cave. That's what I have been thinking. We're no closer to finding my brother. We're no closer to learning the secret of my life."

"Yes, but—"

"My brother is trapped, and he needs *me* to find him." Wanda looked up to the sky, as if the stars could show her the way. "I cannot fail him—but that is exactly what I am doing. I am failing him, and I am failing myself."

"But, Wanda—"

"No, Voltaire. There are no 'buts.' I have faded to smoke, nearly been drowned, and turned into a squid—"

"Yes, however—"

"—torn limb from limb practically twice, and came close to exploding—"

"Yes, Wan— Exploding? Really? I seem to have missed that."

"Oh, it was terrifying. It happened right after you flew off," Wanda said. "Voltaire! I almost forgot! I need to apologize. I think I insulted you. All these things that happened—none of them were your fault. But I said they were, and so I don't blame you for leaving me. Not one bit . . ."

Voltaire, who had been fluttering above Wanda's head, lowered himself for an eye-to-eye talk. "Wanda, there is no need to apologize. You did not insult me. I merely flew off in search of a safe path to take. The right path to take. I was trying to protect you from further harm. And I have succeeded. I have found it. I have found the right path. And that is what I have been trying to tell you."

"The right path! That's excellent news!" Wanda's eyes gleamed with new hope. "Which is the right path?"

"The one that will take us to the cave, of course."

Oh, nooo. Wanda moaned. *Another dead end.*

Voltaire rose in the air. He flew a few yards ahead, to a path edged in little white flowers. "And here it is!"

"Really?" Wanda asked, feeling hopeful again. She practically skipped to the trail. It was an uphill path that wound its way in and out of the trees.

"While I was searching the woods, I suddenly realized

that these bunchberry flowers will direct us to the top of the mountain—exactly where we need to go!"

"What good luck that this came to you!" Wanda said.

"Yes, I believe I always knew it, of course. But it slipped from my mind, as these things can. And then it slipped right back in again—like magic, I'd say."

So, under the glow of the moon and the light of the stars, the two followed the path of the bunchberries. They were hungry and tired, but now that they knew the right path to take, Wanda thought that nothing could stop them. . . .

Until something did.

TWENTY-TWO

What Took You So Long?

The bunchberry path was steep and difficult to climb, but Wanda was strong and determined. A promise made was a promise kept, and Wanda had promised herself that she would not fail her brother or herself. So she climbed and climbed and climbed.

The air turned chillier the higher they went. The flowers thinned out and soon disappeared. The moon drifted behind the clouds and abandoned them, too.

Wanda shivered. She hadn't eaten all day, and her empty stomach churned with hunger. But even though she was famished and cold, her good mood could not be snuffed out.

"I have a wonderful feeling about this new path," she told Voltaire. "We will find the cave. I know it now more than ever. And nothing can stand in our way."

And that's when they came to an unexpected halt. As they rounded a curve, an old shack rose up on the path, and the path ended right at its door.

The shack was tucked into a stand of trees. It was made from the same wood and blended in so well that it nearly faded from sight.

Its walls were splintered and rotted, with places gouged by the blows of an ax. In the front were the remains of a covered porch—a wooden rail hanging, floorboards crumbling.

Wanda gazed up at the shack's rusted tin roof. It sagged in the middle, and a crooked chimney poked through one side.

The front of the shack had no windows, only a door with jagged scars etched in its wood. One couldn't help but imagine that a horrible thing might be hidden inside.

If a house can look evil, this one certainly does, Wanda was thinking, when Voltaire's voice broke through.

"A shack. How delightful! Let's go inside."

"Voltaire, I don't think so." Wanda pointed to the chimney and its dirty gray smoke billowing into the sky.

"Someone is in there." She hugged herself to ward off the chill that ran through her.

"Even better," he said. "We're tired and hungry. It's a good place to rest. And if someone *is* there, they'll have food to share."

"No, I don't like the looks of it," Wanda said. "Let's go around it and be on our way."

But the bird ignored her and flew to the door. He peered into a gap between two planks. "There's lovely candlelight inside, and a stove, and a pot that is pleasantly steaming." He tried to convince Wanda to stay. "You must eat and rest. Please, knock on the door."

Wanda tried to hold back, but suddenly she couldn't resist a warm place to sit and hot food to eat. It had been days since she'd had a cooked meal.

She stepped slowly onto the rickety porch. The wood creaked under her weight, so she waited a moment to make sure it would hold her. She stared at the door. It hung askew on its hinges, and the doorknob, once bronze, had turned flaky and green.

She raised her hand and knocked twice.

"Hello?" she called out.

No one answered.

"Oh, well, we'll have to go," she said, relieved that no one had replied.

"Hold on. Just give it a minute." Voltaire hopped on her shoulder, but Wanda turned to leave. And just as she did, the door slowly scraped open.

In the flickering light stood a hunched old woman. Her face was a perfect oval with high, full cheekbones. Her dry black hair looked lifeless and scratchy and hung on each side of her head like the whisks of a broom.

Her skin was brown and wrinkled. Wanda's glance moved from the bright pink lipstick smeared on her lips to her big eyeglasses and large round eyes, blacker than night.

She was wearing a bright flowered shirt and orange pants with an apron tied around her waist. A crisp white apron splattered with ugly red stains.

"Come in, Wanda," she said. Her black eyes narrowed. "What took you so long? You're late."

TWENTY-THREE

100% Accurate 30% of the Time

"How do you know my name?" Wanda asked, speaking loudly to mask the tremble in her voice. "How did you know we were coming?"

"I know everything. I am the All-Knowing Phyllis," the woman said, and yanked Wanda inside. Voltaire flew in behind her and landed on a small square table in the center of the room.

"The All-Knowing Phyllis?" Wanda rubbed her arm where the woman had gripped it.

"Yes, I am the All-Knowing Phyllis."

"So nice to meet you," Voltaire said. "Do you really know everything?"

"Yes, I do," the woman confirmed.

"Then let's begin right away. There's so much I've forgotten. Please tell me all of it."

"Not *that* kind of everything." The woman shook her head. "I just know the future." Then she pushed Wanda toward one of the two chairs at the table.

"Have a seat." She slammed the shack door. "You never know who you'll meet in the Scary Wood. Can't be too careful." She slid two bolts across the door, then, for good measure, locked it with a key.

While Wanda sat, the woman tucked the key deep inside her apron pocket, which made Wanda very uncomfortable. She tried to hide her distress by gazing around the room. A shabby couch stood against one wall. An old refrigerator, stove, and sink lined another. Stubs of flickering candles sat on a small table in front of an armchair. A crackling fire warmed the shack.

"Why do you live in the Scary Wood?" Wanda asked. "If you're worried about what's out there, I mean."

"I like the quiet," Phyllis said. "It's peaceful here—except for the occasional scream."

Was that a joke? Wanda wondered. She didn't think so—Phyllis wasn't smiling. "Well, if you know everything, what can you tell us?" Wanda asked, trying to hide her fear.

Phyllis took a seat facing Wanda and the bird. "I can

see what is to be seen. I can tell what is to be told," she said. "Usually."

"Yes. Right. You're a fortune-teller," Wanda said. "Where's your crystal ball?"

"I don't use a crystal ball. I look into your eyes. Then you look into my eyes. That sort of thing."

"And that works?" Wanda's fear of the woman started to fade. *She doesn't seem dangerous at all,* Wanda thought. *More likely, she's crazy.*

"You don't believe me?" Phyllis said. "I bet you think I'm crazy." She leaned forward and stared deeply at Wanda—and Wanda could see that the woman's black eyes were like mirrors. She saw herself reflected in each of them.

"So thrilling!" Voltaire said. "Wanda, don't blink. She's going to tell you your future."

Phyllis stared hard into Wanda's eyes.

Wanda stared back.

"Yes, yes, look into my eyes . . ." Phyllis said, "and I will learn what there is to be learned. I am one hundred percent accurate thirty percent of the time."

"But that means you—" Wanda started.

"Shush!" Phyllis narrowed her eyes. "Yes, there it is. You are headed for danger."

"What kind of danger?" Voltaire flapped his wings. "What do you see? What do you see?"

"I see . . . a cave," she declared. "You are searching for a cave."

"Outstanding!" Voltaire chirped. "So true!"

"Your destiny is to reach the cave."

That prediction made Wanda very happy. Although her confidence in the bird might have wavered at times, her faith in him had remained intact. But still, it was comforting to hear news of the cave from someone else. Comforting and encouraging. And now she was convinced that this strange woman did, indeed, have some sort of power.

"And I see a boy in the cave."

"Voltaire, you were right! He *is* in the cave!"

The bluebird puffed out his chest, so proud.

"And I see dragons. They live near the cave."

"Dragons? No, you don't see dragons." Voltaire shook his head. "Please don't see dragons."

"The All-Knowing Phyllis is never mistaken. Generally. Typically. Well, not often. Anyway, I see dragons."

"What do we do about these dragons?" Wanda asked, trying to stay calm.

"Depends," said Phyllis.

"Depends on what?" Wanda asked.

"Depends on if they're the nice dragons or the not-so-nice dragons."

"Well, which ones are they?" Wanda asked.

"You're not supposed to ask questions," said Phyllis. "Nobody asks questions. They just *ooh* and *aah*. Why are you asking so many questions?"

"Well, it's kind of important to know," Wanda said. "Which dragons are they?"

"Another question. No more questions!" The All-Knowing Phyllis's gaze was broken. She blew out an exasperated breath. "Listen, I don't like people. But you seem okay, so I'm trying to help you. *Be patient!* The information doesn't all come at once."

"Maybe we could try again tomorrow?" Wanda asked.

Phyllis stood up from her chair. "We'll see. Now, stop talking. Let's eat. I knew you'd be hungry, so I cooked."

Wanda tried to press Phyllis to go on, but the woman had already walked to the stove. She removed the lid on the pleasantly steaming pot, and the room filled with the wonderful aroma of freshly made stew.

Wanda's stomach gurgled at the smell. She was *very* hungry . . . and the stew smelled *so* delicious . . . but

Wanda worried. She didn't know a thing about this woman. She *did* know these woods, though. She had been kidnapped in them, turned to smoke, and nearly changed into a squid. Could she trust anyone who lived here? Wanda stared at her plate.

"Eat it. It won't kill you," Phyllis said. "That's one hundred percent accurate."

Wanda looked at Voltaire. Was that a flicker of fear in his eyes?

She took a deep breath—and inhaled the stew's incredible aroma. It was hypnotizing, and she couldn't resist it a moment longer.

They ate at the foot of the fire. Wanda finished every morsel and licked the fork clean. She hadn't felt this cozy in days, and soon she and Voltaire fell asleep in front of the hearth, just as the All-Knowing Phyllis knew that they would.

***

The next morning, Wanda woke up to Voltaire's happy tweets. "You're in a good mood," she said.

"It's always a fine day when you discover you haven't been poisoned," he chirped.

"Voltaire," Wanda said, shaking her head, "if you were worried about the stew, why didn't you say something last night—*before* we ate it?"

"Because, Wanda dear, it wasn't a problem *before* we ate it. It would only become a problem *after* we ate it."

I guess that makes sense, Wanda thought. *Sort of. Oh, well, it really doesn't matter now. The important thing is we're still alive!*

The fortune-teller was nowhere to be seen. While they waited for her to return, Wanda and Voltaire reviewed what they had learned the night before.

"We will reach the cave—that's a sure thing," said Wanda. "But there will be danger nearby."

They wondered which dragons they would meet. And what they would do when they met them. And, most of all, they wondered what made the not-so-nice dragons not so nice.

"Even though we know about the dragons and the danger and my destiny, I'm more puzzled now than I was before," Wanda said. "Isn't it strange that the more we learn, the less we seem to know?"

"A million questions just lead to a million more," Voltaire agreed.

Just then, Phyllis came through the door with a stack of firewood in her arms.

"Oh, good," said Wanda. "You're back. We didn't want to leave without saying good-bye."

"I know," said Phyllis.

"And I wanted to talk to you one last time."

"I knew that, too."

Wanda took a deep breath. "Please, Phyllis, could you look into my eyes again and see what can be seen?" she asked. "Who is holding my brother in the cave? Why is he there?"

"Sorry." The All-Knowing Phyllis turned her hands up and shrugged. "I've already told you all there was to tell."

"How about the dragons?" Wanda wouldn't give up. "Can you tell us what they do?"

"Aha! I did have a vision of that as I closed my eyes late last night. The not-so-nice dragons turn people to ash with one single breath."

"And the nice ones?" Wanda asked.

"They don't."

"That's it?" Wanda asked.

"Afraid so," Phyllis replied.

She stood in the open doorway as Wanda and Voltaire got ready to leave.

"It's been—" Wanda started.

"A real pleasure, I know," Phyllis said. "You were

happy to meet me, and you hope to see me again soon."
With a gentle push, she guided them out.

Phyllis's dark gaze followed Wanda and Voltaire as
they made their way down the path. "Be careful and
good luck!" she called after them. "You'll need it. . . ."

TWENTY-FOUR

A Sign

"This apple is delicious!" Wanda took another bite. "So juicy. Want a piece?" She offered it to the bird on her shoulder.

Wanda had new clothes, food, a quickly drawn map, and a new rucksack to put it all in. Phyllis had known exactly what Wanda would need and had packed the rucksack full. Wanda was very grateful.

She and Voltaire picked up the trail that wound its way around the mountain. With boulders on one side and trees on the other, it was a tricky climb. Small stones along the path caused Wanda to stumble. Large leaps were required to jump over big rocks. At times the path became so narrow, her arm scraped up against the boulders. The ride became too bumpy for Voltaire, who decided to fly instead.

But through it all, Wanda remained cheerful. After a night at the shack, she felt revived and refreshed and more than ready to continue their quest.

"A mood improves quickly when you're not hungry or tired," Voltaire said.

"Yes, it does," Wanda agreed, taking another bite of her apple.

"You know, that's the secret to getting things done." Voltaire flew just ahead of her. "Throughout life, the most important decision you make is to be in a good mood." Then he flew back to her. "Today will require a very good mood if we are to battle dragons."

Dragons.

Wanda had been thinking about dragons all morning, and the mention of them caused her stomach to flip. How could a girl and a bird defeat such fearsome creatures?

"Voltaire, you know so much about so much. Do you have any idea how to fight dragons?"

"Yes, of course," Voltaire said. "There are many ways to eliminate, obliterate, annihilate, exterminate, eradicate, or decimate a dragon."

"Well, how 'bout we start with three," Wanda said. "Tell me three ways to slay a dragon."

"Certainly," Voltaire said. "You can poke him in the eyes. Then slay him when he can't see. Or you can stab him once and quickly, directly in the heart—a very sensitive spot. But if you lack something sharp, poison will work just as well."

Hmm. Wanda set her mind to thinking. *I wonder if a dragon would be willing to trade—take someone in our place. We could give the dragon my brother Zane. A beast for a beast. That could work out very nicely.* She didn't say any of this aloud, because she had promised herself to try to be kinder, especially where Zane was concerned. Instead, she asked, "Exactly how many of those methods have you seen actually work?"

"Let's see . . ." Voltaire fell behind Wanda as he counted. "Exactly . . . none," he pronounced. "Very good, Wanda," he yelled up ahead. "You've made an excellent point. I can't say with certainty that any one of those would work."

"I suppose it *is* very good, because they all seem too cruel," she called back.

She rounded a steep curve and lost sight of Voltaire. She took a few more steps, then reached into her rucksack for Phyllis's map. The old woman had done a quick job with the drawing, but it was clear that soon after this curve, the dragons would be in sight. Wanda's heart clenched at the mere thought of seeing them.

"Well, if you cannot bring yourself to slay a dragon, then we should give up our quest," Voltaire shouted.

"Give up our quest! Voltaire, did you really say that? I will never give up my quest to find my brother—no matter what danger lies ahead."

There was no question that Wanda meant what she said, but with each step that brought her closer and closer to the dragons, she grew more and more anxious.

Which dragons will we meet? she wondered.

The nice ones, she hoped—and that's what she was thinking when she tripped and lurched into a wooden post on the path. "Voltaire, come quick," she called. "I've found a sign."

"A good sign or a bad sign?"

"It's a real sign," she answered. "Come see what it says."

Voltaire's wings flapped hard as he caught up to Wanda. He found her shaking her head, staring at the small wooden post with a top carved in the shape of an arrow. And the words:

"How very thoughtful." Voltaire headed in the direction of the arrow.

"No! Come back!" Wanda said. "I think this could be a trap."

"A trap?" Voltaire returned. "How so?"

"Isn't it strange for someone to leave a sign to a hidden cave that we happen to be searching for? No one with good intentions would leave a sign like that," Wanda reasoned. "If we go that way, a trap surely awaits us. So we should go the opposite way. . . ."

"Very good." Voltaire started to fly off in the other direction.

"Unless they want us to think we should go the opposite way—and *that's* where the trap lies. So, in that case, following the arrow would be the right thing to do."

"Just where I was going." Voltaire started again.

"Unless . . ."

Voltaire stopped. "Wanda, I will follow you to the ends of the earth—but only in one direction. You must choose a path."

Wanda paced in front of the sign, trying to decide which direction to take. She consulted Phyllis's map again, but it lacked the detail they needed.

"Voltaire, you know these woods better than I do. What do your instincts tell you? Which way should we go?"

The bird perched on top of the sign. He looked to the left, and he looked to the right. He looked up; he looked down. "Gadzooks! I know this place! We'll follow the arrow."

TWENTY-FIVE

A Hunch

Wanda worried about the path they were on. She would have worried no matter which path they had taken and no matter who had selected it. And no matter how logical the choice had seemed. She worried because she knew that the only thing you could count on in the Scary Wood was that you couldn't count on anything here.

Were they headed into a trap? Her anxiety chased all thoughts of dragons from her mind as they made their way up the mountainside.

As they neared the crest, the path became rougher, then narrower. Finally it ended at two huge boulders, skyscraper tall and just as wide.

Wanda studied the stone giants. There was just a slice of daylight between them. With Voltaire on her shoulder, she drew in her breath to make herself thinner. She pressed her arms tightly to her sides and slowly wedged her way through the tight space.

"Good work!" Voltaire cheered when they stepped free of the stone. "And look where we are!"

They had reached the very highest point of the mountain. At last.

On one side of them grew a thicket of trees. Directly in front stretched a wide-open space—a rocky plateau, ending at a dizzying cliff. Wanda moved to the edge. She looked down at the terrifying drop. She had never stood on anything this high before—and it caused her to swoon. She quickly moved away from the rim.

"Voltaire, we're here! We're finally here. My brother is so close—I can feel it!"

The bluebird fluttered happily over Wanda's head. "Yes! We have done it! The cave must be right through those trees. And look, Wanda, there's not a dragon in sight. Let's hurry!"

The two had just started off again when a powerful roar shattered the heights. It made the ground rumble, and the trees shook from their roots.

And suddenly, thundering through the grove,

stomped four startling dragons, one blue, one green, one purple, and one red. As they charged from the trees into the sunlight, their scales flared and shimmered. It made for a dazzling spectacle, both splendid and fearsome.

When the dragons reached the clearing, they all spread their wings wide. Their span was enormous. Wanda had never seen such an astounding display.

With a slow grace and at exactly the same time, the dragons lifted their wings over their heads. When they spotted Wanda, they started beating their wings with fury, all the while their feet remaining firmly planted on the ground.

Wind whipped and dust churned around Wanda. The treetops bowed low. Voltaire tumbled in the air, and the gusts pushed Wanda back, back, back toward the edge of the cliff.

"Oh, noooo!" she cried.

But just as she was about to topple over the edge, the dragons folded their wings and the wild wind stopped.

Wanda fell to her knees and swallowed great gulps of air.

"Quite impressive, Wanda, wouldn't you say?" Voltaire drifted down to the ground and stared at his own small wings.

"WHO ARE YOU? WHY ARE YOU HERE?" the blue

dragon asked in a voice that was deep and strong and exceptionally loud.

Before Wanda could answer, Voltaire stepped forward.

"No, Voltaire!" Wanda lunged after him. "They will turn you to ash in one single breath."

"Don't worry, Wanda. I have a hunch."

"A hunch?"

"Yes. A hunch," Voltaire said. "Follow me. We will have a talk with these fellows."

As the two moved closer, the dragons' nostrils flared.

"Voltaire, they don't look in the mood for a chat. Are you sure about this?"

"Of course I'm not sure. I have never had a hunch in my life. Although if this one works out, I will make a note to have more."

Wanda halted, but Voltaire nudged her forward. "Now listen closely," he whispered in her ear. "Here's what I think you should say to them. . . ."

TWENTY-SIX

Dragons

"Blue dragon, sir." Wanda slowly approached the four creatures. "Or is it madam? My name is Wanda Seasongood, and I humbly seek your help. We are humbly looking for a cave, and we humbly think you can assist us."

"Very good, Wanda. Exactly as I suggested. Now a little louder and a little closer. Just remember to be respectful," Voltaire coached. "I think that's the key here."

"Do you know where the cave is?" Wanda cupped her hands to her mouth and took two small steps toward the blue dragon. "I ask humbly," she shouted.

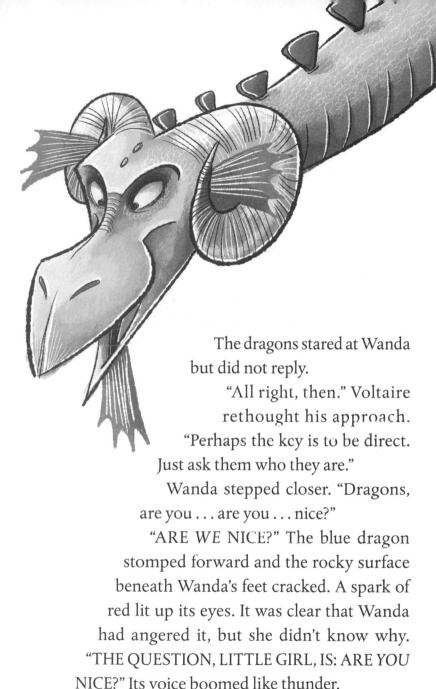

The dragons stared at Wanda but did not reply.

"All right, then." Voltaire rethought his approach. "Perhaps the key is to be direct. Just ask them who they are."

Wanda stepped closer. "Dragons, are you . . . are you . . . nice?"

"ARE WE NICE?" The blue dragon stomped forward and the rocky surface beneath Wanda's feet cracked. A spark of red lit up its eyes. It was clear that Wanda had angered it, but she didn't know why. "THE QUESTION, LITTLE GIRL, IS: ARE YOU NICE?" Its voice boomed like thunder.

Wanda hadn't expected that reply, and she didn't know what to make of it. So she fell into a dumbfounded silence.

The red dragon stepped forward. "If you are nice, we will let you live, and we will help you. If you are not nice, we will kill you."

"Oh." Wanda took a giant step back. "Then you must be the not-so-nice dragons."

"NO. We are the nice dragons. The not-so-nice dragons would kill you whether you're nice or not," the red dragon continued.

"This is very confusing," Wanda said.

"Well then, pay attention," snapped the purple dragon. "If you are pleasant and warm and kind and good-natured . . ."

"And trusting and caring and giving," continued the green one, who seemed a little more patient, "we wouldn't think of harming you. How could anyone harm such a fine person like that? But if you're not those things, we will kill you. It's simple, really."

"SO WHICH ARE YOU . . . NICE OR NOT NICE?" The blue dragon snorted. "THINK CAREFULLY. YOUR LIVES WILL DEPEND ON IT."

"We're nice! We're definitely nice. We're all of those

things. Absolutely," Wanda said boldly, hoping the dragons did not notice her worry.

Her thoughts about her parents and brother hadn't always been nice. Did the dragons have the power to detect that? She'd sworn to be kinder, and she was very serious about it, but she couldn't erase her past. Still, a promise to do better should count. Would the dragons think so? Wanda's palms turned clammy with fear.

The dragons put their heads together to consider Wanda's claim. They spoke among themselves, at first quietly, in a very different tone from their recent roars, and Wanda couldn't hear them. Then their voices rose as their debate continued.

"Do you think she's telling the truth?" the blue dragon grumbled. "I sense she's hiding something."

"Could be." The red dragon snorted. "She looks shifty."

"Rotten to the core, I think," said the purple dragon. "And not terribly smart, by the way."

Wanda's shoulders slumped.

"The bird is a dimwit, too." The green dragon scowled at Voltaire. "Probably can't tell which way is up."

Voltaire let out a sad peep.

"That's enough!" Wanda shouted. "Turn me to ash, if that's what you want, but don't insult my friend!"

"Wanda, no!" Voltaire screeched.

"WELL, NOW YOU'VE DONE IT!" the blue dragon roared. "THAT'S WHAT WE WERE WAITING FOR." The dragons put their heads together once again.

They're probably deciding how to kill me. Wanda's body stiffened.

As her eyes scanned the trees searching for a way to escape, the blue dragon turned to her. "We have come to a determination. By defending the bird, you have passed our test. Wanda Seasongood, we *do* believe you are kind and nice and caring."

Wanda's muscles sagged with relief.

"*Of course* she is kind and nice and caring." Voltaire lifted his head high. "In fact, we're here to save Wanda's brother—that's a very kind and nice and caring thing to do."

"Ah, yes. The boy in the cave," the red dragon said.

Wanda gasped. "The boy in the cave! Do you know my brother? Have you seen him?"

"We have never seen the boy. We hear he lies deep inside the cavern. But the witch who imprisoned him visits the cave often," said the blue dragon.

"Yes, as recently as today, in fact," said the red one.

"She might be there still," said the green one. "With the young lass, Wren—the one who is always by her side.

So, if you are going to the cave, consider going later," he suggested. "You don't want to meet up with them."

"A witch?" Wanda inhaled sharply. "A witch has imprisoned my brother?" Her knees went wobbly. She sank to the ground to steady herself.

A witch. A few days ago, I was simply a girl wondering where I belonged—and now I am a girl who has to save her brother from the clutches of a witch.

"Voltaire, I've never fought a witch before. How can I know if I'm up to the challenge?" Wanda held her head in her hands.

" 'We know what we are, but know not what we may be,' " Voltaire quoted Shakespeare.

"But that still doesn't tell me—am I a girl who can fight a *witch*? Am I a girl who can fight a witch and win?"

"Of course you can. Or maybe not." Voltaire scratched his head. "Do you have a different question I could try to answer?"

Wanda climbed to her feet and brushed herself off. She walked up to the dragons and stood so close to them she could feel their sweltering breath on her face. "Can you please tell me more about the witch?"

"Her name is Raymunda," the purple dragon said. "All the creatures of the Scary Wood fear her. I'm surprised you've never heard of her."

It seems I haven't heard of a lot of things, Wanda thought, but she only shrugged in reply.

"Raymunda rules over these mountains and all the witches who live here," the purple dragon went on.

"You mean there's more than one?" Wanda asked in astonishment. Who knew so much was going on in these woods so close to her home?

"There are many, many witches here. Now, please, do not interrupt me," the purple dragon groused. "It's not nice. There was a time, years ago, when Raymunda's powers began to weaken," he went on. "The other witches held a meeting in the deepest part of the darkest valley, and a new witch was selected to take her place. When Raymunda heard of it, she let out a shriek that echoed to the top of this mountain. And she refused to give up her throne."

The blue dragon spoke next, lowering its head to gaze directly into Wanda's eyes. "Raymunda has worked very hard to strengthen her magic. She has vowed never to be challenged again. We hear her power is fearsome now—and no witch will defy her."

"They say she can crush any creature with a mere crook of her finger," said the red dragon.

"I heard she can make your skin boil," the purple

dragon added. "And the things they say she can do with the blood of a pig would give you nightmares."

"Voltaire," said Wanda, "we must leave here at once. We need to find out why this witch took my brother— and we must save him. Let's get to the cave quickly— before it's too late."

"I'm afraid quickly is not possible," the green dragon said. "The way to the cave is thick with brambles. You'll have a slow, hard time of it."

"Then would you be so kind and blaze a trail for us with your fiery breath?" Wanda asked.

"No. We cannot," the blue dragon replied. "We are dragons, but we are not the kind who breathe fire. That is not a way we can help."

"Can you fly us up there swiftly instead?" Wanda asked.

"We have mighty wings, but we do not fly," the red one answered.

"You do not breathe fire and you do not fly." Wanda was baffled. "Just what kind of dragons are you, besides nice, that is? What *do* you do?"

"We are the dragons who knit," said the green dragon. "We create heartwarming scenes of hearth and home. Scenes of lovely fireplaces and cozy rooms in yarn of red, blue, green, and purple." He pointed to each dragon as he recited the colors.

Knitting dragons. Wanda shook her head. It was hard to believe. "How can you help us if that is what you do?"

"Because what we do is what you'll need," the blue dragon said. "And now it's time to take your measure." He called out to the others. "We have one small bird with a very large task. And an average-size girl with oversize courage."

And then they began to knit. . . .

Which is how it came to be that, a short while later, a girl and a bird set off through the brambles, wearing identical sweaters with matching hats—on their way to meet a witch.

TWENTY-SEVEN

Are You for Me or Against Me?

"Raymunda."

Wanda now had a name to say and a person to picture—although it was hard for her to imagine anyone so wicked.

"Raymunda. Raymunda."

She said it over and over again as they trudged through the brambles. It rolled on her tongue and left with a sting.

"Wanda, how do I look in my sweater and hat?" Voltaire asked.

Wanda knew he was trying to break the hold the name had on her. And it worked, at least for a moment. She looked at the bird and laughed. His sweater, just like hers, had a scene of a roaring fireplace in a room with two overstuffed chairs. A dog snoozed on a rug in front of the fire. A painting of an eagle hung on a wall over the chairs. It was just as the dragons had described—a cozy view of hearth and home. It was a sweater Wanda would never have seen on herself, and most definitely not on a bird. The same could be said of their hats, which were knitted in stripes of red, blue, green, and purple—with a red pom-pom on each at the top.

It was amazing that the dragons had made them—and even more amazing that they could knit things small enough for a bird. The sweater and hat fit Voltaire perfectly. And Wanda had to admit that in this mountain chill, the sweater was keeping her nice and warm.

"You look very good." Wanda smiled, then returned to her monotonous chant. "Raymunda. Raymunda. Raymunda." She sighed. "Voltaire, can you imagine such a horrible person?"

"Wanda, let's not judge her too harshly. After all, she sent me to you. I wouldn't have met you if it weren't for her."

Wanda stopped walking. Her head started to spin. "*What?!* Wait! You know her?"

"Why, yes, now that you mention it," Voltaire chirped. "And it's a real stroke of luck for us, wouldn't you say?"

"Voltaire, are you sure Raymunda sent you?"

"Oh, yes. It just came to me, clear as day." Voltaire perched on Wanda's arm. "Raymunda is the one who tied the note to my neck. She is the one who set us off on our little adventure. I feel so much better now that I've remembered it."

This news pressed all the air from Wanda's lungs. The witch had sent Voltaire to her. The witch had kidnapped her brother. Why? What did it all mean?

Wanda started to walk again, but she remained silent as she tried to puzzle it out. And then another thought began to take shape. The words formed in her mouth, but they stuck to her tongue. She forced herself to say them. "Voltaire, are you for me or against me?"

"Well, both, I think. I seem to be of two minds on this point. It's a bit of a muddle, I'd say." He ruffled his feathers. "But no need to harp on it—because here we are."

They had reached the cave.

Its mouth was as black as a starless night. Wanda peered in, but she couldn't see anything through the inky darkness.

Now it was Wanda who was of two minds. Part of her wanted to rush right in to find her brother; part cautioned her to wait—the witch might still be inside.

She took but a moment to decide and stepped toward the cave. "Let's go. My brother might be in danger. We'll stick to the shadows."

She reached into her rucksack for the small flashlight Phyllis had given her. "Hop on my shoulder," she told the bird. There was no time to ponder his loyalty now. Her brother was here and so were the answers to every important question she'd ever had. Heart pounding, she entered the cave.

TWENTY-EIGHT

The Boy in the Cave

The cave was musty, chilly, and damp.

The path inside sloped down and descended quickly. Wanda placed a hand on the cave wall to keep her balance. She carefully and quietly inched her way through the darkness. She wanted to shine her flashlight up ahead so she could see where she was going, but she didn't want to alert the witch. Instead, she aimed it at her feet, where it made a very small circle of light.

She and Voltaire followed the wall through twists and turns. It was difficult walking this way. And frightening. Soon she lost track of how far they'd traveled, and even though she hadn't yet found her brother, she started to fret about finding their way back out again.

As they moved farther into the cave, the temperature dropped, and she shivered. "Are caves always this c-c-cold?" she whispered.

"Isn't it marvelous? I believe this is an ice cave," Voltaire chirped. "It's very unusual. These caves have ice even in summer."

Wanda didn't think it was marvelous at all. The cold started to settle into her limbs, and she stumbled, kicking some pebbles and sending them thudding.

She stopped—and held her breath.

Did the witch hear that?

No one leaped out at them. It appeared they were safe, at least for the moment.

They continued to follow the wall—then she tripped again, this time over a rock.

Her hand flew up. The flashlight's beam lit the passage in front of them—and she gasped.

She was in a large cavern with a craggy domed ceiling. Directly in front of her the cave narrowed, and she could see that the path was about to end in a small alcove.

Wanda focused her light on the alcove—and saw a solid block of ice, about the size of a coffin.

She took a few steps closer, and the air turned from cold to frigid. Now she and the bird were shaking and shivering. "This is an unnatural c-c-cold." Wanda's teeth chattered, and she could see her breath when she spoke.

"Oh, d-d-dear. I b-b-believe you are r-r-right," the bird agreed. "This is no ordinary ice c-c-cave. What g-g-great g-g-good f-f-fortune it is that we have these s-s-sweaters." But even the sweaters did not sufficiently warm them.

Wanda forced herself to walk into the alcove. The air here was even colder and bit her skin. She swept her light across the block of ice—and cried out. "Voltaire! Look! We've f-f-found my b-b-brother!"

A boy of about fifteen was encased in the frozen block. Even through the layers of ice, Wanda could see that he was very handsome. He had a chiseled jawline with a strong chin. High cheekbones and a perfect nose. And a crown of thick, lustrous black hair. Wanda imagined that if he opened his eyes, they would be the deepest blue. He was the most striking boy she had ever seen.

"V-v-very nice-looking lad," Voltaire said. "What a p-p-pity he's d-d-dead."

"We're t-t-too late!" Wanda moaned. She had known sadness before, but nothing that had tortured her heart this way. Her knees started to fold. She touched the block of ice to steady herself—and a frigid shock coursed through her fingers. It shot up her arm and pierced her chest like a dagger.

She let out a gasp. "Voltaire, I c-c-can't move my arms or my legs!" Her knees and elbows had begun to harden in place. Her skin started to stiffen. She struggled to breathe and fought to fill her lungs with air.

"Wanda, I b-b-believe this c-c-cave is under R-R-Raymunda's spell. Our b-b-blood is turning to ice. She is f-f-f-freezing us to d-d-death from inside and out."

The air grew more frigid. The walls in the cave became coated with frost. Wanda's bones and skin turned brittle. "I think I'm b-b-beginning to c-c-crack," she rasped.

And then, just as their blood was about to turn solid, their sweaters and hats began to glow. The cozy scenes on their sweaters flickered to life. The fire in the fireplaces appeared to blaze, and it cast a red glow on the cave walls.

All the yarn began to shimmer, and it lit up the cave in radiant hues of blue, red, green, and purple.

The air quickly grew warmer.

The frost on the walls began to melt.

And Wanda could feel her blood flowing through her veins again. Her arms and legs tingled with warmth.

"The dragons' sweaters are saving our lives!" She hugged herself and ran her fingers over the magical yarn.

"Voltaire, how are you feeling?" she asked, concerned about the fragile bird.

"My hat is heating my head very nicely," Voltaire observed. "I never considered wearing a hat before, but now I shall think twice about leaving home without it."

Wanda and Voltaire continued to grow warmer—and so did the air around them.

Drip. Drip. Drip.

The air had grown so warm, the coffin of ice began to melt.

The magical sweaters continued to glow. They glowed until the air in the cave was extremely toasty—and all that was left of the icy coffin was a very large puddle on the cave floor. Then they stopped.

"Look!" Wanda's gaze rested on the boy, whose eyelids had begun to flutter. "He's alive! He's alive!"

Wanda and Voltaire watched in silence as the boy moved his arms and legs, bending them, stretching them, testing them. Then he opened his eyes and caught sight of the girl and the bird.

"Hello." His voice was dry and whispery. "Hello," he tried again, and this time it came out stronger and clearer. "My name is William."

"My—my name is Wanda. I'm your long-lost sister!"

Wanda's heart filled with a joy she had never known before.

William slowly sat up. "I've been under a terrible spell," he said. "And somehow you've managed to free me. But I believe you have mistaken me for someone else."

"I'm not mistaken," Wanda said, nodding with confidence, "although I can understand your shock. I am your sister."

The boy smiled at Wanda. "I hate to disagree with you, since you've just saved my life, but I am very certain of it—I am not your brother."

TWENTY-NINE

I've Made a Slight Error

Voltaire hopped on the boy's knee. "Evidently, this young man is in some sort of stupor," he said to Wanda.

"Try to concentrate," he suggested to William. "You've been in a deep freeze, and perhaps your brain has not quite defrosted. This is Wanda. Wanda, your sister."

The boy listened to Voltaire, then turned to Wanda. "I'm sure it would be very nice to be related to you, but if you were my sister, I would know it."

"Voltaire, how can this be?" Wanda's face creased in confusion.

"Let me think." The little bird paced in front of the boy. "Yes! Something has just come to me!" He stopped and looked up at Wanda. "I've made a slight error. The boy in the cave is not your brother." He turned to William. "But aren't you somebody's brother?"

"Yes, I am." William rose to his feet and tested his legs. "I am a brother to a brother—and his name is Zane."

"ZANE?!" Wanda cried. "That's impossible. Zane is *my* brother."

"No, Wanda. Zane is *his* brother," Voltaire chirped.

"What do you mean Zane is his brother?" Wanda slumped against the cave wall. The threads of her life were suddenly unraveling, and she felt like loose, dangling strings of cloth.

"I recall it all now. Pity I couldn't remember it sooner," Voltaire said. "The witch told me everything—but I've simply mixed up the brothers. Sometimes things get a bit jumbled up here." The bird lifted his foot and scratched his head.

"I thought I had at least one brother," Wanda said, "and now I have none."

"Not to worry, Wanda," Voltaire said. "A brother was missing and a brother was found. A good day all around, don't you think?"

Wanda's thoughts were in a whirl. She took a deep breath to calm herself. "Voltaire, you said the witch told you everything. What else did she say?"

"I believe you know all of it now, dear Wanda. Oh, wait. Did I tell you about my mission?"

Wanda held her breath. She slowly shook her head no.

"The witch told me to lead you into the Scary Wood, where you'd most certainly die. It would stop you from snooping. From uncovering her secret. From ruining all her plans."

"Oh, no." Wanda gasped. Voltaire had been plotting against her this whole time. The ground beneath her began to spin.

I was right, she thought with a heavy heart. *Voltaire led me to the Groods, and the swamp goblin, and the horrible nixie.* Wanda trembled at the thought of it. She could barely look at the bird she had considered her one true friend. Her head hung down in despair.

"Is there anything else you need to tell me?" she asked.

"That's it"—he gave a satisfied nod—"except for one last thing. . . ."

She held her breath while Voltaire tried to recall the one last thing. She reached out for the wall, unsure if she could remain standing for yet another surprise.

"Aha! Now I remember. I refused to help her. I wanted no part of it. But then things became foggy—well, foggier than usual—and the next thing I knew, I was flying into your window."

"The witch must have put you under one of her spells," William told Voltaire. "They tend to make you dizzy and muddle the mind. It's the sort of thing she loves to do."

"How do you know what the witch loves to do?" Wanda asked. "Do you know her that well?"

"I know her quite well," he answered. "The witch is my mother."

THIRTY

An Exemplary Witch

Wanda sat down on the cold cave floor.

"The witch—Raymunda—is your mother?" She had heard William perfectly, but she needed to say it again and out loud for it to become real.

"Yes, yes, she is," William said, and shrugged.

How could a mother bury her son in ice? And how could a son seem to take it so calmly?

It was all so . . . *unthinkable.*

Wanda insisted that they leave the cave and find a place to sit under a tree. A place where she could catch her breath. Absorb everything she had heard. And try to find out how she fit into this mess.

William was excited to leave the cave—to see flowers and trees, the sky and the sun, the whole world again. "Is it day or night?" he asked, bounding ahead before Wanda had a chance to aim her flashlight.

"It's probably dark out by now," she said. She pointed the light in front of her—and caught sight of a shimmering object on the cave floor. She picked it up and placed it in the palm of her hand.

It looked like part of a necklace. *A locket?* she wondered. The case was made of lapis, and Wanda admired its deep blue color. *The color of the sky at midnight,* she thought. She stared at the streaks of glittering gold that ran through it. "Like little moonbeams," she whispered as the rays stretched out to her. She tucked the beautiful trinket safely in her pocket to study it later in better light.

Once out of the cave, William took deep, deep breaths, as if trying to inhale all the lost time he'd spent in his tomb. Then he sat under a tree next to Wanda with Voltaire perched on the top of Wanda's hat.

"I hope you don't think I'm rude," Wanda said to William, "but I have so many questions. And you seem to be fine, so I'll just start right in." Wanda knew she was inches away from learning the secret of her life, and she simply couldn't wait any longer. "Why did your mother put you under this horrible spell, and why does she want to destroy me? Do you know the answers?"

"Yes, I do," William replied. "But first—how much do you know about witches?"

"Not much," Wanda said. "Only what I've read in fairy tales. It wasn't until today that I learned that they're real."

"Well, the most important thing to know about witches is that they love one thing above all else, and that is power. Anyone who stands in the way of them getting it, keeping it, or growing it stronger is doomed," he said. "And you are in my mother's way. The same is true for me and for Zane."

"Wanda, isn't this thrilling?" Voltaire flew to the ground and hopped up and down. "A witch is out to get you! Now you'll have something exciting to write in your diary." He gathered some leaves to settle into a comfy seat.

"How can I be in your mother's way?" Wanda asked, trying to focus on what William was saying. "I don't even know her."

"Actually, you do, although somewhat by accident," William said with a smile.

Though William's smile was a little sad, Wanda thought it was still very nice. She looked into his eyes and saw that they were the exact shade of blue she had imagined. There was something mesmerizing about this boy, and she suddenly wished they didn't have to spend any more time talking about witches.

"A witch's power needs to be fed," William continued. "Some witches feed on hatred. Others on greed, jealousy, fear, or lies. There's a coven for each of these traits— five covens in all—and every witch belongs to one of them."

"Which coven does your mother belong to?" Wanda thought it would be important to know.

"None of them," William replied. "Mother is what they call an *Exemplary*. She feeds on all of those things. That's why she is so powerful, and why she is the leader of the covens. Exemplaries are very rare. But you know two of them—my mother and Zane."

"Zane is a witch?" Wanda couldn't believe it at first, but then she had to admit it made sense. He was definitely evil enough. . . .

Then a piercing thought stabbed Wanda. "That means you must be a witch, too. . . ." She shifted away from William.

William shook his head. "No, I have no magical powers of any kind." He gazed down as if embarrassed, then lifted his head to look at Wanda. "Of course, one can learn to become a witch. You don't have to be born into it. But I don't seem to have the talent to learn, either." He laughed. Then his smile faded as he continued his story. "Over the course of her life, my mother has had many enemies—and one of them cast a deadly spell on her. An extraordinary spell. Day by day it weakened her powers and slowly drained her life away. Everyone knew that the time would soon come when Zane would have to take her place."

"This is all very fascinating," Voltaire said. "But what exactly does it have to do with our Wanda?"

"Exactly this," William replied. "My mother craves power and will do *anything* to hold on to it. She would never allow *anyone* to take her place, including Zane."

Wanda's toes curled inside her shoes. She didn't know where this was heading, but she knew it wasn't going to be good.

"She tried to turn Zane into an animal. But she was too weak, Zane was too strong, and the spell didn't quite work. She turned him into something half boy, half creature, and he ran away."

That certainly sounds like Zane, Wanda thought. She wondered what he was like before the spell, but she didn't want to interrupt William to ask.

"We found him in your arbor, growling and howling," William continued, "and he refused to return with us. So, with the little magic she had left, she bewitched your family. She made you all think that Zane was one of your own. She put your parents in a trance, convincing them to tend to Zane above all else. Then she silenced me in a prison of ice—a spell that you managed to break." William slouched against the tree and relaxed. "Thank you for that."

The haze over Wanda's life had finally cleared. Now everything made sense. The strange way her parents treated her. Zane's beastly behavior. The constant feeling that something wasn't quite right.

She felt a sudden lightness and knew that the witch's spell no longer clung to her. Any lingering weight of the curse had lifted. The locket in her pocket grew warm, and she took it out to gaze at it.

"What's that?" William asked, seeing the glow in her hand.

"Just something I brought from home." Wanda slipped it back in her pocket, not ready to share what she had found. "And speaking of home, I must go back and break the spell on Zane and my parents." Wanda jumped up. "How do we do that? We must do it at once!"

William lowered his head to think. "We'll have to go to the witches' garden, in the darkest part of the deepest valley. That's where the plants for the potions grow. We can gather what we need there to end the spell."

When he gazed up, his eyes gave away a new thought taking shape. But he offered nothing more—except a narrowed glance and a slow, mysterious smile.

THIRTY-ONE

The Witches' Garden

The next morning, as the dark surrendered to a brightening sky and the flicker of the last star faded, the three prepared to leave. It was important to get an early start. It would take all day to make their way down the mountain, then till evening to reach the witches' garden.

There was a chill in the air, and Wanda and Voltaire still wore their matching sweaters and hats. Now that William could see them clearly in the morning light, he couldn't help but stare. "Do you two always dress alike?" he asked.

"These sweaters saved our lives," Wanda explained. "And yours, too." She told him about their encounter with the dragons and how the sweaters had melted the ice.

"The nice dragons—of course. I should have recognized their knitting." He touched the yarn on Wanda's sleeve. "There's nothing like dragon yarn. Legend says it has many ways of protecting someone from harm."

Voltaire stuck out both wings. "And the colors really look splendid against my blue feathers, don't you think?"

As they traveled down the mountain, the air grew warmer. Wanda and Voltaire removed their sweaters and hats, and Wanda made sure to tuck them safely in her rucksack.

They followed a winding path until it split in two. William had been guiding them, but he hesitated at the fork.

"I must admit," he said. "I'm not entirely sure which path to take. My memory seems a little foggy." He squinted and gazed down each trail. "I guess my mind hasn't cleared yet from my mother's deep chill."

"Your mother is a horrible, terrible, despicable person," Wanda said. "She confused Voltaire the same way, and because of her, I was nearly killed three times before I found you."

William frowned but didn't say anything.

"I'm feeling much more myself now," Voltaire said,

fluttering above them. "I think I can deduce the way from here. We will take the path on the right. Then we'll look for the moss on the trees—it grows only on the north side. Eventually we will turn left at the dwarf pitch pines and head south. And then we'll be there. It's simple, really."

"How do you know all this?" William asked.

"Voltaire is very smart. When he isn't all mixed up, that is." Wanda smiled and started along the path the bluebird had suggested.

"Thank you, Wanda," said Voltaire. "Nice of you to notice."

They continued in silence, each deep in their private thoughts. Wanda's drifted between Zane and her parents.

"You don't have to worry—your brother is fine." Even though William hadn't asked about Zane, she thought he would want to know. "He hasn't been easy to live with, though," she let slip. "He has the manners of a beast."

"Understandable," said William, "since Mother turned him into one, at least partially." His face lit up with a grin.

"Oh, sorry. That's right," Wanda apologized. "It will be wonderful to break the spell he and my parents are under and have them back the way they should be. I wonder what the real Zane will be like."

"Well, before the spell, he was very charming. Even as a baby he could make anyone give him whatever he wanted." William grinned. "But that was okay, since he shared everything with me."

"Being so close—it must have been nice," Wanda said.

"Yes, it was," William agreed. "We were brothers, and we were best friends."

"I wish I had a brother or sister to go home to," Wanda said.

Wanda wasn't certain William had heard her. A shadow passed over his face and his smile faded. "My mother always said that Zane had incredible power from the day he was born. Now that he's older, I'm sure his powers have grown even stronger. Having that much power can be dangerous." William shook his head and grew quiet. All talk of Zane ended there.

As night approached and they neared the darkest part of the deepest valley, the topic returned to covens and witches.

"Every time someone lies or is greedy or jealous, a witch is encouraged," William explained. "Anytime someone acts with hatred or causes fear, a witch grows stronger. Evil feeds evil, and there seems to be no end to it. It's all very good for the witches." He shrugged.

"Yes, dear boy," Voltaire said. "But evil only wins if we

choose to do nothing about it. And we're doing our part, aren't we?" Voltaire's eyes narrowed with determination. "Look—I believe we're here!"

Just ahead of them Wanda saw an old stone house with a flight of stone steps leading up to it. The house was completely surrounded by tall trees, and Wanda had to peer between the tree trunks to get a glimpse of it. The light of the moon made it easy enough to see.

The house stood two stories high. It was made of gray stone, but most of it was covered with a thick green blanket of moss. The slate roof came to a point, and just beneath the roof's peak, a small, round window was set into the front of the house. Although the other windows in the house were dark, a soft yellow glow filled this one.

"I think someone's inside," Wanda whispered.

"Probably so," William said. "The witches come here to meet and practice their spells. It's a safe place for them."

They walked closer, with Voltaire flying just ahead of them, and Wanda could see that the house was larger than a first glance revealed. It extended far back into the woods. There was another stone staircase at the back. "Those steps will take us down to the garden," William said, and headed toward them. "Let's try to be quiet.

Witches have excellent hearing, and it would be best not to disturb them."

They stepped very carefully, trying to avoid anything on the ground that might snap or crunch. When they reached the bottom of the stairs, Wanda saw a huge plot of land with trees far in the distance. But there was not a single plant in sight. The land was bare.

"Where is the garden?" she whispered.

"It's right here." William took Wanda by the shoulders and positioned her directly in front of him, facing out. "Now you should be able to see it." Voltaire settled on the top of her head.

As Wanda stared at the vacant earth, shafts of moonlight twisted and bent until they were shining directly on the empty field. Then the air began to shimmer— and plants sprouted from the ground, taking shape as if summoned into being.

Wanda gasped. "Did *you* do that?" She turned to William. "I thought you said you weren't a witch."

William shook his head. "It's the magic of the garden."

Within minutes, the garden was lush with colorful and fragrant flowers. Bright reds and pinks. Iridescent blues, yellows, and greens. Glimmering purples. And black flowers, too. They sprouted around oddly shaped

trees and bushes with bright orange berries. William told her that the flowers she thought looked the prettiest and smelled the sweetest were the most poisonous.

Stone walkways appeared, winding through the trees and flowers. And trellises with snaking vines. Common herbs grew next to strange plants Wanda had never seen before.

In the very center of the garden, there was a large circular mosaic embedded in the earth. Arranged around it were elaborately carved benches where one could sit and view the garden.

Wanda focused on the mosaic. Glittery gold and silver tiles had been set into it to form a crescent moon surrounded by twinkling stars. And Wanda saw that all the winding walkways throughout the garden eventually led to the moon.

As they walked through the shrubbery, William identified the plants they would need to undo his mother's spell.

Wanda's rucksack quickly filled with the leaves and berries they would use to make the potion. She and Voltaire sat down under a tree to arrange them all in her bag and to make room for more.

"Ah. Here's what I was looking for," William said from somewhere nearby. "The stinging nettle."

"Be careful," a silky voice warned, floating over the breeze. "Those can burn at the touch."

Wanda peered out from behind the tree. A tall, thin woman stood at the top of the stone stairs. She wore black pants, a shiny black blouse, and a long black cape that flowed to her knees. Her skin was creamy, and her jet-black hair hung in waves to her waist. Wanda's stomach twisted in fear. Was this one of the witches from the house?

"I didn't expect to see you here," the woman said.

"Is that so?" William replied without emotion. He didn't seem concerned as he stepped toward the tree where Wanda was hidden.

He's trying to block me from view, Wanda realized and moved farther back into the shadow of the tree.

But William didn't stand in front of her. Instead, he reached for Wanda's arm. He pulled her from the shadows and yanked her into a patch of moonlight. "And I bet you didn't expect to see *her,* either, Mother."

THIRTY-TWO

Never Trust a Witch

M*other?!* This was Raymunda! Wanda swayed in shock. She nearly fell over, but William held her arm firmly. Voltaire fluttered up into a tree.

"Wanda. How lovely." Raymunda folded her arms tightly in front of her. She was a daunting figure—straight-backed and regal. "I don't know how you escaped the cave. I assume the nice dragons had a hand in breaking my spell. But, I must admit, I'm not totally disappointed. Thank you, William. This is a very thoughtful gift." She sauntered down one of the walkways. "It will be much more satisfying to see Wanda suffer here, where I can watch her closely."

Wanda yanked free of William. "How could you do this to me? I thought we were friends. I saved you! I trusted you!"

"William cannot be trusted." Raymunda meandered toward the center of the garden. "You have learned an important lesson, Wanda, but you've learned it too late—never trust a witch."

Wanda turned to William. "You *are* a witch? But you said . . ." She had foolishly believed him, and he had betrayed her—and she didn't know which one felt worse.

"Sorry, Wanda." His mouth twisted into a grin. "I belong to the Coven of Lies. I feed off deceit. Even my own. With every lie I told you, I felt stronger and stronger. Thanks for your help."

"You're a scoundrel!" Voltaire's wings beat hard as he flew circles around William. "Wanda, I suggest that you end your friendship with this boy at once and cut all ties to him."

"I don't think that will be a problem." Raymunda laughed. "Wanda is about to cut all ties with everyone she knows."

Wanda's heart pounded faster than Voltaire's beating wings. Everything had turned sour so quickly. But she would not allow these witches to witness her fear. "You don't frighten me," she said to Raymunda.

"Oh, but I will," the witch replied. "I will soon terrify you. And there will be no one here to help you this time. No little Grood. No nice dragons." She turned to her son. "Now, William—if you want to remain free, you must promise to leave Zane where he is. Otherwise, I will be forced to do something worse than imprison you in ice."

"That won't be necessary, Mother." William smiled. "I see that your health and powers have returned—and I would very much like to learn and work by your side."

"Good," said Raymunda. "The Five Covens have accepted my reign. They fear a war is coming with the witches from the South, and they need me to lead them. My place is secure here—unless Zane is freed. I understand that boy well. He is so much like me. He would kill me in an instant to take my place."

"I have no desire to help him or to hurt you," William said. He took Wanda's arm again. "Now, what should we do with this one?"

"Tie her up and set her at my feet." Raymunda took a seat on one of the garden benches.

"And the bird?" William asked. Voltaire had settled on Wanda's shoulder, which gave her a little comfort.

"He is no danger to us. I'll see to him later." She reached into the folds of her cape and took out her wand. "Now I will gather the other witches. I want them to witness how I deal with my enemies." She waved her wand and muttered some words that Wanda guessed were a summoning spell.

William pulled out a wand he had hidden in his jacket. With a simple flick of it, a rope appeared around Wanda's wrists. As William tested the knot, Voltaire pressed up against Wanda's ear. "I will fly without rest to bring back help," he whispered. "And if you fall into despair, just remember the words of F. Scott Fitzgerald. 'You mustn't confuse a single failure with a final defeat.' See? I've said it, and I feel better already!"

And with that he flew off.

"You're right about Voltaire," William said as he tightened the knot around Wanda's wrists. "He is a smart bird. You'll never see him again."

Wanda didn't bother responding. This lying boy, raised by such a cruel and evil mother, knew nothing about the true nature of friendship.

Then, as William marched her to sit at the feet of the horrible witch, she forced all fearful thoughts from her mind to concentrate on one thing only—her plan to escape.

THIRTY-THREE

Wanda's Brew

A thousand and two witches.

The Five Covens came for Raymunda's show. Men and women of every age, race, shape, and size. They walked in through the woods, fell from the sky, or just materialized in the air with a *pop!* One old witch with a long beard arrived on a bicycle, pedaling furiously, apologizing for his lateness. Their arrival was at once spectacular and frightening.

But for Wanda, the most terrifying part was how they looked. They appeared to be everyday people—a storekeeper, a neighbor—there was nothing that set them apart from the people Wanda saw daily. *There are witches among us, and it's impossible to tell who they are.* Wanda shivered and hoped that William, standing right behind her, hadn't noticed.

The witches gathered around the circle mosaic and spilled onto the winding paths. They stood on the steps that led to the garden and on the leafy ground at the sides of the house. They surrounded Wanda, and she could not see a way to flee from them.

When the last witch, a young girl named Wren, joined them, Raymunda rose from her seat. She stepped into the middle of the circle. "Welcome, my friends. This is Wanda. Her meddling has landed her here, where no mortal should ever be. I have invited you to enjoy her punishment."

The other witches murmured their approval.

Raymunda turned to Wanda. "I thought about all the wonderful ways I could hurt you. I could make your bones twist until they crack."

"Ooh," the crowd said.

"Or have all your blood drain out through your ears."

"Aah," said the onlookers.

"I even considered having pieces of you simply fall off—your nose, a foot, a finger, an arm, every part of you dropping away, one by one."

"Ouch," said a few of the witches, clutching their noses or ears.

"But in all of these choices, you would die very quickly," said Raymunda, "and where's the fun in that?"

The witches nodded in agreement.

"No. None of those would do." Raymunda stepped toward Wanda. "I have a much better solution—a potion. Concocted especially for someone who asks too many questions."

Wanda's head buzzed with fear. She looked to the sky. Where was Voltaire? Had he found help? She wished he would hurry.

With a wave of her wand, a tarnished and dented goblet appeared in Raymunda's palm. Whatever was inside it was giving off smoke. "I call this Wanda's Brew. After just one cup of it, you will never ask another question. When you speak, it will sound like gibberish. When you write, it will come out in scribbles. *Poor Wanda,* people will say. *Her mind has turned to slush.*"

Wanda had to admit that she couldn't think of a more frightening punishment for herself, someone who had a lot to say . . . someone who wanted to be taken seriously . . . someone who needed to set things right.

Raymunda thrust the cup between Wanda's bound hands. "Drink it."

Wanda searched the sky one last time.

No Voltaire.

She looked out at the witches, who returned her gaze with cold, vacant stares.

She glanced behind her at William, who simply nodded.

She thought about her parents, and even Zane. Who would save them now?

No one. Wanda had failed them, and herself.

She had no choice.

She took the cup and drank.

THIRTY-FOUR

Give It Back!

The liquid was bitter and harsh.

Wanda spit it out.

"Drink it!" the witch commanded. "Drink it all."

Wanda's heart pounded in terror as the sour potion slid down her throat. *I will not let this drink turn my mind to slush. I will not. I will not. I will not.* She repeated this over and over again, certain that her determination would defeat the poison.

The goblet slipped from her hands as the last stinging drop rolled down her tongue.

Raymunda watched as Wanda swallowed the final bit of brew. She let out a sigh. The muscles in her face began to relax.

She waited for the potion to attack Wanda's brain. Then she allowed herself the smile she had earned.

"Who are you?" Raymunda asked. Wanda could see that she was ready to savor the gibberish she would hear.

"I am Wanda."

Gasps echoed from the crowd of witches.

"What?!" Raymunda's anger flared. "How can this be?" She asked again, "Who are you? Why are you here?"

"I am Wanda Seasongood. I am here to make a potion that will free my parents from your terrible spell."

The observers looked at each other in shock.

"This isn't possible!" Raymunda's body turned rigid with fury. She stared out at the witches. "Who is responsible for this?" she demanded. "Show yourself and claim this deed."

No one came forth.

The witches stared at Wanda, bewildered. Was this girl a witch? Did she have powers greater than Raymunda's?

Raymunda whirled around in confusion.

Then her eyes narrowed with horror.

Her hands flew to her throat, frantically searching her neck. "Where is it?" she howled at Wanda. "Give it back!"

"I don't have anything that belongs to you," Wanda replied.

"Do. Not. Lie. To. Me." Raymunda's jaw tightened in anger. She raised her wand in the air. "Where is it?"

"I have no idea what you're talking about," Wanda said, and it was clear to all who heard her that she was speaking the truth.

"She wants the Enlightener. The locket in your pocket," William whispered. "Don't give it to her. It has great power. It will protect you from her spells."

Why was he telling her this? she wondered. And could she believe this liar, this witch?

But something *had* protected her from Raymunda's brew. . . . Had William been trying to fool his mother all this time? Wanda didn't know what to think.

"Give it back NOW!" Raymunda shrieked.

"I am here!" Wanda heard the call from above, and she thought it was the sweetest sound she'd ever heard. Voltaire had returned! "And I have brought help!" The bird landed at her feet.

"Yes!" Wanda cheered. With help she was certain that she could find a way through this dark horde. But she let out a moan when she saw who Voltaire had found to rescue her.

"Hello, Princess." The frog hopped out of the crowd and onto her knee. "I heard you were in trouble. Kiss me."

THIRTY-FIVE

Blast Him

"Oh, nooo!" Wanda let out a long, loud groan.

"Kiss me, Princess. Give me another chance. Kiss me and we'll hop out of here together. It's you and me forever. Kiss me. Kiss me." The frog scrunched up his lips for a smooch.

"Voltaire, how can this frog help us?"

"He saved your life once. Perhaps he can do it again!" Voltaire chirped.

Raymunda stopped shrieking when she caught sight of the frog. She shifted her anger to the slimy pest. "William, get him!" she ordered.

William leaned over and grabbed the frog, but the wet creature slid easily from his grasp.

Wanda gazed out at all the witches gathered before her. "Voltaire, I would need a thousand and two frogs to do any good here." She shook her head, watching William at her feet, trying to pounce on the frog that kept hopping away.

"Use your wand and blast him!" Raymunda ordered her son.

"No!" Wanda cried. "Don't hurt him!"

William raised his wand.

And that's when the idea came to her. "William, if you truly want to help me, please turn this frog into a thousand and one more."

William took aim at the frog.

Wanda held her breath.

The wand came down . . .

And Wanda gasped as a hot green spark flew from it.

Kiss Me

Kiss Me

Kiss Me

iss me. Kiss me. Kiss me. **Kiss me.** KISS ME. KISS ME. Kiss me. Kiss me. Kiss me. KISS ME. KISS ME. KISS ME. Kiss me. **Kiss Me.** Kiss me. KISS ME. Kiss me. Kiss me. Kiss me. Kiss me. Kiss me. Kiss me. Kiss me. Kiss me. KISS ME. **KISS ME.** Kiss me. Kiss me. Kiss me. KISS ME. KISS ME. KISS ME. Kiss me. KISS ME. Kiss me. KISS ME. Kiss me. Kiss me. Kiss me. Kiss me. KISS ME. KISS ME. **Kiss Me**

KISS ME. Kiss me. Kiss me. Kiss me. KISS ME. KISS ME. KISS ME. Kiss me. KISS ME. Kiss me. KISS ME. Kiss me. Kiss me. Kiss me. Kiss me. KISS ME. KISS ME.

Kiss me. Kiss me. Kiss me. KISS ME. KISS ME. KISS ME. Kiss me. KISS ME. Kiss me. Kiss me.

Kiss me. Kiss me. Kiss me. Kiss me. KISS ME. KISS ME. Kiss me. Kiss me. Kiss me. KISS ME. **KISS ME.** KISS ME. Kiss me. KISS ME. Kiss me. KISS ME. Kiss me. Kiss me. Kiss me. Kiss me. Kiss me. Kiss me. Kiss me. Kiss me. KISS ME. KISS ME. Kiss me. Kiss me. Kiss me. KISS ME. KISS ME. KISS ME. Kiss me. KISS ME. Kiss me. KISS ME. Kiss me. Kiss me. Kiss me. Kiss me. KISS ME. KISS ME.

KISS ME. Kiss me. **Kiss me.** Kiss me. KISS ME. KISS ME. KISS ME. Kiss me. KISS ME. Kiss me. KISS ME. Kiss me. Kiss me. Kiss me. Kiss me. KISS ME. **KISS ME.** Kiss me. Kiss me. Kiss me. KISS ME. KISS ME. KISS ME. Kiss me. **KISS ME.** Kiss me.

The garden reverberated with the croaking of 1,002 frogs. They hopped on the witches. Hurled at them. Dove at them. One thousand and two frogs with lips puckering up.

The witches tripped over them. Slipped over them. They darted and dodged them. Swat, smacked, and whacked them. But that only encouraged the frogs to hop higher and faster.

KISS ME. Kiss me. KISS ME. Kiss me. KISS ME. KISS ME. Kiss me. KISS ME. Kiss me. KISS ME.

KISS ME. Kiss me. KISS ME. Kiss me. KISS ME.
Kiss me. **Kiss me.** Kiss me. KISS ME. Kiss me.

KISS ME. Kiss me. KISS ME. Kiss me. KISS ME. KISS ME. Kiss me. KISS ME. Kiss me. **KISS ME.**

KISS ME. Kiss me. KISS ME. Kiss me. KISS ME. Kiss me. Kiss me. Kiss me. KISS ME.

The garden was awhirl with hopping frogs and leaping witches, and Wanda lost sight of Raymunda in the frenzy.

"Run!" William said—and the ropes that tied Wanda magically fell to the ground. "Tell Zane to meet me at the cave. Now go!"

Wanda grabbed her rucksack and ran. She raced up the garden stairs. Hurdled over witches and frogs. Dashed by the front of the house. At the edge of the trees, she took one last look back. The young girl Wren stood at the top of the garden stairs and watched her flee. Wanda felt the power of her gaze follow her as she escaped into the woods.

194

THIRTY-SEVEN

Run Faster

As the night faded and darkness lifted, it became easier to run through the woods. For a time Wanda could still hear the chattering frogs, but soon she was left with only the sounds of her pounding footsteps and her thudding heart.

She leaped over rocks and crashed through the bushes. She raced easily when there were paths to follow and struggled when there were none. But she never stopped, and she ran with only one thought in mind, and that was to run faster.

Wanda was sorry she'd had to leave Voltaire behind, but he could fly to safety and she couldn't. She hadn't had a chance to thank the royal Prince Frog, either. She was so grateful she could have . . . kissed him.

She finally slowed when she saw a flicker of light through the trees. She had reached the edge of the Scary Wood. Wanda hoped it was a magical boundary Raymunda and the other witches couldn't cross. Just beyond the tree line was an open meadow. The morning sun was on the rise. It lit up the goldenrod, and the air shimmered with a yellow glow. For Wanda it was a most beautiful sight. She stepped into the golden light and finally sat down to rest.

In her rucksack, she held everything she needed to brew a tea that would end the witch's curse. Zane would no longer be part beast, and he would return to where he belonged. Her parents would once again become the calm, caring people she had dreamed they would be. They would be proud of her for breaking the spell. And they would love her.

There would be no more great puzzle in her life, she thought—except, perhaps, for William.

Had he offered her up to his mother knowing the Enlightener would save her? Had he freed her just so she could cure Zane? What was the truth behind all his lies?

Well, it really doesn't matter, Wanda thought. *I'll never see him again.* And that brought her to the real reason she was still sitting at the edge of the Scary Wood instead of hurrying home.

Where was Voltaire? Would she ever see *him* again?

She peered into the forest, hoping he would come fluttering out. *Wanda! Wanda!* She imagined him calling her name. But she waited and waited, and he didn't appear. At first she feared he had fallen prey to the witches, but that worry quickly slipped away—Voltaire was quite capable of taking care of himself.

No, his mission is over, and he is on to something new, Wanda thought, *if he can keep in mind what the new thing is.* She smiled. Then she stood up and headed home, triumphant and sad, wondering how her heart could feel both heavy and light at the same time.

THIRTY-EIGHT

The True Zane

"I'm home!" Wanda opened the peeling and cracked yellow door to her house. She had been away for just a few days, but so much had happened to her since then. So much had changed.

Her parents rushed to the door to meet her.

"Wanda!" Her father looked puzzled. "What are you doing here?"

"You've returned too soon!" her mother shouted.

Zane bullied his way between the two and charged right into Wanda. She reeled to the left, swung an arm out for balance, and knocked over a delicate vase. It clattered to the floor with a great crash. Zane gazed down at the scattered shards, then peered up at Wanda and grinned.

"Your grandmother's vase." Her mother sighed.

"You're so clumsy." Her father shook his head in despair.

Wanda took a deep breath. She held her rucksack in front of her and gripped it tighter, protecting the plants she needed to break the spell. *William was supposed to help with this part,* she thought. *I don't know the first thing about potions.* But if she was worried, her pleasant smile didn't betray her. "Let's go into the kitchen," she said, "and I'll make some tea."

***

Wanda's mother set down her teacup and leaned back in her chair. "That tasted heavenly." A peaceful smile formed on her lips. Wanda hadn't seen her mother's smile in years.

"Yes, delicious," her father agreed, the wrinkles in his forehead slowly smoothing away.

Wanda was deliriously happy to see that, even though she'd had to guess about the recipe, the brew she had prepared was beginning to work. She turned to Zane— and jumped up from her chair, startled.

"Very good tea, Wanda. Thank you." The eight-year-old boy-beast was gone, and in his place stood a young man of eighteen, the true Zane. Wanda didn't think it was possible, but he was even more handsome than William.

"Who's your friend, Wanda?" her mother asked. "Aren't you going to introduce us?"

"His name is Zane," Wanda replied. Her parents didn't recognize him, and she realized it would take time to explain everything to them. To avoid more questions—at least for now—she guided him out of the kitchen.

"Nice to meet you, Zane." Wanda's father waved after them. "Come back soon!"

"Zane, you're your-self again!" Wanda whispered in the living room. "And you're . . . you're . . . older." She couldn't get accustomed to the real Zane, and she tried not to stare. "How does it feel to be free of your mother's curse?"

"My mother's curse . . ." Zane said slowly, as if tasting the words. "Yes, I am free." He studied Wanda closely, with an icy stare that seemed to cut her.

Wanda took a step back. The eight-year-old Zane was a bother for sure, but this one was truly frightening. "Your brother, William, is waiting for you." She told him what had happened and instructed him to head to the cave. She encouraged him to leave at once.

"Thank you, Wanda," he said again, but with a coldness that sent a chill down her spine. He still had a dark, wild look in his eyes, and Wanda suspected it had always been there, even before his mother's spell. "I will not forget this."

She reached into her pocket and gripped the Enlightener. She knew it would protect her from him, but still, when he headed out the door, she was relieved to see him go.

THIRTY-NINE

Where's Wren?

Wanda stepped back to admire the fresh yellow paint she had just brushed on the front door.

"So cheerful." Her mother wrapped her in a warm hug.

"And the garden looks lovely." Her father, sitting on the garden bench, smiled at the magenta, purple, and golden pansies that he and Wanda had planted.

The garden did look wonderful, and Wanda was quite satisfied with all the colorful flowers they had selected, especially the pink and red blossoms the butterflies seemed to like, too. For a moment, she recalled the witches' garden, but she quickly banished it from her mind. She preferred not to think about it, not now, not ever.

This week had been the best of her life. Her parents were the family she had always dreamed of having. They were kind and thoughtful, and it was clear that they loved her very much.

"Tell us again." Her mother took a seat on the garden bench, too. "Who is Zane?"

Wanda's parents were still recovering from the spell. They couldn't fathom where the time had gone. They had no idea what had transpired over the last few years. And they were slowly remembering what their life had been like before Raymunda. Wanda felt confident that, in time, their minds would clear and their memories would return completely.

"Zane is the witch's son," Wanda explained again. Then she told them once more about her adventure in the Scary Wood and the ghastly creatures that had attacked her.

"What a frightful time!" Her mother's face flooded with worry and horror. "You were in such danger"— she took a deep breath—"and we weren't there to help you."

"Wanda, we are so grateful to you," her father said.

"You were incredibly brave. You risked everything to return our lives to us."

"Yes." Her mother's eyes filled with tears. "Now we can be a happy family again."

Wanda's father started drawing a circle in the soil with the top of his boot, but he didn't close the loop. "I'm happy, yes, but I can't help but feel that something is missing. . . . I can't quite put my finger on what it is, though. . . ."

Just then a bird flew down to perch on the edge of the birdbath. Wanda was disappointed, as always these days, that it wasn't Voltaire.

"Mother," said Wanda, "have you seen any bluebirds around lately?"

"Bluebirds?" Her mother shook her head. "No, just robins and sparrows."

"Birds . . ." Wanda's father murmured. "I think it has something to do with a bird." He stared up into the tree as if the missing thing might be hidden up there. Then he jumped to his feet. "That's it! How could we have forgotten? Wren!"

Wanda's mother stood up and cast a frantic glance left and right. Then behind her. "Wren! Yes! Where is Wren?"

For a moment, Wanda was confused. Why were her parents searching for a wren? *Oh, wait,* Wanda realized. *Not a bird. A person.* The name seemed familiar to her, but she couldn't recall exactly where she had heard it. "Who?" Wanda asked.

"Wren!" her mother replied. "Your sister!"

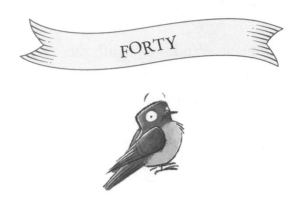

FORTY

It Started with a Thud

*I*t has been one week and five hours since I returned home from the Scary Wood. It's wonderful here without Zane. But today I learned that I have a sister. She's one year older than me, and her name is Wren. She's been gone so long I don't remember anything about her. When I see her, it will be like meeting her for the first time.

It could be excellent to have a big sister. But since I'm a very honest person, I have to admit it would be much better if I didn't have to rescue her from a witch. Is that unkind? I don't want to be mean again. Still, I wish that there was someone else who would go save her instead. My parents are too frightened to do it. They *say there has to be another way, but so far they haven't come up with it yet. And anyway, it would be too dangerous for them. They're still in a daze from Raymunda's spell.*

When they look at me, they see me now. They see who I am, and they are proud of me. But they also see what's missing. Each time they look at me, I am a reminder that they have another daughter who is gone. It shows in their eyes.

So now I must return to the Scary Wood. I just packed my dragon sweater and hat and Voltaire's, too, in case I should see him. I'm ready to go, but I'm having a hard time with the actual leaving. Raymunda wants me dead, and I'm headed her way, and I think that would be enough for anyone to decide to stay home. But my parents need Wren, and Wren needs me to find her.

Wanda continued to write in her diary—but stopped when she heard a loud THUD. She looked up to see a little blue lump crumpled on her windowsill.

Voltaire!

She leaped up from her bed, opened the window, and scooped up the bird.

"Voltaire, are you all right?" She held him up to see if he was breathing. Then she set him down on her dresser, and he opened his eyes. He bent his neck from side to side, fanned his feathers, and stood up.

"My neck is a bit stiff, but that seems to be the worst of it. Wanda, dear, if I'm going to be visiting, you might think about keeping the window open."

"I'm so happy to see you! I have something to tell you—the girl dressed in yellow? The one in my visions? She's my sister, Wren! And we think that Raymunda is holding her prisoner! I'm about to sneak off to go look for her."

"Wren? What a coincidence! That's why I am here! So good of you to remind me." He started to pace back and forth across the dresser. "I have discovered that there is a girl with the witch—and she is your sister. Oh. You know this already. Not very helpful, I suppose."

"But it *is* helpful! The witch has Wren—now we're sure of it," Wanda said.

"Hold on! There's something more you should know." Voltaire stopped his pacing and looked into Wanda's eyes. "And you should know it before you leave."

"What is it?" Wanda asked.

"It's . . . Let me see . . . Wait. . . . I knew it when I left, but apparently I have arrived without it. No worries, dear Wanda. We shall go off together, posthaste, to find Wren . . . and along the journey, I'm almost certain I'll remember it."

Wanda smiled. She grabbed her rucksack from the bed and hefted it over her shoulder. "If we do not find anything pleasant, at least we shall find something new."

"How true! I couldn't have said it better myself!" Voltaire chirped, then flew out the window. "Follow me!"

Wanda leaped down the stairs two at a time to join her friend.

Voltaire's Acknowledgments

I would like to acknowledge me, the world-famous Voltaire, for all of my wonderful and witty quotes that you found in this book. It was a pleasure to share them with you and my dear Wanda. I created them back in the 1700s, but there isn't a bit of dust on them. Here they are again. Take another look:

"Doubt is not a pleasant condition.
But certainty is an absurd one."

"The longer we dwell on our misfortunes,
the greater is their power to harm us."

"If we do not find anything pleasant,
at least we shall find something new."

"The biggest reward for a thing
well done is to have done it."

"One should always aim at being
interesting rather than exact."

"The most important decision you
make is to be in a good mood."

And I would like to acknowledge you, dear reader, for reading all the way to this very page. I am going to thank you personally . . . just as soon as I can remember your name. . . .

Author's Acknowledgments

One morning, I was staring out the window of my office when I saw a bird fluttering nearby. My window was shut, and the bird was heading right for it . . . and that's where Wanda's story began. I sat down at my computer and quickly wrote the first page of this book. Then I read it to my friend and colleague Jane Stine. What ensued was a very high-level editorial discussion.

I said, "Do you think this could be something?"

Jane said, "It could definitely be something."

As you can see, Jane and I speak the same language. I can't thank her enough for her enthusiasm and encouragement from that first page to the last draft.

Pat Fortunato, Diana Guiseppone, and Ellen Steiber read the second draft, offered sage advice, and didn't even complain when I asked if they could read any faster. True friendship.

My husband, Lou Venezia, was there for all the drafts. I trust his judgment because he has the heart of a ten-year-old and the mind of a scholar, although he might say it's the other way around. Lou read every single draft, and he was required to listen when I read them aloud, and yet he remained enthusiastic, supportive, and in a pretty good mood. I would have to say that's true love.

Abraham Lurie, Leila Lurie, and Ryan Lorello, my father, sister, and nephew, are always there for me no matter what, and I think they think I'm much better at this than I really am, which can carry a person a long way, believe me.

In addition to writing, I also edit children's books. One of the authors I work with is the brilliant R. L. Stine, who has instilled a love of reading in kids all around the world with his Goosebumps book series. I've edited nearly 150 Goosebumps books so far, and along the way I've learned a thing or two from Bob about storytelling. I hope it shows. I'm very grateful.

Thank you so much to Wanda Seasongood's amazing illustrator, Jenn Harney. Working with Jenn has been total magic. Her artwork is incredible, and I can't imagine Wanda any other way. And thanks to designer Tyler Nevins for making this book look spectacular. And much appreciation to everyone at Disney Hyperion!

Which brings me to Stephanie Lurie. We're not related, but I wish we were. Stephanie is an extraordinary editor. She pinpoints with laser-like precision where a manuscript needs a second look. Her suggestions are insightful and always elevate the story. She's tireless in her review and comments, extremely patient, and incredibly polite about it all! Stephanie, thank you, thank you, thank you.

And finally . . . deepest thanks to all my elementary school teachers and librarians. They made me want to read and write. I can't imagine anything better than that.

Don't miss Wanda's next
exciting adventure

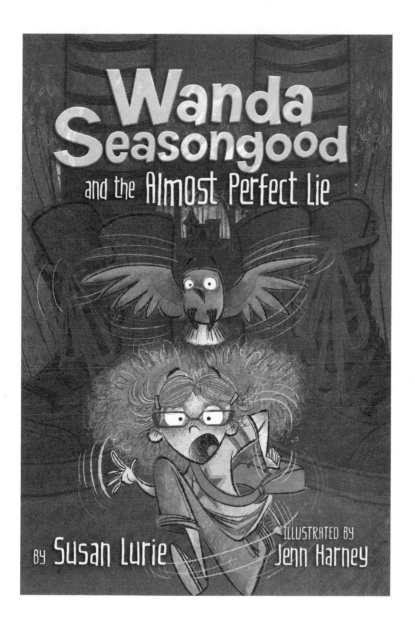

Wanda
Seasongood
and the Almost Perfect Lie

by Susan Lurie

ILLUSTRATED BY
Jenn Harney

FREEDOM FOR THE
THOUGHT
THAT WE HATE

A BIOGRAPHY OF THE FIRST AMENDMENT

ANTHONY LEWIS

MJF BOOKS
NEW YORK

Published by MJF Books
Fine Communications
322 Eighth Avenue
New York, NY 10001

Freedom for the Thought that We Hate
LC Control Number: 2011923197
ISBN-13: 978-1-60671-098-2
ISBN-10: 1-60671-098-2

MJF Books and the MJF colophon are trademarks of Fine Creative Media, Inc.

QF   10 9 8 7 6 5 4 3 2 1

To Margie
Who makes everything possible

CONTENTS

INTRODUCTION

Ours is the most outspoken society on earth. Americans are freer to think what we will and say what we think than any other people, and freer today than in the past. We can bare the secrets of government and the secrets of the bedroom. We can denounce our rulers, and each other, with little fear of the consequences. There is almost no chance that a court will stop us from publishing what we wish: in print, on the air, or on the Web. Hateful and shocking expression, political or artistic, is almost all free to enter the marketplace of ideas.

Other countries that we think of as like our own—Britain, for example—have many more restrictions on what can be said. Why are we different? Where does our extraordinary freedom come from? The answer commonly given is "the First Amendment." That amendment to the United States Constitution provides, among other things, that "Congress shall make no law . . . abridging the freedom of speech, or of the press. . . . "

But those fourteen words cannot in themselves account for our great freedom, because over many decades they did not protect critical expression. In 1798, just seven years after the

First Amendment was added to the Constitution, Congress passed a law that punished disrespectful comment on the president; editors were imprisoned for mocking President John Adams. A century later, under another congressional statute, men were sentenced to twenty years in prison for criticizing a policy decision by President Woodrow Wilson.

Today every president is the target of criticism and mockery. It is inconceivable that even the most caustic critic would be imprisoned for his or her words. If such a prosecution were attempted, the courts would throw it out as in conflict with the First Amendment. So something has happened to the fourteen words of the speech and press clauses. Their meaning has changed. Or, more accurately, the understanding of those words has changed: judges' understanding and the public's.

To say that is to open the way to appreciating a mysterious and remarkable process: the changing interpretation of our fundamental law. "We are under a Constitution," Chief Justice Charles Evans Hughes said, "but the Constitution is what the judges say it is." That may sound today like a cynical description of what critics on the Right call "judicial activism." But Hughes, who said it in 1907, three years before he was first appointed to the Supreme Court, thought he was stating the obvious. Someone has to interpret the words of our eighteenth-century Constitution and its amendments; under our system as it has developed, that is the job of the courts.

Judges do not operate in a vacuum. They are influenced by the attitudes of their society, and the society in turn may be influenced by what the courts say. So history, law, and culture contribute to the process of defining what the Constitution commands.

When we say today that the First Amendment guarantees our freedom, we mean not only its brief text but the vast body of law that judges have built up over the years in applying it to issues brought before them. When a dissident burns the flag to protest official policy, is that a form of expression protected by the First Amendment? Is political campaign spending immune from regulation as protected "speech"? What about a false and damaging attack on a politician: Can he or she collect damages for libel?

In answering such questions, courts look to what earlier judges have said on more or less analogous issues. Each decision becomes a precedent for others. It is called the "common-law method," because for centuries, English and then American judges built up the rules of property, contracts, and the like in what was called the "common law": law defined not by explicit statutes but by judicial decisions.

The defining of our fundamental laws in this way is a drama, and nowhere more so than in the law of the First Amendment. It has been a drama since 1791, and it still is today: a tale without end. First Amendment law poses hard questions, for judges and the rest of us. How unregulated a society do we really want? Where should the line be drawn between liberty and order? Is the demand for "no law" abridging the freedom of speech and press an absolute? Those are some of the questions I shall discuss in this book as I explore the meaning of the First Amendment in law and society.

The story of the First Amendment is powerful testimony to the crucial role of judges in a political system that rests on a foundation of law. Voters are the ultimate sovereigns in a republic, as James Madison and the other Framers of the Constitution said. But transient political majorities cannot be expected to articulate the fundamental values of a constitution, least of all when the majority's immediate interest conflicts with those values—as, from time to time, it will. Judges, serving for long terms and bound by their commissions to look beyond momentary partisan conflicts, are in the best position to give voice to the deeper values.

So the American experience teaches. Until World War II it was a uniquely American practice to give courts, especially the Supreme Court, a significant role in the structure of governance. No other democratic society had a constitution enforced by judges. In Britain and its empire, the doctrine of parliamentary supremacy prevailed; whatever a parliament did—however discriminatory, however unjust—was law. But the tyrannies of the twentieth century brought a change.

Aharon Barak, then the president of the Israeli Supreme Court, explained the change in a 1998 lecture. In the past, he said, people thought that respect for basic values "could be guaranteed by relying on the self-restraint of the majority." But after the Nazis, the lesson was that there must be "formal limits on the power of the majority. The concept that 'It is not done' needs to receive the formal expression, 'It is forbidden.'"

And so, country after country adopted *constitutional* democracy, giving the last word to judges on basic issues. That was the pattern in a state with as profound a republican system as

France, and then in a reconstructed Germany. It was followed in the great former British territories, notably India and South Africa. And the countries of Europe adopted a European Convention on Human Rights, enforced by a Court of Human Rights. In time, even Britain agreed that its own courts should be bound by the European Convention.

As the history of the First Amendment shows, putting a guarantee into a charter is no assurance that it will be enforced. After all, it took more than a century for the courts to begin protecting dissenting speakers and publishers from official repression in the United States. Or to put it another way, it took time for judges to build on the fundamental promise of those fourteen words in the First Amendment: that this would be a country of free speech and freedom of the press. Time and imagination and courage. Timid, unimaginative judges could not have made America as extraordinarily free as it is.

Freedom to speak and write as you wish is the inescapable necessity of democracy. The judges of the European Court of Human Rights understood that when, in 1986, they considered the right to criticize political leaders. They did not consider the issue in a vacuum; they built on American experience and decisions.

An Austrian journalist, Peter Michael Lingens, had written articles charging a politician with the "basest opportunism." The politician sued for libel, and the Austrian courts awarded him damages. Lingens went to the European Court of Human Rights, which found that the libel judgment against him violated the Convention on Human Rights—its clause guaranteeing freedom of expression. That freedom, the court said, "constitutes one of the essential foundations of a democratic society. . . . It is applicable not only to 'information' or 'ideas' that are favorably received or regarded as inoffensive . . . but also to those that offend, shock or disturb. Such are the demands of that pluralism, tolerance and broadmindedness without which there is no 'democratic society.'" In other words, as Justice Oliver Wendell Holmes Jr. of the United States Supreme Court said, "freedom for the thought that we hate."

When a constitutional provision has no discernible history, as is true of the First Amendment—no meaningful discussion by its authors of what they meant—how do judges begin to build on its words to decide concrete cases? That is a subject of endless debate. But one thing is sure. Judges, however bold, are part of their society and are influenced by its attitudes. To give a stark example: The Nazi experience made more Americans, and judges, understand the devastating character of religious and racial discrimination.

Justice Ruth Bader Ginsburg of the Supreme Court, speaking at the University of Cape Town, South Africa, in 2006, said: "What caused the Court's understanding to dawn and grow? Judges do read newspapers and are affected, not by the weather of the day, as distinguished constitutional law professor Paul Freund once said, but by the climate of the era."

Justice Ginsburg was talking about gender discrimination. But her point applies to the drama of the First Amendment's expanding interpretation since early in the twentieth century. Great judges like Holmes saw, before most judges and most Americans, that freedom of thought was an essential element in the success of our diverse society. But judicial commitment to openness of expression grew as citizens' did; each informed the other. And it is worth remembering that the 1798 statute criminalizing criticism of the president, which was enforced by judges, was rejected by American voters in the election of 1800 as incompatible with the First Amendment and with American ideals.

The meaning of the First Amendment has been, and will be, shaped by each American generation: by judges, political leaders, citizens. There will always be authorities who try to make their own lives more comfortable by suppressing critical comment. There will always be school principals like the one in Wilton, Connecticut, who in 2007 canceled a student play about the war in Iraq because it might disturb some families. But I am convinced that the fundamental American commitment to free speech, disturbing speech, is no longer in doubt.

1

Beginnings

The American commitment to freedom of speech and press is the more remarkable because it emerged from legal and political origins that were highly repressive. The colonists who crossed the Atlantic in the seventeenth century came from an England where it was extremely dangerous to utter a thought that differed from official truth. The state defined what was allowable in politics and, perhaps even more rigorously, in religion.

Repression was accomplished by two different devices. The first was preventive: a licensing system for all publications. In England in 1538, King Henry VIII issued a proclamation requiring anyone who wanted to print something to get a license first. The requirement applied to everything: books (Bibles were the biggest seller), pamphlets, shipping schedules. The system created valuable printing monopolies, and it prevented the publication of unorthodox opinions.

The licensers were bureaucrats who operated with utter arbitrariness. They took as long as they wished to decide whether something could be printed, and they gave no reasons for their decisions. When they said no, there was no appeal. This system of previous restraints on publication, as they were called, provoked the classic protest against censorship, by the poet and essayist John Milton: "Areopagitica—A Speech for the Liberty of Unlicensed Printing."

When Parliament overthrew King Charles I in the civil war of the 1640s, it abolished the royal licensing system. But as is so often the case, the rebels became less tolerant of dissent when they exercised power. In 1643 Parliament enacted its own licensing statute. It lasted until 1694, when Parliament let it die by failing to renew the law.

The second repressive device may have been even more intimidating. It was the law of seditious libel, which made it a crime to publish anything disrespectful of the state or church or their officers. The premise of seditious libel was that these institutions had to have respect for the country to avoid the terrible danger of social chaos. If you published something critical—a charge, say, that an official had taken a bribe—it did you no good to prove that the statement was true. Truth was no defense to a charge of seditious libel. The crime lay in reducing public respect for the official, so a truthful criticism might be even worse than a false one. A defendant was entitled to trial by jury, but the judge alone (appointed by the state) decided whether the publication was seditious; the jury considered only whether the defendant had published it. Punishment upon conviction included the death penalty, carried out by the lingering horror of being hanged, drawn, and quartered.

Curiously, from our viewpoint today, critics of the licensing system often did not object to the rigors of subsequent punishment. "It is of greatest concernment in the Church and Commonwealth," Milton wrote, "to have a vigilant eye how books demean themselves as well as men: and therefore to confine, imprison, and do sharpest justice on them as malefactors."

Sir William Blackstone was the leading authority on the common law, including seditious libel. Like Milton, he drew a sharp distinction between it and prior restraint by licensing. "Where blasphemous, immoral, treasonable, schismatical, seditious or scandalous libels are punished by the English law," he wrote in 1769,

> the liberty of the press, properly understood, is by no means infringed or violated. . . . [It] consists in laying no *previous* restraints upon publications, and not in freedom from censure for criminal matter when published. . . . To punish (as the law does at present) any dangerous or offensive writings, which, when published, shall on a fair and impartial trial be adjudged of a pernicious tendency, is necessary for the preservation of peace and good order, a government and religion, the only solid foundations of civil liberty.

Blackstone's eminence notwithstanding, there was not much protection in his talk of a "fair and impartial trial" when judges relied on the slippery concept of "a pernicious tendency" to decide whether something was seditious and truth was not a defense.

Colonial America began with little tolerance of dissent. Puritans crossed the ocean for freedom to practice their religion, but they did not extend that freedom to others. Massachusetts hanged Mary Dyer in 1660 because she insisted on advocating her Quaker views. Colonial judges applied the common law of England, including the law of seditious libel. But the public began, after a time, to resist. That was the lesson of the first great legal test of press freedom in America, the case of John Peter Zenger.

Zenger was a New York printer. He printed—though he had nothing to do with the content—a newspaper, the *New-York Weekly Journal*, that attacked the royal governor of New York, William Cosby. Cosby had Zenger prosecuted for seditious libel. At his trial in 1735 Zenger's lawyer, Andrew Hamilton of Philadelphia, argued that the criticisms of Governor Cosby in the newspaper were accurate. That was irrelevant under seditious libel law, as Hamilton knew—truth was not a defense. The judge, a Cosby appointee, so ruled. But Hamilton appealed to the jurors to ignore the judge's ruling, make up their own minds, and free Zenger if they found the newspaper's criticisms of Cosby to be true. The jury found Zenger not guilty: an extraordinary decision that could not formally change the law but that reverberated around the colonies and discouraged further prosecutions for seditious libel.

The newspapers of eighteenth-century America were raggle-taggle affairs, nothing like the highly capitalized metropolitan press known to us. Anyone could put out a newspaper by bringing the copy to a job printer like Peter Zenger. The papers were highly partisan, the editors often political party men. The *New-York Weekly Journal* that got Zenger in trouble was started and written by a political faction opposed to Governor Cosby. There was little pretense of objectivity. Even a figure as lofty as George Washington was not above rancid criticism. When he retired from the presidency in 1797, the *Philadelphia Aurora* called him "the source of all the misfortunes of our country" and said every American heart "ought to beat high with exultation that the name of Washington from this day ceases to give a currency to political iniquity."

In a 1960 book, *Legacy of Suppression*, professor Leonard Levy argued that at the end of the eighteenth century—when the First Amendment was adopted—the much-vaunted liberty of the press in America was freedom only from prior restraint, not from punishment for disapproved words. The law of seditious libel was alive and well then, he said. His book caused a scholarly stir. But twenty-five years later, Levy mostly took it back. In a new edition of the book, retitled *Emergence of a Free Press*, he said further research had shown him that though legal theory remained repressive, in practice "the press conducted itself as if the law scarcely existed." It was highly critical of politicians, indeed "habitually scurrilous."

Prosecutions for seditious libel dwindled in the last decades of the eighteenth century, no doubt in part because the authorities feared they would outrage the public. But as late as 1803 an editor in Hudson, New York, Harry Croswell, was prosecuted in the state courts for an attack on President Thomas Jefferson. The story in his newspaper, *The Wasp*, said that while vice president under John Adams, Jefferson had paid a journalist to write savage assaults on Adams and

Washington. (The journalist called Washington "a traitor, a robber and a perjuror.") Croswell was convicted—but got out of jail when the New York legislature, a year later, made truth a defense against seditious libel charges.

In that turbulent mix of repressive law and an audacious press, the idea arose of committing governments to the principle of press freedom in their fundamental documents. Virginia was the first to act, in 1776. The Declaration of Rights that its colonial legislature adopted in that momentous year included this statement: "The freedom of the press is one of the greatest bulwarks of liberty, and can never be restrained but by despotic Governments." By the time the federal Constitution was drafted in 1787 and the First Amendment added in 1791, nine of the original thirteen states had such provisions in their constitutions or other basic documents.

Writers and printers were no doubt gratified to have their freedom hailed in state constitutions. But what did these provisions actually mean by "the liberty of the press"? Blackstone was highly influential in American courts; and many legal authorities agreed with him that the liberty meant only freedom from prior restraint, not from prosecutions for seditious libel. In that view, the warm words about freedom of the press did not mean much, since prior restraints had died out after England abandoned the licensing system for printing in 1694. Blackstone in effect offered freedom from a restraint that hardly existed any more.

And there was an even more profound doubt about the usefulness of the state calls for freedom of the press. Today we take it for granted that the words of a constitution are enforceable as law, a superior law that in lawsuits can trump current legislation. But that was not the received view in the eighteenth century. Some people did speak of constitutional provisions as legally enforceable. But they were generally thought of as mere admonitions to state legislatures, encouraging but not binding. The phrasing of the press-freedom clause in Virginia's Declaration of Rights, quoted above, certainly sounds more like exhortation than law.

The first time judges enforced a constitutional provision to strike down an established common-law practice occurred in Massachusetts. In 1780, it acquired a constitution, largely drafted by John Adams, that began, "All men are born free and equal." Three years later the Supreme Judicial Court of the commonwealth heard the case of Quock Walker, a Negro slave who said he had been promised his freedom and, when it was not forthcoming, ran away. His master, Nathaniel Jennison, found him and beat him. Jennison was prosecuted for assault and battery. He argued in his defense that slavery was long established in Massachusetts, and he had the right to seize and punish a runaway. But what was the significance of the language about "free and equal"? Chief Justice William Cushing said it was incompatible with slavery, which therefore could "no longer be tolerated." With that, slavery ended in Massachusetts.

The federal Constitution of 1787 had no bill of rights—no guarantee of free speech or press or any other right. But it quickly acquired one under exigent political circumstances. When the Constitution was put to conventions in the states for ratification, opposition was fierce. The opponents included such notable advocates of liberty as Patrick Henry and George Mason of Virginia, who feared that the new federal government would have too much power and could oppress the people.

Conventions in the key states of Massachusetts, New York, and Virginia were leaning against ratification. Then, in Massachusetts, John Hancock came up with a device that persuaded some of the doubters. He proposed that the convention ratify the Constitution and at the same time call on the first Congress elected under it to adopt a bill of rights. With that, the Massachusetts convention voted for ratification, 187 to 168. The New York convention followed, by a vote of 30 to 27, and Virginia's by 89 to 79. By such narrow margins did the United States come into being.

James Madison, a leading figure in the making of the Constitution, opposed the idea of a bill of rights at the time. He feared that listing some specific rights would lead to the view that others, overlooked in the drafting, were not valued. For protection of freedoms he relied on the fact that the Constitution gave only limited, named powers to the new federal government—so it would have no power over matters not mentioned, including the press. And he did not believe that declarations of rights were effective. In a 1788 letter to Jefferson, who was in Paris as the American minister, Madison dismissed what he called "parchment barriers" and said that bills of rights had been repeatedly violated "by overbearing majorities in every State." He was evidently thinking of bills of rights as admonitions to legislatures, not as law enforceable in courts.

(In reply to Madison, Jefferson said there was one argument in favor of a bill of rights that "has great weight with me; the legal check which it puts in the hands of the judiciary." Jefferson was evidently anticipating that the courts would enforce a bill of rights by holding unconstitutional legislation that was inconsistent with its provisions. But when Chief Justice John Marshall, in *Marbury v. Madison* in 1803, found a congressional statute invalid as a violation of the Constitution, Jefferson, now president, fumed that Marshall's decision would "make the judiciary a despotic branch." Consistency was not one of Jefferson's virtues.)

Madison, despite his previous opposition to a bill of rights, pushed for one when he took his seat as a member of the House of Representatives in the first Congress. The contrary view had persuaded him, and perhaps he felt an obligation to carry out the wishes of the key state ratifying conventions. He got twelve constitutional amendments through the House and Senate. What is now the First Amendment was third on the list. The first two, dealing with the number of representatives and congressional salaries, were not approved by the necessary three-fourths of the states. The remaining ten were added to the Constitution on December 15, 1791, when the last needed state, Virginia, ratified them.

Some judges and lawyers argue today that judges should interpret a provision of the Constitution by looking to the "original intention" of its Framers. According to the "Originalists," as they are called, this is to be done by reading statements of the members of Congress who proposed a constitutional amendment, the debates over it, and the comments during the ratification process. But such exploration has little to say about the First Amendment. Madison proposed the idea in the House, the language was changed in committee and in the Senate, and nothing of note was said. Indeed, the Senate then kept no record of its debates. The birth of the First Amendment threw no light on how its scope should be understood. But it was not long before the Constitution and the country underwent a profound test of what was meant by "the freedom of speech, or of the press."

2

"Odious or Contemptible"

On July 4, 1798, the United States Senate passed a bill to make seditious libel a federal crime. Its backers, in the Federalist Party, had chosen the date to identify the legislation with patriotism. The House, also under Federalist control, passed the bill on July 10. President John Adams, a Federalist, signed it into law on July 14. Ten days from start to finish: a swift course for a fateful statute.

The Sedition Act made it a crime to write or publish "any false, scandalous and malicious writing or writings against the government of the United States, or either house of the Congress . . . or the President . . . with intent to defame . . . or to bring them, or either of them, into contempt or disrepute; or to excite against them or either or any of them, the hatred of the good people of the United States." Violators were subject to imprisonment for up to two years and a fine of up to $2,000.

What was the rush in legislating against "sedition"? The law was needed, it was said, to defend the country against terrorism: French terrorism. The French Revolution of 1789 had led to Jacobin Terror and the guillotine. Some Americans, especially those of conservative outlook, feared that France would export its ideology. The French had provided crucial support in the American Revolution, but feelings of gratitude for that faded with the bloody events in Paris.

Fear of French terror was used for a political purpose in the Sedition Act. The party system was just emerging, and the Federalists spoke for what could be called the established forces. The rising opposition, more populist, called themselves Republicans. (Despite the name, they were the ancestors of the modern Democratic Party.) They supported the vice president, Thomas Jefferson. Partisan feelings were fierce. Abigail Adams, the president's wife, wrote a friend in 1798 that "the French party"—the Republicans—were busy "sowing the seeds of vice, irreligion, corruption and sedition."

The Federalists designed the Sedition Act to suppress pro-Jefferson comment in the run-up to the presidential election of 1800, when Jefferson would oppose Adams. Its political cast was made transparent by the fact that it punished criticism of the president and Congress, but not of the vice president. The act itself provided that it would expire on March 3, 1801, the day before the next presidential inauguration. In the little more than two and one-half years of its existence, fourteen men were prosecuted under the act. Among them were the editors and proprietors of the leading Jeffersonian newspapers: the *Philadelphia Aurora*, the *Boston Independent Chronicle*, the *New York Argus*, the *Baltimore American*, and the *Richmond Examiner*. Most of the cases came to trial in the very year of the election, 1800. Adams's secretary of state, Timothy Pickering, encouraged prosecutions that would silence pro-Jefferson papers during the election year.

The law's stated requirement that a statement be "false" to be criminal was described by its sponsors as a liberalizing reform of the common law of seditious libel, which did not allow the truth of criticisms as a defense. But in practice it was a distinction without a difference. Judges made those charged with violating the Sedition Act bear the burden of proving that their statements were true in all respects, and men were prosecuted for expressions of opinion, which could not be proved true.

The repressive nature of the law was made clear by the first prosecution. It was of a Republican member of Congress, Matthew Lyon of Vermont. He was charged for a letter to the editor he had written to the *Vermont Journal*. It said the president was engaged in "a continual grasp for power, in an unbounded thirst for ridiculous pomp, foolish adulation and selfish avarice." It was political slanging, hardly to be judged true or false. But an indictment charged that Lyon's words were "scurrilous, feigned, false, scandalous, seditious and malicious." Supreme Court Justice William Paterson presided at Lyon's trial. (The justices then had to act also as trial judges, riding a judicial circuit.) He charged the jury that it had to decide whether Lyon could have written his letter "with any other intent than that of making odious or contemptible the president and government, and bringing them both into disrepute." Lyon was convicted and sentenced to four months in prison and a fine of $1,000.

Another Sedition Act prosecution that drew much attention was of a political pamphleteer, James T. Callender. As the campaign of 1800 got under way, he published a book that called President Adams a "hoary headed incendiary" and said the choice was "between Adams, war and beggary, and Jefferson, peace and competency." (Harry Croswell was prosecuted for seditious libel under New York law in 1803, as mentioned in Chapter 1, for saying that Jefferson had paid Callender to publish that attack on Adams.) Callender was convicted in a trial before Supreme Court Justice Samuel Chase, whom Republicans regarded as virulently pro-Federalist. (Chase was impeached by the House after Republicans won a majority there in 1800, but not convicted in the Senate.) The jurors in the Callender trial were all Federalists. Modern research has found that judges and federal marshals packed juries with Federalists in Sedition Act trials.

Prosecutions like those of Matthew Lyon and James Callender aroused wide protests—remarkably wide, considering the difficulty of communication at the time. Lyon's prison term was due to expire on February 9, 1799, but he was unable to pay the fine and had to stay in prison. But leading Republicans around the country contributed to a fund for him. Senator Stevens T. Mason of Virginia brought the money in gold to Vermont, and Lyon was released to a triumphal parade in his honor.

The Federalists' design to use the Sedition Act for political advantage badly miscarried. Jeffersonians denounced the prosecutions as attempts to take America back to the tyranny of George III; they published the transcript of Callender's trial as evidence of that intention. The law became a campaign issue, contributing to the defeat of Adams by Jefferson in 1800. In that election the Federalists also lost control of both houses of Congress, and the party began fading into oblivion.

It was a great political debate. From the viewpoint of the twenty-first century, what is surprising is that it *was* political rather than legal. Today, opponents of such a statute would rush to court to assert that it violated the First Amendment. The Sedition Act's constitutionality was never tested in the Supreme Court during its brief life. If it had been, the Court would almost certainly have upheld the law. Three of the six members of the Supreme Court in 1800, Justices Chase, Paterson, and Bushrod Washington, had presided at Sedition Act trials without intimating any constitutional doubts.

But the Constitution and the First Amendment were not overlooked in the debate. They were invoked by critics as reasons for Congress and the public to oppose the law. In fact, the political and public debate over the Sedition Act brought out, at that early stage in United States history, arguments about the freedom of speech and press that are still with us.

In the House debate, Federalists argued that a power to prevent seditious attacks in the press—though it was not one of the powers specifically given to the new federal government by the Constitution—was a necessary incident of any government. Representative John Allen of Connecticut told the House to look at newspapers in Philadelphia, where the government then sat. They showed, he said, that a "dangerous combination" existed to "overturn and ruin the government," urging people "to raise an *insurrection*." There were indeed Philadelphia newspapers hostile to the Adams administration, but they urged that it be turned out not by insurrection but by the ballot box.

Federalists rejected the relevance of the First Amendment because, they said, its clause guaranteeing "the freedom of the press" disallowed only prior restraints—and the Sedition Act called for subsequent punishment. It was Blackstone's argument. In reply, Albert Gallatin of Pennsylvania (who became secretary of the treasury in Jefferson's administration) said it was "preposterous to say that to punish a certain act was not an abridgment of the liberty of doing that act." He called the Blackstone view "absurd" when applied to the free-speech clause of the First Amendment: How could a government apply prior restraints to men speaking, by sealing their mouths or cutting their tongues?

Representative John Nicholas, a Republican from Virginia, made an argument that anticipated free-speech theory two centuries later. Federalists defended the statute as liberal because it applied, at least in theory, only to false statements. Nicholas answered that any attempt to distinguish true from false was inconsistent with freedom. Any vigorous political criticism would be charged with falsehood, he said, and printers would be "afraid of publishing the truth as, though true, it might not always be in their power to establish the truth to the satisfaction of a court." In 1964, in the case of *New York Times v. Sullivan*, the Supreme Court said that "erroneous statement is inevitable in free debate, and . . . it must be protected if the freedoms of expression are to have the breathing space that they need to survive."

Nicholas made another important argument when the Republicans moved, unsuccessfully, in 1799 to repeal the Sedition Act. Its thinking, he said, came from Great Britain, which had a very different political structure. "The King is hereditary," he said, "and according to the theory of their government, can do no wrong. Public officers are his representatives, and derive some portion of his inviolability." But in America, "the officers of government are the servants of the people, are amenable to them, and liable to be turned out of office at periodical elections."

The most important voice heard in opposition to the Sedition Act was James Madison's. After its passage, he and Jefferson set out to arouse state legislatures against it. They acted in secret, for fear that they would be prosecuted themselves under the act—a leading drafter of the Constitution and the vice president of the United States! Jefferson wrote a resolution that the Kentucky legislature approved later in 1798. It made the argument of federalism—that the Constitution left to the states any power to adopt laws on the press. Madison wrote resolutions for the Virginia legislature making a classic argument that freedom of speech and of the press are the essential guardians of a republican political system.

The Virginia Resolutions, approved by the legislature in 1798, protested against "the palpable and alarming infractions

of the Constitution" in the Sedition Act. It exercised, the resolutions said,

> a power not delegated by the Constitution, but, on the con-
> trary, expressly and positively forbidden by one of the
> amendments thereto—a power which, more than any other,
> ought to produce universal alarm, because it is leveled
> against the right of freely examining public characters and
> measures, and of free communication among the people
> thereon, which has ever been justly deemed the only effec-
> tual guardian of every other right.

(John Adams had expressed virtually the same idea thirty-
three years earlier in his treatise "A Dissertation on the
Canon and Feudal Law." He wrote: "Liberty cannot be preserved without a general knowledge among the people, who
have a right . . . and a desire to know; but besides this, they
have a right, an indisputable, unalienable, indefeasible, divine
right to that most dreaded and envied kind of knowledge, I
mean of the characters and conduct of their rulers.")

Madison's phrase "the right of freely examining public
characters and measures" really expresses the premise of the
American political system: the Madisonian premise, we may
call it. It tells us why Americans should scent danger when a
government tries to stop a newspaper from disclosing the origins of an unsuccessful war, as the Nixon administration did
when the *New York Times* began publishing the Pentagon Papers on the Vietnam War in 1971, or accuses a newspaper of
endangering national security by disclosing secret and illegal

wiretapping without warrants, as the administration of George W. Bush did during the Iraq War in 2006.

Madison expounded his ideas further in a "Report on the Virginia Resolutions" that the legislature approved in January 1800. Under our Constitution, he said, "The people, not the government, possess the absolute sovereignty." That was "altogether different" from Britain—the point that Representative Nicholas had made: "Is it not natural and necessary, under such different circumstances, that a different degree of freedom in the use of the press should be contemplated?" In America, Madison said, "the press has exerted a freedom in canvassing the merits and measures of public men, of every description, which has not been confined to the strict limits of the Common Law. On this footing the freedom of the press has stood; on this foundation it yet stands."

There were dissenters in the Virginia House of Delegates, and they published a "minority address" in support of the Sedition Act—drafted by Henry Lee, a Revolutionary War hero known as Light Horse Harry Lee (and the father of Robert E. Lee). It posed in stark terms the choices that any society had to make then, and does now, about freedom of political expression. The minority argued:

> To contend that there does not exist a power to punish writings coming within the description of this law would be to assert the inability of our nation to preserve its own peace, and to protect themselves from the attempts of wicked citizens who, incapable of quiet themselves, are incessantly employed in devising means to disturb the public repose. Government

is instituted and preserved for the general happiness and safety; the people therefore are interested in its preservation, and have a right to adopt measures for its security, as well against secret plots as open hostility. But government cannot be thus secured if, by falsehood and malicious slander, it is to be deprived of the confidence and affection of the people.

That minority address was a fascinating expression of the political premises that underlay the Sedition Act. It saw government as a sovereign that had to be protected from "wicked citizens" rather than as a body chosen by sovereign citizens to govern temporarily. And it saw danger in speech as unconspiratorial as Matthew Lyon's mocking of John Adams.

When Jefferson became president in 1801, he quickly pardoned all the men who had been convicted for violating the Sedition Act. He gave his reasons in an 1804 letter to Abigail Adams. (Despite their bitter relations before the election of 1800, Jefferson had a long and friendly correspondence with Abigail and, after a while, John Adams. They were close until the two ex-presidents died—on the same day, July 4, 1826, the fiftieth anniversary of the Declaration of Independence.) Jefferson wrote Mrs. Adams: "I discharged every person under punishment or prosecution under the Sedition Law, because I considered, and now consider, that law to be a nullity, as absolute and palpable as if Congress had ordered us to fall down and worship a golden image; and that it was as much my duty to arrest its execution in every stage, as it would have been to have rescued from the fiery furnace those who should have been cast into it for refusing to worship the image."

The Sedition Act inadvertently made a significant contribution to American freedom. It made numbers of Americans appreciate the importance of free speech and freedom of the press in a republic: the Madisonian premise. Whether or not the authors of the First Amendment intended to eliminate the crime of seditious libel, ten years after it was added to the Constitution the weight of American opinion was that such a crime was inconsistent with constitutional values.

But one feature of the Sedition Act did not disappear: the political use of fear to justify repression. Again and again in American history the public has been told that civil liberties must be sacrificed to protect the country from foreign threats. There have been repeated examples of what Richard Hofstadter called "the paranoid style in American politics." As in 1798, when the Federalists spoke of French terror to justify the Sedition Act, so in the twentieth century Congress passed many laws branding as infamous anyone who was suspected of a Communist taint; politicians from the 1920s through Richard Nixon and Joe McCarthy won votes by charging their opponents with being soft on communism. In the "war on terror" in the twenty-first century, President George W. Bush persuaded Congress to deprive alleged "enemy combatants" of legal rights in order, he said, to keep the country safe.

James Madison foresaw the problem. Two months before the Sedition Act was passed, in a letter to Vice President Jefferson, he wrote: "Perhaps it is a universal truth that the loss of liberty at home is to be charged to provisions against danger, real or pretended, from abroad."

3

"As All Life Is
an Experiment"

The First Amendment today is regularly and successfully invoked in lawsuits. The Supreme Court and other courts enforce its guarantees of free speech and freedom of the press. So it is astonishing to realize that the first time a Supreme Court opinion ever supported a claim of freedom under the amendment was in 1919—and that was a dissenting opinion. It was only 120 years after the Sedition Act that the speech and press clauses became a serious issue of law.

There were reasons for that long silence. The federal government had no laws restricting speech or publication from the end of the Sedition Act in 1801 until 1917. And the First Amendment, by its terms, applied only to federal laws, not state. ("*Congress* shall make no law . . . ") In 1833 the Supreme Court, in an opinion by Chief Justice Marshall, made clear that the entire Bill of Rights, the first ten amendments, covered only federal action.

The Fourteenth Amendment, added after the Civil War, provided that no state could "deprive any person of life, liberty, or property, without due process of law." The Supreme Court soon began to read that clause as guaranteeing individuals' property rights against state regulation, but at first it did not apply the clause to personal liberties of the kind protected by the first ten amendments, like freedom of speech.

When free-speech claims did reach the Supreme Court in the nineteenth century, it gave them the back of its hand, treating freedom of expression as an unimportant interest. The Court's approach was to allow repression of any speech that had a "bad tendency." That meant speech that might offend right-thinking people: a category so vague that it really offered no protection to speakers or writers. As late as 1907 this doctrine was used by a great Supreme Court justice, Oliver Wendell Holmes Jr., in a case called *Patterson v. Colorado*. Thomas M. Patterson, an editor, had been held in contempt of court for criticizing a judge. Under the old common-law rule, he was not allowed to argue that his criticism was true; Patterson argued that that denied him due process of law. Justice Holmes, following Blackstone, said "the main purpose" of the free speech guarantee was to prevent "previous restraints upon publication." The guarantee, he said, did "not prevent the subsequent punishment of such as may be deemed contrary to the public welfare." Even true statements could be punished if they did social harm, as criticism of a judge might in lowering respect for the administration of justice. That view echoed English seditious libel law. It gave no meaningful protection to speech or press, because just about anything might be "deemed contrary to the public welfare."

Justice John Marshall Harlan, dissenting, urged that the Fourteenth Amendment should be understood to have incorporated the guarantees of free speech and press in the First— and said that the judgment of contempt imposed on the editor violated those guarantees. Harlan's opinion was brief, three paragraphs, and without any discussion of the nature or scope of the freedom of speech and press. But it should be noted as a prescient call for applying those rights to state cases: a step that the Supreme Court did not take until 1925.

A dozen years later, Justice Holmes changed his mind—with profound consequences for American freedom. It is a remarkable story, still marked by a bit of mystery. The story starts with American entry into World War I, in 1917. The mood of the country turned jingoistic. Dissent from the war was not tolerated. German names were changed; sauerkraut became "liberty cabbage." In that atmosphere President Woodrow Wilson sought, and Congress passed, a sweeping Espionage Act. The act made it a crime to "cause or attempt to cause insubordination, disloyalty, mutiny, or refusal of duty in the military or naval forces" in wartime or to "willfully obstruct the recruiting or enlistment service." Hundreds of people were prosecuted under the act for merely speaking or writing critically. The most innocuous criticism of government or the war was found to violate the Espionage Act; judges told juries to convict if they found a defendant's words "disloyal."

In March 1919 three cases involving the Espionage Act were decided by the Supreme Court—all three unanimously, all three in opinions by Justice Holmes, all three upholding criminal convictions for violation of the act. At first glance there was little solace in the opinions for believers in freedom of speech.

In the first case, *Schenck v. United States*, the defendants had given leaflets denouncing conscription as slavery to men called up in the draft. Justice Holmes said, with what seemed reluctance, that "it may well be" that the First Amendment's guarantee of free speech "is not confined to previous restraints, . . . as intimated in *Patterson v. Colorado*." But in exigent circumstances speech could be punished, he said, producing an analogy that has become famous but is not really a fair analogy to criticizing government policy: "The most stringent protection of free speech would not protect a man in falsely shouting fire in a theater and causing a panic."

Then Justice Holmes offered a formula for deciding when speech can be punished. "The question in every case," he said, "is whether the words used are used in such circumstances and are of such a nature as to create a clear and present danger that they will bring about the substantive evils that Congress has a right to prevent." Those Delphic words have been scrutinized by generations of scholars. Holmes said years later that the concept of "clear and present danger" came from the discussion of attempted crimes in his 1881 book, *The Common Law*. An attempt can be punished, he said then, if "its natural and probable effect" would in time have led to a crime. That approach did not seem protective of speech, and Holmes almost certainly did not intend it to be. It did not help the *Schenck* defendants—or those in the two

other cases decided at that time, *Frohwerk v. United States* and
Debs v. United States.

The *Debs* case made plain how far-reaching punishment for
speech could be. The defendant was a well-known political
figure: Eugene V. Debs, leader of the Socialist Party and five
times its candidate for president. He was prosecuted for a
speech he made in Canton, Ohio. It was mostly about social-
ism, but he began by telling the audience that he had just visited three men who were in jail nearby for aiding another man
in failing to register for the draft. As Holmes put it in his
opinion, Debs said the three "were paying the penalty for
standing erect and for seeking to pave the way to better con-
ditions for all mankind." Debs was convicted and sentenced to
ten years in prison. (He was released after three years, having
run for president in 1920 from a federal penitentiary.)

Holmes brushed off First Amendment arguments made
for Debs, saying that his opinion in the *Schenck* case had dis-
posed of them. He said there was evidence to "warrant the
jury" in finding that Debs's opposition to the war and conscription "was so expressed that its natural and intended effect would be to obstruct recruiting." To appreciate how
little weight Holmes gave to freedom of speech in the *Debs*
case, think of the later American wars in Vietnam and Iraq.
They were denounced in words far rougher than Debs's, but
no one was prosecuted for mere speech. What Debs said in
Canton did not actually harm recruiting efforts, but Holmes
evidently felt that the clear and present danger test was met
because the potential harm in wartime, however unlikely,
was so great.

Just eight months later, in November 1919, the Supreme Court decided a fourth Espionage Act case, *Abrams v. United States*. Four radicals, refugees from the pogroms and tyranny of czarist Russia, protested President Wilson's decision to send American troops into Russia after the Bolshevik Revolution. They threw leaflets from the top of a building in New York's Lower East Side, urging a general strike in protest against Wilson's intervention. The four were charged under amendments to the Espionage Act, passed by Congress in 1918, which made it a crime to "utter, print, write or publish any disloyal, profane, scurrilous, or abusive language" about the Constitution, the armed forces, military uniforms, or the flag. The charge was that their leaflets, though they discussed the Russian intervention, were an attempt to hurt the war against Germany. All four were convicted. Three men were sentenced to twenty years in prison; Mollie Steimer, a twenty-year-old woman, to fifteen years.

The Supreme Court affirmed the convictions. But this time Justice Holmes dissented in an opinion joined by Justice Louis D. Brandeis. Holmes said he did not doubt the rightness of the three earlier Espionage Act decisions. The United States, he said, had the power to "punish speech that produces and is intended to produce a clear and imminent danger that it will bring about forthwith certain substantive evils." Holmes said he was merely restating his "clear and present danger" test, but he had added two crucial adjectives, "imminent" and "forthwith."

"Now nobody can suppose," Holmes wrote, "that the surreptitious publishing of a silly leaflet by an unknown man, without more, would present any immediate danger that its opinions would hinder the success of the government arms. . . . In this case sentences of twenty years imprisonment have been imposed for the publishing of two leaflets that I believe the defendants had as much right to publish as the Government has to publish the Constitution of the United States now vainly invoked by them." Holmes called the leaflets "poor and puny anonymities" and said that even if they could be found unlawful, only "the most nominal punishment" could be justified unless the defendants were really being punished for their radical views—views, he said, "that I believe to be the creed of ignorance and immaturity" but that "no one has a right even to consider in dealing with the charges before the Court."

It was a powerful dissent. Holmes made the case that savage sentences had been imposed for the publishing of words that only wartime zealotry could stretch into disruption of the war effort. But where had the opinion come from? Holmes always denied that his view in the *Abrams* case differed from what he had said in the three earlier Espionage Act decisions. But not only the outcome but the reasoning was quite different. By the standards of this opinion, Debs should not have been convicted for uttering a few sentences about meeting men who were imprisoned for advising on how to avoid draft registration.

How and why Holmes changed his mind, or at least changed his emphasis profoundly, cannot be said with certainty; that is where mystery remains. But there are clues. For one, the *Debs* decision had drawn widespread criticism from scholars and commentators who were usually admirers of Justice Holmes. We know that he read at least one of these criticisms, because he wrote a letter to the author—but did not mail it.

Another possible influence was Learned Hand, a federal trial judge in New York who later went on to the Court of Appeals and became probably the most respected judge in the country. Hand and Holmes met on a train in 1918. They evidently talked about freedom of speech, for they exchanged letters on the subject immediately afterward. Hand had written a striking opinion in favor of free speech in a case involving the radical magazine *The Masses*. The postmaster general had excluded it from the mails because of an issue that attacked the war and the draft. Judge Hand, ruling for the magazine in a suit against the exclusion order, *Masses Publishing Co. v. Patten* (1917), said speech that directly incited "violent resistance" could be punished—but not speech that merely criticized government policy, whether temperately or by invective. The distinction, he said, was "a hard bought acquisition in the fight for freedom." He added that a country with our constitutional commitment depended on "the free expression of opinion as the ultimate source of authority." That was a remarkable, telling point about political legitimacy. (Hand was reversed by the Court of Appeals, but his ideas survived.)

Hand wrote to Holmes, privately, after the *Debs* decision. Consistently with his *Masses* judgment, he said that speech should be punishable only when "directly an incitement" to illegality. He made a further point that was highly relevant in the wartime atmosphere. It was wrong to let juries decide whether words had a "tendency" to some bad result, he said, because the cases arise "when men are excited." Holmes replied, "I am afraid that I don't quite get your point." That seems most unlikely.

But the greatest influence on Holmes in this period was an article in the *Harvard Law Review* by Professor Zechariah Chafee Jr. of the Harvard Law School. Chafee was a scholar on freedom of speech, and he marshaled evidence from history to argue that the First Amendment gave broad protection to speech even in the agitated circumstances of wartime. He said the Framers of the amendment intended "to wipe out the common law of sedition and make further prosecutions for criticisms of the government, without any incitement to law-breaking, forever impossible in the United States."

Chafee might have been expected to attack the three decisions of March 1919 upholding Espionage Act convictions. To the contrary, he praised Holmes's "clear and present danger" formula, saying it would make "the punishment of words for their bad tendency impossible." He did say that the *Debs* jury should have been required to find a clear and present danger of illegal actions.

The Chafee article, entitled "Freedom of Speech in War Time," appeared in the *Harvard Law Review* issue of June 1919. It could not have been better timed. Holmes read it that summer, and years later he told Chafee in a letter that he had been "taught" by it about the historical roots of the First Amendment. But it would be a mistake to attribute Holmes's thinking entirely to this or that source. He was a phenomenal reader: He often read a book a day, and he read books in various languages.

When he came to write the *Abrams* dissent, Holmes relied on his own rhetorical power—which was extraordinary. He did not stop with the passage quoted above. He went on in words that forever changed American perceptions of freedom:

Persecution for the expression of opinions seems to me perfectly logical. If you have no doubt of your premises or your power and want a certain result with all your heart, you naturally express your wishes in law and sweep away all opposition. . . .

But when men have realized that time has upset many fighting faiths, they may come to believe even more than they believe the very foundations of their own conduct that the ultimate good desired is better reached by free trade in ideas—that the best test of truth is the power of the thought to get itself accepted in the competition of the market, and that truth is the only ground upon which their wishes safely can be carried out.

That at any rate is the theory of our Constitution. It is an experiment, as all life is an experiment. . . . While that experiment is part of our system I think that we should be eternally vigilant against attempts to check the expression of opinions that we loathe and believe to be fraught with death, unless they so imminently threaten immediate interference with the lawful and pressing purposes of the law that an immediate check is required to save the country. . . .

Only the emergency that makes it immediately dangerous to leave the correction of evil counsels to time warrants making any exception to the sweeping command, "Congress shall make no law . . . abridging the freedom of speech." Of course I am speaking only of expressions of opinion and exhortations, which were all that were uttered here, but I regret that I cannot put into more impressive words my belief that in their conviction upon this indictment the defendants were deprived of their rights under the Constitution of the United States.

No other judge, then or since, could have written "It is an experiment, as all life is an experiment"—or "opinions that we loathe and believe to be fraught with death." Holmes was the closest we have had to a poet judge.

There was a remarkable episode on the way to Holmes's dissent in the *Abrams* case. It was unknown until Dean Acheson, the former secretary of state, told the story in 1965 in his memoir, *Morning and Noon.* Acheson was Justice Brandeis's law clerk in the 1920 Supreme Court term. His friend Stanley Morrison had clerked for Justice Holmes the year before, the *Abrams* year. Morrison told him that before the decision was announced, three other justices had called on Holmes, bringing Mrs. Holmes with them. Acheson wrote:

They laid before him their request that in this case, which they thought affected the safety of the country, he should, like the old soldier he had once been, close ranks and forego individual predilections. Mrs. Holmes agreed. The tone of the discussion was at all times friendly, even affectionate. The justice regretted that he could not do as they wished. They did not press. Thus, fortunately, survived a most moving statement of liberal faith in freedom of thought and speech.

Holmes had been a Union soldier in the Civil War, and had been gravely wounded three times. (When he died, his Union Army uniform was found hanging in his closet.) His colleagues and his wife appealed to his patriotism, but he would not yield. He dissented in his action as in his words—a perfect symbol of the point he was arguing, the legitimacy of dissent.

Justices Holmes and Brandeis were together in a stream of dissenting opinions in free speech cases over the next decade. They were a remarkable pair, alike in powerful intellects but differing sharply in other ways. Holmes was a Boston Brahmin, a lover of wine and women. Brandeis, the first Jewish member of the Supreme Court, was something of a Puritan who did not drink. After a brilliant record at the Harvard Law School, Brandeis made a fortune in private legal practice but devoted himself increasingly to legal work on behalf of the public. He was a social reformer; Holmes believed such efforts pointless. They had in common, though, a willingness to let governments experiment with such reforms as maximum hour laws, which led them to dissent when the Court held economic reform legislation unconstitutional. After Holmes's shift in 1919, they did not apply their deference to legislatures when free speech was at issue.

Claims for free speech regularly lost in the Court through the 1920s. There was just one notable victory. In *Gitlow v.*

New York (1925) Benjamin Gitlow challenged his conviction under New York law for a publication urging a "revolutionary dictatorship of the proletariat." The Court ruled against him, with a Holmes dissent joined by Brandeis. But the majority for the first time said that the Fourteenth Amendment applied the free-speech clause of the First to the states. Most free-speech cases in the Supreme Court from then on dealt with repression by state authorities.

Dissenting opinions are an appeal to "the brooding spirit of the law," Charles Evans Hughes said. That is, they call on future courts to rethink decisions. In fact, that rather seldom happens. But the dissents by Holmes and Brandeis between 1919 and 1929 did in time overturn the old, crabbed view of what the First Amendment protects. It was an extraordinary change, really a legal revolution. And it showed the power of words to change minds. Holmes and Brandeis had only two votes of nine. But their rhetoric was so powerful, so convincing, that it changed the attitude of the country and the Court.

Three opinions in that decade stand out. The first was Holmes's dissent in 1919 in the *Abrams* case. The second came in 1927 in the case of Anita Whitney, a member of a socially prominent family who helped to found the Communist Labor Party of California; she was convicted of membership in an organization advocating "criminal syndicalism," a term for radical groups, and sentenced to one to fourteen years in the San Quentin penitentiary. In *Whitney v. California* (1927), Brandeis wrote an opinion, joined by Holmes, that many regard as the greatest judicial statement of the case for freedom of speech. It said in part:

Those who won our independence . . . believed liberty to be the secret of happiness and courage to be the secret of liberty. They believed that freedom to think as you will and to speak as you think are means indispensable to the discovery and spread of political truth; that without free speech and assembly discussion would be futile; that with them, discussion affords ordinarily adequate protection against the dissemination of noxious doctrine; that the greatest menace to freedom is an inert people; that public discussion is a political duty; and that this should be a fundamental principle of the American government. They recognized the risks to which all human institutions are subject. But they knew that order cannot be secured merely through fear of punishment for its infraction; that it is hazardous to discourage thought, hope and imagination; that fear breeds repression; that repression breeds hate; that hate menaces stable government. . . . Believing in the power of reason as applied through public discussion, they eschewed silence coerced by law—the argument of force in its worst form. Recognizing the occasional tyrannies of governing majorities, they amended the Constitution so that free speech and assembly should be guaranteed.

Fear of serious injury alone cannot justify suppression of free speech and assembly. Men feared witches and burnt women. . . .

Brandeis's opinion did not then represent the law, but it helped Anita Whitney. A month after the Supreme Court turned down her appeal, the governor of California, C. C.

Young, pardoned her, quoting the Brandeis dissent at length in his pardon message.

(The fate of the four radicals who lost in the *Abrams* case was different. They were released from prison in 1921 on condition that they go to the Soviet Union. Mollie Steimer and Jacob Abrams were unhappy with the tyranny they encountered under Leninism and left for Mexico. Hyman Lachowsky and Samuel Lipman stayed in the USSR—and died at the hands, respectively, of Soviet and Nazi terror.)

The third great dissent of that decade was in the case of *United States v. Schwimmer*, decided by the Supreme Court in 1929. Rosika Schwimmer was a pacifist, an immigrant from Hungary who applied for citizenship. The rules at the time required her to swear that she would take up arms to defend the United States—which as a pacifist she refused to do. She was denied the right to become a citizen, and the Supreme Court upheld the denial. Justice Holmes, who was then eighty-eight years old, said her refusal to swear was irrelevant, "as she is a woman over fifty years of age, and would not be allowed to bear arms if she wanted to." He said he did not agree with her pacifism and did not think "that a philosophical view of the world would regard war as absurd." But he concluded his opinion as follows:

> Some of her answers might excite popular prejudice, but if there is any principle of the Constitution that more imperatively calls for attachment than any other it is the principle of free thought—not free thought for those who agree with us but freedom for the thought that we hate. I think that we

should adhere to that principle with regard to admission into, as well as to life within this country. And recurring to the opinion that bars this applicant's way, I would suggest that the Quakers have done their share to make the country what it is, that many citizens agree with the applicant's belief and that I had not supposed hitherto that we regretted our inability to expel them because they believe more than some of us in the teachings of the Sermon on the Mount.

I add a personal note on how I first came to read Justice Holmes's opinion in the *Schwimmer* case. Some time around 1960, when I was reporting on the Supreme Court for the *New York Times*, I was talking with Justice Felix Frankfurter in his chambers. Suddenly, to make a point, he rose and strode across the room to his shelves of *United States Reports*, the volumes of Supreme Court opinions. He pulled one off the shelf, opened it, and handed it to me. It was the Holmes dissent in *United States v. Schwimmer*. I read. When I came to the final paragraph, ending ". . . Sermon on the Mount," I felt the hair rise on the back of my neck.

4

Defining Freedom

A majority on the Supreme Court began enforcing the constitutional guarantee of freedom of speech in 1931, in the case of *Stromberg v. California.* A California law forbade the display of a red flag "as a sign, symbol or emblem of opposition to organized government." The Court held the statute unconstitutional: the first time it had ever done so in the name of the First Amendment. Chief Justice Charles Evans Hughes, who had joined the Court a year earlier, wrote the opinion for a 7-to-2 majority. "The maintenance of the opportunity for free public discussion to the end that government may be responsible to the will of the people and that changes may be obtained by lawful means," Hughes wrote, "is a fundamental principle of our constitutional system." The rhetoric had not the thrill of Holmes or Brandeis, but it operated from their premise: that free speech was a basic American value, that repression was not to be tolerated to prevent some dim and distant bad tendency.

Once the Court embarked on enforcing the First Amendment as law, it faced a new task: defining from case to case what the words of the amendment mean. That may sound simple. What could be more direct than the command, "Congress shall make no law . . . abridging the freedom of speech, or of the press"? But in fact, giving concrete meaning to those words was a daunting, and endless, job.

The language of the amendment sounds all-embracing, but does it really mean that the law cannot act against anything spoken or printed? Hardly. Blackmail is carried on by speech or writing, but the First Amendment does not protect the blackmailer—or the gangster who threatens violence if his demands are not met. The First Amendment is not a license to publish a copyrighted work without permission.

Conversely, the First Amendment has been interpreted to protect some actions that are not literally spoken or printed. That is true of the *Stromberg* case. Yetta Stromberg did not use words; she was prosecuted for carrying a red flag. The Supreme Court saw that as symbolic speech, the beginning of a long line of cases in which expressive acts have been protected. A notable example was the 1989 decision in *Texas v. Johnson*, reversing, on First Amendment grounds, a conviction for burning the American flag in a political demonstration.

How, then, is a judge to interpret the First Amendment? One approach would be to look at what James Madison, its drafter, and those who voted for it in 1791 thought they were doing. After all, they prohibited Congress from "abridging the freedom of speech. . . ." The word "the" can be read to mean what was understood at the time to be included in the concept of free speech.

The trouble with that approach, or one trouble, is that it is not at all clear what the Framers of the First Amendment had in mind. No definitions of freedom were offered in the congressional consideration, so far as we know, and it is impossible to get any useful guidance on the views of the many state legislators who voted to ratify the amendment.

The evident truth is that those who gave us the First Amendment did not provide a detailed code of how it was to be applied—and did not want to. They deliberately wrote a spacious amendment—a "sweeping command," as Justice Holmes put it in his *Abrams* dissent—and left it to later generations to apply its broad call for freedom to particular situations.

Holmes himself made one of the classic statements on the futility of looking to 1791 or 1787 for answers to constitutional questions. He wrote in 1920: "When we are dealing with words that also are a constituent act, like the Constitution of the United States, we must realize that they have called into life a being the development of which could not have been foreseen completely by the most gifted of its begetters. . . . The case before us must be considered in the light of our whole experience and not merely in that of what was said a hundred years ago."

Chief Justice Hughes also addressed the issue, in 1934: "If by the statement that what the Constitution meant at the time of its adoption it means today, it is intended to say that the great clauses of the Constitution must be confined to the interpretation which the Framers, with the condition and outlook of their time, would have placed upon them, the statement carries its own refutation."

Fifty years after Hughes wrote that, a legal movement arose that took the position he regarded as self-evidently wrong. Its supporters, including some judges and professors, became known as Originalists—because they advocated giving clauses of the Constitution their "original meaning." Their argument was that, in a sea of possible interpretations, the only course that kept judges from reading their own preferences into constitutional language was to look for the intention of the Framers. The most prominent Originalist was Justice Antonin Scalia of the Supreme Court. He and others ran into the difficulty, noted above, of finding an original intention when the authors or supporters of a clause in the Constitution had not expressed one, indeed had not even imagined the problem now at issue. Justice Scalia, a strong believer in freedom of expression, applied the First Amendment often without any reference to original intent. He joined, for example, in the decision finding unconstitutional the law against flag-burning.

Justice Hugo L. Black, whose long service on the Supreme Court (1937–1971) was marked by devotion to freedom of expression, sought in a different way to limit the interpretive discretion of judges. He read the First Amendment, he said, as "an absolute" that forbade any official restrictions on expression. But on occasion Justice Black found ways to uphold restrictions, saying for example that speech had occurred in an inappropriate place or was not really speech. When a young protester against the Vietnam War was prosecuted by California for wearing a jacket inscribed with the phrase "Fuck the Draft" in *Cohen v. California* (1971), the Supreme

Court found the protest protected by the First Amendment; but Justice Black joined a dissent that called it an "absurd and immature antic, . . . mainly conduct and not speech."

One important issue, in applying the amendment over many decades, was whether it gave any protection to false statements. The early cases were about beliefs and opinions, which cannot be judged true or false—"expressions of opinion and exhortations," as Holmes put it in his *Abrams* dissent. But what about statements of fact? If they include falsehoods, are they entitled to constitutional protection?

In 1925 the Minnesota legislature decided to close down scandal-mongering newspapers that often attacked legislators and other public officials. It passed a curiously named Public Nuisance Law that allowed the courts to enjoin—shut down—any "malicious, scandalous and defamatory newspapers." The statute allowed a newspaper to defend itself by showing that it had published the truth—but only if it had done so "with good motives and for justifiable ends." That condition effectively canceled the defense of truth, allowing judges to appraise the character of publishers.

A weekly paper called the *Saturday Press*, put out by Jay M. Near, became a target of the law in 1927. Near was a virulent anti-Semite. His paper regularly charged that Jewish gangsters, in league with officials, were corrupting government. After only nine issues, the *Saturday Press* was closed by court order. Near appealed to the Minnesota Supreme Court, which turned him down. "Our constitution," the court said, "was never intended to protect malice, scandal and defamation when untrue or published with bad motives or without justifiable ends. It is a shield for the honest, careful and conscientious press."

The established newspapers of Minnesota, no doubt thinking themselves honest, careful, and conscientious, took no interest in Jay Near's plight. But Robert Rutherford McCormick, the splenetic conservative publisher of the *Chicago Tribune*, recognized that leaving it to judges to decide who was a nice publisher would eviscerate freedom of the press; he decided to support Near. His lawyer, Weymouth Kirkland, took the case to the Supreme Court of the United States.

James E. Markham, deputy attorney general of Minnesota, who argued *Near v. Minnesota* for the state, may have hoped for help from Justice Brandeis because of Near's anti-Semitism. But from the bench Brandeis, who had obtained and read the nine published issues of the *Saturday Press*, told Markham that Near had tried to expose "combinations between criminals and public officials." We know, he added, "that just such criminal combinations exist to the shame of some of our cities." For a newspaper to expose them was bound to involve defamation, he said; if they got it wrong, they could be sued later for libel.

That was where the Supreme Court came out. By the narrowest of majorities, 5 to 4, the Court found the ban on the *Saturday Press* in violation of the First Amendment, as applied to the states by the Fourteenth. It was a turning point for freedom of the press.

Chief Justice Hughes, for the majority, found that the injunction against Near was a prior restraint of the kind rejected by Blackstone. He quoted Madison on the need for a free press. "The impairment of the fundamental security of life and property by criminal alliances and official neglect," he wrote, "emphasizes the primary need of a vigilant and courageous press, especially in great cities." Robert R. McCormick had those words inscribed in the lobby of his new building in Chicago, the Tribune Tower.

The four dissenters, in an opinion by Justice Pierce Butler, quoted from a treatise on the Constitution by an early, much-respected Supreme Court justice, Joseph Story. The First Amendment, Story said, meant only that "every man shall be at liberty to publish what is true, with good motives and for justifiable ends"—the very condition asserted by the Minnesota law. "Without such a limitation," Story added, the amendment "might become the scourge of the republic, . . . by rendering the most virtuous patriots odious through the terrors of the press, introducing despotism in its worst form." Contemporary critics of the press could not do better than his warnings against the press's "terrors" and "despotism."

I have taken my description of the *Near* case from a wonderful book by Fred Friendly, *Minnesota Rag.* Friendly was a CBS executive, a colleague of Edward R. Murrow, and later a vice president of the Ford Foundation. In writing the book he had an experience that is an illuminating coda to the case of *Near v. Minnesota.* At lunch one day in the Ford Foundation, Friendly spoke about his work on the book. A foundation trustee, Irving Shapiro, then the CEO of the DuPont Corporation, came over and said, to Friendly's astonishment, that he had known Jay Near. Shapiro's father owned a dry-cleaning store in Minneapolis. One day gangsters came in and demanded protection money. When Mr. Shapiro said no, they sprayed the clothes hanging in the store with acid. Irving, a young boy, watched from the back of the store. The established local papers did nothing with the story. But Mr. Near came in, wrote about the attack—and the gangsters were prosecuted. Fred Friendly tells the story.

Near v. Minnesota was and remains a bulwark of American press freedom. Because of that decision, it is very difficult to persuade a judge to issue a prior restraint on the press. It is a sharp contrast from the law in Britain, where courts routinely do such things as prohibit the publication of a book when someone asserts that he will be libeled in it.

Just five years after the *Near* decision the dissenting justices abandoned their opposition. Huey Long, the dictatorial populist governor of Louisiana, put through a newspaper tax to punish papers critical of him. The Supreme Court unanimously held it unconstitutional in *Grosjean v. American Press Co.* (1936). The opinion of the court, by Justice George Sutherland, one of the four conservative dissenters in 1931, cited the *Near* case. It rested on the informing function of the press, the point that Brandeis had made at the argument of the *Near* case and that Chief Justice Hughes had described in his opinion. The people, Sutherland wrote, are entitled to "full information in respect of the doings or misdoings of their government; informed public opinion is the most potent of all restraints upon misgovernment."

In his *Near* opinion Hughes did not rule out all prior restraints. No one would doubt, he said, that the government could prevent "publication of the sailing dates of transports or the number or location of troops." Forty years later, that language—the *Near* exception, it was called—became the crux of one of the greatest conflicts over freedom of the press, the Pentagon Papers case. In June 1971, the *New York Times* began publishing top-secret documents from a secret official history of the Vietnam War. The war was still on, and President Richard M. Nixon asserted that the stories threatened the national security. The courts temporarily stopped publication. Lawyers and judges debated whether what was in the papers amounted to Hughes's sailing dates of troopships.

In *New York Times v. United States*, a 6-to-3 majority of the Supreme Court, ruling just two weeks after the case began, held that the *Times* and other newspapers could resume publication of the Pentagon Papers. There were ten different opinions, offering diverse arguments. The most powerful, and no doubt the most lasting, came from Justice Black. It was his last opinion, before his illness and death that summer. Justice Black wrote:

The press was protected [in the First Amendment] so that it could bare the secrets of government and inform the people. Only a free and unrestrained press can effectively expose deception in government. And paramount among the responsibilities of a free press is the duty to prevent any part of the government from deceiving the people and sending them off to distant lands to die of foreign fevers and foreign shot and shell. In my view, far from deserving condemnation for their courageous reporting, the New York Times, the Washington Post and other newspapers should be commended for serving the purpose that the Founding Fathers saw so clearly. In revealing the workings of government that led to the Vietnam War, the newspapers nobly did precisely that which the Founders hoped and trusted they would do.

The *Near* decision freed the author of a damaging statement from the need to prove its truth before publication; with rare and extreme exceptions, judges must reject demands for prior restraints without examining the character of the statement. But what about a libel suit after publication? Could the target of an offensive newspaper story demand then that the author or publisher prove its truth? That question was resolved by the Supreme Court in 1964 in one of its most dramatic and far-reaching First Amendment decisions, *New York Times v. Sullivan.*

The case arose out of the civil rights movement in the American South. Its leader, Dr. Martin Luther King Jr., was convinced that the public in the North would reject racial segregation and discrimination if confronted with their cruelty. His strategy, based on the nonviolent approach of Mahatma Gandhi, was to demonstrate against racism and show Americans, most of whom knew little about its brutal reality, what it meant. The press—newspapers, magazines, broadcasting—had a crucial role in that strategy, bringing the reality home to national audiences.

On March 29, 1960, the *New York Times* published an advertisement by supporters of Dr. King. At that date, six years after the Supreme Court decision in *Brown v. Board of Education* holding segregation in schools unconstitutional, not only schools but state universities remained segregated by race throughout the Deep South. In a number of states, blacks were prevented from voting by threats and murderous violence.

The advertisement said that racist southern officials had used lawless tactics against the civil rights movement—for example arresting Dr. King seven times on trumped-up charges and mistreating demonstrators. The ad mentioned no names. It spoke of "Southern violators of the Constitution." But one official, L.B. Sullivan, a commissioner of the city of Montgomery, Alabama, sued the *Times* for libel. He claimed that he could be identified as one of the "violators" because he was in charge of the Montgomery police and the ad charged them with misconduct.

The atmosphere in the white South was so hostile that a *New York Times* lawyer who went down to the libel trial from New York was advised to stay in a motel 40 miles from Montgomery under an assumed name. (Justice Black, who was from Alabama, observed in a concurring opinion in the case that if white people in Montgomery had happened to see the ad and connect it with Commissioner Sullivan, his "political, social and financial prestige" had "likely been enhanced.")

The trial took place in a state court before a judge, Walter B. Jones, who so admired the Confederacy that on the anniversary of its founding he seated the jurors in his courtroom in Confederate military uniforms. Judge Jones ruled that the advertisement was libelous and left just two questions to the jury: Did the ad refer to Sullivan, and if so, what damages should he get? The jury awarded him all he asked, $500,000, at that point the largest libel award in Alabama history.

Under Alabama law, any publication that was challenged in a libel action was presumed to be false; the burden was on the publisher to prove it true. That burden of proof, as it is called, is a crucial factor, because proving truth can be difficult. It was the rule in libel cases in the common law, and it remains the rule in English law today—one reason why British newspapers so often give up and settle when they are sued for libel. At the time of the *Sullivan* case it was the law in a number of states, not just Alabama.

Another traditional rule in libel cases, followed in Alabama and elsewhere, was that damage was presumed. The person suing did not have to prove actual damage, say to his career, as he or she would have to prove in other civil damage cases, such as medical malpractice. It was enough in libel to show that the challenged publication was of a kind that would harm reputation.

A third libel rule was that the publisher's fault was presumed. In other damage cases the plaintiff had to show that the doctor, say, had not followed approved practice and hence was negligent. In the common law of libel, it did not matter whether the publisher had printed his statement negligently or with any other fault. Even if he did his best to get the truth, he paid if he could not prove it. Lawyers called these the "three galloping presumptions" of libel law.

The *New York Times* could not meet the demand that it prove the ad true in all material respects. It admitted that there were some misstatements in it: Dr. King had been arrested four times, not seven, for example; the dining hall of a black college was not padlocked, as the ad said. The advertisement was therefore libelous, as Judge Jones found, under Alabama law.

The $500,000 judgment against the *Times* was a large blow to the paper. It was barely profitable in 1960. Moreover, other Montgomery commissioners and the governor of Alabama, John Patterson, also sued over the advertisement, and one of the commissioners soon won $500,000 from a jury. The *Times* seemed likely to owe $3 million—enough to put it out of business, its general counsel, James Goodale, said later. But more important than the financial problems of the *New York Times* was the effect on the civil rights movement. The *Sullivan* lawsuit could discourage not only the *Times* but all national press institutions from covering the movement because of the legal risks. Indeed, the suit may have been planned with that idea in mind. The *Montgomery Advertiser*—edited by Grover C. Hall Jr., a friend of Commissioner Sullivan—headlined a story about the libel cases, "State Finds Formidable Legal Club to Swing at Out-of-State Press." So the suit threatened Dr. King's whole strategy of displaying racism to the country. In the most fundamental way, it threatened the informing purpose of the First Amendment.

The *Times* took the case to the Supreme Court. It looks now like an easy case to win: a huge, menacing libel judgment for a plaintiff not even named in the advertisement. But it was not easy at the time, not at all. Libel had always been considered outside the protection of the First Amendment. No libel judgment had ever been found to violate the guarantees of freedom of speech and press.

That was the challenge facing the *Times*'s lawyer, Professor Herbert Wechsler of the Columbia Law School. He would have to ask the justices to do what courts are extremely reluctant to do: reverse a long-unchanged course of legal history. Wechsler decided to meet that history with another page of history: the record of the Sedition Act of 1798. He argued that the libel law of Alabama, as applied in this case, punished criticism of public officials just as the Sedition Act had done. And he said the Sedition Act, though never tested in the Supreme Court, had in effect been found unconstitutional when the voters rejected President Adams in 1800 and installed Thomas Jefferson, the act's critic, in his place.

Wechsler argued that there could be no test of truth for criticism of public officials. To allow libel judgments for any misstatement, he said, would discourage the press and individual citizens from voicing criticism lest they make a mistake. He told the Court: "This is not a time—there never is a time—when it would serve the values enshrined in the Constitution to force the press to curtail its attention to the tensest issues that confront the country."

At the oral argument of the case, Justice William J. Brennan Jr. asked Wechsler whether there were "any limits whatever" to the First Amendment's protection for criticism of officials. That is, was he proposing an absolute privilege for such criticism? Wechsler said he was. "If I take my instruction from James Madison," he said, "I can see no toying with limits." Justice Potter Stewart asked whether he would make the same argument if a newspaper accused an official of taking a bribe. "Certainly," Wechsler replied. "Of course, in the historic period in which Madison was writing, charges of bribery were common, and it was this type of press freedom that he saw in the First Amendment."

Justice Brennan delivered the opinion of the Court on March 9, 1964. It was a decisive victory for the *New York Times*, and a sweeping assertion of the values of free speech and freedom of the press. Quoting from Madison, Hand, and Brandeis, Justice Brennan adopted their views as the law of the Constitution. He said: "Thus we consider this case against the background of a profound national commitment to the principle that debate on public issues should be uninhibited, robust and wide-open, and that it may well include vehement, caustic, and sometimes unpleasantly sharp attacks on government and public officials."

Justice Brennan put the Sedition Act of 1798 at the heart of his analysis. The controversy over it, he said, "first crystallized a national awareness of the central meaning of the First Amendment" —the right to criticize what Madison called "public characters and measures." "Although the Sedition Act was never tested in this Court," Brennan said, "the attack upon its validity has carried the day in the court of history." With that, the Sedition Act was found unconstitutional 163 years after it expired.

Letting libel defendants escape damages by proving the truth of their criticism was not enough, Justice Brennan said: "Would-be critics of official conduct may be deterred from voicing their criticism, even though it is believed to be true and even though it is in fact true, because of doubt whether it can be proved in court or fear of the expense of having to do so." It was the same point made by Representative John Nicholas in the House debate on the Sedition Act in 1798.

But Justice Brennan did not go all the way with Madison and Wechsler. He did not say that the First Amendment required an absolute privilege for criticism of officials. Instead, he said that officials could not win libel damages from their critics unless they proved that a false, damaging statement had been made with knowledge of its falsity—a deliberate lie—or in "reckless disregard" of its truth or falsity. Later cases explained that "reckless disregard" meant the author or publisher was aware of the statement's probable falsity.

Six members of the Supreme Court joined in that resolution of *New York Times v. Sullivan.* Three—Justices Black, William O. Douglas, and Arthur Goldberg—said in concurring opinions that they would have gone farther and disallowed all libel actions by officials over criticism of their official conduct. Commentators have wondered why Justice Brennan did not agree with them. The *Sullivan* case was decided just after Senator Joseph McCarthy's demagogic career of denouncing as Communists or disloyal such persons as General George C. Marshall, a revered former secretary of state. Justice Brennan never spoke to the McCarthy problem as such, but in a lecture the year after the *Sullivan* decision he said:

At the time the First Amendment was adopted, as today, there were those unscrupulous enough and skillful enough to use the deliberate or reckless falsehood as an effective political tool. . . . That speech is used as a tool for political ends does not automatically bring it under the protective mantle of the Constitution. For the use of the known lie as a tool is at once at odds with the premises of democratic government and with the orderly manner in which economic, social or political change is to be effected.

New York Times v. Sullivan revolutionized the law of libel in the United States. What had always been a matter of state law became, in most cases, a subject that turned on federal constitutional law. The old common-law doctrine putting the burden on libel defendants to prove truth was reversed; decisions following the *Sullivan* case made clear that the plaintiff had to prove falsity in order to win—and had to prove fault on the part of the author or publisher, not just an innocent mistake.

The law of other countries was affected, too. Over the years since 1964, a number of courts abroad have adjusted their law of libel to give the authors of criticism more protection. Even the House of Lords, Britain's highest court, did so. But no other country went as far as the rule laid down by Justice Brennan.

The immediate consequence of the decision in this country was to open the way for intense coverage of the racial struggle in the South by a press freed from the threat of endless libel actions. Just as Dr. King had hoped, the violence directed at civil rights supporters made the brutal nature of racism clear to many in the North. There, on television, were grown men and women screaming obscenities at little black children trying to go to desegregated schools. Professor Alexander M. Bickel of the Yale Law School said, "The moral bankruptcy, the shame of the thing, was evident."

Public outrage put pressure on Congress to act, and it did. In 1964 it outlawed discrimination in public accommodations, schools, and jobs. In 1965 it passed the Voting Rights Act, which finally enabled black Americans to vote in the Deep South. The politics of the region was transformed, with blacks elected to many offices and southern Democrats moving en masse to the Republican Party. The First Amendment had worked exactly as Madison had hoped it would. Freedom of speech, and of the press, had empowered citizens in a democracy.

The effects of the *Sullivan* case were not limited to the immediate racial context. Over the years it emboldened the American press, encouraging it to challenge official truth instead of acting as a mere stenographer. Within a decade this new spirit of journalism produced two of the press's great modern achievements: penetrating coverage of the Vietnam War and Watergate. Young reporters on the ground in Vietnam found that the American war was not going well, and said so. Officials all the way up to presidents John F. Kennedy and Lyndon B. Johnson put heavy pressure on editors and publishers to curb their reporters, but they did not give way. The new spirit was symbolized by the decision of the *New York Times* to publish the Pentagon Papers in 1971. The next year, Bob Woodward and Carl Bernstein of the *Washington Post* began their epic exploration of the official crimes of Watergate. Officials threatened the publisher of the *Post*, Katharine Graham, with loss of the company's television channels; but she held fast. In 1974, after investigations provoked by the press, President Nixon was forced to resign.

In later cases the Supreme Court extended the *Sullivan* decision so that not only officials but "public figures" had to prove deliberate or reckless falsification to win damages for libel. It defined "public figures" to include people who are universally famous, like movie stars, or who thrust themselves into "the vortex of controversy" on some public issue—for example, a citizen who plays a significant part in a local zoning dispute. The press was pleased that more libel plaintiffs had to bear the heavy burden, but I was and remain unpersuaded. If a supermarket tabloid prints a sensational story about a movie actress, why should she have to meet the same test as a politician if she sues for libel? What does she have to do with what the *Sullivan* decision called "the central meaning of the First Amendment," the right to criticize government officials?

The *Sullivan* decision has been roundly criticized by some politicians who say it makes their life more difficult. It undoubtedly does. The decision has probably played a part in the vulgarization of the public dialogue in recent years—which affects all of us. Professor Vincent Blasi, a First Amendment scholar at Columbia University and the University of Virginia, put it this way: "Today's talk radio, wide open and factually casual, is the result of *Sullivan*." You can say practically anything about a public person without fear of having to pay damages.

The cacophony of talk radio and the bloggers can certainly be depressing. But it is very much like what existed in Madison's day, when newspapers were aggressively partisan and often reckless. After he had been president for six years, Jefferson wrote a friend: "Nothing can now be believed which is seen in a newspaper. Truth itself becomes suspicious by being put into that polluted vehicle."

Whatever the disagreements about the impact of *New York Times v. Sullivan*, one thing is clear. The decision finally put an end to the idea of seditious libel in this country. That is no small thing. In the twenty-first century many countries still prosecute people for saying things that lower the prestige of political leaders. A Turkish citizen who visited the home of modern Turkey's founder, Kemal Ataturk, wrote in the guest book an uncomplimentary comparison with the current prime minister—and then was punished with a hefty fine. Between 1995 and 2005, citizens of Indonesia, Malaysia, Swaziland, and Pakistan were prosecuted on charges of seditious libel or its equivalent for comments they had made about public officials or institutions. A law added to Russia's criminal code in 2006 made it a crime, punishable by up to three years in prison, to engage in "public slander directed toward figures fulfilling the state duties of the Russian Federation."

For many years the great American advocate of uninhibited political speech was Alexander Meiklejohn. He believed that the concept of seditious libel was inconsistent with the role of the citizen in a democracy. He was ninety-two years old when the *Sullivan* case was decided. When someone asked him what he thought about it, he replied, "It is an occasion for dancing in the streets."

5

Freedom and Privacy

The long struggle to give meaning to the First Amendment established that freedom of speech and of the press is a fundamental value in American society. But is it a paramount value, overriding others when they conflict with it? The question arises again and again, in the courts and in everyday life. All kinds of interests are involved: the right to a fair trial without inflammatory press coverage, the protection of racial or religious groups from hateful speech, the safeguarding of national security. Nowhere is the conflict likely to be more personal or more painful than on issues of privacy.

A child is paraded as a genius by a domineering father. Grown up, he rebels and retreats into hermit-like anonymity. But a magazine writer finds him and writes a mocking exposure. Should he be able to win damages from the magazine for destruction of his privacy?

That is the case, the tormenting case, of William James Sidis. Born in 1898, he was mentally force-fed by his father, Boris, a psychologist. William was reading the *New York Times* by the age of eighteen months. So said his father, who trained him relentlessly and issued bulletins on his accomplishments to the press. William entered Harvard at age eleven, and the *Times* described him as the "wonderfully successful result of a scientific forcing experiment."

As might have been predicted, Sidis rebelled against the life of fame, seeking obscurity. He escaped press attention for years—until, in 1937, *The New Yorker* published a piece about him by Jared L. Manley. Under the headline "Where Are They Now?" was the subhead "April Fool," a play on the fact that Sidis was born on April 1. The article treated him with contempt, noting his "curious laugh," his interest in the lore of the Okamakamesset Indians, his collection of streetcar transfers. (Sidis had actually published, anonymously, a book called *Notes on the Collection of Transfers*; a biographer, Amy Wallace, called it "arguably the most boring book ever written.") Manley's article described Sidis as living a lonely life in "a hall bedroom in Boston's shabby South End."

Sidis sued for violation of his privacy. The case, *Sidis v. F-R Publishing Corporation*, was decided in 1940 by the United States Court of Appeals for the Second Circuit. The opinion was by a particularly thoughtful judge, Charles Clark, a former dean of the Yale Law School. Judge Clark expressed sympathy for Sidis. He described the Manley article as "merciless," a "ruthless exposure of a once public character" who had gone to "pitiable lengths . . . to avoid public scrutiny" in his "passion for privacy." The judge said there was no reason to doubt Sidis's claims that the article had held him up to "public scorn, ridicule and contempt," causing him "grievous mental anguish."

But Judge Clark rejected Sidis's legal claim. The court would not, he said, "afford to all the intimate details of private life an absolute immunity from the prying of the press." It would, rather, permit "limited scrutiny of the 'private' life of any person who has achieved, or has had thrust upon him, the questionable and indefinable status of a 'public figure.'" Sidis had not challenged the truth of the painful descriptions in the *New Yorker* piece, and Judge Clark said they must be allowed unless the revelations were "so intimate and so unwarranted in view of the victim's position as to outrage the community's notions of decency." In this instance, he concluded, the public had a legitimate interest in learning how the onetime boy genius had turned out.

"Thrust upon him," that phrase of Judge Clark's, is what makes the outcome of the case seem so cruel. Sidis was subject to public mocking for the rest of his life because of the fame his father had forced upon him. That was the balance Judge Clark struck between the freedom of journalism and the right to privacy. Might it have made a difference if the judge had known more about the journalism in this case?

In her book *Secrets*, Sissela Bok told us some surprising things about the *New Yorker* article on William Sidis. Its supposed author, Jared L. Manley, did not exist; it was a pseudonym for James Thurber, one of *The New Yorker*'s most esteemed writers. And apparently Thurber never met Sidis. The article said a woman, unnamed, had "recently succeeded in interviewing him." One wonders whether she disclosed that she was acting as an agent for Thurber, or posed as friendly to the lonely Sidis so she would be invited to visit him in the shabby South End and inspect his collection of street-car transfers. When Sidis's lawsuit went to court, Thurber explained that he wanted to "help curb the great American thrusting of talented children into the glare of fame and notoriety" by showing how the children suffered later. But Sissela Bok observed drily that such a purpose was not evident in Thurber's article, "the less so as its author did more than anyone else to renew the glare of notoriety for Sidis. What comes across, rather, is a distant and amused contempt for those judged to be doing less than they might, and living boring lives in one-room apartments."

Four years after the Second Circuit decision, Sidis, unemployed and destitute, died of a cerebral hemorrhage. He was forty-six.

There is an aspect of the Sidis case that must seem puzzling today: Judge Clark's opinion does not mention the First Amendment. That is because privacy, like libel, was then considered to be outside the scope of the amendment—a view that did not change until the *Sullivan* decision in 1964. But Judge Clark dealt with the case exactly as if the First Amendment were in it. He balanced Sidis's interest in privacy against the society's interest in freedom of comment. He decided the latter had greater weight because of the free-spoken society we are. Once someone becomes a public figure, however unwillingly, he or she is forever fair game for the press.

The interest of privacy was first authoritatively weighed against the First Amendment's guarantee of free expression by the Supreme Court in 1967, in the case of *Time, Inc. v.*

Hill. It is a remarkable case in several ways: the closeness of the competing interests, the surprising course of decision inside the Court, and the tragic nature of the denouement. James Hill, his wife, and five children lived in a suburb of Philadelphia. In 1952 three escaped convicts took over their home, keeping the Hills hostage but treating them respectfully. After the convicts left, they were caught. The press covered the story intensely, to the distress especially of Mrs. Hill. To escape publicity, the family moved to Connecticut and sought obscurity.

Two years later a play called *The Desperate Hours* opened on Broadway. It was about a family held hostage in its home by escaped convicts. Unlike the convicts who came to the Hills' home, the convicts in the play carried out a reign of terror: brutality, sexual threats, and general menace. The play was set in Indianapolis. But *Life* magazine, doing a feature on the opening, photographed the actors in the former home of the Hills near Philadelphia and described the play, with all its terror, as a reenactment of what had happened to the Hills. The *Life* story was devastating to the Hill family. Mrs. Hill suffered a psychiatric breakdown. Mr. Hill said he could not understand how *Life* could publish such a piece without at least telephoning him to check the facts. "It was just like we didn't exist," he said, "like we were dirt."

Mr. Hill sued Time, Inc., the publisher of *Life*, for violation of the New York privacy law. By associating his family with horrors that it had not in fact experienced, he said, the article showed the family in a false light. (Privacy law embraces four different concepts. One is called "false light privacy," which describes cases in which there are errors but no damage to reputation, as there is in libel. Other branches of privacy will be described later in this chapter.)

In the New York courts, Mr. Hill won damages of $30,000. But Time took the case on to the Supreme Court. There Mr. Hill was represented by Richard M. Nixon, who practiced law in New York in the years before his successful campaign for president in 1968. The case was argued on April 27, 1966; the justices thought Nixon performed well.

What happened then inside the Court was a secret until the appearance in 1985 of a book by Professor Bernard Schwartz, *The Unpublished Opinions of the Warren Court.* His account, taken from the papers of retired justices, has not been challenged. In their next conference after the argument, the justices voted 6 to 3 to uphold Mr. Hill's modest judgment. Chief Justice Earl Warren assigned the opinion to Justice Abe Fortas. His draft, which the Schwartz book reproduces, began with a stinging attack on *Life*'s handling of the story—and sarcastic comments on the behavior of some journalists:

> Needless, heedless, wanton and deliberate injury of the sort inflicted by *Life*'s picture story is not an essential instrument of responsible journalism. Magazine writers and editors are not, by reason of their high office, relieved of the common obligation to avoid inflicting wanton and unnecessary injury. The prerogatives of the press—essential to our liberty—do not preclude reasonable care and avoidance of casual infliction of injury. . . . They do not confer a license for pointless assault.

The Fortas draft also included an eloquent comment on the meaning of privacy and its place in a civilized society:

> It is of constitutional stature. . . . It is not only the right to be secure in one's person, house, papers and effects, except as permitted by law; it embraces the right to be free from coercion, however subtle, to incriminate oneself; it is different from, but akin to the right to select and freely to practice one's religion and the right to freedom of speech; it is more than the specific right to be secure against the Peeping Tom or the intrusion of electronic espionage devices and wiretapping. All of these are aspects of the right to privacy; but the right of privacy reaches beyond any of its specifics. It is, simply stated, the right to be let alone; to live one's life as one chooses, free from assault, intrusion or invasion except as they can be justified by the clear needs of community living under a government of law.

But Justice Fortas's words were never published by the Supreme Court. In the weeks after argument, members of the Court began to rethink their views. The justices ordered the case argued again the following fall. And then a new majority decided against Mr. Hill's privacy claim.

Before the reargument Justice Black, the Court's most passionate advocate of freedom of expression, sent a memorandum to his colleagues. It is printed in the Schwartz book. "After mature reflection," he wrote, "I am unable to recall any prior case in this Court that offers a greater threat to freedom of speech and press than this one does." His point was that the press, imperfect as it inevitably is, would be forced into self-censorship if it were subject to damages for mistakes that did not damage anyone's standing in the community—did not, that is, rise to the level of libel.

The decision came down in January 1967. A 5-to-4 majority set aside Mr. Hill's judgment in an opinion by Justice Brennan. He had written the landmark libel opinion three years earlier in *New York Times v. Sullivan*, holding that public officials could not recover damages for false and damaging reports unless the falsities were deliberate or reckless. Now Justice Brennan applied the same formula to the privacy claim of James Hill. *Life*'s falsifying of the Hill family's story had not been proved knowing or reckless, he said, so *Life* was entitled to a new trial at which a jury would decide that question. But the *Sullivan* case had turned on what Justice Brennan called "the central meaning of the First Amendment," the right to criticize the government. How did that apply to speech about private citizens like the Hills? Justice Brennan gave this explanation:

> The guarantees for speech and press are not the preserve of political expression or comment upon public affairs, essential as those are to healthy government. One need only pick up any newspaper or magazine to comprehend the vast range of published matter which exposes persons to public view, both private citizens and public officials. Exposure of the self to others in varying degrees is a concomitant of life in a civilized community. The risk of this exposure is an essential incident of life in a society which places a primary value on freedom of speech and press.

That passage in Justice Brennan's opinion amounts to a rejection of privacy as an important value. The most obscure American, it says, one who wants urgently to avoid the public gaze, must accept "exposure of the self to others." That is the price of "life in a civilized community." I am a great admirer of Justice Brennan, but I disagree with his conception of a "civilized community."

Justice Fortas dissented, in an opinion that lacked the angry rhetoric of his draft. (His overheated tone there may have helped change justices' minds.) His opinion was joined by Chief Justice Warren and Justice Tom C. Clark. Justice John Marshall Harlan, grandson and namesake of the first Justice Harlan, wrote a separate dissenting opinion, making the vote 5 to 4 against the Hills. I find the Harlan opinion persuasive.

The Hill case, Justice Harlan said, did not involve an official or public figure, someone who could command an audience. If Mr. Hill protested the *Life* story, who would publish his comments? So the "marketplace" of free speech in which Justice Holmes said ideas must compete did not work. Justice Harlan said that raised the danger of "unchallengeable untruth." Accordingly, he would have required Mr. Hill to prove merely that *Life*'s editors had been negligent in making their mistakes, rather than what is harder to prove, that their falsification was deliberate or reckless.

When Schwartz's book was published and the internal course of decision in *Time, Inc. v. Hill* became known, Richard Nixon—by then a resigned president—asked his former White House counsel, Leonard Garment, to look into it. Garment had worked on the Hill case as Nixon's law partner.

After reading the Schwartz account, Garment wrote an article for *The New Yorker*. He described Nixon's meticulous preparation for the two arguments of the case in the Supreme Court. He also described telephoning Nixon with the news that the Court had decided against him. Nixon said: "I always knew I wouldn't be permitted to win a big appeal against the press."

Garment noted a statement in Justice Harlan's opinion that unwanted publicity carried a "severe risk of irremediable harm . . . [to] individuals exposed to it and powerless to protect themselves against it." Garment said there had been testimony at the trial in New York that the *Life* article had caused "lasting emotional injury" to Mrs. Hill. Then Garment wrote: "Two eminent psychiatrists had explained the causal dynamics of the trauma inflicted on her. Both said she had come through the original hostage incident well but had fallen apart when the *Life* article brought back her memories transformed into her worst nightmares and presented them to the world as reality. Both said she was and would for an indefinite time remain a psychological tinderbox. In August, 1971, Mrs. Hill took her life."

The legal debate about privacy traces back to an extraordinary law review article: "The Right to Privacy," by Louis D. Brandeis and Samuel D. Warren, published in 1890 in the *Harvard Law Review*. It was extraordinary because it had more effect on the law than anything else ever written for a law review. In its wake most states have adopted rules of law to protect privacy by either legislation or judicial decisions.

The Brandeis-Warren article spoke of "the right to be let alone." Thirty-eight years later, Brandeis, a man of lasting convictions, used that phrase again in dissenting from a Supreme Court decision that said wiretapping was not a search subject to the restraints of the Fourth Amendment to the Constitution, which regulates searches and seizures by government agents. In *Olmstead v. United States* (1928) Justice Brandeis wrote:

> The makers of our Constitution . . . recognized the significance of man's spiritual nature, his feelings and his intellect. They knew that only a part of the pain, pleasure and satisfactions of life are to be found in material things. They sought to protect Americans in their beliefs, their thoughts, their emotions and their sensations. They conferred, as against the government, the right to be let alone—the most comprehensive of rights and the right most valued by civilized men.

The wiretapping decision from which Brandeis dissented was overruled by the Supreme Court in 1967, when taps were made subject to the Fourth Amendment. "The right to be let alone" has become a familiar phrase in law and life. (Justice Fortas used it, without attribution, in the tribute to privacy in his draft opinion in *Time, Inc. v. Hill*.) But the Brandeis-Warren law review article arose not from any general assault on privacy but from a particular fact: Pictures of Warren's wife had been used without her permission.

Using someone's likeness without permission has developed as one of the four branches of privacy law. A second is false light privacy, exemplified by the *Hill* case: putting someone in a false light by, for example, fictionalizing a story about him or her. (A colorful biography of a baseball pitcher invents a childhood scene in which his mother says, "Lefty, why do you keep throwing a ball at that chicken?") The third branch of privacy law, known as intrusion, is invasion of one's personal space by means, for example, of an eavesdropping device. The fourth is publication of truthful but embarrassing private facts.

The first of these, known as appropriation, has produced some colorful cases involving "look-alikes": people who look like famous individuals and masquerade as them. Woody Allen successfully sued to keep companies from using Phil Boroff, who looked like him, in advertising. Bette Midler was awarded $400,000 in damages by a jury from an advertising agency that used a sound-alike mimicking her famous voice.

Jacqueline Kennedy Onassis sued, and won, to stop a model who looked like her, Barbara Reynolds, from seeming to be her in advertisements. In her case, unlike others, she was not complaining of unfair commercial competition; she wanted the right not to have her face appear commercially. Reynolds claimed that her impersonation was constitutionally protected as art. Justice Edward J. Greenfield of the New York Supreme Court disagreed. "To paint a portrait of Jacqueline Kennedy Onassis is art," he said. "To look like Jacqueline Kennedy Onassis is not."

The third branch of privacy law, intrusion, was fascinatingly explored in a California case, *Shulman v. Group W Productions*, decided by the state Supreme Court in 1998. Like the cases of William Sidis and James Hill, the *Shulman* case saw the interest of free expression in conflict with poignant claims of privacy. Ruth Shulman was driving on a California highway when her car was hit by another and rolled down an embankment. She was gravely injured, ending up as a paraplegic. A rescue helicopter came to the scene of the accident and flew Shulman to a hospital. Without her knowledge, a member of the rescue party, a nurse, was wearing a microphone and recorded her conversation with Shulman at the scene and in the helicopter; someone else filmed her with a video camera. A program made from these recordings appeared on television, and Shulman sued for invasion of her privacy.

The California Supreme Court decided that Shulman could maintain her suit. Justice Kathryn M. Werdegar, rejecting First Amendment objections, said that government may not dictate what the news media "should publish and broadcast, but neither may the media play tyrant to the people by unlawfully spying on them in the name of news-gathering." She found that Shulman may reasonably have expected that her conversations with the nurse at the accident scene and in the helicopter were in a zone of privacy. It was up to a jury, she said, to decide whether the defendant broadcasters had invaded that zone, and whether such an invasion was "highly offensive to a reasonable person." That was in effect a narrowly defined exception to the broadcasters' First Amendment right to do a story on a newsworthy event. Two justices, dissenting, would have thrown out the lawsuit. But Justice Werdegar was surely in the spirit of Brandeis when she wrote:

A jury could reasonably believe that fundamental respect for human dignity requires the patients' anxious journey to be taken only with those whose care is only for them and out of the sight of prying eyes. . . . A reasonable jury could find that defendants, in placing a microphone on an emergency treatment nurse and recording her conversation with a distressed, disoriented and severely injured patient, without her consent, acted with highly offensive disregard for the patient's personal privacy.

The broadcasters settled the case, paying Shulman an unstated amount in damages. They must have guessed what jurors would think of their behavior.

The fourth branch of privacy law, publication of truthful but embarrassing facts, has produced some notable examples of conflict between the claims of privacy and freedom to publish. President Gerald R. Ford left the St. Francis Hotel in San Francisco on September 22, 1975, when a woman waiting there, Sara Jane Moore, raised a gun and pointed it at him. A former Marine in the crowd, Oliver S. Sipple, leapt forward and struck her arm. The shot missed the president; Sipple may have saved his life. Newspapers across the country described his daring. Two days later a well-known columnist in the *San Francisco Chronicle*, Herb Caen, wrote that Sipple was gay and was a hero in the city's gay community. Others copied the story, and across the country Sipple was identified as gay. He sued for violation of his privacy, arguing that he was indeed homosexual but was entitled to damages for disclosure of a fact that would embarrass him in some circles. The California courts ruled against him without resolving the conflict between his privacy and the press's freedom. They said his sexual orientation was known to many before the Caen column and hence was not really "private."

For decades the California courts were unusually hospitable to damage claims for publications that were truthful but embarrassing. The case of *Melvin v. Reid*, decided in 1931, involved a former prostitute who had been accused of murder but acquitted. In the years following, she had reformed, married, and become a respected member of the town where she lived. Then a movie called *The Red Kimono* was made about her life. It had an adverse effect on her social position, and she sued for violation of her privacy. She won the case. As late as 1971 the California Supreme Court followed that precedent, holding that even though a scandalous event was publicized at the time, a later story reminding readers of it could be a violation of privacy.

That view was in direct conflict with Judge Clark's decision in the *Sidis* case that once someone is a subject of public attention, he or she cannot escape that condition. More recently, the more generous interpretations of the First Amendment by the Supreme Court make it clear that the press may call attention truthfully to old facts, however embarrassing. In her opinion in the *Shulman* case, Justice Werdegar indicated that the California Supreme Court would no longer adhere to the precedent of the Red Kimono case. The American legal culture as it is today would not accept a prohibition on publication of facts already public. And search engines on the Internet have made just about everyone's past available to the public at a click. Once known, no fact of private life can be buried. But that still leaves open the question whether a prurient reporter or tabloid can be held liable for fresh invasions of privacy.

The press has urged the Supreme Court to hold that it may always publish the truth, no matter how much it may trouble someone. The Court has repeatedly refused to decide that large issue, instead resolving a series of cases on narrower grounds.

One example involved a Georgia statute prohibiting the publication of a rape victim's identity. In the case of a young woman who was raped and murdered, a court clerk allowed a television reporter to see an indictment that included the name of the victim—which was then broadcast. The victim's father sued the broadcaster for publication of private facts. When this case, *Cox Broadcasting v. Cohn* (1975), went to the Supreme Court, the broadcast company argued that the state statute barring its use of the victim's name violated the First Amendment. But the Court did not reach that question. It held that the broadcaster could not be penalized because it had obtained the name from public records, the document shown to the reporter by the court clerk. Justice Byron R. White wrote: "By placing the information in the official court records the State must be presumed to have concluded that the public interest was thereby being served." I find that assertion of Justice White's puzzling. Why would the action of a court clerk— very likely a mistake on his or her part—be taken as more indicative of Georgia's policy than the state statute finding that it was not in the public interest to publish the name of rape

victims? To avoid a hard question, the Supreme Court seems
to have engaged in judicial sleight-of-hand.

Cox Broadcasting v. Cohn was followed by other cases in
which newspapers published matters that state statutes had
required to be kept confidential: the name of a state judge
whom a state commission considered investigating, the names
of juvenile offenders, and again the name of a rape victim. In
each case, the Supreme Court declined to adopt a general rule
that such statutes violated the First Amendment; instead it
found particular circumstances, every time, that freed the
newspaper from the consequences of noncompliance. One's
conclusion had to be that the Supreme Court was not greatly
moved by the interests of privacy, even when those interests
were embraced in state statutes.

Then, in 2001, the Supreme Court dealt with a federal law
protecting the privacy of telephone and other conversations.
The Omnibus Crime Control and Safe Streets Act of 1968
made it a crime to intercept such conversations or to disclose
what was intercepted. The law also allowed civil damage suits
for interceptions. In the case before the Court, *Bartnicki v.
Vopper*, someone unknown taped a cell-phone call between
two union officers in Pennsylvania during a strike. One said
to the other: "If they're not gonna move for 3 percent, we're
gonna have to go to their, their homes. . . . To blow off their
front porches. . . . " The unknown intercepter sent the tape to
a union opponent, who gave it to a radio station. The tape
was played on the radio.

The union officers who were taped sued the radio station
for damages. In the Supreme Court, the broadcaster argued

that the law against disclosure of illegally taped conversations had to yield to the station's interest, protected by the First Amendment, in broadcasting the tape. A divided Supreme Court decided in favor of the broadcaster. Justice John Paul Stevens, in an opinion for a six-justice majority, gave short shrift to the privacy interests. But two of the six, justices Stephen Breyer and Sandra Day O'Connor, joined in a separate concurring opinion, written by Breyer, that gave much greater weight to the privacy claim.

Discussing the importance of privacy, Justice Breyer made a novel point. Giving people an assurance of privacy not only protects "the right to be let alone," he said, but encourages them to speak freely: It "helps to overcome our natural reluctance to discuss private matters when we fear that our private conversations may become public. And the statutory restrictions consequently encourage conversations that otherwise might not take place." In other words, there is a free-speech argument for protecting the privacy of conversations. Justice Breyer indicated that he and Justice O'Connor joined Justice Stevens here only because the intercepted call involved a matter of "unusual public concern, namely a threat of physical harm."

The Breyer opinion suggests that American law may yet put limits on the crushing of privacy in the name of freedom. We are in the age of exposure now: self-exposure on television, exposure of every kind of human fault or flaw by the press, tabloid and otherwise. We have come a long way from the modest indignity that provoked Brandeis's great defense of privacy, the use of pictures of his partner's wife without her consent. Not only the press but the law itself mercilessly exposes private lives. Kenneth Starr, the independent counsel who tried to drive President Bill Clinton from office, used his power to obtain Monica Lewinsky's letters and personal jottings from her personal computer—and included them in the report he sent to the House of Representatives. Despite Lewinsky's plea, he also included in the report computer messages Lewinsky had received from a woman friend telling about conflict with her husband. Starr issued a subpoena demanding that a Washington bookstore produce a record of all the books Lewinsky had bought there.

When Judge Charles Clark rejected William Sidis's privacy suit, he said he could imagine situations in which a "public character" like Sidis could succeed in getting damages for violation of his privacy: if "revelations" were so "intimate and unwarranted . . . as to outrage the community's notions of decency." Nowadays it is hard to imagine any revelation so intimate that it would offend the public's sense of decency.

The press is right that judges must not let their disapproval of rancid journalism lead them to censor anything that offends them. An English judge, Lord Chief Justice Woolf, got it right in 2002 when he set aside an injunction obtained by a football player to keep a tabloid newspaper from telling the story of his extramarital sexual relations with two women. Courts "should not act as censors or arbiters of taste," Lord Woolf said. "The fact that a more lurid approach will be adopted by the publication than the court would regard as acceptable is not relevant." Moreover, he said, a man who indulges in multiple affairs cannot complain if one of the women kisses and tells. Lord Woolf added: "The courts must not ignore the fact that if newspapers do not publish information which the public are interested in, there will be fewer newspapers published, which will not be in the public interest." British courts in the past had been all too ready to stop the press, so Lord Woolf's judgment marked a change—a step, one might say, toward the First Amendment's premise of an open society.

But it does not follow—not for me, at any rate—that an open society must allow the publication of private facts no matter how cruel or antisocial the publication would be. The reason was well expressed by Professor Thomas Nagel of New York University:

> The distinction between what an individual exposes to public view and what he conceals or exposes only to intimates is essential to permit creatures as complex as ourselves to interact without constant social breakdown. Each of our inner lives is such a jungle of thoughts, feelings, fantasies and impulses that civilization would be impossible if we expressed them all. . . . Just as social life would be impossible if we expressed all our lustful, aggressive, greedy, anxious or self-obsessed feelings in ordinary public encounters, so would inner life be impossible if we tried to become wholly persons whose thoughts, feelings and private behavior could be safely exposed to public view.

Secrecy is a red flag to journalists, rightly so. Governments use it to hide corruption and incompetence and to increase their unaccountable power. Their power has grown enormously. But a substantial part of it is the power to intrude in the lives of citizens by electronic and other means that were unimaginable to Brandeis when he predicted in his wiretapping dissent in 1928 that the state would find methods even more intrusive than wiretapping. When the press joins the government in intruding on privacy, it is not playing its essential role as a check on the power of the state.

When Czechoslovakia was under Communist control, the police secretly recorded the conversations of a leading dissident, Jan Prochazka, with another dissident friend. One day the state radio began broadcasting the tapes. The great Czech writer Milan Kundera said the tactic nearly succeeded in its purpose of denigrating Prochazka. People were shocked, Kundera said, because "in private a person says all sorts of things, uses coarse language, acts silly, tells dirty jokes . . . floats heretical ideas he'd never admit in public and so forth." But gradually people realized, Kundera wrote, "that the real scandal was not Prochazka's daring talk but the rape of his life; they realized, as if by electric shock, that private and public are two essentially different worlds and that respect for the difference is the indispensable condition, the sine qua non, for a man to live free. . . . "

In an interview in 1985, Kundera summed up his views on privacy:

We live in an age when private life is being destroyed. The police destroy it in Communist countries, journalists threaten it in democratic countries, and little by little the people themselves lose their taste for private life and their sense of it. Life when one can't hide from the eyes of others—that is hell. Those who have lived in totalitarian countries know it, but that system only brings out, like a magnifying glass, the tendencies of all modern society. . . . Without secrecy, nothing is possible—not love, not friendship.

The First Amendment's guarantees of freedom of speech and of the press are fundamentals of our freedom, but they are not the only essentials of a healthy society. If they succeed in totally overriding the interest of privacy, it would be a terrible victory.

6

A Press Privilege?

Marie Torre was a television columnist for the *New York Herald Tribune* in the 1950s. In 1957 she wrote a column about Judy Garland, the great stage and movie star, that made First Amendment history. Garland had signed a contract with the CBS television network to do a series of specials, but she was proving evasive about setting a date for the first program. The Torre column said a CBS executive, unnamed, had told Torre that something was bothering Garland—"I don't know, but I wouldn't be surprised if it's because she thinks she's terribly fat." Later biographies said Garland was in fact overweight at the time and was taking too many diet pills.

Judy Garland sued CBS for libel and breach of contract, seeking $1.4 million in damages. In pretrial proceedings, her lawyers demanded that Torre name the CBS executive who was the alleged source of the quotation. She refused to do so, saying that if she did, "nobody in the business will talk to me again." A federal judge held her in contempt and ordered her to serve ten days in prison. She appealed to the United States Court of Appeals for the Second Circuit.

Torre's lawyers argued that the First Amendment protected her against having to disclose her source—gave her a testimonial privilege, in the language of the law—because breaking her promise of confidentiality to the source would, as she said, curdle her relations with other potential sources. It was the first time that constitutional argument had ever been made: the beginning of what has become a familiar legal debate about the rights of journalists. The outcome in the Torre case was a preview of the ultimate fate of the claim that journalists have a constitutional privilege unavailable to others.

The opinion on appeal was written by a judge visiting from the Sixth Federal Circuit, Potter Stewart, who later became a Supreme Court justice. He said he accepted "the hypothesis that compulsory disclosure of a journalist's confidential sources of information may entail an abridgment of press freedom by imposing some limitation upon the availability of news." But freedom of the press is not an absolute, Judge Stewart wrote. It "must give way under the Constitution to a paramount public interest in the fair administration of justice." Quoting an opinion in another case, he went on: "'The right to sue and defend in the courts is the alternative of force. In an organized society it is the right conservative of all other rights, and lies at the foundation of orderly government.'" And in this case, he said, the testimony demanded was not of "doubtful relevance"; it "went to the heart of the plaintiff's claim."

In that first exploration of the problem, Judge Stewart fairly laid out what have become the debating points ever since. Crucially, he made clear that the journalist's interest is not the only one to be considered. The press does have a real interest: that of maintaining an ability to use sources who will not speak to a reporter unless promised confidentiality. But on the other side in this kind of civil case, there is the interest of the person whose good name has been sullied. Would we want to deprive someone whose reputation has been trashed by an anonymous source of any real chance of repairing that reputation in court? I would not.

Marie Torre asked the Supreme Court to hear the case, but it refused. She went to jail for ten days, still refusing to name her source. Then Judy Garland dropped the case. Why? Perhaps she had developed sympathy for Torre. Or perhaps she decided that the publicity over the litigation was making her look bad.

The Supreme Court took up the issue of reporter's privilege, as it had come to be called, in 1972. It agreed to review three cases in which reporters had been subpoenaed to appear or testify before grand juries in criminal proceedings, and had refused to do so. The decision took the name of the first case, *Branzburg v. Hayes*. Paul Branzburg, a reporter on the *Courier-Journal* of Louisville, Kentucky, had written an article describing young people synthesizing hashish. State authorities wanted to know their names.

By a vote of 5 to 4, the Supreme Court rejected the reporters' claims. Justice Byron R. White wrote the opinion of the Court, beginning with a flat statement of the result. "The issue in these cases," he said, "is whether requiring newsmen to appear and testify before state or federal grand juries abridges the freedom of speech and press guaranteed by the First Amendment. We hold that it does not."

Justice White made what seemed a reluctant concession, expressed in a double negative, to the press argument. He did not suggest, he said, "that news gathering does not qualify for First Amendment protection; without some protection for seeking out the news, freedom of the press could be eviscerated." But he went on to point out that while the First Amendment protected the press from prior restraints and subsequent penalties for what it published, the press was also traditionally barred from many sources of news. "Despite the fact that news gathering may be hampered," he wrote, "the press is regularly excluded from grand jury proceedings, our own conferences, the meetings of other official bodies gathered in executive session. . . . " The obligation to testify is critical to the functioning of our criminal justice system, he said, and exceptions to that duty are frowned upon. He added a historical note: that Chief Justice John Marshall, in 1807, "opined that in historical circumstances a subpoena could be issued to the President of the United States." (The *Branzburg* case was decided on June 29, 1972—twelve days after the break-in at the Watergate that led eventually to a subpoena for President Nixon's tapes and then his resignation from office.)

Practical reasons against granting a constitutional privilege to the press were also advanced by Justice White. One was the difficulty of defining who counts as "the press" and thus would qualify for the privilege. The traditional idea, Justice White said, is that "liberty of the press is the right of the lonely pamphleteer . . . just as much as of the large metropolitan publisher." How would courts define those who were entitled to the privilege? (This concern has become far more compelling since then, with the rise of the Internet and millions of bloggers who circulate what they may regard as news.) Justice White went on to make a related point:

> The informative function asserted by representatives of the organized press in the present cases is also performed by lecturers, political pollsters, novelists, academic researchers, and dramatists. Almost any author may quite accurately assert that he is contributing to the flow of information to the public, that he relies on confidential sources of information, and that these sources will be silenced if he is forced to make disclosures before a grand jury.

Again, the concern expressed by Justice White has been borne out. In a postlude to the Pentagon Papers case the Nixon administration subpoenaed an assistant professor of government at Harvard, Samuel Popkin, to appear before a grand jury and identify sources for a scholarly paper he had written on Vietnam. He refused—and went to jail for a week. The president of Harvard, Derek Bok, then appeared as his lawyer and embarrassed the government into ending the grand jury term and thus freeing Popkin.

There was a skeptical tone at places in Justice White's *Branzburg* opinion. The press "is far from helpless to protect itself from harassment or substantial harm," he said; it "has at its disposal powerful mechanisms of communication." But the opinion ended with what may have been meant as a reassuring note, expressed in another double negative: "News gathering is not without its First Amendment protections," Justice White said, "and grand jury investigations if instituted or conducted other than in good faith, would pose wholly different issues for resolution under the First Amendment."

In the *Branzburg* case the press did not seek an absolute privilege for journalists: one that would protect them from having to testify before grand juries in all circumstances. A brief filed by the *New York Times* explained that a subpoena should not be enforced against a journalist unless: (1) the government showed there was probable cause to believe the journalist had information relevant to a specific probable crime; (2) the government showed that it could not obtain the information from other sources; and (3) the government showed "a compelling and overriding interest in the information."

Three justices, dissenting, would have given journalists a qualified privilege against having to testify by imposing those three requirements on governments. The opinion was by Justice Stewart, who denounced what he called the majority's "crabbed view of the First Amendment," which he said "reflects a disturbing insensitivity to the critical role of an independent press in our society." As a Sixth Circuit judge, Stewart had required Marie Torre to identify the unnamed CBS source of the defamatory comment on Judy Garland; to some, that may have seemed inconsistent with his dissenting opinion in *Branzburg*. Justice Stewart merely noted the *Garland* case in a footnote, quoting the statement in his *Garland* opinion that the demand for the source's name "went to the heart of the plaintiff's claim." Perhaps he meant that, if something like the qualified privilege test were applied in a civil case, Judy Garland had met the test because she could not get the critical information from anyone other than Marie Torre.

The fourth dissenter, Justice William O. Douglas, would have given journalists an absolute First Amendment privilege against having to testify before a grand jury unless they were themselves involved in a crime. Justice Douglas denounced the *Times* for taking what he called "the amazing position that First Amendment rights are to be balanced against other needs or conveniences of government." The Framers of the First Amendment cast it "in absolute terms," he said, not "the timid, watered-down, emasculated versions of the First Amendment which both the Government and The New York Times advance."

The *Branzburg* decision was the Supreme Court's first judgment on the press privilege claim, and the last for decades. As of 2007, the Court has not agreed to hear another case raising the issue. And so, one would think, the question was settled. Wrong. Far from it, in fact. Over the decades, journalists in a variety of situations declined to disclose their confidential sources—and continued to claim that the First Amendment gave them that privilege. Sometimes lower courts agreed with them, sometimes not. It was an extraordinary legal pattern. A Supreme Court decision that was evidently meant to be the last word on a problem was being widely ignored or explained away.

Why? One reason was that one of the five justices in the *Branzburg* majority, Lewis F. Powell Jr., wrote a brief opinion of his own. He joined the opinion of the Court by Justice

White and rejected the journalists' claims in the three cases before the Court. But Justice Powell said journalists could still challenge orders to testify in other cases: "if a newsman believes that the grand jury investigation is not being conducted in good faith," for example, or if the information sought from him bears "only a remote and tenuous relationship to the subject of the investigation." That sounded a good deal like the qualified privilege that Justice Stewart proposed in dissent. And Justice Powell said judges should balance freedom of the press and the need for testimony in criminal matters "on a case-by-case basis."

Many lower courts, state and federal, read Powell's concurring opinion as effectively modifying Justice White's flat rejection of the journalists' privilege claim. In civil cases especially, judges accepted his invitation to weigh the interests of press confidentiality and the need for the information case by case.

There was another reason for the peculiar status of the *Branzburg* decision. The press simply did not accept it. Editors and publishers, and their lawyers, spoke of "the First Amendment privilege" against compelled disclosure of sources as if that privilege existed. In 1981, for example, a *Washington Post* story that won the Pulitzer Prize—a story about an eight-year-old heroin addict in the Washington, D.C., slums—turned out to have been fabricated. When the hoax was discovered, an editorial in the *Post* warned against using the episode "to discredit the various First Amendment protections that were activated . . . when the conflict sharpened between the paper and the authorities on the question of identification of sources." Translated, that remarkable statement meant that the Washington police and other authorities looking into the supposed crime of hooking an eight-year-old on heroin were prevented by the First Amendment from pressing the reporter for the real names of the characters in her story. It is hard to believe that any court, even one using the balancing test, would go that far.

But the press's privilege claims were not usually as absurd as the one made about the fraudulent *Washington Post* story. Some of the most important work journalists do can only be accomplished by relying on confidential sources. That was dramatically so, for example, when the *New York Times* in 2005 reported that President George W. Bush had ordered the National Security Agency to tap international telephone calls without obtaining the warrants required by law. It was a vitally important story, bringing to light—and to a degree of accountability—a lawless executive activity. And of course the facts could only have come from confidential sources inside the government. The response of the government was a threat to subpoena the reporters who wrote the story and demand the names of the sources: that is, to focus on the leak instead of the flagrant violation of law in the program that the story exposed.

The last half of the twentieth century and the first years of the twenty-first saw a vast growth of executive power in the United States, very often exercised in secret, without scrutiny by Congress. President Bush claimed the unilateral power not only to eavesdrop on American citizens but to imprison them forever without trial on suspicion of being "enemy combatants." The press, with all its defects, is often the only defense against the abuse of power. Watergate was a signal example—

and that exposure of the Nixon administration's abuses depended famously on unnamed sources.

If a journalist promises to keep a source's name confidential, he or she absolutely has to keep that promise. That is an ethical demand, and one of common sense: As Marie Torre understood, who will talk to you in the future if you break a promise? Disclosing a name that you undertook to keep secret can also have legal consequences. When a Republican operative told reporters for Minnesota newspapers that the Democratic candidate for lieutenant governor had a criminal record, the newspapers published the story and—despite a promise to keep his name secret—disclosed the source. The source sued for violation of the promise. The newspapers argued that it would violate the First Amendment to make them pay damages, but the Supreme Court rejected that argument in a 1991 decision.

The clash between journalists' need to keep their promises of confidentiality and court orders to name their sources occasionally produces a dramatic denouement: a writer going to prison for contempt of court. An extreme example was the case of Vanessa Leggett, a Texas woman who had never published anything but set out to write a book about a notorious murder. After she had conducted many interviews, a federal grand jury subpoenaed her and demanded her notes and the names of her sources. She said no—and spent 168 days in jail for contempt.

Vanessa Leggett was not a journalist. That is an embarrassing fact for the editors and press lawyers who say the First Amendment should be read to provide a testimonial privilege for journalists. They feel uncomfortable about excluding

Leggett from their legal theory, as well they should. But including such writers would bring them back to the problem Justice White foresaw in his *Branzburg* opinion: the difficulty of defining who is to qualify for a journalists' privilege. White said freedom was as much for "the lonely pamphleteer" as for the *New York Times* reporter. Bloggers, in all their millions, are the modern version of lonely pamphleteers. Vanessa Leggett surely qualified as the purveyor of information to the public. But if the courts are to define, case by case, who qualifies for a testimonial privilege and who does not, then judges will be issuing something like journalists' licenses—which are required in some countries but are utter anathema to the American press, which rightly regards press licensing as a form of official control.

The press, unable to get assured protection from subpoenas through its First Amendment argument in the courts, has pushed for statutes giving journalists a testimonial privilege. Almost all states have adopted such shield laws, as they are called. (The state laws do not apply in federal courts, where some of the most controversial privilege cases have arisen.)

Shield laws do not dispose of all the doubts about exempting journalists from the universal citizens' duty to testify in court when called. Those doubts are illustrated by the case of Wen Ho Lee, a scientist at the Los Alamos National Laboratory who was described in various press stories in the late 1990s as an atomic spy. The stories, evidently the result of leaks from government sources, said Lee was suspected of giving secrets to China. He was arrested, charged with fifty-nine felony counts, and held for nine months in solitary confinement.

Then the government dropped all but one of the counts, a charge that he mishandled information that had been retroactively classified as "secret." The judge handling the case apologized to Lee and said officials had "embarrassed our entire nation and each of us who is a citizen of it." A *Boston Globe* editorial said the suspicions about Lee came from an intelligence official "with a reputation for right-wing zealotry and racist behavior."

Lee sued the government for violation of his privacy in the leaks to the press. His lawyers subpoenaed five reporters and asked about the sources of their stories. They refused to answer, and they were held in contempt and ordered to pay fines of $500 a day until they agreed to respond. Then five news organizations—ABC News, the *Los Angeles Times*, the *New York Times*, the *Washington Post*, and the Associated Press—settled the case and ended the contempt sanctions by agreeing to pay Lee $750,000. The government also contributed $895,000 toward his lawyers' fees and taxes.

In settling the case, the news organizations made no apology for their contemptible treatment of Wen Ho Lee. They said they agreed to settle "to protect our journalists from further sanctions" and to protect their ability to obtain information that can come "only from confidential sources." In other words: We don't care what we did to Wen Ho Lee; we care only about our needs. The *Boston Globe*, which had not been part of the attack on Lee, saw the real situation in an editorial on the settlement. It said: "It is important to remember what was done to Lee because powerful institutions rarely admit abuse of their powers, and because the rule of law is imperiled when the government and a compliant or gullible press tramples on the rights of a single private citizen."

Suppose that a federal shield law had existed when Wen Ho Lee sued to seek some compensation for his nightmare ordeal. The journalists who wrote the damaging stories would have had their subpoenas dismissed, and without the names of the leakers Lee would probably have had to give up his lawsuit. Is that what a decent society should want? Would that have really benefited the press? Or would it have added to the evident public feeling that the press is arrogant, demanding special treatment?

The press, as James Madison told us long ago, can be a crucial force in countering abuse of official power. But it is not always the good guy. It can be a compliant or gullible handmaiden of government abuse. Or it can be something even worse, as a South African case shows.

During the time of racial oppression in South Africa, a news magazine called *To the Point* published an article about a black minister, the Reverend Dr. Manas Buthelezi. It said that while he spoke publicly of the need for peaceful change, according to "reliable sources" he privately advocated "violence." That was an extremely damaging charge in apartheid South Africa, one that could have brought Dr. Buthelezi's imprisonment or even execution. He sued *To the Point* for libel—and demanded to know the names of the "reliable sources." The editor claimed a privilege to keep them secret. The court rejected the claim and decided the case in favor of Dr. Buthelezi, awarding him damages. Some time later, in what South Africans called the "Information Scandal," disclosures from the Ministry of Information showed that the article in *To the Point* had actually been written by the secret police.

When an American public figure sues for libel after a devastating attack, the Supreme Court's libel rule requires him or her to prove that the author of the charge made it knowing that it was false or in reckless disregard of its truth or falsity. That gives great protection to the press. It really means that the victim must find out what the author knew before publishing. If journalists were immunized from having to respond to questions, the injured person would essentially be stymied. Someone whose life was ruined by a false report could not sue successfully to repair his or her reputation. That should not be an acceptable result in a civilized society. The press, having won great protection in libel cases, cannot expect to have a testimonial privilege in those cases as well.

The solution in libel suits is not to put a journalist in jail if he or she refuses to name the confidential source who made a charge against the plaintiff. It is for the judge to tell the jury that it can assume there was no such source. That formula would effectively force the press to have at least one named source for any pejorative story, or be prepared to pay libel damages if sued. Such an approach has been used in a number of states.

When a journalist's testimony becomes an issue in criminal prosecutions, it is usually the prosecutor who wants the testimony. But it can be the defendant, and then our sense of what justice requires may be different. If a reporter has confidential information that could help a defendant charged with murder, can he or she properly withhold it?

Something like that scenario played out in the case of Myron Farber, a *New York Times* reporter. In 1975 Farber wrote a series of articles about deaths in a Hackensack, New Jersey, hospital—deaths that were unexplained. The articles said that a doctor in the hospital—Farber called him Doctor X, withholding the name—had murdered five patients with the poison curare. New Jersey authorities reopened their investigation of the deaths and indicted a surgeon, Dr. Mario Jascalevich. Jascalevich's lawyer subpoenaed Farber's notes, arguing that they could show inconsistencies between what his sources had said to him and what they might say on the stand. The judge ordered Farber to provide the notes—and, when he refused to, sentenced him to six months in jail for contempt. The *Times* had to pay a fine of $100,000 plus $5,000 a day while the subpoena was defied. New Jersey had a journalists' shield law, and Farber relied on it. But the state supreme court held that it had to yield to the defendant's constitutional right to evidence.

After Farber spent forty days in prison, he was pardoned by the governor of New Jersey, Brendan Byrne, who also returned $286,000 that the *Times* had paid in fines. There was no doubt that Myron Farber had taken his stand on principle, and the chance of the defendant's lawyer actually finding something useful in his notes seemed rather remote. But it is easy to see that in an appropriate case it would be morally testing for a journalist to withhold information from a criminal defendant.

The truth is that there are ethical and other compelling interests on both sides of the privilege issue. The press does need to use confidential informants; sometimes parties seeking to clear their names—a Wen Ho Lee, a Manas Buthelezi— have an indisputable reason. The fact that there are interests on both sides should make journalists be cautious in relying on unnamed sources in what they write. For one thing, it is plainly wrong to quote anonymous sources in pejorative comments on individuals. ("The mayor has taken bribes in his office," an informed source told the *Daily Bugle*.) That is not just unfair to the mayor; it is asking for a confrontation over a demand for the name of the "informed source" if the mayor sues. The press has come to understand the possibility of abuse in using unnamed sources. The *New York Times*, for example, has internal rules requiring that an editor be told the reason for the confidentiality, and specifically barring the use of anonymous pejorative comments.

Thirty-five years after the *Branzburg* decision it is clear that the First Amendment is not going to provide a solution to the conflict between the press's need for confidential sources and the occasional need of the legal process for journalists' evidence. In a number of high-profile cases lower courts have rejected the press's constitutional arguments. The Supreme Court has shown no interest in reexamining the issue; the chance that it will read the First Amendment to give journalists a testimonial privilege is zero.

The trouble with the constitutional claim is that it fits awkwardly with the general course of First Amendment decisions on the freedom of the press. Starting in 1931, the Supreme Court largely immunized the press from prior restraints (in *Near v. Minnesota*) and subsequent penalties for what it published (in *New York Times v. Sullivan*). It hardly ever read the

First Amendment as assuring the acquisition of information, and then only when the complaint was against closed courtrooms. And in those courtroom cases the Supreme Court gave no special access to the press, deciding rather that courtrooms must be open to the public at large. To prevail with its constitutional argument on the privilege issue, the press would have to persuade the Supreme Court to take two new steps: First, it would have to decide that the First Amendment gives the press (however defined) access to information not given to the public, and then it would have to decide that keeping sources secret is crucial to that access.

Journalists and their lawyers often speak as if the First Amendment, in guaranteeing the freedom of "the press," protected an institution—the organized press. Indeed, Justice Stewart made that assumption in a lecture. But in the eighteenth century there was nothing like the organized press institutions that developed later. In promising "the freedom of speech, or of the press," the amendment surely meant merely to cover both oral and written expression: pamphlets and books just as much as newspapers. Once the premise of a specially protected institution is put aside, the constitutional claim for special treatment of journalists in the courts becomes more difficult to sustain.

All this suggests that the question of a testimonial privilege for journalists is really one of public policy rather than of constitutional law. The Constitution did not create the privileges familiar in Anglo-American law: the assurances that a lawyer need not testify against a client, a doctor against a patient, one spouse against another. They were adopted by courts and legislatures in response to felt needs. In 1975 Congress formalized the process for federal courts by explicitly authorizing them to develop privileges in keeping with "the principles of the common law as they may be interpreted . . . in the light of reason and experience." Under that authority, the Supreme Court recognized privileges for communications between lawyers and clients, wives and husbands, psychotherapists and patients.

In 2005 a judge of the United States Court of Appeals for the District of Columbia Circuit, David Tatel, proposed that the federal courts use the authority of the 1975 statute to adopt a qualified privilege for journalists. He said "reason and experience" called for that step because the press had such an important role in exposing official abuse of power and because forty-nine states (all but Wyoming) had adopted some form of press privilege by statute or judicial decision.

Judge Tatel spoke of the "clash between two truth-seeking institutions: the grand jury and the press." He suggested a qualified privilege that would balance interests, but one different from the three-part test advocated by Justice Stewart in dissent in the *Branzburg* case. The latter would not work when the government was seeking the source of a leak, he pointed out; the only people who would know would be the leaker and the journalist, so the government could always show that it had no alternative witnesses. Instead, Judge Tatel said, courts should balance the interest in compelling disclosure, measured by the harm the leak caused, against the public interest in newsgathering, measured by the leaked information's value. Thus, for example, if the government wanted to learn who leaked the

story of President Bush's order for wiretapping without required warrants, a court would weigh the harm caused by that
leak against the importance of the information to the public. In
my view the latter would plainly prevail, and the reporters
would have a privilege not to disclose their source.

Judge Tatel's qualified privilege would not assure a victory
for the press every time, not at all. That was clear from the
very case in which he put forward his idea: the contempt proceedings against Judith Miller of the *New York Times* and Matt
Cooper of *Time* magazine. The underlying issue there was a
leak about Iraq's supposed weapons of mass destruction. In a
speech in 2003, President Bush said Saddam Hussein's determination to have those weapons was shown by an intelligence
report saying that Iraq was trying to buy uranium ore in Niger,
in Africa. On July 6, 2003, the *Times* published an op-ed piece
by Joseph Wilson, a former ambassador, saying that he had
been sent to Niger to investigate that report and found it false.
His article infuriated the Bush administration. Soon Robert
Novak, a conservative columnist, wrote that high sources had
told him that Wilson's wife, Valerie Plame Wilson, was a secret agent at the CIA and had suggested he be sent on that
mission. It can be a crime to disclose the name of a secret intelligence agent. A special prosecutor was appointed to investigate. He called Miller and Cooper before a grand jury to
testify on who had told them about Wilson and Plame; they
refused to answer. Cooper eventually did reply, but Miller
spent eighty-five days in jail before she said she had permission
from her source to give his name—Lewis Libby, chief of staff
to Vice President Dick Cheney. She was then released.

When the contempt orders were before the Court of Appeals, on appeal by Miller and Cooper, Judge Tatel proposed his idea of the court adopting a qualified privilege. His colleagues did not agree with him, but he wrote an opinion applying his proposal to the facts of this case—and concluded that there should be no testimonial privilege for the two journalists. On the one hand, he said, what was leaked—the name of an intelligence agent—was a serious matter, possibly even criminal. On the other, the news value of Valerie Plame's name and employment was "marginal."

David Tatel had a high reputation as a judge, including a particular sensitivity to First Amendment interests. The press and its lawyers could not persuasively dismiss his opinion as the product of bias or unfairness. The press might better have taken the case as a warning against pressing its claims too far and separating itself from the mainstream of the law and public opinion.

A warning against doing that had come, years before, from one of the press's greatest friends, Justice William J. Brennan Jr. of the Supreme Court. In 1979, when press organizations had lost a case in the Supreme Court and cried out that the Constitution was unraveling, he urged them to be more careful and more understanding in their claims. He added: "This may involve a certain loss of innocence, a certain recognition that the press, like other institutions, must accommodate a variety of important social interests."

7

Fear Itself

Early in 1918, the year after the United States entered World War I, Montana adopted a state sedition law. The act made it a crime, punishable by a fine of up to $20,000 and a prison term of up to twenty years, to "utter, print, write, or publish any disloyal, profane, violent, scurrilous, contemptuous, slurring, or abusive language" in wartime about the government, the Constitution, the flag, or the military uniforms of the United States, or to say anything calculated to bring them "into contempt, scorn, contumely, or disrepute."

In the next year, seventy-nine Montanans were convicted of violating that vague language. A real estate man was convicted for having said, "Because I don't buy Liberty Bonds and don't carry the goddamn flag they call me pro-German." A sheep rancher was convicted after being accused by tenants he had been trying to evict. A traveling salesman for a wine company was found guilty for having called wartime food regulations "a big joke." He was sentenced to from seven and one-half to twenty years at hard labor. Many of the convictions were for comments made in saloons.

State and local committees enforced their ideas of patriotism. The Montana Council of Defense issued an order forbidding the use of the German language in schools and churches. (Montana had some communities of German origin.) In Lewistown a mob went into the high school, took all the German textbooks, and burned them in the street. Newspapers worked up fear of German plots. The editor of the *Helena Independent*, Will Campbell, warned against poisonous beans being sneaked into the country; after hearing about tales of mysterious airplane sightings, he wrote, "Are the Germans about to bomb the capital of Montana?"

Montana, so far from the war in Europe, might have been thought the last place to be gripped by fear of The Enemy. Its unlikely record was forgotten until it was unearthed in a book published in 2005: *Darkest Before Dawn: Sedition and Free Speech in the American West*, by Clemens P. Work of the School of Journalism at the University of Montana in Missoula. I have taken my examples from him. The book had an extraordinary consequence. Law students in a class at the university looked into the sedition cases, got in touch with family members of those who were convicted, and helped draft a pardon petition. In May 2006 Governor Brian Schweitzer posthumously pardoned seventy-eight Montanans convicted of sedition under the 1918 law. (One had been pardoned earlier.) Schweitzer made a statement that he said should have been made by the governor who proposed the law, Sam Stewart: "I'm sorry, forgive me and God bless America, because we can criticize our government."

The patriotic hysteria in Montana during World War I was a sample of a national phenomenon. In fact, the Montana sedition law was used as the model for a federal Sedition Act—the first since 1798—passed by Congress at the urging of President Wilson. The federal law differed from Montana's in only three insignificant words. It was the statute used against the radicals who threw pamphlets from a rooftop in New York City in *Abrams v. United States,* in which Justice Holmes wrote his first, memorable free-speech dissent. ("It is an experiment, as all life is an experiment.")

The federal Sedition Act and the wartime statute it amended, the Espionage Act of 1917, swept up all kinds of obscure victims apart from those known to us because the Supreme Court considered their cases. Clemens Work's book cites the case of Clarence Waldron, a Pentecostal minister in Windsor, Vermont, who was prosecuted for telling his Bible class that "a Christian can take no part in the war" and "Don't shed your precious blood for your country." The jury found that his words showed an intent to "cause insubordination, disloyalty, or refusal of duty." He was convicted and sentenced to fifteen years in prison. More than 2,000 Americans, most of them no more dangerous than Clarence Waldron, were prosecuted under the Espionage and Sedition Acts.

It is a seeming characteristic of American society that it is periodically gripped by fear— fear manipulated by politicians. In 1798 it was French Jacobin terrorists who were supposedly going to infiltrate; even someone as sensible as Abigail Adams was touched by that fear. In the middle of the nineteenth century the Know-Nothing Party warned against the dire influence of immigrant Roman Catholics. After World War I demagogues persuaded many Americans that they were in mortal danger from political radicals.

Of course no society is immune from the poison of fear. Germany was a country of high culture, and Jews had an important place in it, before it was taken over by an anti-Semitic mass murderer. But America, though it has faced economic troubles more than once, has never experienced anything like the distress of Weimar Germany. With its continental reach and vast resources, it might have been expected to be less susceptible to panic. That proved untrue time and again. Even in a time of strong economic growth, the years after World War II, another Red Scare developed. Congressional committees hunted Communists with considerable public support: a phenomenon that reached its peak in the 1950s in the maestro of fear and hate, Senator Joe McCarthy.

The excesses of patriotic fervor during America's participation in World War I were succeeded, after the war, by the outrages of the first American Red Scare. The Bolshevik Revolution in Russia aroused fear of all kinds of radicalism—fear of socialists, communists, anarchists. Industrialists saw the hand of revolutionaries in strikes, particularly in the activities of the feared radical union, the Industrial Workers of the World (IWW). Politicians played on the fear. Twenty states adopted legislation banning "criminal syndicalism." These laws made it a crime to join an organization with the doctrine of advocating violence for political ends—whether or not a defendant personally held those views or had acted on them. (California's Criminal Syndicalism Act was the one used against Anita Whitney in *Whitney v. California*, the case that evoked Brandeis's classic argument for freedom of speech.)

In 1919 the United States House of Representatives refused to seat Victor Berger, who had been elected in Wisconsin as a member of the Socialist Party. In 1920 the New York State Assembly unseated five elected Socialists. That action brought a powerful response from Charles Evans Hughes, former governor of New York and former Supreme Court justice who narrowly lost to Woodrow Wilson as the Republican candidate for president in 1916. (He was appointed chief justice in 1930.) Hughes said it was "a most serious mistake to proceed against masses of our citizens . . . by denying them the only resource of peaceful government; that is, action by the ballot box. . . . "

Woodrow Wilson, who ran as a progressive Democrat and introduced important economic reform measures as president, left an abysmal record on civil liberties—including freedom of speech and of the press. He proposed the repressive Espionage Act of 1917 and Sedition Act of 1918. He urged Congress to make it a crime to publish anything that might be useful to the enemy in wartime. (Congress rejected that proposal after a barrage of critical newspaper editorials.) His postmaster general, Albert Burleson, barred from the mails any publication that he deemed critical of the war effort. For example, he explained, "papers may not say that the Government is controlled by Wall Street or munitions manufacturers, or any other special interests."

But it was Wilson's attorney general, A. Mitchell Palmer, who put his mark on the era most dramatically. At his direction, Department of Justice agents conducted raids in November 1919 and again the following January, arresting more than 4,000 supposed radicals. The Palmer Raids, as they were called, targeted aliens, about 800 of whom were deported. The most famous may have been Emma Goldman, who sounded a bit like Charles Evans Hughes when she said at her deportation hearing: "The free expression of the hopes and aspirations of a people is the greatest and only safety in a sane society."

The First Amendment is meant to assure Americans that they can believe what they will and say what they believe. But repeatedly, in times of fear and stress, men and women have been hunted, humiliated, punished for their words and beliefs. We look to the courts to maintain our faithfulness to freedom. This book, like others, tends to chart the state of American liberty in judicial decisions. But courts have hardly been consistent guarantors of free speech.

Courts did nothing to restrain the harsh consequences of the Sedition Act of 1798. The law's constitutionality was never definitively resolved before it expired, but justices of the Supreme Court acting as trial judges enforced it with no sign of reluctance. It was Madison, Jefferson, and their supporters who made the libertarian case against the Sedition Act. They—politicians, not judges—persuaded the contemporary public, and history, that it violated our commitment to freedom. The courts did nothing to stop the Palmer Raids and other government repressions during and after

World War I. Policies gradually changed then because of the force of criticism by Charles Evans Hughes, Professor Zechariah Chafee, and other liberal-minded men and women. The established press, it should be noted, was not in the vanguard in the defense of freedom; it tended to echo the government. More leadership came from private organizations such as the American Civil Liberties Union, founded in 1920.

Judge Learned Hand spoke at a wartime rally for freedom in Central Park, New York, in 1944. His speech, entitled "The Spirit of Liberty," included this often-quoted passage: "I often wonder whether we do not rest our hopes too much upon constitutions, upon laws and upon courts. These are false hopes, believe me, these are false hopes. Liberty lies in the hearts of men and women; when it dies there, no constitution, no law, no court can save it; no constitution, no law, no court can even do much to help it. While it lies there it needs no constitution, no law, no court to save it."

Judge Hand's rhetoric was memorable, and there was a kernel of truth in what he said. A society that does not value freedom cannot be kept free by a court. But his words were a misleading overstatement. Modern history shows that courts can do much to help, by inspiring devotion to freedom. Holmes and Brandeis had neither sword nor purse, as Alexander Hamilton said of courts. But they had words, and their words played a significant part in American society's growing attachment to freedom of speech later in the twentieth century—in the fitful realization of the promise of the First Amendment.

Consider cases decided by the Supreme Court a dozen years apart, in 1925 and 1937. In 1925, the Court upheld the conviction of a radical in the case of *Gitlow v. New York*. Benjamin Gitlow was prosecuted for publishing the manifesto of a small left-wing group that called for mass action to bring about a "revolutionary dictatorship of the proletariat." There was no charge that he sought immediate revolution or violence. Justice Holmes, dissenting with Justice Brandeis, rested on his clear and present danger test. He said there was "no present danger of an attempt to overthrow the government by force on the part of the admittedly small minority who shared the defendant's views." Holmes continued:

It is said that this manifesto was more than a theory, that it was an incitement. Every idea is an incitement. It offers itself for belief and if believed it is acted on unless some other belief outweighs it or some failure of energy stifles the movement at its birth. The only difference between the expression of an opinion and an incitement in the narrower sense is the speaker's enthusiasm for the result. Eloquence may set fire to reason. But whatever may be thought of the redundant discourse before us, it had no chance of starting a present conflagration. If in the long run the beliefs expressed in proletarian dictatorship are destined to be accepted by the dominant forces of the community, the only meaning of free speech is that they should be given their chance and have their way.

Holmes's astringent characterization of Gitlow's manifesto as a "redundant discourse" put this case—and others like it—

in realistic perspective. Benjamin Gitlow was not a threat to American society. Decades later, one can only wonder why the authorities bothered with him. The same was true of hundreds of prosecutions brought under state statutes like the Montana sedition law and the federal Espionage and Sedition Acts. But the majority of the Supreme Court was still fixed on upholding the convictions of radicals whose words might have a "tendency" of which they disapproved. (The *Gitlow* decision was in fact important for another reason. The majority opinion, by Justice Edward T. Sanford, for the first time accepted the argument that the First Amendment's protections of speech and press from federal repression were applied to the states by the Fourteenth Amendment. From then on, most of the development of First Amendment freedoms came in state cases.)

In 1937 the Supreme Court made two decisions that turned away from fear of radicalism. In *De Jonge v. Oregon*, Dirk De Jonge had been convicted of violating Oregon's criminal syndicalism law when he helped to conduct a meeting held under the auspices of the Communist Party. There was no charge that "criminal syndicalism" or violence was advocated at the meeting. The sole basis of the conviction was the fact that the Communist Party had called the meeting.

The Supreme Court unanimously reversed De Jonge's conviction. The opinion, by Chief Justice Hughes, did not take up the debate about whether there was a clear and present danger of some substantive evil. Instead, the chief justice focused on the general importance of freedom of speech and freedom of assembly, which is also protected by the First

Amendment. ("Congress shall make no law . . . abridging the freedom of speech, or of the press; or the right of the people peaceably to assemble, and to petition the Government for a redress of grievances.") Hughes wrote: "The right of peaceable assembly is a right cognate to those of free speech and free press and is equally fundamental. . . . Peaceable assembly for lawful discussions cannot be made a crime. The holding of meetings for peaceable political action cannot be proscribed. Those who assist in the conduct of such meetings cannot be branded as criminals on that score."

Dirk De Jonge was in a different legal situation from that of Benjamin Gitlow and the others who had lost all the early cases. But underneath those differences one can sense a change in judicial attitude, a much greater sensitivity to the demands of free expression. De Jonge would not have prevailed in 1919, when the *Abrams* case was decided over Holmes's dissent, or in 1927, when Anita Whitney's was.

The 1937 Court had greater difficulty in the case of *Herndon v. Lowry*, decided in favor of a free-speech claim by a vote of 5 to 4. Angelo Herndon was a black man who acted as an organizer for the Communist Party in Georgia: a role that must have required extraordinary courage. He was convicted of "attempt to incite insurrection" in violation of a Georgia law because of his place in the Communist Party. The party advocated "self-determination" for predominantly black areas of the South, but there was no evidence that Herndon had personally advocated this program or urged it on those he tried to enlist in the party.

Justice Owen J. Roberts, in the opinion of the Court, focused on the character of what Herndon had been shown to have said, or not shown. His "membership in the Communist Party and his solicitation of a few members," Roberts wrote, "wholly fail to establish an attempt to incite others to insurrection. In these circumstances, to make membership in the party and solicitation of members for that party a criminal offense, punishable by death, in the discretion of a jury, is an unwarranted invasion of the right of freedom of speech." The dissenting opinion, by Justice Willis Van Devanter, spoke of the vulnerability of Herndon's target audience: southern blacks. The literature he carried, Van Devanter wrote, was "largely directed to a people whose past and present circumstances would lead them to give unusual credence to its inflaming and inciting features."

The two 1937 cases, *De Jonge* and *Herndon*, show how the fear of radical ideology that dominated the earlier decisions had ebbed as an influence in the Court—and freedom of speech had been given pride of place. One other case should be mentioned as an indication of how far the ideal of free speech had gone: *Cantwell v. Connecticut*, decided in 1940. An itinerant Jehovah's Witness preacher was convicted of breach of the peace when he denounced the Roman Catholic Church in a largely Catholic neighborhood. The case did not involve fear of radical doctrine; the legal issue was different. But Justice Roberts, in the opinion reversing the conviction, made plain where free speech now stood in the Court's hierarchy of interests:

In the realm of religious faith, and in that of political belief, sharp differences arise. In both fields the tenets of one man may seem the rankest error to his neighbor. To persuade others to his own point of view, the pleader, as we know, at times resorts to exaggeration, to vilification of men who have been, or are, prominent in church or state, and even to false statement. But the people of this nation have ordained in the light of history that, in spite of the probability of excesses and abuses, these liberties are, in the long view, essential to enlightened opinion and right conduct on the part of the citizens of a democracy.

World War II was a far more menacing conflict for the United States than World War I had been. A significant part of the American fleet was destroyed at the outset in the surprise Japanese attack on Pearl Harbor on December 7, 1941. Soon after that, President Franklin D. Roosevelt set in motion what was very likely the greatest blow to constitutional rights in all the wars and times of stress in American history. He authorized military commanders to exclude from the West Coast all persons of Japanese ancestry. About 120,000 people were removed from their homes on the coast, more than 80,000 of them American citizens, and confined behind barbed wire in desert "relocation camps." Why? Again, fear was the dominant reason—fear, spread by politicians, that Japan was about to invade the United States. Someone as profoundly humane as Earl Warren—then attorney general of California, later governor, and then chief justice of the United States—pressed for the removal because, he said, it was impossible to tell the difference between a loyal Japanese American and a disloyal one. In fact, not one was charged during the war with any form of disloyalty.

The Supreme Court made this civil-liberties disaster worse by refusing to pronounce it unlawful. In 1944, in *Korematsu v. United States*, the Court upheld the conviction of Fred Korematsu for being in California in violation of the military order. Justices Frank Murphy, Owen J. Roberts, and Robert H. Jackson dissented. Justice Jackson wrote:

> A military order, however unconstitutional, is not apt to last longer than the military emergency. [But] once a judicial opinion rationalizes such an order to show that it conforms to the Constitution, or rather rationalizes the Constitution to show that the Constitution sanctions such an order, the Court for all time has validated the principle of racial discrimination in criminal procedure and of transplanting American citizens. The principle then lies about like a loaded weapon ready for the hand of any authority that can bring forward a plausible claim of an urgent need.

The Japanese relocation program did not engage the First Amendment. In terms of freedom of speech and press, the society's record was far better in the second world war than in the first. There were a few prosecutions of German sympathizers, but not the mass hysteria that sent harmless men and women to prison for long terms. In World War I, Americans were prosecuted for objecting to the purchase of Liberty Bonds. In World War II, a test of patriotism was joining in the salute to the flag. Children were expelled from public school for refusing to do so; they were Jehovah's Witnesses who said their religion forbade such obeisance. In 1940, in *Minersville School District v. Gobitis*, the Supreme Court rejected an appeal by such children; only the chief justice, Harlan F. Stone, dissented. But the decision was widely criticized, and just three years later the Court changed its mind. A 6-to-3 majority in *West Virginia Board of Education v. Barnette* (1943) found that compelling the flag salute violated the First Amendment. Justice Jackson, writing for the majority, said:

> Compulsory unification of opinion achieves only the unanimity of the graveyard. It seems trite but necessary to say that the First Amendment to our Constitution was designed to avoid these ends by avoiding these beginnings. . . . We can have intellectual individualism and the rich cultural diversity that we owe to exceptional minds only at the price of occasional eccentricity and abnormal attitudes. When they are so harmless to others or to the State as those we deal with here, the price is not too great. But freedom to differ is not limited to things that do not matter much. That would be a mere shadow of freedom. The test of its substance is the right to differ as to things that touch the heart of the existing order.
>
> If there is any fixed star in our constitutional constellation, it is that no official, high or petty, can prescribe what shall be orthodox in politics, nationalism, religion or other matters of opinion or force citizens to confess by word or act their faith therein.

Justice Jackson's point that the First Amendment does not allow the state to compel speech was applied thirty-four years later by the Supreme Court to reverse the conviction of a Jehovah's Witness couple who had taped over the motto on New Hampshire license plates, "Live Free or Die." Chief Justice Warren E. Burger said that First Amendment freedom of thought "includes both the right to speak freely and the right to refrain from speaking at all."

At the end of World War II the First Amendment seemed to be in a strong position in the courts and in the country. The legal doctrines that had sent men and women to prison for years because they criticized the government or its officials were history. But within a few years the country was in the grip of another Red Scare. Fear ate away at freedom of speech and association. And the courts did not respond to the challenge in a timely and effective way.

The Cold War with the Soviet Union underlay the fear. Soviet imposition of Communist rule in Eastern European countries it had taken from German occupation by the end of the war—Poland, Czechoslovakia, and the rest—raised the specter of Soviet armies marching west. Germany itself, divided between East and West, was a source of particular tension. Inside the United States, ambitious politicians stoked the fear that disloyal Americans were helping the Communist cause. When Republicans won control of the House of Representatives in 1946, they used hearings of the House Committee on Un-American Activities to paint a disturbing picture of Communist infiltration into schools, universities, the press, and even Hollywood. Movie directors and writers were subpoenaed, and ten refused to testify—the Hollywood Ten. They were cited for contempt of Congress and prosecuted on that charge.

The unfriendly witnesses, as they were called, argued that forcing them to testify about their associations, and to name others, violated their freedom of speech and belief under the First Amendment. When that argument failed, some went to prison for contempt. Even those who avoided contempt citations were publicly humiliated and pictured as subversives. The Hollywood figures were blacklisted by the film industry. (Some wrote scripts under assumed names.) A magazine called *Red Channels* published lists of broadcast performers who it said were pro-Communist, and many were unable to appear on radio or television.

The Supreme Court considered the First Amendment issue in 1959 in *Barenblatt v. United States.* Lloyd Barenblatt, an instructor at Vassar College, had refused to tell the Un-American Activities Committee about past or present membership in the Communist Party. The Court rejected his constitutional arguments by a vote of 5 to 4. Justice Harlan, for the majority, said the interest of Congress in investigating subversive activity outweighed Barenblatt's interest in the privacy of his beliefs. He said the Court could not consider whether, as Barenblatt alleged, the committee was not interested in legislating but was engaged in exposure for exposure's sake. Justice Black, dissenting, said: "[The majority] leaves out the real interest in Barenblatt's silence, the interest of the people as a whole in being able to join organizations, advocate causes and make political 'mistakes' without later being subjected to governmental penalties for having dared to think for themselves. It is this right, the right to err politically, which keeps us strong as a nation."

There was one case in those years in which the Supreme Court found that a legislative investigation violated the First Amendment. The case arose from a curious procedure in New Hampshire that made the state attorney general a one-man investigating committee for the legislature. (New Hampshire at the time was dominated politically by the Far Right.) Paul Sweezy, a left-wing economics professor, refused to answer the attorney general's questions about a lecture he had given at the University of New Hampshire and about the Progressive Party, a left-wing third party. His contempt conviction was reversed by the Supreme Court by a vote of 6 to 3. The crucial opinion, focusing on the First Amendment, was a concurring opinion by Justice Frankfurter, joined by Justice Harlan—two who were the leading conservatives on the Court at the time. Justice Frankfurter weighed the competing interests as follows:

> The inviolability of privacy belonging to a citizen's political loyalty has so overwhelming an importance to the well-being of our kind of society that it cannot be constitutionally encroached upon on the basis of so meagre a countervailing interest of the State as may be argumentatively found in the remote, shadowy threat to the security of New Hampshire allegedly presented [by the Progressive Party]. . . . When weighed against the grave harm resulting from governmental intrusion into the intellectual life of a university, justification

for compelling a witness to discuss the contents of his lecture appears grossly inadequate.

Frankfurter had been a professor at the Harvard Law School before being appointed to the Supreme Court by President Roosevelt in 1939. His defense of academic freedom in that opinion was often cited by embattled universities and their faculties in later years. The statement that the First Amendment protects academic life was also an answer, in its way, to the press's frequent (though unsuccessful) claim that it had a preferred position under the First Amendment.

But the Sweezy case stood alone for some years in granting First Amendment protection to a witness accused of Communist associations. Those who looked to the courts to stand against the political manipulation of fear were disappointed. Senate committees vied with the House Committee on Un-American Activities in exposing assertedly Red-tainted individuals. The Permanent Investigations Subcommittee became the most famous—or notorious, depending on one's view—when it was chaired by Senator Joe McCarthy. But the executive branch was equally important in the anti-Communist crusade of the late 1940s and 1950s.

President Harry S. Truman instituted a government-wide loyalty program that removed government employees found to be of doubtful loyalty because of supposed dangerous associations. Loyalty boards that passed these judgments acted on the basis of charges by informants whose names and testimony were often withheld from the accused. Efforts were made over many years to have the Supreme Court find that these methods, reminiscent of the denunciations that sent French victims to the guillotine in the years after the Revolution, denied the victims the due process of law guaranteed by the Constitution. But the efforts failed. The loyalty program and other anti-Communist measures by the Truman administration were a product of the Cold War and in part reflected genuine concern about Communist infiltration. But they were also an attempt to counter Republican charges that Democrats were "soft on communism," a political theme that reached its apogee in Senator McCarthy's talk of "twenty years of treason" dating back to Franklin Roosevelt's first inaugural in 1933.

Government employees suspected of disloyalty under the Truman program were offered hearings before special boards, but the hearings lacked essential elements of fair process. The charges were based on statements by unnamed informers who were not subject to cross-examination, and the charges themselves often wandered far afield from what could rationally be considered threats to government security. Dorothy Bailey, who had a nonsensitive federal job, was asked by a board member at her hearing, "Did you ever write a letter to the Red Cross about the segregation of blood?" Bailey was black, a graduate of Bryn Mawr. In volume 12 of the history of the Supreme Court being written and published with funds left to the United States by Justice Holmes, William M. Wiecek relates that episode and observes: "The prevalent racism and sexism of the era infected the security screening process, and some investigators hoped to root out civil rights activists and civil libertarians."

Dorothy Bailey was denied permanent federal employment because "reasonable grounds exist for belief that you are disloyal. . . . " She sued, challenging the denial of a right to confront her accusers. The United States Court of Appeals for the District of Columbia Circuit ruled against her by a vote of 2 to 1. The Supreme Court divided equally, 4–4, one justice not sitting; that had the effect of upholding the Court of Appeals decision. The Supreme Court never did squarely resolve the troubling issue of the use of unnamed informants in loyalty-security proceedings.

The great legal test of the period came in the Truman administration's prosecution of leaders of the Communist Party, which ended in the Supreme Court's 1951 decision in *Dennis v. United States*. Eleven defendants were charged with conspiring to "teach and advocate the overthrow and destruction of the Government of the United States by force and violence." They were not charged with actually attempting the overthrow, or with conspiring to do so, but only with conspiring to advocate it—a distinction often lost in the theatrics that surrounded the trial. The party's own documents abjured the use of violence, but former party members who testified for the prosecution said that these professions of support for peaceful change were "Aesopian language" concealing violent intentions. The jury convicted the eleven.

The United States Court of Appeals for the Second Circuit affirmed the conviction in an opinion by that most respected judge, Learned Hand. He offered a new formula for Holmes's clear and present danger test: "whether the gravity of the 'evil,' discounted by its improbability, justifies such invasion of free speech as is necessary to avoid the danger." If the perceived danger is very great, then, repression is allowable even if there is only a minimal chance of the danger actually occurring. This sliding scale was adopted by Chief Justice Fred M. Vinson in the Supreme Court, and the convictions were upheld.

The niceties of legal doctrine could not conceal what was really happening in *Dennis*. In the world, the Soviet Union presented profound dangers. In the United States, the open Communist Party presented no threat to the American system of government. What was a threat was the spy network maintained by the Soviet Union. The extent of this espionage effort was disclosed by the publication in 1995 of what were called the Venona documents, cables from Soviet agents intercepted and decrypted by the United States. They showed that the USSR used American Communists and secret supporters intensely to try to obtain security information. But U.S. officials, knowing the Venona findings contemporaneously, chose not to prosecute Communist leaders for conducting or supporting espionage but instead to charge them, in *Dennis*, with conspiring to teach and advocate the necessity of revolutionary violence. Why? Professor Martin H. Redish of Northwestern University Law School wrote, convincingly to me, that a possible explanation was the intended goal of FBI Director J. Edgar Hoover: to send the message to the country, "Engage in unpopular political thought at your own risk." In short, the decision to prosecute Dennis and the others for teaching and advocacy was political in origin and consequence.

Moreover, there was a deep irony in the legal legacy of the case, Judge Hand's reformulation of the clear and present danger test. Hand had never liked the test or considered it a wise reading of the First Amendment. He said of Justice Holmes's authorship of it, "For once, Homer nodded." During World War I, as a federal trial judge, Hand had proposed a different approach when the radical magazine *The Masses* challenged an order by Postmaster General Burleson barring it from the mails. Hand thought the crucial question should be whether the speech or writing that led to the government action was expressly intended to bring about an unlawful result. But his approach was rejected on appeal at the time and was forgotten by the time of the *Dennis* case. Hand felt obliged to follow the Holmes approach, though his version of it was much weaker than what was intended by Holmes—who would have protected intentional appeals to lawlessness if they had no immediate danger of succeeding. Personally, Hand took a dim view of the *Dennis* prosecution. He wrote a friend, "Personally I should never have prosecuted those birds."

Justices Black and Douglas dissented in the Supreme Court. Black wrote: "Public opinion being what it is now, few will protest the conviction of these Communist petitioners. There is hope, however, that in calmer times, when present pressures, passions and fears subside, this or some later Court will restore the First Amendment liberties to the high preferred place where they belong in a free society."

Freedom of speech and belief was seriously damaged during the second Red Scare. The congressional hearings, the

Dennis prosecution, the federal loyalty program, and numerous other state and federal anti-Communist laws encouraged all but the bravest Americans to stick to conformist views. The First Amendment, which from 1930 to 1943 (when the *Barnette* flag-salute case was decided) had been interpreted ever more broadly by the Supreme Court, was left in a shrunken state. The Court had shown that it was not inclined to stand against what Justice Black called popular "passions and fears."

But in time the situation changed, in the country and the Court. The public's support for Red-hunting ebbed with the disgrace and death of Senator McCarthy after he was condemned by the Senate in 1954. In 1957, in *Yates v. United States*, the Supreme Court in an opinion by Justice Harlan read the law as prohibiting advocacy of violent overthrow only when it was accompanied by an effort at action to that end, not mere abstract advocacy.

The law that prohibited advocacy of violent overthrow, the Smith Act, also made it criminal to be a member of a party with such a program. In order to sustain the membership clause's constitutionality, the government prosecuted Communists who it said were "active" members. (A Justice Department lawyer ironically explained to me at the time, off the record: "It's not enough to be a member of the party; you have to be a"—raising his voice—"*member.*") On that basis, the Supreme Court by a 5–4 vote affirmed the conviction of Junius Scales, a Communist in North Carolina. A Columbia Law School professor who had been a war crimes prosecutor at Nuremberg, Telford Taylor, asked the Kennedy administration to commute Scales's five-year sentence. Despite fears of a political backlash, Attorney General Robert Kennedy recommended the commutation and President Kennedy granted it. Scales was the last Smith Act prisoner.

In 1969 the Supreme Court adopted a new test for advocacy of violent or unlawful action. In *Brandenburg v. Ohio* a Ku Klux Klan leader had denounced blacks and Jews at a rally. The Court reversed his conviction. To pass constitutional muster, it said, a conviction must be for advocacy (1) directed to "inciting or producing imminent lawless action," and (2) "likely to produce such action." The first element, the speaker's intent, followed Judge Hand's approach. The second, and the word "imminent," incorporated Justice Holmes's. The *Dennis* conviction would not have passed the test.

The calmer times for which Justice Black had hoped had evidently arrived, and the First Amendment was restored to its high position. The Supreme Court proceeded to hold a number of anti-Communist laws unconstitutional. An especially interesting case was *Lamont v. Postmaster General*, decided in 1965. As the Cold War intensified, the government adopted a program to discourage Americans from receiving Soviet publications such as *Pravda*. When a copy arrived at the post office, officials would send a notice to the addressee with a postcard that he could return saying that he wanted the "Communist political propaganda" to be delivered to him. The Kennedy administration abolished the practice—whereupon Congress, under pressure from anti-Communist zealots, wrote it into a statute. Many of the addressees were libraries, which could brave the stigma of saying they wanted

"Communist political propaganda." One individual sub-
scriber, Corliss Lamont, challenged the law in court. The
Supreme Court held it unconstitutional. Justice Douglas said
requiring return of the postcard "is almost certain to have a
deterrent effect. . . . Public officials, like school teachers who
have no tenure, might think they would invite disaster if they
read what the Federal Government says contains the seeds of
treason." The Lamont decision, surprisingly, was the first that
ever found a federal law in violation of the First Amendment.

The times did not remain calm. Not long after the *Lamont*
decision the country was bitterly, savagely divided over the
Vietnam War. The 1968 Democratic Convention in Chicago
saw street battles between antiwar protesters and squads of
police who brutally attacked the protesters. President Lyndon
Johnson privately fulminated against his critics, saying that
such eminent newspaper columnists as Walter Lippmann and
James B. Reston were dupes of communism. But he did not
use the federal prosecutorial power, as President Wilson had,
for widespread attempts to suppress political disagreement.
There were some prosecutions, notably of the antiwar group
that came to be known as the Chicago Seven. Their case
turned into a shouting match with an irascible, antagonistic
judge, Julius Hoffman. In the end, all convictions resulting
from that trial were overturned on appeal.

Divisions if anything deepened after the election of
Richard M. Nixon as president in 1968. Leading universities
were disrupted by student protests; Nixon referred to the protesters as "these bums." Speaking to the nation from the
White House on April 30, 1970, Nixon said he was widening

the war into Cambodia lest the United States be seen in the world as "a pitiful helpless giant." A few days later, at Kent State University in Ohio, national guardsmen fired their rifles at a group of unarmed students, killing four.

The Supreme Court's response to the Vietnam turmoil was utterly different from the Court's submission to the Wilson administration's prosecutions in 1919. The signal decision was in *Bond v. Floyd* in 1966. Julian Bond was elected to the Georgia House of Representatives, but the House voted to exclude him on the ground that he could not honestly swear—as required of members—to support the Georgia and federal constitutions. Bond, a significant black figure in the civil rights movement, had endorsed a statement by the movement's Student Nonviolent Coordinating Committee. It said, "We are in sympathy with, and support, the men in this country who are unwilling to respond to a military draft."

Bond explained to a Georgia legislative committee that he was not urging people to break laws but was simply trying "to say that I admired the courage of someone who could act on his convictions knowing that he faces pretty stiff consequences." The Supreme Court held unanimously that exclusion of Bond from the legislature violated the First Amendment. Chief Justice Warren's opinion said it needed no discussion to show that Bond could not, constitutionally, have been convicted of a crime for his statements. Eugene Debs, the Socialist Party leader, had been convicted in World War I and sentenced to ten years in prison for making very similar comments about the draft—and in 1919 the Supreme Court unanimously upheld his conviction.

Eugene Debs was pardoned by President Warren G. Harding in 1921. In 1920, Congress repealed the Sedition Act of 1918. In 1976, President Gerald Ford said the day the Japanese-Americans were removed from the West Coast in 1944 was "a sad day in American history"; in 1988, Congress passed and President Ronald Reagan signed an act giving modest compensation to survivors of the 1944 relocation program and saying that it had been motivated largely by "racial prejudice, wartime hysteria and a failure of political leadership."

Repeatedly, then, times of fear and stress were followed, some years after the fear ebbed, by regret and apology. But that pattern was challenged by the first episode of fear in the twenty-first century: the great national fear of terrorism after the attacks of September 11, 2001, on the World Trade Center and the Pentagon. President George W. Bush used that fear to adopt a series of programs that broke sharply with American law. He authorized the use of torture and other harsh methods of interrogation on suspected terrorists detained in a prison at Guantanamo Bay, Cuba, and elsewhere in secret CIA prisons. (Such treatment was in violation of the Geneva Conventions—treaties to which the United States was a party—and of a federal criminal statute.) He ordered wiretapping of Americans' international telephone calls, in violation of a criminal law. He detained American citizens suspected of terrorist ties indefinitely, without trial or access to counsel.

The war on terror, as President Bush called it, differed from the past times of war and fear in its endless quality. It was hard to envisage a point of victory when the world's terrorists would surrender: hard to imagine the most-publicized terrorist leader, Osama bin Laden, boarding an American ship to surrender as Japanese leaders did at the end of World War II. So it was difficult to see when a time might come for regret and apology for the cruel excesses of the war on terror.

Measures such as indefinite detention and torture did not engage the First Amendment. They were reminders that the freedoms of speech and of the press are not the only tests of a humane and free society. Freedom from arbitrary arrest, detention, and physical abuse is just as crucial. The central concern among the Framers of the American Constitution was concentrated power, and the checks and balances they built into our system of government were intended to prevent that kind of power. The aim of the Bush measures was to give the president precisely what the Framers had wanted to avoid: unilateral power unchecked by the other branches of government—and unchecked by the press. The Bush administration worked to exclude press scrutiny—and hence public accountability—by the most sweeping secrecy in American history. Even documents that had long been public were recalled and classified. Journalists who succeeded in exposing secret measures like the wiretapping order were threatened with prosecution for espionage.

Even in a country with constitutional guarantees of freedom, something more is needed to resist fear and its manipulators. That is courage. And there have been men and women of courage, lawyers and journalists and citizens, in all of America's crises. Two were in Montana in World War I, and they will serve as examples: Burton K. Wheeler, the

United States district attorney for the state (famous later as an isolationist senator before World War II), and the single federal district judge for Montana, George M. Bourquin. As described in Clemens Work's book, Wheeler persuaded a grand jury not to indict forty-eight Montanans brought in on sedition complaints in 1918. (The grand jurors had to be courageous, too, because their names were published.) Wheeler drafted a statement that the grand jury issued: "In many cases . . . it has been found by us that reports of so-called "seditious utterances" and "disloyal statements" were highly colored and greatly exaggerated. . . . The testimony disclosed complaints of words of a most trivial character showing a specie of hysteria prevalent in the minds of people in many communities. . . . "

Thanks to Wheeler, and to Judge Bourquin, there were no successful Espionage Act prosecutions in Montana. Judge Bourquin heard a petition for habeas corpus from a man who had been convicted of sedition under the state law for refusing to kiss the American flag. Bourquin decided that a federal judge could not intervene, but he wrote:

> Like religion, patriotism is a virtue so indispensable and ex-
> alted, its excesses pass with little censure. But when . . . it de-
> scends to fanaticism, it is of the reprehensible quality of the
> religion that incited the massacre of St. Bartholomew, the
> tortures of the Inquisition, the fires of Smithfield, the scaf-
> folds of Salem, and is equally cruel and murderous. In its
> name, as in that of Liberty, what crimes have been commit-
> ted! In every age it, too, furnishes its heresy hunters and its

witch burners, and it, too, is a favorite mask for hypocrisy, assuming a virtue which it haveth not.

I wonder whether Justice Robert H. Jackson was aware of Judge Bourquin's words when he wrote, decades later, in a case about a woman who was supposedly a risk to American security, Ellen Knauff: "Security is like liberty, in that many are the crimes committed in its name."

8

"Another's Lyric"

On February 22, 1971, in the Supreme Court chamber, Professor Melville B. Nimmer of the Law School of the University of California at Los Angeles rose to argue in the case of *Paul Robert Cohen v. California*. Before he could say a word, Chief Justice Warren E. Burger addressed him. "The Court is thoroughly familiar with the factual setting of this case," he said, "and it will not be necessary for you, I'm sure, to dwell on the facts." Nimmer said he would keep his statement of the facts brief. His client had been convicted of "engaging in tumultuous conduct," he said. "What this young man did was to walk through a courthouse corridor in Los Angeles County . . . wearing a jacket on which were inscribed the words 'Fuck the Draft.'"

Those were of course the words that Chief Justice Burger did not want to hear in the courtroom. (He may have been particularly sensitive because a group of nuns were there that day.) But Nimmer understood that to shy away from the words was in a sense to give his case away. He was courageous, he was wise, and he won the case. By a vote of 5 to 4, the Supreme Court reversed

Cohen's conviction, holding that it violated his right to free expression under the First Amendment.

Justice John Marshall Harlan, writing the opinion of the court, made of this trivial incident a luminous statement on freedom of expression. "One man's vulgarity is another's lyric," he said. In the context of the Vietnam War, the "unseemly expletive" Cohen used was a form of political protest. Justice Harlan went on:

> The constitutional right of free expression is powerful medicine in a society as diverse and populous as ours. It is designed and intended to remove governmental restraints from the arena of public discussion, putting the decision as to what views shall be voiced largely into the hands of each of us, in the hope that use of such freedom will ultimately produce a more capable citizenry and more perfect polity and in the belief that no other approach would comport with the premise of individual dignity and choice upon which our political system rests. . . . That the air may at times seem filled with verbal cacophony is, in this sense, not a sign of weakness but of strength.

Justice Harlan emphasized the political in his analysis of Cohen's use of the expletive. But it was sexual offensiveness that got Cohen arrested, and official disapproval of sexual content was a staple element in American legal conflict for many decades.

In the early years of the twentieth century such serious literary works as D.H. Lawrence's *Lady Chatterly's Lover* and

Theodore Dreiser's *An American Tragedy* were banned as obscene. Judges found a work obscene if any passage in it might have an unfortunate effect on susceptible readers, such as children. Then, in 1933, U.S. Customs seized a copy of the French edition of James Joyce's *Ulysses* as it was brought into the country. The novel, now generally considered a masterpiece, had been banned since 1920 when the New York Society for the Suppression of Vice complained about an episode in which Joyce's leading character, Leopold Bloom, masturbated. But after a trial over the customs seizure, Federal District Judge John M. Woolsey found that *Ulysses* was not obscene. He used a new test, judging a work by the effect of its dominant theme on an average reader. This more permissive standard—we might say more grown-up—was widely adopted.

In 1948 what was widely expected to be an important test case reached the Supreme Court. It was a ban on *Memoirs of Hecate County*, a novel by the eminent literary critic Edmund Wilson. (The objection was apparently to a passage about a woman's orgasm.) But one justice did not sit, and the Court then divided equally, 4 to 4. That was probably the last time the Supreme Court allowed a ban on a serious book to stand.

The Court's first broad pronouncement on censorship of the supposedly obscene came in 1957, in *Roth v. United States*. Sam Roth had been convicted of mailing an obscene publication in violation of a federal law. The Supreme Court affirmed the conviction. But the opinion seemed to look both ways, taking obscenity outside the protection of the First Amendment but defining it narrowly. Justice Brennan said that anything with "even the slightest redeeming social importance—unorthodox ideas, controversial ideas, even ideas hateful to the prevailing climate of opinion" was protected by the First Amendment. But history, he said, showed that obscenity had been treated as "utterly without redeeming social importance." In 1792, thirteen of the fourteen states that had ratified the Constitution provided for the prosecution of libel—and made "either blasphemy or profanity, or both, statutory crimes." So it was "apparent," Justice Brennan said, that obscenity, like libel, was "outside the protection intended for speech and press." (It was unusual for Justice Brennan, who was anything but an originalist in interpreting the Constitution, to rely on such history. And just seven years later, in *New York Times v. Sullivan*, he ended the historic exclusion of libel from the amendment's protection.)

"However," Justice Brennan went on, "sex and obscenity are not synonymous. . . . The portrayal of sex, e.g. in art, literature and scientific works, is not itself sufficient reason to deny material the constitutional protection of freedom of speech and press. Sex, a great and mysterious motive in human life, has indisputably been a subject of absorbing interest to mankind through the ages; it is one of the vital problems of human interest and public concern." So Justice Brennan propounded this test of what is censorable: "whether to the average person, applying contemporary community standards, the dominant theme of the material taken as a whole appeals to the prurient interest."

Justices Douglas and Black dissented, hewing to their position that the First Amendment ordains absolute freedom.

Justice Douglas's opinion said the amendment was intended to "preclude courts as well as legislatures from weighing the values of speech against silence." Douglas said he had "the same confidence in the ability of our people to reject noxious literature as I have in their capacity to sort out the true from the false in theology, economics, politics or any other field."

Movies engaged the Supreme Court as much as books. For a long time films were thought to be outside constitutional protection. But in 1952 the Court ended that assumption. In *Burstyn v. Wilson* it set aside a New York ban on a movie called *The Miracle* that had been found contemptuous of Christian religion. The Court said such thematic censorship was unconstitutional; Justice Tom C. Clark put it that the state had "no legitimate interest in protecting all or any religions from views distasteful to them. . . ."

Censorship of films with controversial themes was one thing. Provocative sexual scenes were quite another, and tortuously difficult for the Supreme Court to handle. The test for obscenity laid down by the *Roth* case was hardly self-executing. Judges, like everyone else, disagreed on whether particular films "appealed to the prurient interest" and on what "contemporary community standards" were. For a period of years the Supreme Court dealt with the problem by actually viewing the films at issue in a screening room set up in the court building. Justices Black and Douglas never came; they thought nothing could be banned. The other justices did. Justice Harlan, whose eyesight by then was severely impaired, brought a law clerk with him to tell him what was going on.

The result was chaos. In case after case the Supreme Court simply issued a brief order reversing or upholding a ban, with little or no explanation of how it came to that conclusion. In others, various justices issued conflicting opinions with no majority view emerging. In 1964, in *Jacobellis v. Ohio*, Justice Stewart offered, for himself, a much-quoted pronouncement, saying that criminal antiobscenity laws could be applied constitutionally only to "hard-core pornography." He doubted that he could intelligibly define what that was, Justice Stewart said; "but I know it when I see it, and the motion picture involved in this case is not that." Justice Brennan added a further element to the test he laid down in the *Roth* case: that, to be bannable, material must be "utterly without redeeming social value." A majority of the Court withdrew that requirement in 1973, giving local communities greater rights to define, and ban, obscenity. Justice Brennan, dissenting, said he had come to the view that his attempt to lay down a standard in *Roth* had not worked. He would abandon all restraints on alleged obscenity, he said, except those imposed to protect children and to prevent "unconsenting adults" from having pornography thrust upon them.

In those years the Court acted like a national film licensing board. It was a hopeless task, performed clumsily. Some critics argued that it was not only a daunting notion but one outside the proper scope of the First Amendment. Professor Robert H. Bork of the Yale Law School said the amendment's protection of speech and press should be limited to political expression. "There is no basis," he said, "for judicial intervention to protect any other form of expression, be it scientific, literary or that variety of expression we call obscene or pornographic." To go beyond the explicitly political, Bork argued, was to involve courts in value judgments that should be left to the political process. He also argued, in disagreement with Holmes and Brandeis and the whole course of constitutional interpretation since 1930, that the First Amendment should not protect advocacy of law violation or overthrow of the government. (Bork became a judge, was nominated to the Supreme Court by President Reagan, and rejected by the Senate.)

On the particular issue of protecting sexual expression, critics made a number of arguments. One was that allowing pornography made for a coarser society. Bork suggested that it caused a "pollution of the moral and aesthetic atmosphere precisely analogous to smoke pollution," altering "attitudes toward love and sex . . . and views of social institutions such as marriage and the family."

Perhaps reflecting the idea that pornography can be a form of pollution, or perhaps in accordance with Justice Brennan's concern about unconsenting adults having it thrust upon them, a number of cities limited the locations where adult theaters could operate. In 1986, by a vote of 5 to 4, the Supreme Court upheld a local zoning law providing, among other things, that such a theater could not be located within 500 feet of a residential area. Television and radio broadcasting, regulated by the Federal Communications Commission (FCC), has been seen by the Court as posing a danger of offending unconsenting listeners and viewers. In 1978 the Court upheld an FCC finding that a radio station had violated the law by broadcasting a monologue by the comedian George Carlin on "seven dirty words."

Another argument against constitutional protection for pornography, made by a leading feminist law professor, Catherine MacKinnon, was that it was a way of subordinating women. The city of Indianapolis adopted an ordinance criminalizing pornography on that basis, but the United States Court of Appeals for the Seventh Circuit held it unconstitutional. In 1986 a commission appointed by President Reagan's attorney general, Edwin L. Meese, found that sexually violent material could cause antisocial conduct and that "degrading" material could "increase acceptance of the proposition that women like to be forced into sexual practices." The data offered by the commission were widely questioned.

There are powerful reasons to disagree with the critics and support constitutional protection for artistic, literary, and scientific expression, including the sexual. Zealots have made their mark in American history with censorship of all kinds. Politicians often find it easier to play to what H.L. Mencken, that coruscating critic of American foolishness, called the "booboisie." Independent judges like John M. Woolsey can stand against the mob that wants to ban a *Ulysses*, usually without having read it. The Supreme Court is well-placed to counter local pressure groups that have persuaded politicians to ban a film like *The Miracle*. A national, constitutional forum has its value. The expression that opens the minds of a people is not limited to the political.

Moreover, sex and politics can be intermingled. That was true in *Cohen v. California*. And it was true in a case that came before the Supreme Court in 1988, *Hustler v. Falwell*. Its facts made Paul Robert Cohen's rude jacket look like a Sunday school lesson. Campari, the aperitif, had run a series of magazine advertisements labeled "the first time"—the first time those portrayed had tasted Campari but, by innuendo, their first sexual encounter. *Hustler* magazine ran what it called a "parody advertisement" saying that the Reverend Jerry Falwell's "first time" was with his mother in an outhouse. Falwell sued for libel and intentional infliction of emotional distress. A jury rejected the libel claim, reasoning that the ad could not be taken as fact, but awarded $150,000 for emotional distress.

In the Supreme Court, a brief as friend of the court was filed by the Association of American Editorial Cartoonists. It consisted of political cartoons from American history, starting with one that showed George Washington as an ass and including the famous Thomas Nast cartoons of Boss Tweed and his Tammany Hall political gang as vultures. At the argument—an extraordinary one—the justices repeatedly referred to the cartoons. At one point, counsel for *Hustler* said the George Washington example showed that in the open American society even revered leaders had been subjected to vicious lampooning. Justice Scalia responded that he thought "old George" could stand that, "but with your mother in an outhouse?" The Court unanimously set aside Falwell's damage judgment. The opinion, by Chief Justice William H. Rehnquist, relied on the libel decision in *New York Times v. Sullivan*. Even when couched as a claimed deliberate infliction of emotional distress, Chief Justice Rehnquist said, a suit for damage to a public figure's amour propre could not succeed unless he or she proved that what was said was deliberately or recklessly false—and a lampoon could not be factually false.

Americans today would find it hard to believe what was suppressed in the past, and not only the distant past. In 1956 a San Francisco bookseller, Lawrence Ferlinghetti, was prosecuted for selling Allen Ginsberg's poem "Howl." A municipal judge, Clayton W. Horn, ended that repressive folly. "The best method of censorship is by the people," he said, "as self-guardians of public opinion, and not by the government."

As to suppression of pornography on film, in the end courts became irrelevant. Technology and public opinion overtook all the legal logic-chopping. By the end of the twentieth century, millions of Americans were watching, on their computers or on cable television, what Justice Stewart would have described as hard-core pornography. The Federal Communications Commission stuck doggedly to its role as nanny, imposing heavy fines on broadcasters who televised the 2004 Superbowl game in which Janet Jackson, in a halftime show, unexpectedly exposed a breast. But most Americans probably couldn't care less.

Or most people in other Western societies. Britain, for example, was long regarded as a straitlaced country. For centuries, plays had to be submitted to the Lord Chamberlain for approval before they were produced; he blue-penciled anything suggestive or disrespectful of authority. Parliament abolished that requirement in 1968. And the top-selling tabloid in Britain (and the world), Rupert Murdoch's *Sun*, publishes every day a photograph of a topless model with much more of a come-hither look than Janet Jackson.

The critics' objections may be futile now, but they are right to worry about the flood of pornography and the general coarsening of our societies. There is a difference between *Ulysses* and adult movies, so called. When literature no longer has room for subtle intimations of love and sex—no room, say, for Jane Austen—we are the losers. But the bluenoses who kept Americans from reading Joyce and Lawrence made censorship intellectually unacceptable, and attempts to draw a line somewhere else—by judges and politicians— did not work.

9

"Vagabonds and Outlaws"

In Dickens's *Martin Chuzzlewit*, the eponymous hero sails to America on a packet boat. In New York harbor it is boarded by newsboys who cry out the latest in their papers—the *New York Stabber*, the *Peeper*, the *Family Spy* and so on. "Here's the Sewer!" shouts one. "Here's the Sewer's exposure of the Wall Street Gang, and the Sewer's exposure of the Washington gang, and the Sewer's exclusive account of a flagrant act of dishonesty committed by the Secretary of State when he was eight years old; now communicated, at a great expense, by his own nurse."

The nineteenth-century American press could certainly be, well, piquant. But the odd thing is that a century later American newspapers had moved toward respectability, while the British press could be almost beyond Dickensian parody in the extravagance of its make-believe.

In 1982 an unemployed Englishman, Michael Fagan, got into Buckingham Palace one night and made his way into the Queen's bedroom, where he had a chat with her. The *Sunday People*, a weekly, said it had polled its readers on what should be done, and the answer was that the Queen and Prince Philip should share a double bed. The story ran on page one under the headline, "Give Her a Cuddle, Philip."

My favorite example of British tabloid style began on February 25, 1987, when *The Sun* published a story with this lead: "Elton John is at the center of a shocking drugs and vice scandal involving teen-age 'rent boys', The Sun can reveal today." "Rent boy" is British journalese for male prostitute. The story said its source was one "Graham X." The next day's *Sun* relied on Graham X for a story saying, "Kinky superstar Elton John loved to snort cocaine through rolled-up $100 bills." John denied both stories and brought two libel actions against *The Sun*. Over the following months, there were many more stories, each followed by a libel writ. The last was headlined "Mystery of Elton's Silent Dogs." John, it said, had had his "vicious Rottweiler dogs" silenced by a "horrific operation." John sued again: his seventeenth libel action since the start of *The Sun*'s campaign.

For some reason, possibly the English fondness for dogs, the last of the suits was scheduled for trial first: on December 12, 1988. That morning, *The Sun*'s banner headline was "Sorry Elton." *The Sun* had settled the seventeen lawsuits by paying John 1 million pounds in damages and about half as much again for his legal fees. "We are delighted that The Sun and Elton have become friends again," the paper said, "and we are sorry that we were lied to by a teenager living in a world of fantasy." The "apology" was for the boy's lies, not for the editors' credulousness or, more likely, coaching.

British editors and reporters stayed longer than their American counterparts with the old model of their trade: raffish, disrespectful. But the classic portrayal of the old style was American: the 1930s stage comedy *The Front Page* and its movie version, *Our Gal Friday*. Reporters sat around the press room drinking whiskey out of paper cups and trading lies. The hero hid an escaped criminal in a rolltop desk. The demon editor demanded that the exclusive story have the paper's name in the lead paragraph (like the first of *The Sun*'s fictions about Elton John). They were ruffian reporters, street-smart but without intellectual or social pretensions.

In the mid–twentieth century, American reporters began drinking white wine. They had college, some even graduate degrees. And their ambitions climbed. They wanted to be in Washington, the center of the world. They wanted to go to dinner parties with the secretary of state. That is a bit of a caricature, but not much. Reporters used to be outsiders, badly paid. Now they, at any rate those in Washington and others among the top in the profession, are part of the establishment, upper-middle class in outlook. They call themselves journalists instead of reporters. There is a danger in all that: the danger of becoming too close to power. It is a palpable danger in Washington. Writing critically about a cabinet member is hard after sitting next to his or her spouse at a dinner party.

A notable British columnist, Bernard Levin of *The Times* of London, warned tellingly against the press's assuming "responsibility"—using that word in an English sense of commitment to official institutions. "The press," he wrote, "has no duty to be responsible at all, and it will be an ill day for freedom if it should ever acquire one. . . . We are and must remain vagabonds and outlaws, for only by so remaining shall we be able to keep the faith by which we live, which is the pursuit of knowledge that others would like unpursued and the making of comments that others would prefer unmade." (Levin loved champagne and opera, as it happened, but that did not stop him from scourging the mighty when they went wrong.)

The highest duty of the press—to inform the public about its governors—was defined in the earliest days of the United States by James Madison. In a republic, he said, the people are the ultimate sovereigns; they depend for their information on the press, which must therefore be free to "canvass the merits and measures of public men." Madison was something of a romantic about the press. He wrote in 1799: "To the press alone, chequered as it is with abuses, the world is indebted for all the triumphs which have been gained by reason and humanity over error and oppression."

The American press has to perform its Madisonian function today in relation to a federal government that Madison could scarcely have imagined. It was tiny in his day, and it remained modest in size and role until Franklin Roosevelt's New Deal in the 1930s; as New Deal programs went into effect, new governmental agencies were born and the government in Washington began to assume responsibilities that had formerly been exercised by the states or by no government. Now the federal government is huge and powerful. Its officials often operate in secret, and they are protected by armies of spokesmen. A government that George Washington warned to avoid foreign entanglements is entangled politically and militarily around the world.

Coping with a government of that character requires press institutions with large resources. The raggle-taggle newspapers of the eighteenth century could not have coped with the Pentagon, and neither can their contemporary equivalent, bloggers. It took a newspaper as established as the *Washington Post* to carry off the investigation of Watergate, and as the *New York Times* to publish the Pentagon Papers. Each of those episodes required, as well, proprietors of courage in the face of economic and legal threats: Katharine Graham of the *Post* and Arthur Ochs Sulzberger of the *Times*.

In his opinion in the Pentagon Papers case, Justice Stewart said the role of the press was especially important in matters of national security. In that area, he said, the usual legislative and judicial checks and balances on executive power scarcely operate; Congress and the courts tend to defer to the president. So, he wrote, "the only effective restraint upon executive policy and power . . . may lie in an enlightened citizenry—in an informed and critical public opinion. For this reason, it is perhaps here that a press that is alert, aware and free most vitally serves the purpose of the First Amendment. For without an informed and free press there cannot be an enlightened people."

To Justice Stewart's adjectives—informed, free, alert, aware—must be added courageous. By those standards, the American press failed sadly when it met its next great test after Vietnam: the government's policy and power after the terrorist attacks on New York and Washington on September 11, 2001.

Within a few months of those attacks President George W. Bush claimed the power to detain any American citizen as an enemy combatant and hold him or her indefinitely, without trial or access to counsel. His attorney general ordered thousands of aliens swept up and held for months on suspicion, often humiliated and physically abused. (Not one was convicted of an offense related to terrorism.)

President Bush and his aides set about preparing the way for a war on Iraq by trying to persuade the American public that the Iraqi regime of Saddam Hussein had been involved in the September 11 terrorist attacks. Their propaganda campaign was extraordinarily successful. By March 2003, just before the war was launched, polls showed that 45 percent of Americans believed Saddam Hussein was "personally involved" in the September 11 attacks, and 44 percent said that some of the men who hijacked planes that day were Iraqis. Both beliefs were untrue, indeed preposterous. So much for the "enlightened citizenry" that Justice Stewart said was essential.

Where was the press in that period? The kindest answer would be: out to lunch. When the government seized two American citizens and detained them without trial as "enemy combatants," there were brief newspaper stories—with no sense of the constitutional stakes. The sweep of aliens got little attention until it was long over. The march toward war in Iraq had so little scrutiny that both the *Washington Post* and the *New York Times* later apologized for their failure. When a protest march took place in Washington before the Iraq invasion, a story in the *Post* mocked the demonstrators as "dudes" and "Patchouli girls."

Watergate and Vietnam had seemed to signal a new attitude on the part of what could be called the establishment press. In the years after World War II, it had treated federal officials with deferential respect. The leading correspondents and columnists shared the government's viewpoint on the commanding issue of the day, the contest with the Soviet Union. They credited officials with good faith and superior knowledge. Those assumptions collapsed in the Vietnam War. Correspondents there reported the situation far more accurately than official statements, and high officials engaged in deliberate deception.

Professors Harold Edgar and Benno Schmidt Jr. of the Columbia Law School wrote afterward that the *Times*'s decision to publish the Pentagon Papers symbolized "the passing of an era in which newsmen could be counted upon to work within reasonably well understood boundaries in disclosing information that politicians deemed sensitive." There had been a "symbiotic relationship between politicians and the press," they said, but now the press "intended to become an adversary."

What happened to those brave words after September 11? Instead of acting as a critic, or even a skeptic, the press performed more like a stenographer for official views. It printed President Bush's statements about his "war on terror" without paying particular note to the extraordinary power he was asserting. It hardly raised an eyebrow when the attorney general, John Ashcroft, told a Senate hearing: "To those who scare peace-loving people with phantoms of lost liberty, my message is this: Your tactics only aid terrorists, for they erode our national unity and diminish our resolve. They give ammunition to America's enemies."

Why was the press so submissive after 9/11? One reason was that, like the American public generally, editors were stunned by the terrorist attacks and felt the need for national unity against the perpetrators. That meant, for most, uniting behind the president. Moreover, to criticize the president in the atmosphere of fear could seem unpatriotic. Indeed, Attorney General Ashcroft had said that disagreement was unpatriotic. The sense of intimidation came also from the extreme right-wing voices on radio and television talk shows, one of whom said she regretted that the offices of the *New York Times* had not been bombed.

The extent of press submissiveness to the White House was demonstrated by broadcasters a month after 9/11. When five major television networks broadcast a taped message by Osama bin Laden, the terrorist leader, President Bush's national security adviser, Condoleezza Rice, got top executives of the networks on a conference telephone call. She urged them to eliminate "inflammatory language" from any future bin Laden tapes they used. She also warned that his talks might include coded instructions to terrorists—a singularly unpersuasive point, since his tapes had first been broadcast on an Arabic-language network. The American network executives agreed to broadcast only short segments of any future tapes. One of them said, "We're not going to step on the landmines she [Rice] was talking about." A more candid statement would have been, "We don't want to look unpatriotic."

In time, the press began to recover from its fear and lassitude. The brazen character of President Bush's claims of unilateral power became increasingly hard to overlook. One of his Justice Department lawyers advised him that he could order the torture of alleged terrorist detainees, and that Congress was without power to stop him. As a result of that legal opinion, dozens of foreign detainees were tortured, and some killed. Pictures of tortured men in Abu Ghraib prison in Iraq shocked the country.

The end of the deferential time was signaled by the decision of the *New York Times* to publish a story disclosing that President Bush had secretly ordered wiretapping of Americans' international telephone calls without obtaining the warrants required by law. The order was an explicit violation of a federal criminal statute. Once again, as in the legal memorandum claiming a presidential power to order torture, the assertion was that the president was above the law. That was the exact opposite of what was thought to be the lesson of Watergate: that the law applied to the high as to the low. The press could not, and did not, miss the growing evidence of abuse of power. Right-wing voices accused the *Times* of "treason" for publishing the story about warrantless wiretapping, and the reporters who wrote it were threatened with subpoenas for their sources. But the paper stood its ground, and the reporters won the Pulitzer Prize.

Because I spent years in England, I find informative the difference between British and American attitudes toward press freedom. In 1981 a civil-liberties organization brought suit on behalf of a prisoner who said he had been mistreated in a British jail. The prisoner's lawyer, Harriet Harman, asked for documents on the prison rules. The government objected, but the trial judge ordered that some of them be given to Harman. She read them out in open court. A newspaper reporter, uncertain of his shorthand, asked her for a copy. She gave it to him—and for that was convicted of contempt of court. On appeal, Lord Denning said: "There was no public interest in having the highly confidential documents in the present case made public. It was in the public interest that they should remain confidential. The use made of them by the journalist in the present case was highly detrimental to the good ordering of our society. They [were] used to launch a wholly unjustified attack on ministers of state and high civil servants who were only doing their best to deal with a wicked criminal."

That statement, one must remember, was made about the "disclosure" of a document that had already been read out in open court. It was made about someone who may have been a wicked criminal but was, at the time, in the custody of government officials, so that any cruelty to which he was subjected was a matter of public concern. But Harman's conviction was affirmed.

The outrage of the Harman case could not happen in Britain today. The law has caught up with the demands of a free society. Parliament passed a law making the provisions of the European Convention on Human Rights apply in British courts. One of those provisions calls for freedom of the press.

A case like Harriet Harman's could not have happened in the United States, not unless some distracted judge ignored the law—the law of the First Amendment. The use of the contempt power of judges to silence comment on legal matters was rejected by the Supreme Court in 1941 in the historic case of *Bridges v. California.*

Harry Bridges was the left-wing leader of the West Coast longshoremen's union. When a California state judge decided a case that affected his union in a way he did not like, Bridges sent a telegram to the U.S. secretary of labor criticizing the decision. The judge held him in contempt of court for that criticism. The Supreme Court considered the contempt order along with another from California, against the *Los Angeles Times.* Its offense was the publication of editorials about a criminal case in which two members of the Teamsters Union had been convicted of assault. The editorials said the trial judge would make "a serious mistake" if he sentenced them to probation; the community needed "the example of their assignment to the jute mill." (There was a fine irony in the coupling of the *Times* and Bridges on the same side in the Supreme Court. The *Times* was a strongly conservative, anti-union paper then, and its particular bête noir was Harry Bridges.)

In the Supreme Court, a drama was played out behind the scenes that only came into public view more than forty years later, in an exploration of Justice Black's papers after his

death. The case was first argued in October 1940. In conference, the justices voted 6 to 3 to affirm the two contempt convictions. Chief Justice Hughes assigned the majority opinion
to Justice Frankfurter. Frankfurter greatly admired English
law, and that came through in the draft opinion he circulated
to his colleagues. The power of judges to punish outside comment on matters pending in their courts, he said, is "part and
parcel of the Anglo-American system of administering justice.
. . . It is believed that all the judicatures of the English-speaking world . . . have from time to time recognized and exercised the power. . . . "

Justice Black circulated a dissent that said:

[T]he basic fallacy of the Court's opinion is the assumption
that the vitalizing liberties of the First Amendment can be
abridged . . . by reference to English judicial practice. . . . In
my judgment, to measure the scope of the liberties guaranteed by the First Amendment by the limitations that exist or
have existed throughout the English-speaking world is to
obtain a result directly opposite to that which the framers of
the Amendment intended. . . . Perhaps no single purpose
emerges more clearly from the history of our Constitution
and Bill of Rights than that of giving far more security to the
people of the United States with respect to freedom of religion, conscience, expression, assembly, petition and press
than the people of Great Britain had ever enjoyed. . . . The
First Amendment is proof conclusive that the framers of our
government were well aware of the suppression of conscience and expression that had been indulged in abroad,

both in England and elsewhere, and intended by the First Amendment to see that they did not happen here.

In the spring of 1941 one justice in the *Bridges* majority retired, and another changed his mind. That made the vote 4 to 4, and the Court ordered the case reargued the following fall. Before then Hughes retired, so it was 4 to 3 for reversal of the contempt convictions. Two new justices split, Robert H. Jackson for reversal and James F. Byrnes to uphold the convictions. Justice Black had a 5-to-4 majority and now wrote the opinion of the Court.

The *Bridges* decision was announced by the Supreme Court on December 8, 1941. The justices went on the bench after walking over to the Capitol in the morning to hear President Roosevelt denounce the Japanese attack on Pearl Harbor. ("Yesterday, December seventh, 1941, a date which will live in infamy. . . . ") In the circumstances, the decision did not get much attention. But it was in fact a turning point in constitutional history. It was the opening round in years of conflict between Justices Black and Frankfurter over whether the First Amendment guarantee of freedom of speech should be read broadly, as Black urged, or in a more limited way. The majority opinion in the *Bridges* case was a declaration of independence from the English legal tradition. That revolution was carried on twenty-three years later in *New York Times v. Sullivan*, breaking decisively with the English common-law rules that heavily favored libel plaintiffs.

The American press has been given extraordinary freedom by the Supreme Court's interpretations of the First Amendment.

In return, it owes society courage. It must resist the lure of obeisance to power. Its reporters and editors must remain freebooters—vagabonds and outlaws, as Bernard Levin put it. Only then can they perform the press's patriotic function of holding government to account.

10

Thoughts That
We Hate

It was in the case of a pacifist that Justice Holmes spoke of "freedom for the thought that we hate." But suppose it were not a pacifist but a Nazi. Would that change her right to freedom of expression? Should it?

Hate speech, it is called: virulent attacks on Jews, blacks, Muslims, homosexuals, or members of any other group. It is pure hatred, not based on any wrong done by an individual. A German may have been a practicing Roman Catholic; but if the Nazis found that he had a Jewish grandfather, off he went to a death camp.

The United States differs from almost all other Western societies in its legal treatment of hate speech. In Germany it is a crime, a serious one, to display the swastika or any other Nazi symbol. In eleven European countries it is a crime to say that the Holocaust did not happen, that Germans in the Nazi years did not slaughter Jews. So it is in Canada, and the Canadian Supreme

Court has decided that Holocaust deniers can be prosecuted and punished despite that country's constitutional guarantee of free expression. In the United States, the First Amendment protects the right to deny the fact of the Holocaust.

At one point the Supreme Court took a different view of bans on hateful speech. In 1952, in the case of *Beauharnais v. Illinois*, it sustained an Illinois law that made it a crime to distribute any publication that "portrays depravity, criminality, unchastity or lack of virtue of a class of citizens, of any race, color, creed or religion," exposing them to contempt or being "productive of breach of the peace or riots." Joseph Beauharnais had distributed a leaflet urging Chicago authorities to stop the "invasion of white . . . neighborhoods and persons by the Negro."

Justice Frankfurter, writing the opinion for a 5–4 majority, saw the Illinois law as a group form of criminal libel—which had existed in the American states from the beginning. "Illinois did not have to look beyond her own borders or await the tragic experience of the last three decades," Frankfurter said, "to conclude that wilful purveyors of falsehood concerning racial and religious groups promote strife. . . . " He instanced the murder in 1837 of Elijah Parish Lovejoy, a newspaper editor in Alton, in southern Illinois, because he favored the abolition of slavery, and recent race riots in the Chicago area. "Libellous utterances," he said, were not "within the area of constitutionally protected speech." Justice Black, dissenting, said that the Illinois law was entirely different from statutes against libel of individuals, and much more subject to abuse. Any minority group that welcomed the decision, he said, should remember Pyrrhus's statement: "Another such victory and I am undone."

The logical premise of Justice Frankfurter's *Beauharnais* opinion was undone by the 1964 decision in *New York Times v. Sullivan*, which ended the exclusion of libel from the protection of the First Amendment. Under *Sullivan* and cases stemming from it, public officials and public figures cannot recover damages for libel unless they can prove that a false statement of fact was published knowingly or recklessly. The generalized smear of hate speech—a Beauharnais pamphlet, for example—does not lend itself to the factual analysis contemplated by these later decisions, however vicious the smear may have been. That was so, the Court indicated, even when the viciousness was directed at an individual, as in *Hustler* magazine's attack on Jerry Falwell.

Moreover, the Court in 1969 put extremely tight restrictions on criminal punishment for speech attacking racial or religious groups. That was the case of *Brandenburg v. Ohio*, discussed in Chapter 7. The speaker there, a Ku Klux Klan leader, said, "Personally, I believe the nigger should be returned to Africa, the Jew returned to Israel." The Supreme Court unanimously reversed his conviction because there was no proof that the speaker was inciting "imminent lawless action" or that such action was likely to occur.

The issue of free speech for Nazis is symbolized in American law by the word "Skokie." Skokie is a village near Chicago that in 1977 had a large Jewish population, including a substantial number who were survivors of Nazi concentration camps. An American Nazi party announced that it would hold a demonstration in Skokie, with the demonstrators wearing a swastika, the Hitler symbol. The village authorities passed ordinances that among other things prohibited the dissemination of anything, including signs and clothing, that "incites hatred against persons by reason of their race, national origin, or religion." The authorities also sought an injunction to the same effect from the Illinois courts. Cases went through state and federal courts. The ultimate judgment was by the United States Court of Appeals for the Seventh Circuit, which held that the village ordinances designed to stop the demonstration were unconstitutional. The Nazi group then canceled its plan.

The Skokie episode created wide controversy among civil libertarians. Many members of the American Civil Liberties Union resigned because the ACLU had supported the Nazis' right to march. But the ACLU leadership did not budge, and in the end its stand probably improved its public standing and enlarged its membership.

Roger Errera, a French legal scholar and jurist, said that Europeans would not accept American tolerance for hateful speech, as in the Skokie case. The American view, he suggested, must be based on "an inveterate social and historical optimism"—which Europeans could not be expected to share after their tragic experience at the hands of the Nazis and Communists. Hitler had made his murderous intentions plain enough in *Mein Kampf*. Wouldn't it have been better to imprison him for such expression before he could organize his words into horrendous reality?

That is the dominant view in Europe, but it is not the only one. *The Economist*, the British weekly with an orientation toward the United States, made strong arguments in 2006 against laws criminalizing Holocaust denial and other forms of racist speech. Such laws, it warned, could be interpreted to punish or restrain speech that "merely causes offense." It instanced the example of Oriana Fallaci, the great Italian journalist, who when she died in 2006 was awaiting trial for offending Islam in a critical essay about the religion. "The big danger," *The Economist* wrote, "is that, in the name of stopping bigots, one may end up by stopping all criticism."

A notorious English Holocaust-denier, David Irving, served thirteen months in an Austrian prison in 2006–2007 for speeches he made in that country. Irving had sued an American author, Deborah Lipstadt, for libel for calling him a denier; an English judge, in a devastating judgment, found that the characterization was true. But Lipstadt said she regretted his imprisonment in Austria, which made him "a martyr to free speech."

The conflict over how to deal with hate speech grew more intense with the rise of Islamic extremism and terrorist acts at the beginning of the twenty-first century. Britain, one of several European countries with a substantial Muslim population, faced the issue particularly acutely. A number of imams allegedly urged violent jihad in sermons in their mosques. One was prosecuted and convicted for soliciting murder and racial hatred. A leader of a British Islamist group, Atilla Ahmet, said: "You are attacking our people in Muslim countries, in Iraq, in Afghanistan. So it's legitimate to attack British soldiers and policemen, government officials and even the White House." In July 2005 four Muslim suicide bombers killed fifty-two people in London subways and on a bus. A militant spokesman, Abu Izzadeen, called the bombings "praiseworthy." In 2007 he was arrested for a later speech and charged with encouraging terrorism.

The great statement of reasons for allowing even the most noxious speech was made by Brandeis in his opinion in *Whitney v. California:* "Discussion affords ordinarily adequate protection against the dissemination of noxious doctrine," he wrote. And, "The fitting remedy for evil counsels is good ones." But even the Supreme Court's highly tolerant decision in *Brandenburg v. Ohio* in 1969 would allow legal action against speech that is intended to incite imminent lawlessness and is likely to do so. Doesn't a call for the murder of police and other officials pass that test, given the fact of actual murders in the Islamist cause? Given the context—an actual terrorist bombing in Britain—the *Brandenburg* requirement of imminence seems to me inappropriate.

One of the arguments for allowing hateful speech is that it makes the rest of us aware of terrible beliefs and strengthens our resolve to combat them. This argument was rudely countered by Jeremy Waldron, an Englishman who emigrated to teach law in the United States. He wrote:

> The costs of hate speech . . . are not spread evenly across the community that is supposed to tolerate them. The [racists] of the world may not harm the people who call for their toleration, but then few of them are depicted as animals in posters plastered around Leamington Spa [an English town]. We should speak to those who are depicted in this way, or those whose suffering or whose parents' suffering is mocked

by the [Skokie neo-Nazis] before we conclude that tolerating this sort of speech builds character.

Something like Jeremy Waldron's view animated a movement, in the 1980s and 1990s, to ban hateful speech on university campuses. Spurred by members of minority groups, the movement aimed at racist speech. Proponents of banning hate speech against minorities said students who were victimized by such speech were traumatized by it. To deal with the problem, some professors and students called for the adoption of speech codes, with penalties for violations.

A significant number of universities adopted speech codes. In practice, they dealt with hurtful comments on a wide range of matters beyond the original proposal, race. One of the best-known codes, adopted by Stanford University, prohibited "harassment by personal vilification" when it was "intended to stigmatize an individual or a small number of individuals on the basis of their sex, race, color, handicap, religion, sexual orientation, or national and ethnic origin." A code proposed by the University of Massachusetts at Amherst in 1995 added to those subjects "age, marital status, veteran status." The graduate students' union there wanted to add "citizenship, culture, H.I.V. status, language, parental status, political belief and pregnancy."

The lengthening list of characteristics to be protected from harassing speech brought ridicule on the speech-code campaign. In 1989 a federal court held the University of Michigan code unconstitutional. Stanford's failed a legal test a few years later. And the campaign ebbed.

No one can doubt that black students and others had historically been subjected to viciousness at some universities, not limited to speech. But once the attempt to deal with the problem by speech codes got going, it became too easy a target for critics of political correctness. Even a sense of humor seemed endangered. A Harvard Law School professor drew protests when he quoted an opinion by Justice Robert H. Jackson. The trouble was that Jackson had used a quote from a poem by Byron: the famous lines about Julia, "who, swearing she would ne'er consent, consented."

The attempt to censor what is said at universities has not been limited to such foolishness. In 2003 the House of Representatives passed a bill called the International Studies in Higher Education Act. It would have required the secretary of education, in allocating federal funds to universities, to consider whether foreign language or area studies courses reflected diverse perspectives. It would have created an advisory board to "study, monitor, appraise and evaluate" university programs supported by federal funds. A principal supporter of the bill, Representative Howard Berman of California, said he was concerned about "anti-American bias" in Middle East studies programs. There was evidence, he said, that many Middle East studies grantees had a point of view that "questions the validity of advancing American ideals of democracy and the rule of law" in the Middle East and elsewhere.

Most American colleges and universities get federal aid of one kind or another. Under such legislation, their faculties and administrators would have had to worry about whether their classes conformed to the ideas, and very likely the ideology, of a federal board. Yet the very premise of Representative Berman's argument for it, that "advancing American ideals of democracy" in the Middle East was a wise idea, was controversial, to put it mildly. That premise played a large part in creating the disaster of the Iraq War. Universities above all should be places where ideas are challenged.

The largest controversy about offensive speech in modern America concerned not a verbal utterance but symbolic expression: burning the flag. During the Republican National Convention in 1984 a group of demonstrators marched through the streets protesting the policies of the Reagan administration. One of them, Gregory Lee Johnson, set an American flag on fire in front of the Dallas City Hall. He was convicted of violating a Texas law that prohibited desecration of a "venerated object." The Supreme Court, by a vote of 5 to 4, reversed his conviction, finding the flag-burning expressive conduct that was protected by the First Amendment. "If there is a bedrock principle underlying the First Amendment," Justice Brennan wrote in the opinion of the Court, "it is that the government may not prohibit the expression of an idea simply because society finds the idea itself offensive or disagreeable."

Many Americans indeed found the burning of the flag offensive. Congress came close to approving a constitutional amendment to allow the criminalizing of flag-burning. It did pass a criminal statute, the Flag Protection Act of 1989, to punish anyone who, except to dispose of a worn or soiled flag, "mutilates, defaces, physically defiles, burns, maintains on the floor or ground, or tramples upon any flag of the United States." In *United States v. Eichman* in 1990 the Supreme

Court, by the identical 5–4 vote, held that statute unconstitutional. Justice Brennan, writing again for the majority, said the very list of prohibitions showed that the concern behind the act was "disrespectful treatment" of the flag. Thus the act "suppresses expression out of concern for its likely communicative impact." Justice Brennan concluded: "Punishing desecration of the flag dilutes the very freedom that makes this emblem so revered, and worth revering."

In the catalog of hateful or offensive expression, burning a flag is surely less dangerous than most other examples: anti-Semitic ravings in a Munich beer hall, say, or preaching to young Muslims in England that they should become suicide-bombers. (One worshipper who heard such sermons, Richard Reid, tried unsuccessfully to blow up an airliner with a bomb in his shoe.)

In 1994 broadcasts on a radio station in Rwanda urged Hutus, who were a majority of the population, to kill Tutsis, the minority, and moderate-minded Hutus. A massacre followed, and more than 500,000 people were killed. Years later a Tutsi-led government forbade political parties to appeal to group identity, and public statements promoting "divisionism" were outlawed. Should we in America who have avoided such tragedies tell Rwandans that it is wrong for them thus to limit freedom of speech?

In an age when words have inspired acts of mass murder and terrorism, it is not as easy for me as it once was to believe that the only remedy for evil counsels, in Brandeis's phrase, should be good ones. The law of the American Constitution allows suppression only when violence or violation of law are intended by speakers and are likely to take place imminently. But perhaps judges, and the rest of us, will be more on guard now for the rare act of expression—not the burning of a flag or the racist slang of an undergraduate—that is genuinely dangerous. I think we should be able to punish speech that urges terrorist violence to an audience some of whose members are ready to act on the urging. That is imminence enough.

11

Balancing Interests

Since the middle of the twentieth century, the idea of the First Amendment has acquired a powerful hold on the American imagination. Even conservatives, who had been found on the repressive side of speech controversies, now join in exaltation of freedom of expression. People invoke "the First Amendment" as if those words would settle whatever issue was being debated. But in truth the freedoms of speech and of the press have never been absolutes. The courts and society have repeatedly struggled to accommodate other interests along with those.

A long-running example is the effort to square freedom of the press with protection of the right to fair trial. How can a defendant get an unbiased jury if newspapers and broadcasters have convicted him in graphic terms before the trial begins? The Supreme Court dealt with the issue over a period of nearly forty years. Once again, the starting point was English practice.

In 1949 a series of murder victims were found in London with bite marks in their necks. Inevitably, the popular papers called the unknown murderer "the vampire killer." On March

4, 1949, the *Daily Mirror*, then the largest-selling tabloid, carried the headline: "Vampire—A Man Held." The lead, a tabloid classic of its day, said: "The Vampire Killer will never strike again. He is safely behind bars, powerless to lure victims to a hideous death. This is the assurance which the *Daily Mirror* can give today. It is the considered conclusion of the finest detective brains in the country." The story did not give the name of the person "safely behind bars." But on an inside page, a short piece said a man called John George Haigh was helping the police with their inquiries—tabloidese for being questioned by the police—in an unidentified criminal investigation.

The editor of the *Mirror* was Silvester Bolam, known to his colleagues as Bishop Bolam because he habitually wore a black suit and white shirt. Bolam was summoned to court, where a judge sentenced him to three months in prison for contempt by endangering a suspect's fair trial. Bolam was taken from the courtroom to serve his sentence, and he never worked in journalism again.

That was the British system for discouraging pretrial comment in criminal cases: short and sharp. And it still is, though erring editors are now more likely to be fined than imprisoned. That is what happened, for example, when the *Sunday People* said the way to protect the Queen from marauders in Buckingham Palace was "Give Her a Cuddle, Philip" (see Chapter 9).

The reality in America is different. In 1977 a serial murderer in New York signed notes "Son of Sam." When a suspect, David Berkowitz, was arrested, the *New York Post*'s headline, in red, was: "Caught!" The story named him and said he told the police that he was on the way to kill more victims when he was arrested. Nothing happened to the editor of the *Post*.

American law broke with the stern British view of public comment on pending cases in the 1941 decision in *Bridges v. California*, also described in Chapter 9. The Supreme Court held that such comment could not be punished as contempt unless there was a "clear and present danger" of perverting the course of justice—and no case after that found such a danger. The use of contempt as a device to discourage reporting that might endanger the fairness of a future trial was effectively barred.

But the problem of prejudicial press coverage of sensational cases remained. What else could be done about it? In 1961 the Supreme Court for the first time tried another course. It held that the Constitution required reversal of a murder conviction when pretrial publicity had made a fair trial unlikely. The case was *Irvin v. Dowd*, and the facts were extreme. The defendant was called "the mad dog killer" by the press. When jurors were questioned before the trial, eight of twelve said they thought he was guilty from what they had read—but believed they could still decide on the evidence in court.

Justice Frankfurter, who had dissented in the *Bridges* case, still wanted to take direct action against the press—as he made bitterly clear in a separate opinion: "This Court has not yet decided that the fair administration of justice must be subordinated to another safeguard of our constitutional system—freedom of the press, properly conceived. The Court has not yet decided that, while convictions must be reversed and miscarriages of justice result because the minds of jurors or potential jurors were poisoned, the poisoner is constitutionally protected in plying his trade." That was wishful thinking on Justice Frankfurter's part. The Court had in fact decided that what he called the poisoner, the press, was constitutionally protected—at least against British-style contempt punishment.

Reversal of a conviction was an awkward way to deal with the effects of sensational stories on a jury. By the time an appellate court made such a decision, witnesses might have died or disappeared. The Supreme Court suggested alternatives in the case of Dr. Samuel Sheppard, which became famous in a romanticized movie version, *The Fugitive*. Doctor Sam, as the press called him, was charged with the murder of his wife at their home in a Cleveland, Ohio, suburb in 1954. The press had played a vigorous part in demanding his arrest and prosecution. A front-page editorial was entitled, "Quit Stalling— Bring Him In." In a radio broadcast, a commentator compared Sheppard to Alger Hiss, who was accused of being a Soviet spy in a notorious case of the time. At the trial, reporters filled the courtroom. Jurors and witnesses were photographed and televised when they entered or left the court.

When *Sheppard v. Maxwell* (1966) reached the Supreme Court, Justice Tom C. Clark wrote that "bedlam reigned at the courthouse during the trial." The Court concluded that Sheppard had been denied "the judicial serenity and calm" to which he was entitled as a defendant. It set aside his conviction. Justice Clark, writing for the Court, went on to suggest ways of preventing such travesties. Trial judges could bar statements to the press by the police, prosecutors, and defense counsel. They could and should control the scene in the courtroom. If there was prejudicial publicity, they could delay the trial or move it to another location—a change of venue. They could sequester the jury, insulating it from public comment.

There is a striking curiosity in the Sheppard case. Sheppard was convicted in 1954, and the Ohio courts finally upheld the conviction in 1956. That same year the Supreme Court denied a petition for review. But ten years later the Court agreed to hear an appeal, on a petition for habeas corpus by Sheppard's lawyers, and set aside his conviction. Why did the Court change its mind and act a decade later?

The habeas corpus petition focused on the prejudicial effect of the press behavior before and during the trial. My guess is that the justices found that issue compelling in 1966 because of a powerful intervening event: the assassination of President Kennedy and then the murder, in Dallas police headquarters, of the alleged assassin, Lee Harvey Oswald. Chief Justice Warren was the chairman of the commission that investigated the assassination and its aftermath. The commission wrote stingingly about the behavior of the press in Dallas, among other things its overwhelming presence in police headquarters—which may have helped Jack Ruby come in and shoot Oswald.

The next idea tried out on the fair trial–free press issue was to bar the press, by injunction, from publishing anything before trial that was strongly "implicative of guilt" on the part of an accused. The case arose from the gruesome murder of six family members in the small town of Sutherland, Nebraska, in 1975 in connection with a sexual assault. A suspect named Erwin Charles Simants was arrested, and there was quite naturally intense press interest in the case, local and national. The prosecutor and Simants's lawyer joined in asking the Nebraska courts to limit press coverage lest it become impossible to pick an unprejudiced jury. The Nebraska Supreme Court prohibited reporting of any confession by Simants (who had in fact made one) or other matters "strongly implicative" of him.

The Supreme Court of the United States reviewed that order in 1976. There was considerable expectation that it would approve some restraints on reporting. Other courts had begun issuing such injunctions in aggravated criminal cases. (The press called them "gag orders," a characterization that made them seem illegitimate.) But the Supreme Court did not do so. The Court's opinion, by Chief Justice Burger, said that "prior restraints on speech and publication are the most serious and least tolerable infringement on First Amendment Rights." It ruled out injunctions against press coverage of criminal proceedings before trial unless there was a "clear and present danger" of preventing a fair trial. That always elusive phrase did not really hide the fact that the decision, *Nebraska Press Association v. Stuart*, was a great victory for the press. If a bar on publishing a confession was wrong in so aggravated a situation—a gruesome multiple murder in a small rural town—it was hard to see when one would be permissible. And in fact, none was sustained on appeal after that.

Three years later one more proposal to prevent the prejudicing of juries was tried out. At a pretrial hearing in a murder case in upstate New York, defense counsel moved to close the courtroom to the public, including the press. The prosecutor did not object; and the judge, Daniel A. DePasquale, granted the motion. The Gannett newspaper chain did object, and the case went to the Supreme Court in 1979 as *Gannett Co. v. DePasquale*.

By a vote of 5 to 4, the Court upheld the order closing the courtroom. The majority opinion focused not on the First but on the Sixth Amendment, which says among other things, "In all criminal prosecutions, the accused shall enjoy the right to a speedy and public trial." Justice Stewart said the public-trial right could be invoked only by the defendant, who had waived it in this case, not by outsiders like the press. "Members of the public," he wrote, "have no constitutional right under the Sixth and Fourteenth Amendments to attend criminal trials." For the dissenters, Justice Harry Blackmun disagreed about the Sixth Amendment in an analysis that sounded more like a discussion of the First. The guarantee of public trial, he said, ensures that everyone in the criminal justice system is "subjected to public scrutiny." He said pretrial hearings, like the one in this case, often consider charges of misconduct by the police—and were the only chance for the public to learn about possible official misconduct. He noted that most criminal cases are ended by a plea before trial; in this county, Seneca, not one prosecution went on to a trial in 1976.

The *Gannett* decision was greeted with a chorus of outrage by the press. The chairman of the American Newspaper Publishers Association said it showed that the Supreme Court was "determined to unmake the Constitution." Several members of the Court indicated, unusually, that they were troubled by the criticism.

One year to the day after its *Gannett* decision, the Court reversed its field. In *Richmond Newspapers v. Virginia* it considered the same question, whether courtrooms can be closed to protect the sanctity of juries, under the First Amendment. By a vote of 8 to 1, the Court said the speech and press clauses of the amendment assured the public's right to attend trials. (At the argument, Professor Laurence Tribe of the Harvard Law School, representing the newspapers, had disclaimed any special right of access for the press.) There was no majority opinion. But Justice John Paul Stevens put his finger on the larger significance of the case in a concurring opinion: "Until today the Court has accorded virtually absolute protection to the dissemination of information or ideas, but never before has it squarely held that the acquisition of newsworthy matter is entitled to any constitutional protection whatsoever."

The potential reach of the new constitutional theory that Justice Stevens described was revolutionary. With a right of access under the First Amendment, the press could sue to see secret government documents and attend closed meetings. So it might have seemed. The reality was not like that at all. The Supreme Court confined the new right to situations where there was a tradition of openness—like court proceedings. Attempts to get into other matters failed.

There the effort to find some constitutional way of insulating juries from outside comment stood: in frustration. The Supreme Court had been unable to resolve the tension between the interests of fair trial and freedom of the press—and let the latter prevail.

That is just an example of the many subjects in which freedom of expression has been in tension with other important interests. Another is the effort to limit the corrupting effect of financing political campaigns. The issue is complex enough to justify an entire book. Here it can have only the briefest of summaries.

No other democratic society allows political campaigns remotely as expensive as those in the United States. By the twenty-first century, presidential candidates of the major parties were spending in excess of $100 million just for the primaries and other early stages. In 1971 and 1974, Congress passed legislation intended to control the race for funding—and the influence-peddling that accompanied it. The legislation put limits on individual contributions to candidates, and on expenditures by candidates and by others on their behalf.

In 1976, in the case of *Buckley v. Valeo*, the Supreme Court considered claims that the ceilings violated the First Amendment's guarantees of freedom of expression. The Court upheld limits on contributions, but it found the expenditure ceilings unconstitutional. Political spending, it said, was a form of speech at the heart of the First Amendment. The unsigned opinion said the amendment "denies government the power to determine that spending to promote one's political views is wasteful, excessive, or unwise." The result was to give a great advantage to candidates with personal wealth and to those who were good at attracting contributions. Criticism of the decision was summed up wittily by Professor Paul A. Freund of the Harvard Law School, the leading constitutional scholar of his day: "They say that money talks. I thought that was the problem, not the solution."

Before long, politicians and their supporters had bored loopholes in the contribution limits that the Supreme Court had upheld. In 2002 Congress made a new attempt to stem the flood of money. It banned what had been unlimited contributions to the political parties, and it outlawed some television advertising paid for by corporations and labor unions during campaigns. Critics from right to left—from the National Rifle Association to the American Civil Liberties Union—objected that the law violated the First Amendment. But the Supreme Court rejected the critics' claims. There were multiple opinions and differing judicial lineups, by votes of 5 to 4—an indication of how sharp the tension was between the conflicting interests of campaign reform and freedom of expression. Despite the legal victory for reform, the reality was that campaign spending kept going up. Its heaviest cost, even worse than the opportunities for corruption, was the burden the money race put on politicians. In 2007 the Supreme Court, with two new members, turned away from reform. It held that restrictions on political spending by independent entities in the period just before the elections violated the First Amendment. Members of the Senate and House had to spend endless time raising money for their next campaigns.

The role of the First Amendment in election campaigns arose in a different context: elections of judges. Most states elect their judges, unlike the appointive system followed in other Western countries and in the federal government. (The federal practice was based on the Massachusetts constitution of 1780, which was drafted by John Adams and is still in force.)

Judicial elections used to be tame affairs, attracting little attention. In states where judges had fixed terms or had to face a periodic vote on whether they should continue, incumbents routinely won. But toward the end of the twentieth century, conservative political forces realized that judicial decisions had an impact on issues that mattered to them: social issues such as abortion as well as economic ones like punitive damages. So the conservatives opposed some sitting judges, spent increasing amounts of money to beat them, and succeeded in doing so in many cases.

To limit the politicization of judicial elections, many states adopted rules that barred judicial candidates from stating their views on controversial issues: "I am against abortion" and the like. Minnesota had what it called the "announce clause," forbidding candidates for judgeships to announce their views on legal or political issues. The Republican Party of Minnesota challenged the rule as a violation of the First Amendment, and won in the Supreme Court in 2002. By a vote of 5 to 4, the Court held that politicization of the courts, if it increased, was a price that had to be paid for our system of free speech. Similar rules in many other states were overthrown by the decision. And the cost of judicial elections, which used to be negligible, rose sharply—to over $1 million in campaigns for state supreme court justices.

The Minnesota decision seems to me an egregious misapplication of the First Amendment, treating it woodenly and ignoring the reality involved. The test of judicial decisions is not, as Justice Holmes said of political speech, "the power of the thought to get itself accepted in the competition of the market." Some of the greatest judicial opinions have run against popular opinion—as did those of Holmes and Brandeis when they dissented from the punishment of radical speech. If judges announce their views in election campaigns, in effect telling the voters that they will decide this way or that, they appear to be just another species of politician. The commitment of judges should be to the law, to interpreting it as faithfully as they can, and not to current popular opinion.

When the Supreme Court reaches a debated result by a narrow margin, as in the Minnesota case, there is always a hope among those disappointed by the result that a later Court may overrule the decision. Indeed, it can be more than hope. Opponents of *Roe v. Wade*, the 1973 case upholding a woman's right to choose abortion on constitutional grounds, campaigned fiercely for that decision to be overruled. The Court has said that its constitutional decisions are always open to reconsideration in light of experience and new understandings.

Chief Justice Hughes spoke of dissents as appeals "to the brooding spirit of the law." He described as "self-inflicted wounds" three Supreme Court decisions that had profoundly damaging consequences for the country and the Court itself—decisions that in different ways were overturned.

The first of the three was the Dred Scott case, in which Chief Justice Roger B. Taney wrote in 1857 that black people could not be citizens of the United States. It was overruled by the Civil War and the Fourteenth Amendment, which provides that all persons born in the United States are citizens. The second was one of the legal tender cases of 1869, in which a divided Court held that paper money was unconstitutional; it was overruled by the Court itself two years later. The third came in 1895, when a federal income tax (of 2 percent) was held unconstitutional. That decision was overturned by the Sixteenth Amendment in 1913.

The Court has reversed itself more often lately than in earlier years. A well-known example was the 2003 decision in *Lawrence v. Texas*, overruling a 1986 decision and holding that the states could not criminalize homosexual sodomy. But it is still a notable occasion when the Supreme Court changes its mind. And since the ascendancy of the First Amendment, it has not changed its mind about the central importance of freedom of speech or of the press. The abortion decision, *Roe v. Wade*, has been whittled away; but *New York Times v. Sullivan* and other landmarks of free expression stand unchanged.

12

Freedom of Thought

The freedom of speech and press promised by the First Amendment is not only external but internal: not only "freedom of expression" but "freedom of thought." The latter phrase was used as shorthand for America's promise even before the Constitution. A few weeks after the Declaration of Independence was issued in 1776, Samuel Adams, John's cousin, the fiery orator whose speeches helped to set off the Revolution, told an audience in Philadelphia: "Driven from every corner of the earth, freedom of thought and the right of private judgment in matters of conscience direct their course to this happy country for their last asylum."

Why do we want freedom of thought, of speech and press? The reasons have been canvassed by philosophers and judges and professors. Professor Zechariah Chafee Jr., whose writing on freedom of speech so influenced Justice Holmes, divided the subject into two large categories. "The First Amendment," he wrote, "protects two kinds of interests in free speech. There is an individual interest, the need of many men to express their opinions on matters vital to them if life is to be worth living, and a social interest in the attainment of truth. . . . "

Through a long history, individuals have struggled against repressive forces to express themselves. Their need to speak, as Chafee put it, may have been scientific in origin, or literary, or political. Galileo wanted to publish what he had proved by observation: that the earth moved around the sun. He was finally silenced by the repressive arm of the Catholic hierarchy at the time, the Inquisition. (The story is movingly told in Bertolt Brecht's play *Galileo.*) Boris Pasternak, after years of silence during Stalin's terror in the Soviet Union, wrote *Doctor Zhivago,* managed to have it published abroad, and won the Nobel Prize. But even after Stalin's death, official pressure forced him to renounce his acceptance of the prize. Anita Whitney rebelled against her socially prominent family and courted danger by helping to found the Communist Labor Party of California. Her criminal conviction evoked Justice Brandeis's great statement on free speech.

Perhaps there is something especially American about the need for self-expression if life is to be worth living, as Chafee put it. Albert Einstein used the same phrase in describing what he found when he came to the United States. "From what I have seen of Americans," he wrote in 1944, "I think that life would not be worth living without this freedom of self-expression."

The social interest in freedom of thought has been put in many different ways, most prominently in what Chafee called the interest in the attainment of truth. John Stuart Mill, in his

"On Liberty" in 1859, laid the philosophical groundwork. He argued that a suppressed opinion may contain a whole or partial truth that society needs. Even a false belief is valuable, he argued, because the process of debate about it may test and confirm the truth of the opposing view.

Justice Holmes gave powerful expression to Mill's argument in his *Abrams* dissent in 1919: Men may come to believe, he wrote, "that the ultimate good desired is better reached by free trade in ideas—that the best test of truth is the power of the thought to get itself accepted in the competition of the market." (The phrase "marketplace of ideas" is often used as if it were Holmes's, but he did not exactly say that. Professor Vincent Blasi traced the phrase and found its first use in a letter to the editor of the *New York Times* from David M. Newbold in 1936.)

Unlike many advocates of free speech as a search engine for truth, Holmes was really prepared to risk severe consequences. Professor Blasi put it:

Holmes, the old soldier and proud Darwinist, thought that one of the valuable functions of dissenting speech, including speech that advocates violent revolution, is its capacity to generate some of the grievances, aspirations and mobilizations that force political adaptation and transformation. . . . Probably the most energizing contribution that the freedom of speech can make is simply to leave people free to follow their political thoughts wherever they might lead—free, that is, to think the unthinkable regarding political loyalty, consent, obedience and violence.

James Madison saw freedom of speech, and especially of the press, as essential in a republic—a political system in which "the people, not the government, possess the absolute sovereignty." Madison's latter-day apostle of political freedom, the philosopher Alexander Meiklejohn, said in 1948: "When men govern themselves, it is they—and no one else—who must pass judgment upon unwisdom and unfairness and danger." Thus, for Meiklejohn, no restraint on political speech could be squared with the First Amendment.

A particular aspect of the case for freedom in political speech is what Blasi called "the checking value"—the role of the press and commentators in pointing to, and correcting, abuses of official power. The checking value has become crucial as the imperial pretensions of the executive branch of government have grown ever greater. When President George W. Bush took the United States to war in Iraq on false premises, and then secretly ordered the wiretapping of Americans in violation of law and claimed the right to torture detainees, Congress seemed unable or unwilling to perform the checking role that Madison and the other Framers of the Constitution had envisaged. It was the press that eventually penetrated the secrecy and exposed the abuses. And Bush has not been the only president with imperial ambitions and an exalted view of his power.

A final argument for broad freedom of expression is its effect on the character of individuals in a society. Citizens in a free society must have courage—the courage to hear not only unwelcome political speech but novel and shocking ideas in science and the arts. In his opinion in the *Whitney* case, Brandeis sounded the theme of civic courage:

Those who won our independence by revolution were not cowards. They did not fear political change. They did not exalt order at the cost of liberty. To courageous, self-reliant men, with confidence in the power of free and fearless reasoning applied though the processes of popular government, no danger flowing from speech can be deemed clear and present, unless the incidence of the evil apprehended is so imminent that it may befall before there is opportunity for full discussion. . . .

The courage required in a free society is not alone of those who believe in change, but of journalists and other shapers of opinion. And, not least, of judges. Many of the great advances in the quality—the decency—of American society were initiated by judges: on racial justice, on respect for the equal humanity of women and homosexuals, on freedom of speech itself. Every one of such steps exposed judges to bitter words and, sometimes, physical danger. "We are very quiet there," Holmes said of the Supreme Court, "but it is the quiet of a storm center."

Attacks on the courts grew in ferocity in the latter part of the twentieth century. Much of the antagonism came from those white southerners who wanted to defend their racist institutions from the civil rights progress set in motion by the 1954 Supreme Court decision in *Brown v. Board of Education* that racial segregation in public schools was unconstitutional. The attackers sought to delegitimize the Court and its members. Later, it was decisions upholding the free-speech rights of radicals that brought outcries.

Conservatives used the word "activist" to denounce what they did not like—"activist judges," "activist decisions." The word implied that judges had gone beyond their proper role in interpreting the Constitution, but it was used with so little consistency that it was meaningless except as a way to denounce a result that the critic disliked. The truth is that bold judicial decisions have made the country what it is, from John Marshall's expansive vision of the nation to *Brown v. Board of Education.* Only that kind of judicial boldness—of courage—will preserve a free society in an age of international threats and of governments ready to use them to advance their own power.

Of course a democracy should not wait for courts to save it. Some threats to American freedom never came to a definitive judicial decision. The Sedition Act of 1798 was effectively rejected by the voters in the election of 1800. The Palmer Raids of 1920 finally aroused public discontent. The Supreme Court rejected a challenge to the removal of Japanese Americans from their West Coast homes in World War II, but Congress eventually apologized for the outrage. Public exposure killed one of the most insidious repressive government programs, a harassment system run by the longtime director of the FBI, J. Edgar Hoover. Hoover acted to ruin the lives of those he considered dangerous leftists. The program was exposed when an unknown group raided an FBI office in Media, Pennsylvania, in 1971 and released the name of the program, Cointelpro, and some of its damning actions. Even in a time of fear about communism, Cointelpro was insupportable in the sunlight—"the best of disinfectants," in Brandeis's words.

Secrecy and repression breed fear. Openness can make us confident. Justice Black's sister-in-law, Virginia Durr, put it well when she said of Black: "He felt that when people couldn't discuss issues, then nobody could be free. That's one reason I always had a feeling of safety around him."

In 2006, during the war in Iraq, a Pakistani woman, twenty-five-year-old Nur Fatima, moved to the United States. She settled in Brooklyn, where she was interviewed by a *New York Times* reporter, Andrea Elliott. She told the reporter: "I got freedom in this country. Freedom of everything. Freedom of thought."

Samuel Adams's vision of America still lives.

ACKNOWLEDGMENTS

Vincent Blasi and I have taught a course together at Columbia University's Graduate School of Journalism for the last twenty years. He is a professor of law at Columbia and the University of Virginia; the course is on the constitutional law of the press. Vince has educated me. And he did me an extraordinary kindness by reading the manuscript of this book and making many important suggestions. I owe him much.

The idea for the book came from Wendy Strothman, my literary agent, who went on to give me valuable advice. William Frucht, executive editor of Basic Books, made the idea reality. His assistant, Courtney Miller, was helpful, as were Basic's project editors, Shana Murph and Sandra Beris. The copy editor, Katherine Streckfus, did a wonderful job of correcting and provoking me.

Linda Greenhouse, who covers the Supreme Court for the *New York Times,* helped me puzzle out the elusive meaning of the Court's decisions. Over many years, librarians and researchers at the *New York Times* informed me.

Christina Mathers kept me straight on this project as on much else. My wife, Margaret Marshall, who is a judge, cast a professional and lovingly critical eye on every word.

Thank you all.

TABLE OF CASES

NOTES

The notes use legal methods of citation. Thus *United States v. Schwimmer*, 279 U.S. 644, 654–55 (1929), means that the Supreme Court decided the case in 1929 and that the opinions can be found starting at page 644 of volume 279 of the United States Reports, the official volumes of the Court's decisions; the particular passage quoted or mentioned in the text is on pages 654–55.

Introduction

   x *Hughes:* Speech in Elmira, N.Y., 1907.

  xii *Barak:* Remarks at the Hebrew University Honorary Doctorate Award Ceremony, June 7, 1998.

 xiii *Lingens case: Lingens v. Austria*, 8 E.H.H.R. 407, 409, 418–19 (1986).

 xiv *Holmes: United States v. Schwimmer*, 279 U.S. 644, 654–55 (1929).

 xiv *Justice Ginsburg's speech:* University of Cape Town, Feb. 10, 2006.

  xv *Wilton, Connecticut, school principal:* See New York Times, Mar. 10, 2007, p. 10, col. 1.

Chapter 1

  1 *King Henry's proclamation:* See Frederick Seaton Siebert, *Freedom of the Press in England, 1476–1776: The Rise and*

Decline of Government Controls 48 (University of Illinois Press, 1952).

2 *Milton:* John Milton, "Areopagitica: A Speech for the Liberty of Unlicensed Printing to the Parliament of England," para. 8.

3 *Blackstone:* Sir William Blackstone, *Commentaries on the Laws of England,* Bk. 4, Chap. 2, pp. 151–52 (1765–1769).

5 *Levy books: Legacy of Suppression* (Belknap Press of Harvard University Press 1960); *Emergence of a Free Press* 271 (Oxford University Press 1985).

7 *Quock Walker case:* See Peter W. Agnes Jr., *The Quork Walker Cases and the Abolition of Slavery in Massachusetts: A Reflection of Popular Sentiment or an Expression of Constitutional Law?* Boston Bar J., March-April 1992 at 8, 10. (Walker's first name was spelled in various ways.)

8 *Madison's letter to Jefferson:* Oct. 17, 1788.

9 *Jefferson's reply:* Mar. 15, 1789.

Chapter 2

12 *Abigail Adams:* James Morton Smith, *Freedom's Fetters* 96 (Cornell University Press 1956).

13 *Matthew Lyon:* James Morton Smith, *Freedom's Fetters: The Alien and Sedition Laws and American Civil Liberties* (Cornell University Press 1956), starting at p. 226.

14 *Callender case:* Ibid., starting at p. 334.

16 *Rep. John Allen's remarks:* Ibid., pp. 113–14.

16 *Gallatin's remarks:* Ibid., pp. 122–23, and Leonard W. Levy, *Emergence of a Free Press* 302–3 (Oxford University Press 1985).

16 *Nichols:* Levy, *Emergence of a Free Press* 301–2, 310.

17 *The Virginia Resolutions and Madison's Report:* The relevant one of the Virginia Resolutions is at 4 *Elliot's Debates on the Federal Constitution* 553–54 (Jonathan Elliot ed.) (Lippincott 1836).

19 *Madison's Report on the Resolutions:* 4 *Elliot's Debates* 546–80.

19 *"Minority address"* on the Resolutions: Attributed to John Marshall in Albert J. Beveridge's 1919 *Life of John Marshall*, pp. 401–6. That attribution was persuasively challenged in an editor's note in 3 *The Papers of John Marshall* 499 (William C. Stinchcombe and Charles T. Cullen eds.) (1979). An extended note in 12 *The Papers of John Marshall* 512–524 (Charles F. Hobson ed.) (2006) shows conclusively that Henry Lee was the author and that in fact Marshall made it known that he would have opposed the Sedition Act had he been a member of the House when it was adopted.

20 *Jefferson's letter to Abigail Adams:* 1 *The Adams-Jefferson Letters: The Complete Correspondence Between Thomas Jefferson and Abigail and John Adams* 274–76 (Lester Capon ed.) (University of North Carolina Press 1959).

21 *Hofstadter:* Richard Hofstadter, Harper's, November 1964, p. 77.

21 *Madison's letter to Jefferson:* May 13, 1798.

Chapter 3

24 *Patterson case: Patterson v. Colorado*, 205 U.S. 454 (1907).

26 *Schenck case: Schenck v. United States*, 249 U.S. 47 (1919).

26 *Holmes: The Common Law* (Little, Brown 1881; Belknap Press of Harvard University Press 1963; Dover 1991).

27 *Frohwerk case: Frohwerk v. United States*, 249 U.S. 204 (1919).

27 *Debs case: Debs v. United States*, 249 U.S. 211 (1919).

28 *Abrams case: Abrams v. United States*, 250 U.S. 616 (1919). For a full account of the *Abrams* case and its participants, see Richard Polenberg, *Fighting Faiths: The Abrams Case, the Supreme Court and Free Speech* (Viking 1988).

30 *Masses case: Masses Publishing Co. v. Patten*, 244 F. 535 (S.D.N.Y. 1917).

30 *Hand-Holmes correspondence:* Gerald Gunther, *Learned Hand and the Origins of Modern First Amendment Doctrine: Some Fragments of History*, 27 Stanford L. Rev. 719 (1975).

31   *Chafee article:* Zechariah Chafee, *Freedom of Speech in War Time*, 32 Harvard L.R. 932 (1919).

31   *Holmes's letter to Chafee:* See David M. Rabban, *The Emergence of Modern First Amendment Doctrine*, 50 University of Chicago L. Rev. 1205, 1265–66, 1271 (1983).

33   *Acheson: Morning and Noon* 40 (Houghton Mifflin 1965).

34   *Gitlow case: Gitlow v. New York*, 268 U.S. 652 (1925).

35   *Statement by Hughes:* Charles Evans Hughes, *The Supreme Court of the United States* 68 (1928).

35   *Whitney case: Whitney v. California*, 274 U.S. 357 (1927). The Brandeis opinion starts on p. 374.

37   *Schwimmer case: United States v. Schwimmer*, 279 U.S. 644 (1929).

Chapter 4

39   *Stromberg case: Stromberg v. California*, 283 U.S. 359 (1931).

40   *Flag-burning case: Texas v. Johnson*, 491 U.S. 397 (1989).

41   *Holmes in 1920: Missouri v. Holland*, 252 U.S. 416 (1920).

41   *Hughes in 1934: Home Building and Loan Association v. Blaisdell*, 290 U.S. 398, 442–43 (1934).

42   *Black's comments:* Black joined the dissent in *Cohen v. California*, 403 U.S. 15 (1971).

43   *Near case: Near v. Minnesota*, 283 U.S. 697 (1931).

45   *Friendly: Minnesota Rag* (Random House 1981; Vintage 1982).

45   *Irving Shapiro's story:* Ibid., 40–42, 57–58.

46   *Grosjean case: Grosjean v. American Press Co.*, 297 U.S. 233 (1936).

47   *Pentagon Papers case: New York Times v. United States*, 403 U.S. 713 (1971). Justice Black's opinion in the case is at p. 717.

48   *King advertisement: New York Times Co. v. Sullivan*, 376 U.S. 254 (1964).

54   *Brennan lecture: The Meiklejohn Lecture*, 79 Harvard L.R. 1 (1965).

55   *Bickel: The Least Dangerous Politics: The Supreme Court at the Bar of Politics* 267 (Bobbs-Merrill 1963; Yale University Press 1986).

57   *Extension of the* Sullivan *rule to public figures:* See *Gertz v. Robert Welch Inc.*, 418 U.S. 323 (1974).

57   *Jefferson on the press:* Letter to J. Norvell, 1807.

58   *Russian criminal code:* News Alert, Committee to Protect Journalists (New York), July 28, 2006.

58   *Meiklejohn:* See Harry Kalven Jr., *The New York Times Case: A Note on "The Central Meaning of the First Amendment,"* 1964 Supreme Court Rev. 191, 221 n.125.

Chapter 5

59   *Sidis case: Sidis v. F-R Publishing Corporation*, 113 F.2d 806 (1940).

60   *Manley's article:* The New Yorker, Aug. 14, 1937, p. 22.

61   *Bok: Secrets: On the Ethics of Concealment and Revelation*, 250–52 (Pantheon 1983; Vintage 1984).

62   *Time, Inc. case: Time, Inc. v. Hill*, 385 U.S. 374 (1967).

64   *Schwartz: The Unpublished Opinions of the Warren Court* 251, 272 (Oxford University Press 1985).

67   *Garment article: Annals of Law: The Hill Case*, New Yorker, Apr. 17, 1989, p. 90.

68   *Brandeis-Warren article: The Right to Privacy*, 4 Harvard L.R. 193 (1890).

69   *Olmstead case: Olmstead v. United States*, 277 U.S. 438, 478 (Brandeis's dissent) (1928). *Olmstead* was overruled in *Katz v. United States*, 389 U.S. 347 (1967).

70   *Woody Allen case: Allen v. Men's World*, 15 Media Law Reporter 1001 (1988).

70   *Bette Midler case:* Decision of the United States Court of Appeals for the Ninth Circuit, marked not for publication, July 16, 1991.

70 *Jacqueline Onassis case: Onassis v. Dior,* 472 NYSupp 254 (1984).

70 *Shulman case: Shulman v. Group W,* 955 P.2d 469 (Cal. 1998).

72 *Sipple case: Sipple v. Chronicle Pub. Co.,* 201 Cal. Reporter 665 (Ct. App. 1984).

73 *Red Kimono case: Melvin v. Reid,* 297 Pac. 91 (Cal. App. 1931).

74 *Cox Broadcasting case: Cox Broadcasting v. Cohn,* 420 U.S. 469 (1975).

75 *Other cases involving confidentiality:* See *Landmark Communications v. Virginia,* 435 U.S. 29 (1978); *Smith v. Daily Mail Publishing Co.,* 443 U.S. 97 (1979); *Florida Star v. B.J.F.,* 491 U.S. 524 (1989).

75 *Telephone interception case: Bartnicki v. Vopper,* 532 U.S. 514 (2001).

77 *The English case:* A v. B Plc, 2 All E.R. 545.

78 *Nagel:* Thomas Nagel, *The Shredding of Public Privacy,* Times Literary Supplement, Aug. 14, 1998, p. 15.

79 *Kundera on the Prochazka case:* Milan Kundera, *Testaments Betrayed: An Essay in Nine Parts* (Harper Collins 1995).

79 *Kundera interview: A Talk with Milan Kundera,* New York Times Magazine, May 19, 1985, p. 85.

Chapter 6

81 *Judy Garland case: Garland v. Torre,* 259 F.2d 545 (2d Cir. 1958).

83 *Branzburg case: Branzburg v. Hayes,* 408 U.S. 665 (1972).

85 *Pentagon Papers case: New York Times v. United States,* 403 U.S. 713 (1971).

90 *Damages for disclosing a source: Cohen v. Cowles Media,* 501 U.S. 663 (1991).

91 *United States v. Wen Ho Lee:* Statement of Judge James A. Parker at sentencing, Sept. 13, 1990.

92 *Boston Globe editorial:* June 11, 2006.

93 *To the Point magazine:* Feb. 1, 1970.

93 *Buthelezi case: Buthelezi v. Poorter and Others* (1975), 4 So. Afr.L.R. 608.

95 *Farber decision in the New Jersey Supreme Court:* Matter of Farber, 78 N.J. 259 (1978).

97 *The closed courtroom decision: Richmond Newspapers v. Virginia,* 448 U.S. 555 (1980).

97 *Stewart lecture:* Lecture at Yale Law School, Nov. 2, 1974, reprinted in 26 Hastings L.J. 631 (1975).

98 *Congressional act of 1975:* Rule 501 of the Federal Rules of Evidence.

98 *Tatel's comments:* Judge Tatel explained his proposal in a concurring opinion in *In re Grand Jury Subpoena,* 397 F.3d 964, 986 (D.C. Cir. 2005).

99 *Joseph Wilson on Niger: What I Didn't Find in Africa,* New York Times, July 6, 2003, Sect. 4, p. 9, col. 1.

100 *Justice Brennan:* Address, 32 Rutgers L.R. 173 (1979).

Chapter 7

105 *Charles Evans Hughes:* See Clemens P. Work, *Darkest Before Dawn* 240 (University of New Mexico Press, 2005).

105 *Burleson:* Ibid., 10.

106 *Emma Goldman:* This comment appears in her autobiography, Emma Goldman, *Living My Life,* vol. 2, 704 (Dover Edition 1970).

108 *Gitlow case: Gitlow v. New York,* 268 U.S. 652 (1925).

109 *De Jonge case: De Jonge v. Oregon,* 299 U.S. 353 (1937).

110 *Herndon case: Herndon v. Lowry,* 301 U.S. 242 (1937).

111 *Cantwell case: Cantwell v. Connecticut,* 310 U.S. 296 (1940).

113 *Korematsu case: Korematsu v. United States,* 323 U.S. 214 (1944).

114 *Minersville case: Minersville School District v. Gobitis,* 310 U.S. 586 (1940).

114 *West Virginia case: West Virginia Board of Education v. Barnette,* 319 U.S. 624 (1943).

115 *License plate case: Wooley v. Maynard,* 430 U.S. 705 (1977).

116 *Barenblatt case: Barenblatt v. United States*, 360 U.S. 109 (1959).

117 *Sweezy case: Sweezy v. New Hampshire*, 354 U.S. 234 (1957).

119 *Wiecek's comment on the security screening process:* William M. Wiecek, *The Birth of the Modern Constitution: The United States Supreme Court, 1941–53*, vol. 12 of *The Oliver Wendell Holmes Devise History of the Supreme Court of the United States*, at 583 (Cambridge University Press 2006).

120 *Dennis case: Dennis v. United States*, 341 U.S. 494 (1951). The Second Circuit decision in *Dennis v. United States:* 183 F.2d 201 (1950).

121 *Redish article:* 73 U.Cin.L.R. 9 (2004).

122 *"Homer nodded":* Learned Hand, *The Bill of Rights: The Oliver Wendell Holmes Lectures* 59 (1958; Harvard University Press 1962).

122 *"Prosecuted those birds":* Geoffrey R. Stone, *Perilous Times: Free Speech in Wartime, from the Sedition Act of 1798 to the War on Terrorism* 395 (W.W. Norton 2004).

123 *Yates case: Yates v. United States*, 354 U.S. 298 (1957).

123 *Scales case: Scales v. United States*, 367 U.S. 203 (1961).

124 *Brandenburg case: Brandenburg v. Ohio*, 395 U.S. 444 (1969).

124 *Lamont case: Lamont v. Postmaster General*, 381 U.S. 301 (1965).

125 *"These bums":* Richard Nixon, remarks to Pentagon employees in informal conversation, May 1, 1970.

126 *Bond case: Bond v. Floyd*, 385 U.S. 116 (1966).

128 *Wheeler's statement:* Work, *Darkest Before Dawn* 113.

129 *Judge Bourquin:* Ibid., 118.

130 *Knauff case: Knauff v. Shaughnessy*, 338 U.S. 537 (1950).

Chapter 8

131 *Cohen case: Cohen v. California*, 403 U.S. 15, 24–25 (1971). The transcript of the argument is found in 70 *Landmark Briefs and Arguments of the Supreme Court of the United States: Constitutional Law* 828 (P. Kurland and G. Casper eds. 1975).

133 *Woolsey's opinion: United States v. One Book called "Ulysses,"* 5 F.Supp. 182 (S.D.N.Y. 1933).

133 *Hecate County case: Doubleday & Co. v. New York,* 335 U.S. 848 (1948).

133 *Roth case: Roth v. United States,* 354 U.S. 476 (1957).

135 *Burstyn case: Burstyn v. Wilson,* 343 U.S. 495 (1952).

136 *Jacobellis case: in Jacobellis v. Ohio,* 378 U.S. 184, 197 (1964).

136 *Justice Brennan's "utterly without redeeming social value": Memoirs v. Massachusetts,* 383 U.S. 413, 418 (1966).

136 *Court withdrew that requirement:* The test was rejected in *Miller v. California,* 413 U.S. 15 (1973), Brennan dissenting.

136 *Bork's argument:* Robert H. Bork, *Neutral Principles and Some First Amendment Problems,* 47 Indiana L.J. 1 (1971).

137 *Adult zoning case: City of Renton v. Playtime Theatres,* 475 U.S. 41 (1986).

137 *"Seven dirty words" case: FCC v. Pacifica Foundation,* 438 U.S. 726 (1978).

138 *MacKinnon: Only Words* (Harvard University Press 1993).

138 *Indianapolis case: American Booksellers Association v. Hudnut,* 771 F.2d 323 (1985).

138 *Meese commission:* Final Report of the Attorney General's Commission on Pornography, 1986.

138 *Hustler case: Hustler v. Falwell,* 485 U.S. 46 (1988).

140 *Ginsberg's "Howl":* Judge Horn's unpublished opinion was handed down on Oct. 3, 1957. See Bill Morgan and Nancy Peters (eds.), *Howl on Trial: The Battle for Free Expression* 198 (City Lights Books 2006). See also Ronald Collins and David Skover, *Mania: The Madcap Stories of the Lives That Launched a Nation* (Sourcebooks Forthcoming), Part 4.

Chapter 9

146 *Madison:* Report on the Virginia Resolutions.

148 *The alien sweep:* See Anthony Lewis, *Un-American Activities,* review of David Cole, *Enemy Aliens: Double Standards and*

Constitutional Freedoms in the War on Terrorism, New York Review of Books, Oct. 23, 2003, p. 16.

149 *"Patchouli girls"*: Hank Stuever, *The Art of Peace: Deploying Posters and Body Paint, the Anti-Warriors*, Washington Post, Jan. 20, 2003, p. C1.

149 *Edgar and Schmidt*: Harold Edgar and Benno Schmidt Jr., *Espionage Statutes and the Publication of Defense Information*, 73 Columbia L.R. 929 (1973).

150 *Ashcroft comment*: New York Times, Dec. 7, 2001, p. 1, col. 4.

151 *Bush wiretapping*: James Risen and Eric Lichtblau of the *Times* wrote many stories on NSA wiretapping starting on Dec. 16, 2005, p. A1, col. 1, with *Bush Lets U.S. Spy on Callers without Courts*. Their Pulitzer Prize: See New York Times, Apr. 18, 2006, p. B7, col. 1.

152 *Harman case: Home Office v. Harman*, [1983] 1 A.C. 280.

153 *Bridges case: Bridges v. California*, 314 U.S. 252 (1941).

Chapter 10

158 *Beauharnais case: Beauharnais v. Illinois*, 343 U.S. 250 (1952).

159 *Skokie case: Collin v. Smith*, 578 F.2d 1197 (1978).

160 *The Economist*: Oct. 21, 2006, p. 64.

161 *Irving and Lipstadt*: See New York Times, Dec. 21, 2006, p. A3, col. 1.

161 *"You are attacking . . . "* See New York Times, Aug. 21, 2006, p. A8, col. 1.

162 *"Praiseworthy"*: See New York Times, Feb. 9, 2007, p. A11, col. 1.

162 *Waldron*: See London Review of Books, July 20, 2006, pages 22–23.

165 *Flag-burning case: Texas v. Johnson*, 491 U.S. 397 (1989).

165 *Second flag-burning case: United States v. Eichman*, 496 U.S. 310 (1990).

166 *Rwanda:* See Stephen Kinzer, *Big Gamble in Rwanda,* New York Review of Books, Mar. 29, 2007, p. 23.

Chapter 11

170 *David Berkowitz:* See "Caught," New York Post, Aug. 11, 1977, p. 1. Berkowitz was convicted of six murders and sentenced, for each, to twenty-five years to life. See also New York Times, June 13, 1978, A1, col. 5.

171 *Irvin case: Irvin v. Dowd,* 359 U.S. 394 (1959).

172 *Sheppard decision: Sheppard v. Maxwell,* 384 U.S. 333 (1966).

174 *Nebraska case: Nebraska Press Association v. Stuart,* 427 U.S. 539 (1976).

175 *Gannett case: Gannett Co. v. DePasquale,* 443 U.S. 368 (1979).

176 *Richmond case: Richmond Newspapers v. Virginia,* 448 U.S. 555 (1980).

177 *Buckley case: Buckley v. Valeo,* 424 U.S. 1 (1976).

178 *2002 campaign reform law:* Bipartisan Campaign Reform Act of 2002.

178 *The decision upholding the law: McConnell v. Federal Election Commission,* 540 U.S. 93 (2003).

178 *The decision on the reform act: Federal Election Commission v. Wisconsin Right to Life* see New York Times, June 26, 2007, p. A1: "Justices Loosen Ad Restrictions in Campaign Law," by Linda Greenhouse and David Kirkpatrick.

179 *Republican Party case: Republican Party of Minnesota v. White,* 536 U.S. 765 (2002).

180 *Hughes:* Charles Evans Hughes, *The Supreme Court of the United States* 68 (Columbia University Press 1928).

180 *Dred Scott case: Dred Scott v. Sanford,* 60 U.S. 393 (1857).

181 *Legal tender case:* The first of the legal tender cases was *Hepburn v. Griswold,* 75 U.S. 603 (1869).

181 *The income tax case: Pollock v. Farmers' Loan & Trust Co.,* 157 U.S. 429 (1895).

181   *Lawrence case: Lawrence v. Texas,* 539 U.S. 558 (2003).
181   *Roe v. Wade,* 410 U.S. 113 (1973).

Chapter 12

183   *Samuel Adams:* Speech in Philadelphia, Aug. 1, 1776.
183   *Chafee:* Zechariah Chafee Jr., *Free Speech in the United States* 33 (Harvard University Press 1941).
184   *Einstein:* Walter Isaacson, *Einstein* 480 (Simon & Schuster 2007); see also note 26.
185   *Blasi:* Vincent Blasi, *Holmes and the Marketplace of Ideas,* Supreme Court Rev. 2004, 1, 39.
186   *Meiklejohn:* Alexander Meiklejohn, *Free Speech and Its Relation to Self-Government* (Harper Brothers 1948).
187   *"We are very quiet there":* Oliver Wendell Holmes Jr., "Law and the Court," speech, Feb. 15, 1913.
187   *Brown case:* 347 U.S. 483 (1954).
189   *Durr on Black:* Virginia Foster Durr, *Outside the Magic Circle* 167 (University of Alabama Press 1985; Simon & Schuster/ Touchstone 1987).
189   *Nur Fatima:* See New York Times, Sept. 10, 2006, p. A1.

INDEX